PRIZE-WINNING STORIES
FROM CHINA
1980-1981

By Ke Yunlu, Zhang Xianliang and others

English Text Edited by W. C. Chau

FOREIGN LANGUAGES PRESS   BEIJING

First Edition   1985

Illustrated by
Cai Rong   Zhao Ruichun
Zhou Jianfu   Zheng Shufan**g**
and Zheng Xin

ISBN 0-8351-1313-2

Published by Foreign Languages Press
24 Baiwanzhuang Road, Beijing, China

Printed by Foreign Languages Printing House
19 West Chegongzhuang Road, Beijing, China

Distributed by China International Book Trading Corporation
(Guoji Shudian), P.O. Box 399, Beijing, China

Printed in the People's Republic of China

Editor's Note

The release of creative energy in the post-"cultural revolution" period has continued to produce works of high quality. Appropriately, Mao Dun wrote in his foreword to the first number of *Selections of Stories* which came out in July 1980: "A new spring has arrived. There has never been so much creativity for the past 30 years." The present anthology comprises 16 of the many prize-winning short stories for the years 1980 and 1981.

As contemporary Chinese literature entered a new age, the writers recounted their sufferings during the "cultural revolution". Many of the pieces in the previous anthology, *Prize-Winning Stories from China 1978-1979,* are based on personal experiences of the nightmare of the soul. The term "scar literature" gained currency in the early post-"cultural revolution" period. It is hoped that readers will not jest at these scars — certainly not those who have felt the wounds of life, which may have been of a different kind.

But calm always returns after even the most violent storm, as nature recovers from disorder. Any wound will eventually heal. Time alleviates even the greatest pain, in one's memory, and the mind will sooner or later regain its former peace. Of course, traces of past sufferings, recollected not yet in tranquillity, can still be found in a number of stories which came out in 1980 and 1981. However, in general, the term "scar literature" can no longer accurately describe the body of literature that was produced in those two years. The writers feel it is their mission to give realistic reflections of life and experience in their concerted efforts to create a modern socialist literature. They believe, as does Hamlet when he comments on the purpose of acting, that the artist should "hold the mirror up to nature". Life is not a simple story that can be simply told. The deep commitment to life and experience has been the Chinese writers' source of inspiration and strength.

The socialist writer believes that artistic creation is a lot more than indulgence in self-expression. In his vision of life and society, he sees a strong bond between him and the reader. That sense of responsibility of the Chinese writer has sometimes been overlooked by Western scholars — I dare not use the word "misunderstood".

What do the stories in this anthology have in common? It is love and the sense of discipline that life demands. In these stories, love manifests itself in its different forms and its range is wide: from romantic young love with its joys and agonies, to the love of one's country which may at times turn out to be the cause of frustration — perhaps even resentment, though not blatantly expressed, which springs from the very depths of that intense love itself.

The themes vary; so, too, the style. There is light humour in the story "Phoenix Eyes", unfailing devotion to an ideal in "A Soldier in the Tianshan Mountains", the psychological study of envy in "A Saleswoman", the deep concern about the abuse of power in "Thirty Million", and so on. The writers welcome the new hopes which have dawned on China, but their sensitivity, a rare gift, also enables them to see the new problems which have come with social change. Their literary merits apart, then, these stories may serve as a record, written with imagination, of Chinese life in a new age.

It is too early to predict what new literary trends the writers of the stories in this anthology may have set. What happens after the birth of a new day is open to speculation. Their achievements, even if they may not have been adequately reflected in the English translations, have certainly earned them each a place in the history of modern Chinese literature, which has yet to be written.

W. C. Chau

CONTENTS

THIRTY- MILLION
Ke Yunlu   1

BODY AND SOUL
Zhang Xianliang   58

THE "ON-THE-SPOT" WEDDING
Ma Feng   93

THE IVIED CABIN
Gu Hua   110

OLD SUN SELLS HIS DONKEY
Zhao Benfu   145

PHOENIX EYES
Chen Jiangong   162

THE FLUTTERING FLOWERED SCARF
Chen Jiangong   186

THE MOON ON THE SOUTH LAKE
Liu Fudao   214

A TALE OF BIG NUR
Wang Zengqi   240

THE WOMAN WHO WEARS THE TROUSERS
Wang Runzi   262

BARRIERS ON THE ROAD
Da Li   281

A SALESWOMAN
Hang Ying   313

THE DIARY OF A FACTORY CLERK
Jiang Zilong   331

A SOLDIER IN THE TIANSHAN MOUNTAINS
Li Binkui   360

THE MOON ECLIPSE
Li Guowen   389

ARE YOU A COMMUNIST PARTY MEMBER?
Zhang Lin   417

KE YUNLU

(1947 —   )

Ke Yunlu, or Bao Guolu before he changed his name, was born in Shanghai in 1947. After graduation from a senior middle school in Beijing in 1968, he worked as a peasant in Shanxi Province. Since 1972, he has been working in a polyamide fibre factory in Yuci city.

"Thirty Million" is his first publication. His latest work is "A High-Ranking Cadre Went to Beijing", a short story published in 1981.

THIRTY MILLION

Ke Yunlu

I

Early 1979. A vinylon factory, still under construction.

On the ground between the buildings, heaps of steel bars and planks were lying pell-mell. In the bitter wind, scraps of paper from the cement bags were flying. Members of the factory's Construction Committee were accompanying several high-ranking officials of the Provincial Bureau of Light Industry in their inspection of the building site.

"Thirty million and no cutting down, not even one cent? It's steely, isn't it?" The man who uttered these words was the Bureau's Party Secretary and Director, Ding Meng. His sweeping glance, as he gave everybody a searching look, seemed to suggest that he was plotting something. He had short grey hair. The wrinkles on his forehead were strikingly deep and the lines on his face were like cracks in the rocks, rugged and hard. His usual jesting tone clearly indicated that he was displeased.

Director Ding, who had just been restored to his former post, was a remarkable man. Before the "cultural revolution", he was well known throughout the province for being careful and resolute in performing his duties, and there were numerous accounts of his exemplary work. The object of his present visit was to examine the proposed supplementary budget of the vinylon factory, which, under construction for the past ten years, had indeed acquired the reputation of being an "age-long project". This year, plans had been put forward at last for the completion of the work within the next twelve months. But at the same time, the Joint Construction Directing Committee —

composed of the vinylon factory (Party A) and the Ninth Department of the Provincial Construction Company responsible for the building work (Party B) — submitted a report requesting an increased funding of thirty million yuan. It should be borne in mind that the original budget for the building of the factory was fifty million. Because of over-spending, however, time and again investment had had to be increased. By now, a total of one hundred and fifty million had already been consumed. Undoubtedly, it was absurd to grant another thirty million in order to complete a project which originally required fifty million.

Director Ding knew full well that at present it was an extremely difficult task to cut down investments. Even the Planning Committee, the Construction Committee and the Central Government could not find a proper way to cope with that. Everybody said that the present situation could never be changed. But he wanted to have a go, a good go, at this "present situation", which nobody had the courage to challenge so far. He also felt he was in a favourable position to tackle it: the Party Secretary of the vinylon factory and Chief Director of the Joint Construction Directing Committee, Zhang Anbang, was a cadre trained and promoted by him when they were working in the same textile factory in 1965. He knew Zhang well and naturally believed that he would be a help in his present mission.

However, things did not turn out to be what he had expected. The two of them had not been in contact with each other for well over ten years, and now Zhang Anbang had changed into someone distant and unfathomable. Although he did recognize the warmth and ease with which he was treated as an old superior, there seemed to be a certain barrier subtly erected behind all that politeness and respect. Under Zhang Anbang's arrangement, the examination of the supplementary budget for the past few days seemed to be shrouded in a thick fog. On the surface, everything appeared to be precise and there was no evidence whatsoever of any unjustifiable request for further funds. If one asked for the accounts, a pile of "Budget Reports" and

"Calculation Reports" would be sent in, something like two feet high. The hundreds of pages were filled with thousands of figures worked out by the computer. If one wanted to hear some opinions, well, Party A and Party B of the Joint Construction Directing Committee had already prepared detailed and relevant reports. In short, it all appeared that the budget was authentic and the only thing left to be done was its approval.

Somehow, the perfunctory politeness and the official air irritated Ding Meng more and more. Eventually, he could not help feeling that somebody had spread a cover over everything and that he had not seen the true facts. Who had done this? Zhang Anbang? Ding Meng had yet to decide.

"We've made every effort to trim the budget. It can't shrink any more." The man holding out his hands in reply was no other than Zhang Anbang himself, the Party Secretary of the factory. He had a long and oval fat face, with bright eyes which were full of life. The voice was sonorous even though he was making such a casual remark, but the contrived tone conveying the feeling of closeness was meant to be a special appeal to an old superior for his appreciation of the way a subordinate had been trying hard to cope. After these few words, he smiled cordially at his subordinates, who, all clustered round him, expressed at once their agreement with fawning nods and smiles.

"What's that?" asked Ding Meng, pointing at a building constructed for temporary use. It looked like a ragged warehouse.

"It's the temporary dining hall," Zhang Anbang replied placidly. He pointed at the original dining hall beside it, now filled with cement and machines. "That has become the temporary warehouse because of insufficient storage space, and we've had to build this temporary dining hall. I'm sure you'll agree that the workers shouldn't be eating in the open air."

As he spoke, they entered the "temporary dining hall". Above, were reed mats which served as the ceiling; below were broken bricks which made up the ground. The windows had no frames and the plastic sheets, fixed higgledy-piggledy by wooden strips, were flapping against the wind. Everything had a "temporary" look all right. One of the directors of the Light Industry Bureau's Construction Department confirmed, "They did submit an application for the building of the temporary dining hall."

Ding Meng glanced round the hall and snorted, "What a temporary dining hall! ... Built for temporary use, why do you need cement and mortar for the walls? And the girth? ... Afraid that it's too easy to be pulled down later, eh?" Ding Meng was pointing at various things that caught his eye, full of anger. "Such enormous space, wide doors and wide windows. Look, even the foundation for the partition walls has been laid. So this is a temporary dining hall?... I'll tell you it's going to be a big club; all it needs is some slight alteration.... Well, cooking up a false budget and building something not stated in the plan! It's criminal."

Everybody was stunned by this totally unexpected questioning and kept silent. Embarrassment and apprehension filled the air. Nobody had ever thought that Director Ding could see through everything so easily. The matter was serious.

Zhang Anbang was a little displeased. He looked at everybody and then turned to Ding Meng. Smiling calmly, he said with some regret, "There's no other way really, Director Ding. It's inevitable because of the extreme Leftist policies insisted upon several years ago. What with slogans like 'Production first and living, second', who dare run a club openly. It wouldn't have been approved, as you well know. . . . Most of our workers in the factory are young and we have to look after their cultural interests somehow."

The sympathetic and reasonable defence changed the atmosphere. Everybody was relieved, quietly admiring Chief Director Zhang. Now it seemed that it was Ding Meng's turn to be caught in a dilemma, hard pressed for an answer.

"I see. You can claim credit for that, too, can't you?" said Ding Meng, sarcastically. "It's 1979 now, you know. . . . Why are you still playing games trying to cheat?" He noted that

Zhang Anbang wanted to have more to say in defence and, waving his hand, instantly stopped him.

"First, submit a report on running a temporary dining hall on false pretences and be ready to accept any disciplinary measure."

Everybody was again shocked.

"Then send another report to the bureau and try to get its approval of the club you have in mind. All right?"

These two decisions came fast, like lightning cutting through the clouds. Everybody realized that Director Ding meant business.

Ding Meng went on; his censorious and searching eyes surveyed all the members of the Construction Committee. "It seems to me that your Chief Director is lacking in principles. . . . If he can do things like that, well, what about the other comrades? Why didn't any of you raise any objection, or at least report to the higher-level authorities on the matter?" Nobody said a word. It was truly a wall of silence.

The truth, of course, was that under the banner of "collective benefit", the cadres of an enterprise were often united when they asked the government for more money. That was natural and understandable. It did not pay to sabotage this "collective benefit", for everybody wanted his share, large or small. And everybody wanted to remain at his post in the work unit. That was a very common phenomenon at present, and it had been mocking and enraging Ding Meng for the past few days.

Now, under his fierce eyes, nobody dared look up — except Bai Sha, Dean of the Construction Office of the vinylon factory, a middle-aged woman technician. Nonchalantly, she brushed back a tuft of short hair which was hanging over her forehead uncovered by her blue scarf. She had a quick glance at Ding Meng and resumed her indifferent stare in another direction.

"Comrade Bai Sha, I know you are responsible for the budget. Why didn't you insist on principles?" Ding Meng's eyes fell on her, frankly criticizing her. Instantly, mild anger flushed her cheeks and cold animosity came out of her eyes.

"Director Ding, really I should be held responsible for all this," said Zhang Anbang as he stepped forward. He sounded very sincere. "All the comrades have been working very hard on specific assignments, and it hasn't been easy over the past few years. The faults are all mine; truly, they are not to blame. Besides, this matter of the temporary dining hall has nothing to do with the thirty million. . . .

"Nothing to do with it? You being held responsible? Just you wait. You'll have a lot to answer for," said Ding Meng within himself as he looked askance at Zhang Anbang, whose tricks over the "temporary dining hall" further reinforced his conviction that there was something fishy about the thirty million. He looked at Bai Sha and asked again, "Bai Sha, what's your final comment on the thirty million?"

"Honestly, that's the minimum figure required for the completion of the vinylon factory. Our views on this are one and the same," answered Zhang Anbang instead, smiling and speaking again in the tone of an old subordinate. He very much wanted to relax the tense atmosphere.

"Anbang, it's rather odd, isn't it?" Ding Meng gave him a stern and displeased look. "You're speaking for everybody. She's not dumb, is she?"

Zhang Anbang smiled a little. His expression was one of willingness to accept any criticism from Ding Meng.

"Bai Sha, let's hear your final comment. You can't just be the dependant of your boss," said Ding Meng.

"Dependant? I haven't learned to be one yet." Bai Sha retorted coldly. Ding Meng's words had hurt her self-respect. A woman technician of well over thirty and unmarried, she was pure indifference. In her eyes, there was no need to be serious about anything at all. As long as it did not affect her, if it was thirty million, then let it be thirty million. True, she had taken part in planning the budget, but her heart had never been in it. In the factory, she merely followed the tide and did her eight-hour stint everyday.

"Bai Sha, cool down a bit," said Zhang Anbang reproachfully but protectively. "Director Ding would like to hear your views on the thirty million."

"I don't have any," said Bai Sha, her manner still icy. "Thirty million is probably enough." She did not even look at Ding Meng. Swinging her scarf a little, she turned away and said no more.

"Probably? Is that the word used by someone working in economic planning?" Ding Meng lost his temper. His glances cut through the crowd like a sword; even his cheeks were twitching. Everybody still remained silent. Watching these silent faces, Ding Meng felt that he should keep his cool. Losing one's temper was no more than displaying one's feeling of weakness and helplessness. He desperately wanted to remove the cover which had been concealing the true facts. At once, he thought of that invaluable man, and, eyeing Zhang Anbang with disdain, said solemnly and authoritatively, "All right, if that's how things stand, I'll invite a specialist to investigate the whole matter: Qian — Wei — cong. . . . Ever heard of him?"

Bai Sha instinctively turned round, her eyes betraying her fleeting surprise.

Zhang Anbang had never expected that Ding Meng would make such a move. Nevertheless, he nodded heartily and said, "That's very good indeed! It'll be even more reliable." In his smile, there was not a single trace of uneasiness. He did not know who Qian Weicong was, but believed that even a more astute expert would not be able to find anything to query, in a matter of a few days, in the mass of figures.

"You'd better do the reduction yourselves first. . . . When you are found out, do be careful," said Ding Meng.

II

That afternoon, Bai Sha came to Zhang Anbang's home.

"If the budget needs to be redone, let's do it from scratch. As it is, it won't stand up to the scrutiny of Qian Weicong," she said plainly.

"It can't be that bad," Zhang Anbang shook his head and smiled, not the least perturbed. For, by noon he had done his probing. Qian Weicong was an ordinary engineer in charge of designs at the Bureau of Light Industry. His son, Qian Xiaobo, was a worker in the vinylon factory.

"You may not believe it, but he was a budget expert, well known throughout the country in the past," Bai Sha reminded him.

Zhang Anbang was lost for a little while. He did not know Qian Weicong was a budget expert or how influential these so-called experts were. In order to conceal his bewilderment, he laughed heartily and in his usual, kind and joking tone, when speaking to his subordinates, said, "So you're afraid? Why? It's all part of our work."

"Afraid? What have I got to be afraid of?" Irritated, Bai Sha gave him a sour look. "I only feel it's not worth getting into trouble, that's all. There's no need to." As she finished her words, she turned and left.

Watching her slender shadow disappear outside the door, Zhang Anbang realized the situation was serious and that he had to take counteraction immediately. However, he remained seated in the sofa for a few seconds as if he were in a trance. Then, all of a sudden, he recalled the private talk Ding Meng had with him in the morning after the inspection. His words were so fair, sincere and straightforward that Zhang Anbang was rather moved. At the time, meeting Ding Meng's solemn and kind eyes, he did have second thoughts about the "thirty million".

The telephone on the desk rang. It was a call from the Bureau of Materials demanding the workers recruitment quota. Zhang Anbang had promised a few extra job openings in order that the children of some of the Bureau's Directors could be given positions in the Provincial Construction Company — that had to do with the "thirty million" too. Since people from the Bureau of Materials always gave themselves airs, Zhang Anbang kept saying "It's O.K."

One telephone call, and Zhang Anbang saw everything very clearly. Behind the "thirty million", he saw, however dimly, the faces of many directors and department heads. He put down the receiver and his absolutely plain determination came back: he had to get hold of the "thirty million".

Of course, he would not touch one single cent of the money. But he had to get hold of the whole lot, otherwise he would utterly fail in his many manoeuvres. For example, the assistant secretaries and assistant managers of the factory wanted to live in high-standard houses with individual back-yards. The head of the Administration Department wanted to have a guest house built and put under his control. The director of the hospital wanted another floor added to the Medical Building so that he could have an even more spacious and cosy office. . . . People like these had given him much help in the process of consolidating his position as leader in the factory, and he had to satisfy their demands. That alone was enough to force him to fight for the "thirty million". He could not afford to disappoint them, for that would inevitably lead to loss of future support or even betrayal.

In truth, the object of getting the "thirty million" went beyond all this. Given sufficient ability in exercising stratagems, the Party Secretary of a large factory which had plenty of money and materials, many cars and connections, would certainly be able to gain the invisible authority to command in society. To one who loved the good life, it meant that he could furnish his home with sofas, television and refrigerator, among other much-desired items. To one who loved power, like him, it would lay a solid base for aggrandizement.

Of course, he was not born with this hunger for power. When the "cultural revolution" began, he had been assistant manager of the factory for only a year. Seen as someone belonging to "the group in power", he was sent away and lived in a "cowshed*" for a few days. At the time, what he regretted

---

* The term was used during the "cultural revolution" to describe the place of confinement, where people has to do hard labour.

most was being the assistant manager. But he learned fast. Wisely, he switched sides, declared very clearly where his loyalty lay and stood firmly in line. Then, he struck out, throwing himself recklessly into the tempestuous storm. More and more, he understood the true nature of politics and eventually had a good grasp of its subtleties. True, in the rapid political currents and treacherous whirlpools, he went down many a time. But he always managed to resurface. So, in the process, he buried his old soul and nurtured a new one. In short, he had been moulded. Now, having experienced the vicissitudes of political life for more than ten years, he was naturally in less a hurry to achieve his goals. Nevertheless, he had never lost his indomitable will to carve out a political future for himself.

As things stood, the "thirty million" symbolized the integration of his self-interests and those of numerous others inside and outside the factory. Again, one need not go far in citing examples. If, in the budget, he did not stretch it a little wider for the Provincial Construction Company, he would not be able to obtain the workers recruitment quota he needed for the employment of the children of some of the high-ranking officials of the Bureau of Materials. He had to pursue these matters meticulously. Otherwise, how could he increase and strengthen his social links? Right now, he was thinking of the arrangements for the housing of the relatives of the district Party secretaries in high-standard quarters. He also entertained the thoughts of controlling several of the neighbouring counties through the manipulation of goods and materials. In brief, he understood very well the secrets of political success of the officials these days. If he did not build up a wide network of social links, he would not be able to move ahead. It was as simple as that. These were indeed difficult and complicated times especially in such matters as connections and relations. Promotion or job transfer, he knew full well, for example, was decided not necessarily by one's immediate superior. A word from an unknown junior, carried through a certain channel, would probably do the trick.

In the vinylon factory, he had to know all there was to know about everybody, from the cadres above to the ordinary workers below who had connections with the authorities. Indeed, one of his important "jobs" was to check personal records. You might be only an apprentice, but if your parent or any of your distant relatives was somebody of importance, then he would certainly make it a point of keeping that in mind. When the need arose, he would take "proper care" of you and weave you and your "background" into his net. And he was going to use that net now to catch the "thirty million".

Before he finished the day's work, he phoned the workshop of Qian Weicong's son, asking them to pass on the message that he wanted Qian Xiaobo to come to his home in the evening. He also told the workshop not to assign any work to Qian Xiaobo for the moment because the Party Committee of the factory had some other jobs for him to do.

III

Ding Meng already felt that he had been encircled by Zhang Anbang's activities. Some of the factory's officials, when talking to him, inevitably mentioned in a few words from different angles the need of the "thirty million". A few old friends from his home-town and his nephew, who were all cadres or workers in the factory, came to see him separately in the temporary guest house. Behind their words, it seemed that the long, oval face of Zhang Anbang was faintly visible.

As the encircling forces increased, Ding Meng got more furious; yet, paradoxically, the more furious he was, the cooler he became. When even several old acquaintances from the District Party Committee and one or two old superiors in the province also called on him and expressed their deep concern about the "thirty million", Ding Meng realized well enough that Zhang Anbang was not someone who could be easily brushed aside. Zhang was far different from the man that he had known more than ten years before. Then, he was over thirty, still young, forthright, full of principles and showed great drive in his exemplary work. Although somewhat tainted by pride, he was nevertheless ready to accept criticism and try to improve. Indeed, he was a young cadre with a future, worthy to be nurtured. But now he had changed thus! A classic example of "opportunities producing their own man"!

"Stop playing little tricks and be careful when you're found out! There will be consequences." Ding Meng did not mince his words as he warned Zhang Anbang, who merely smiled a little without giving any explanation, as if saying: "How could I play tricks on Director Ding?"

Ding Meng realized that any verbal rapping would be lost on Zhang Anbang, who would, no doubt, receive it with another perfunctory smile. What was to be done was a thorough investigation of the "thirty million" as soon as possible. He placed all his hopes in engineer Qian Weicong, who would be arriving shortly.

On the very first day of his work at the Bureau of Light Industry, he spotted this man of extraordinary talent bending over the drawing board in a dark and gloomy room. At the sight of this, he could not hold back his feeling of resentment. "Qian Weicong! What on earth is he doing here?" Well over ten years before, Ding Meng had already read his work on the theories concerning budget planning. Imagine such an expert "exiled" here by the National Construction Committee! And for nine years abandoning his special field, living in limbo, pursuing another profession!

Finally, Qian Weicong arrived at the vinylon factory.

When he came out of the jeep, Qian Weicong struck the members of the Directing Committee merely as a short, slightly hunch-backed man, old and somewhat carrying the looks of an intellectual. Ding Meng introduced him as Qian Gong (a shortened title for Engineer Qian), which was how he was usually addressed in the Bureau of Light Industry.

Qian Weicong's appearance was not the least impressive; in fact, he looked rather debilitated. When he spoke, he was overpolite. When he shook hands, he nodded too much and too low.

At the very first sight of him, Zhang Anbang felt: obsequious! In his estimation Qian Gong was rapidly sinking. But Zhang Anbang was adept both at showing his respect properly to his superiors, without any sign of arrogance or servility, and at expressing his warmth and appreciation to his juniors through his amiable smiles. He straightened himself, his belly bulging a little, and in a stylish manner shook hands with Qian Gong, smiling and wittily saying a few words of welcome. Then he turned round and introduced the members of the Directing Committee individually, showing off his poise and prestige as their leader.

Ding Meng, on the contrary, looked upon the visitor as a saviour. He knew that at a glance this expert would have a good idea of the construction cost of a building. In the evening, he sat opposite Qian Gong in his room in the guest house and said, coming straight to the point, "Qian Weicong, you're in complete charge. We depend mainly on you for the examination of the 'thirty million'."

"No, no. Not me, but the leaders," replied Qian Gong, hastily.

"The theory of the sagacity of the leaders, I take it? Without the support of the masses, they're blind in one eye, and without that of the experts they are blind in the other. Damned useful, these totally blind leaders," said Ding Meng. When he saw that Qian Gong still wanted to explain, he stopped him. He pulled out a pile of "Budget Reports" from the drawer and put them on the desk.

"All the figures are in here," he said, "if you want to hear more reports, I'll make the necessary arrangements. If you want to visit the building sites, the Directing Committee will send someone to accompany you. So you make the decisions, and I'll accept all the responsibility. It's going to be our duet. Tell me, how many days do you need? . . . Meals? I'll take them into your room from the dining hall."

Ding Meng handed over the full authority of investigating the "thirty million" to Qian Gong. In addition, he announced clearly at the meeting of the Directing Committee the next day: in

the examination of the budget Qian Gong would be playing the primary role, and he the supplementary. Whatever Qian Gong had to say would count.

Qian Gong now became the focus of attention, being watched closely by everybody. So far, however, he had been doing nothing except nodding politely and making a few courteous remarks. He avoided any question about the budget, and when he had to say something he always sounded rather vague. Obviously, he did not want to get involved in any controversy.

"What shall we do?" anxiously asked the Director of the Construction Department from the Bureau of Light Industry who had come with Ding Meng to examine the "thirty million". Ding Meng was knitting his brows and said nothing, lost in thought.

Nobody realized that Qian Gong was caught in a sharp and violent conflict. That night he was alone in his room and before him lay the slide-rules, calculators and scores of "Comprehensive Budget Reports" on his desk. He was tightly knitting his brows and smoking vigorously, himself shrouded in the dense smoke. Whenever he detected a loop-hole in the reports, he was angered and raised his fist fiercely. But each time it gradually dropped, helplessly, and he again shook his head and sighed.

Ding Meng came in to see him several times and noticed the inner conflicts of Qian Gong, but they were hastily concealed as he mumbled in reply, "Oh, nothing the matter, really." What could he say to Ding Meng? The upheavals in life for well over ten years had daunted his spirits and taken away his courage. Now he felt that he was at his wits' end.

He did recognize the genuine warmth and trust of Ding Meng from the very beginning — he had been used to that kind of treatment by people until things changed during the past ten or more years — so much so that he felt he was driven by a certain unspeakable force. When he saw Ding Meng, after all, the director, bring in meals for him and nodded politely as he put the food down, he appreciated once again the respect and realized all the more the responsibility he was entrusted with.

But, at the same time, he could not forget the words of his wife, who had a very clear idea of his career. Just before he came here, she said to him, "You'll mind your own business, won't you? When you are in the vinylon factory, you just let the leaders do whatever they like and don't try to be smart. Otherwise, you'll never be transferred back to Beijing." These words expressed sufficiently enough their hardship and anxieties of the past several years. Indeed, both of them had done their share of running around and seeing people in their attempts to get transferred back to Beijing, where he felt he could make his contribution through his professional experience of well over half a life-time. But they encountered the same bureaucracy and selfish departmentalism which only increased their discontent. Often enough they were stirred into trembling but ineffectual anger.

Not too long ago, so they heard, the National Construction Committee finally granted permission for his transfer. But, apparently, it went no further, when it got to the Provincial Government and the bureau, and for the past few months he had not been able to get any news whatsoever. When Director Ding asked him to examine the budget of the vinylon factory, his immediate response was one of excitement, for he had an irrepressible passion for his old profession. But after he had been upbraided by his wife, who spoke at length against his involvement, he understood that the work, once started, would make it impossible for him to get away. . . .

His inner conflicts intensified particularly when he realized the significant role that Zhang Anbang could play in all this. The second day he was in the vinylon factory, his son Xiaobo told him that Zhang Anbang's wife worked in the Organization Department of the Provincial Government and that he had promised to help. Upon hearing this, he was overjoyed and said, "We must truly thank him!"

However, unexpectedly, he was met with his son's disdainful looks. "Thanking him? What are you talking about? You just approve the 'thirty million', I'll tell you." In order to remove his doubts, his son went on, "Of course, they won't make it so obvious. Secretary Zhang said that if you wanted to work in your own special field and put your talent to the best use, everybody must try to do something to help. He also said that I don't have to go to work these two days. Instead, I should spend the time taking good care of you. He'd like me to explain to you carefully that a great deal of help is needed from all sides for the early completion of the construction of the vinylon factory. Isn't the message clear enough?" Qian Gong too, was now in Zhang Anbang's net.

Three days had already passed, and Qian Gong was not making any move. Everywhere Zhang Anbang appeared even more relaxed and calm, talking cheerfully. Members of the Directing Committee all said that surely the "thirty million" had been approved. And the Director and Deputy Director of the Construction Department of the Bureau of Light Industry were getting more and more anxious.

Ding Meng, however, kept his silence.

Nobody knew what Ding Meng was waiting for. He said nothing, for he sensed that something unexpected was brewing, unnoticed by the others. Qian Gong's brows were tightly knit whenever he inspected the building site. The grave expression on his face and his silence had now replaced his previous excessive politeness and nods. Zhang Anbang had also noticed these changes in Qian Gong, and he had an unspeakable feeling of apprehensions when he accidentally met Ding Meng's eyes.

Then, the unexpected finally happened when they were inspecting the few dormitories which were near completion.

"You see, the work for these buildings is finished. They cost one hundred yuan per square metre," said the budget planner from the Ninth Department of the Provincial Construction Bureau.

"You can't call it finished, surely?" Qian Gong and the group of people were looking around in a room with chalk white walls. Obviously, he was trying to control himself and said as courteously as possible, "Why aren't the doors and the windows painted? Where are the window panes? The handrail? Also the drainage and the pipes in the washroom? They haven't been fixed yet, have they? . . . You've already spent, for each square metre, one hundred and nine yuan and forty-nine cents!"

"I do admit the building cost is a little bit high," explained the budget planner. "But these buildings are constructed strictly according to the draftsman's design. The quality is relatively better."

"I'm not sure about that. The quality is questionable." Qian Gong pushed the snow-white wall hard and it was shaking.

"The partition wall is made of laths, not bricks, as indicated in the drawing. It's all done according to the drawing."

The repeated explanations eventually angered Qian Gong. He kept pushing the wall hard with his hands and it was shaking perilously while patches of lime were falling on the ground.

"According to the drawing? This kind of lath wall?" queried Qian Gong. Seeing that the budget planner still wanted to explain, he pointed his finger at him, at the same time slapping the wall with his other hand. His eyes were full of anger as he demanded, "Get me the drawing. Go and get it now! There is a drawing which indicates the use of lath walls, I'm sure. But certainly not your kind of lath wall. Scrub away the lime and let's see if the material you've used is up to the standard. You've cheated on the use of material by at least a third." He pushed the wall again and corrected himself in the estimate. "Probably forty per cent. . . . Don't think that by splashing lime on the wall you can cover up everything. According to the regulations, you should pull it down and rebuild it."

The budget planner's face was all red. Silence reigned. Everybody had seen the complete reversal of the humble and courteous Qian Gong. Ding Meng was indignant, cursing in his heart, "All these years, specialists like Qian Gong had been pushed aside. Sheer blindness! No wonder we've been going backwards!"

That night, Ding Meng came into Qian Gong's room and asked him directly, "Well, have you identified the problems?"

"Er. . . ."

"What's on your mind?" Ding Meng picked up several of

the budget reports which were lying on the desk and, patting them with his hands, said, "No problems even in here?"

Qian Gong's forehead was all wet with perspiration. He hesitated and pulled out a cigarette. Ding Meng sat down, struck a match for him and, like an old friend full of understanding, said, "Whatever worries you may have, do let's talk about them. Don't let them be bottled up and trouble you."

After a little while, Qian Gong plucked up a little courage and said that he hoped the Bureau would be able to arrange his transfer back to Beijing. He would of course help in the examination of the budget.

"Oh, this is bargaining. Do you want to haggle about the terms?" Surprised, Ding Meng instantly stood up. Although the day before he had specially made a long distance telephone call requesting the Bureau to study, as soon as possible, the granting of Qian Gong's transfer, he had not expected Qian Gong would talk like that. He went on, "I see. You're going to use the transfer as a condition for your present work. Does it mean, then, if the transfer is not granted, you won't do it?"

Qian Gong's face immediately turned red; he was full of shame and remorse. Ding Meng paced the room. Then he walked to the desk and, piling up all the budget reports, he pushed them towards Qian Gong, saying, "This 'thirty million', give your approval if you like. You've got the authority, long given you. But I'll leave it to your conscience as a budget expert."

Early next morning, the Director of the Construction Department pushed open the door of Ding Meng's room and found him leaning on the desk. His hand was holding his forehead and a grey padded overcoat was draped over his shoulders. He was sitting still, deep in thought. The dim rays of dawn permeated the room through the frosted window panes and, commingling with the gentle yellow light from the desk lamp, shone upon his deeply wrinkled forehead. He was tightly knitting his brows, obviously lost in thought for a long time.

"Lao Ding, you haven't had a wink of sleep?" asked the Director as he came in. "It seems that the lights in Qian Gong's room have also been on the whole night."

"Oh. . . ." Ding Meng nodded slightly, indicating that he was already aware of that.

"It's pretty worrying, isn't it? Even now we don't know how to cut down the 'thirty million'." The Director of the Construction Department sat down, sighing. "Lao Ding, you've been deeply troubled by this for yet another night, haven't you?"

"I've been thinking of what to do after the 'thirty million' has been cut down. . . . Yes, that's it, after we've done it. . . . The specific plans we should follow for the completion of the factory. . . ."

The eyes of the Director of the Construction Department were now wide open.

IV

The next day, something explosive happened at the meeting called by the Joint Commanding Committee to discuss the examination of the "thirty million".

When Ding Meng said "Qian Gong, please say a few words on behalf of the Bureau", everybody felt the meeting was soon coming to an end. Every single face, shrouded in smoke, began to come to life. They relaxed and gladly listened to the polite opening words of Qian Gong, believing that the approval of the "thirty million" had reached its final stage. But almost immediately the scores of faces were frozen by shock; even the smoke which filled the room seemed to stay still. What? There was "a very wide discrepancy" between the proposed supplementary budget and the actual needs?... Even Zhang Anbang was stunned. People looked at one another and then set their eyes on the source of shock.

The tiny and skinny man, Qian Gong, went on, carefully choosing his courteous words, "I hope you understand I represent only myself in expressing this rather premature opinion for my comrades' reference. Mistakes are of course unavoidable in a person's judgement, but based on my preliminary study of the facts available, I've formed this ... impression. The discrepancy is ... shall we say ... rather wide. Of course, I haven't done detailed calculations yet."

Some began agitating. "You reject our budget after skimming through it in a few days, when we've spent more than a month preparing it, going over every item again and again. On the basis of 'preliminary study', not having done 'detailed calculations'. . . . Surely, that's a hasty decision."

His fleeting shock over, Zhang Anbang noted acutely how Qian Gong modified his expression about the "discrepancy", from "very wide" to "rather wide". He also recalled the lath wall incident the day before and how Qian Gong had been enraged by the explanations put forward. He leaned back on the chair, lifted his hand and then lowered it, saying, "Let Qian Gong take his time. We've been rattling away for several days giving him reports. Since he has come here to take part in the inspection work, surely it can't be that he has no opinion to express. I can assure you he is very concerned about the vinylon factory." After these words, he looked at Qian Gong opposite him, smiling as before. His eyes conveyed his calmness and humility and, above all, his respect for and trust in Qian Gong.

But Ding Meng waved his hand and said to everybody, "If you're not convinced, please contradict him. Don't just hold your breath. You have your say and I, mine. That's what it should be. . . . Isn't it, Qian Gong?" He knew Qian Gong had not had any sleep the night before and he also understood what his "impression" implied, as mentioned just now. He wanted to see Qian Gong provoked by the people who had been demanding money left, right and centre.

Some of these people did not realize the sharp conflict between Ding Meng and Zhang Anbang, who had both taken up opposing, irreconcilable positions. Accountant Gong, who had been working for several years for the Ninth Department of the Provincial Construction Company, agitatingly stood up.

He was over thirty, with a dark brown face, and wearing yellow framed glasses, behind which gleamed his sharp, slightly bulging eyes. As he spoke, he gave the whole account, systematically, of how the budget had been prepared so as to prove their serious need of the "thirty million". In giving a series of calculations, he reiterated the need for the increase and the authenticity of the figures. Finally, he pointed at Bai Sha sitting opposite him and said, "Our comrade from Party A has also examined the budget figures in detail." Since, according to practice, Party A and Party B inevitably adopted opposing stands in financial matters, these last words of Accountant Gong carried the most weight. People began to show their agreement with his points. Bai Sha, on the other hand, merely lowered her eyes, staring at the desk without showing any response.

She dared not look Qian Gong in the face. The old engineer appeared haggard and decrepit, entirely different from his old self. However, he was the teacher Bai Sha most respected and felt most grateful to in all her life. In 1965 she was only twenty-two, a graduate in architecture — she was called Li Bei then — and was enrolled in the training class for budget planning, which was run by the National Construction Committee. And Qian Gong was the very person in charge of technical expertise in the training programme. For the past few days, Bai Sha had not been able to find the courage to renew acquaintance with him.

At the meeting, Qian Gong was not completely free from hesitation. When he spoke he was searching hard for the right words, rather like a man looking for the exposed bricks as he was trying to get through a water-logged area. That further increased the airs of the defenders. But precisely because they kept referring to each and every "accurate calculation" or "stipulated clause", Qian Gong was infuriated by their over-rigid arguments. He saw before him no longer courteous and amiable faces but stipulations and official figures. On his face now the traces of humility had completely gone and his looks became piercing and threatening.

THIRTY-MILLION   23

"How does Party B get its management expenses?" He began asking his first question.

"Well, it's entitled to eighteen per cent, according to the government's stipulations." Accountant Gong's eyes rolled behind his glasses and gave a simple, straightforward answer.

"No mistake, then?"

"Certainly not." Slightly bothered, Accountant Gong flicked through the bulky *Book of Stipulations and Regulations*. He stopped at a certain page and put the opened book down on the desk, saying, "Here's the stipulation of the Provincial Revolutionary Committee in 1977: 18%. . . . Before 1977, it was 17%. After that year, it was changed to 18%. No mistake."

At that point, someone was whispering, "The budget expert hasn't been practising his former profession for some time. He remembers only the old 17%. . . ." Immediately, Zhang Anbang tried to smooth away the embarrassment for Qian Gong and, smiling, said, "Qian Gong has been doing a different job and he hasn't had the time to deal with budgets these past few years. He may not have been all that aware of the changes in some of the clauses. The increase of management expenses to 18% is a new regulation. Of course, if we can strive to bring it down to 17% to save money, so much the better."

However, Qian Gong retorted, "18% is 18%. How can you make it 17% just like that? It's not a matter of whether or not you can strive to do that. The stipulations of the state have to be strictly followed and the percentage shouldn't be raised or lowered. It's something firmly fixed, you understand?" He went on, speaking in a tone meant to dismiss any further doubts, "Those who are not clear about the stipulations of the state have no right whatsoever to discuss the budget. The document of the Provincial Revolutionary Committee which Accountant Gong referred to just now, I know, is that of 1977, item number 39. Right? The new measure for expenses came into effect on May 1 of the same year. That document has five clauses, followed by two explanatory notes. Right?"

All eyes now turned from Qian Gong to Accountant Gong,

who was fumbling the documents on the desk unable to utter a single word.

"But that is the stipulation for construction and not management expenses. Right?" Qian Gong paused for a little while and then opened the budget report of the "thirty million". He pointed at one of the pages and said, "Here, why is it that the expenses for the installation of the chemical industrial pipes are drawn up on the same formula as that used for construction? Installation and construction expenses are looked after by the same formula? You mean you don't know that installation expenses are paid according to a different formula? Honestly!"

"There is discrepancy in the expenses. . . ." said Accountant Gong, giving in, as he pushed up his glasses, which had slid down his nose because of his perspiration.

"More than you are entitled to? or less? You have to make that clear."

"Of course, it's a bit more."

"How much is that 'bit'? Our comrade doing the budget should use Arabic numerals in the clarification."

"It's very difficult to work that out instantly. There're different types of pipes and their prices vary, as you know. The installation difficulties and therefore the expenses are not the same either. . . ."

"How many numerals, then? What's the first numeral? Surely, you ought to know."

Accountant Gong was now soaked in perspiration, not knowing what to do or say.

"I have a rough calculation here," sand Qian Gong as calmly as he could. "Three hundred and twenty tons of stainless steel pipes are installed. According to different prices as applied to different tons, we do the calculations separately. Then put the figures all together, and it comes to 14,365,000 yuan, that is the installation expenses. Using the formula for construction expenses instead, you have asked for 2,333,000 yuan more than you're entitled to. That is your 'a bit more', I'm now telling you —2,333,000 yuan."

"The Commanding Committee agreed to this request for money to cover the expenses. . . ." mumbled accountant Gong, caught in a very awkward situation.

Qian Gong was gesticulating wildly. "It won't do," he said. "It won't do, whoever agrees to this. The assignment of funds to cover the expenses is governed by the state's economic stipulations. That's something fixed and unquestionable."

A deadly hush reigned in the conference room.

Ding Meng's eyes fell on Zhang Anbang. Casually but severely, he said, "I see, agreed to by the Commanding Committee. Does that mean you want Comrade Zhang Anbang to do a little explaining?"

Zhang Anbang hastily replied, "I'm held responsible for everything of course, although I must say I don't fully understand all that technical stuff. . . ." Then he caught the dissatisfied look of the officer from the Ninth Department of the Provincial Construction Company and immediately he changed his tone. "But I can assure you I was fully aware of the difficult situation and expressed my agreement. I know well enough that the Provincial Construction Company has very real and practical difficult problems. All in all, I should be held responsible."

"You are being held responsible again?" asked Ding Meng. "I'll make a self-criticism."

"Simple enough, isn't it? All along, you know what's going on. In other words, you've been intentionally violating economic regulations. You'll be properly disciplined by the Party and punished by the law of the state."

Upon hearing these words of Ding Meng, Zhang Anbang could no longer maintain the stand that he should be held singly responsible for everything. He admitted, "As a matter of fact, I'm not all too clear about the detailed and specific quotas in the budget. . . ."

"Then who's clear about them? Have you been deceived by Party B?. . . That party is not my business today. The Construction Bureau will deal with it later. The money swindled through exceedingly high estimate will sooner or later prick your hands,.

you know. Well, Party A, let me ask all of you properly, as director of the Bureau of Light Industry. Are you not clear about the budget figures?" Ding Meng's sharp eyes fell on Bai Sha and he asked, "Comrade Bai Sha, what about you? Are you clear about the budget?"

Now that Ding Meng had lost his temper, Qian Gong felt a little uncomfortable. He was sitting beside Bai Sha and put in a few quiet words by way of advice, "It won't do if the budget planner hasn't learned his lessons well or mastered his trade." Her thick, dark eye-lash lowered, slightly trembling.

Ding Meng demanded, "Bai Sha, aren't you also going to say you don't understand or you're not very clear about the budget figures? That way, you can also get yourself off the hook, you know."

"I haven't said anything." Bai Sha was mildly angry as she looked up briefly and retorted unyieldingly. The atmosphere became even more tense. Everybody was holding his breath, watching intensely how things were going to develop. They all knew very well the personality and temperament of Bai Sha.

Holding on to the table, Ding Meng stood up and said, "Not giving a damn, thinking you're always right and nobody can ever say anything against you. Is that it? . . . But don't forget you are a cadre within the order of the state. Paid by the state, you should be doing some work. Nobody will blame you for not trying to be creative, but you should at least have a sense of responsibility. . . ." Ding Meng was trying hard to speak calmly as he went on. "Let's not talk about you for the moment. We'll do that later. Qian Gong, please carry on."

Qian Gong glanced at Bai Sha and Ding Meng, opened his notebook and went on page by page, pointing out one error after another. Some were made by the Ninth Department of the Provincial Construction Company, many others by Party A, the vinylon factory. The fraudulent figure soon went up from 2,330,000 yuan to 5,000,000.

So, in one morning the thirty million was sliced by five million!

V

Zhang Anbang could no longer underestimate Qian Gong. He fully realized that if Qian Gong went on investigating everything as he had done so far, soon there would be a thorough examination of the budgets and the final accounts of the past few years and the materials in the warehouse. In short, he would be in serious trouble. Certainly, he was not going to risk that.

He came to the Guest House to see Qian Gong. His face was full of cordial smiles and he did not mention one word about the "thirty million". Instead, he made it clear that he had come specially to give Qian Gong news about his transfer. He said that he had just received a telephone call from his wife, saying that the Organization Department of the Provincial Government would soon give its approval. His friendliness was totally beyond the expectation of Qian Gong, who naturally felt extremely grateful.

"That's nothing, really," said Zhang Anbang, waving his hand. "The decision rests mainly with the Organization Department. All I've done is making a few links, that's all. In theory, there shouldn't have been any need for anybody to make these links. . . ." He went on, sighing a little. "But I hope you understand the subtle personal relations at present. There doesn't seem to be any other way. . . ." As he stood up and was about to leave, he started speculating on Qian Gong's behalf. "The last hurdle to be cleared, it seems, is that of the Bureau of Light Industry. . . . Anyhow, we'll see how that can be done. . . ." When Qian again wanted to express his gratitude, he interrupted him and said, "No, no. You can't call it help. Your visit to the vinylon factory has been a great help to our work. . . . About the budget, Qian Gong, I'd like you to understand that our feelings don't count. Do whatever you think is right. It may be a bit difficult for us. . . . But if it's going to be difficult, let it be. No doubt, you understand the practical problems in construction work these few years. Aye. . . ." Zhang Anbang sighed deeply, his heart apparently much troubled as he continued. "I only fear the construction won't be finished. Over ten million yuan's capital and several thousand workers here, and yet we still can't generate production power. That's a waste more serious than anything I've known."

What was weighing on Zhang Anbang's mind, however, could never be disclosed to anybody. When he was sitting in the sofa at home, knitting his brows and deeply thinking, his daughter Haiyan came in and gently sat on the arm-rest, asking, "Daddy, people in the factory all said you're responsible for the mess over the 'thirty million'. Is that true? They also said you had fallen out with uncle Ding. Is that true, too?" He was much bothered by her questions but he did not show any sign of irritation for he loved his only daughter very dearly indeed. (When he was living in the cowshed during the "cultural revolution", Haiyan was only seven. Every day she breezed through the jeering and abusing crowd quietly, like a willow leaf, and brought him food. She had also stood on her toes in order to wipe away the tears at the corner of his eyes.) He patted her hand and said, "Don't worry. Uncle Ding and I equally mean well. Both of us are trying to cut down expenses as much as possible. . . ." He noticed the mischievous looks of his daughter and went on, "You still have doubts? Well, you think your daddy can ever lie to you? Aye, some of the comrades who worked on the budget have been irresponsible. . . ." His daughter believed him, but he now felt very uneasy. He did not want his daughter to know the truth — that absolutely would not do. At the same time, however, he did not want to tell her lies. He still had the kind heart of a father.

He stood up, intending to pace the room and drive away the worries from his mind. Through the window he saw Ding Meng and Xiaobo walking together below. Astounded, his attention was immediately focused on the "thirty million". Now was the crucial moment and he could not afford any slackening.

Ding Meng was coming to see Qian Gong, who was sitting at the desk, all by himself and in low spirits, smoking. That afternoon, he had a row with his son, Xiaobo, who was telling him, "If it's thirty million, then let it be thirty million. Why all that fuss? I wonder how many people are still left with your kind of dead brain." He rejected his son's advice. The quarrel, however, opened his eyes: Zhang Anbang's object was still that he should not go too far, especially in dealing with the issue of clearing the warehouse. He well understood the difficulties in construction work for the past few years. So, the factory project could never be completed? That was entirely possible.

He sensed that Ding Meng had come to discuss the issue of clearing the warehouse. "Director Ding. . . ." He wanted to talk about his worries, but Ding Meng interrupted him, saying, "No, I don't come here to persuade you — there's no such need. You consider in full the question of the warehouse. . . . Incidentally, I had a chat with Xiaobo just now and gave the young man a few words of advice." He sat down and continued. "I want to discuss two things with you. First, I think we should not only simply examine and reduce the budget, but also help to work out a plan which will guarantee the completion of the factory project. We need a series of measures. To plan the budget strictly according to fixed quotas and then get on with the construction work and finish it — that isn't very easy at present.

"That's right." Qian Gong instantly put out his cigarette.

"Well, this is the first thing. We can let it rest for the moment and consider it further while we're clearing the warehouse. The second thing I want to discuss with you demands even greater involvement than the first. We're going to develop the textile industry much further and there will be many new projects, including the expansion of some existing ones. I'd like to invite you to run a budget-planning class for the cadres and the technicians. It will last three months. What do you think?"

"Certainly a good idea. Otherwise, to say that we want to have more effective management while not providing well-trained people at all levels — that's empty talk, surely." Qian Gong was getting excited. With the exception of not letting him go back to Beijing, everything about Ding Meng was excellent.

"Qian Gong, I'm afraid once this training class sponsored by the Bureau of Light Industry starts, the Provincial Construction

Committee will certainly be envious. It will also try to get hold of you, and you will be kept in the province. Then it'll be even more unlikely that you can go back to Beijing. So what will you do?"

"You won't let me go. What else can I do?" answered Qian Gong, helplessly.

"I won't let you go?. . . Such great power!" Ding Meng nodded and said humorously. He stood up, paced the room a little and stopped before Qian Gong. "Please don't make fun of me. I may not have a brain as good as yours, but I do have a conscience. I'm paid by the state every month!" He then told Qian Gong that the bureau had approved his transfer and sent a report to the Organization Department of the Provincial Government that very day.

Qian Gong opened his eyes wide, feeling it was all too sudden.

"You see, you can't accuse me of hoarding talent. But I must say I'm a little guilty of selfish departmentalism. Your three-month teaching of the budget-planning class can be interpreted as service borrowed from Beijing by the Bureau of Light Industry." Ding Meng smiled. "As to the Provincial Construction Committee trying to get hold of you after that, well, I can't interfere, can I? But I'll do my best to have you transferred first. I can't believe that in such a large province there aren't people with talent."

After he had finished his conversation with Qian Gong, Ding Meng went to see Bai Sha.

Bai Sha was sitting at the desk, her hand holding her cheek. Under her elbow was a group photograph of the teachers and students of the budget-planning class organized by the National Construction Committee in 1965. She did not know why she dug it out from the bottom of the box a day or two ago. The photograph showed over one hundred people in three rows. She was wearing a short-sleeved blouse, kneeling in the middle of the front row before the knees of Qian Gong, who was seated in the middle of the second. Then, she was young and vivacious. Her eyes were shining bright with the yearning hopes of the future. Out of the corners of her mouth flowed the joy of her passionate love of life. On the back of the photograph were beautifully written some lines of words in ink:

> Li Bei,
>> Here's to the future woman budget expert of China.
>>> Qian Weicong

Indeed, that was her aspiration at the time. . . . She had taken the photograph out only for a random look, not realizing that the light of those long-forgotten "naive" days, jeered at by herself later, could yet shine through those cold and indifferent years, and these vivid though somewhat unfamiliar rays now hurt her deeply. Together with the events of the past few days, it disturbed her inner peace of mind.

The coming of Ding Meng startled her out of her trance. She sat still, her face registering expressions of icy animosity. Rumour in the factory had it that Ding Meng had taken out her personal file from the Cadre Organization Department with the intention of disciplining her. Zhang Anbang had just been here to talk to her, but his answers to her questions were all too ambiguous: "Concerning the business of the authorities you may as well leave it alone. . . . H'm. . . . As to your personal file being taken out, that's probably also because Director Ding cares about you." At any rate, Zhang Anbang's words confirmed the truth of the rumour which had been circulating in the factory.

"Well, just coming over to have a little chat with you about your work." Ding Meng briefly surveyed the simply but tastefully furnished room and sat down.

"All right. You have the power," replied Bai Sha drily.

"I've come, first to tell you what I think. If I may say so, shirking responsibility in your work, that's your greatest fault. The 'thirty million' is such a big problem. You should also be held responsible for that — the extent of that will be studied later."

"I'll bear the responsibility. If you want to lay on your punishment, please yourself."

"If punishment could solve the problem, you would all have been punished before this."

A slight, cold scorn came out of the corners of Bai Sha's mouth.

"You've studied budget planning before?" Ding Meng asked calmly.

"You can look up my personal file."

"That will be looked after by the Organization Department." A slight alertness flashed upon Ding Meng's mind. He had decided, only the day before, to look into the files of the cadres from the mid-level up. "I'd like to talk to you first, right now." He looked at Bai Sha solemnly and continued, "You may think the world is not worth it. Put the blame on society or your bitter experience, if you like. But you will regret living such a pointless life!"

"That's my choice. So there!"

"I don't believe you were like this before! Neither would I like to see you continuing like this," said Ding Meng as he curtly stood up.

Bai Sha's face instantly turned pale.

Ding Meng pushed the chair aside and walked to the door. He pulled it open, but turned round and said, "Here's your work for the next two days: first, put all the accounts together and be ready to help Qian Gong in checking the materials in the warehouse. Second, think very carefully and see if there're still any problems concerning the 'thirty million'."

Bai Sha's peace of mind, long possessed, was now completely shattered. "I don't believe you were like this before! . . ." What was she like in the past? Her old self in the photograph was smiling at her. Indeed, the life of those ten nightmarish years had changed her into another person, totally different. The buffets of misfortune at home undoubtedly left deep wounds in her, then in her youth. Not only had her political career been taken away; her faith in love and her self-respect had also been devastated by the hypocrisy behind passion and the self-seeking that inevitably led to desertion. Her desire to live had almost been completely destroyed. . . . Precisely because she wanted to forget her past, she changed her name. What she had had to endure for over ten years in the past eventually made her contemptuous of everybody, everything. Understandably, she appeared extraordinarily apathetic, cold and unconcerned.

But why had she suddenly lost her peace of mind in the past few days?. . . Well, any person who could see things objectively would have noticed that in fact her internal disturbance had been mounting for some time. Although no government policy could ever redress the wrongs done in the destruction of her ideals and the ravage of her faith in love, the rehabilitation of her father, who had been done gross injustice, and the thawing of the freezing social atmosphere, nevertheless, let in some rays of sunshine on her heart. . . .

The next day, early in the morning, Bai Sha collected all the accounts concerning the materials in the warehouse and quietly gave them to Qian Gong. But she did not supply any information about the inspection work.

The result of the clearing of the warehouse was: the vinylon factory had to subtract from its budget the proposed operation funds of ten million yuan for stocking materials. So, from the thirty million, another ten had been sliced after the five already taken away. Only fifteen million was now left!

VI

Zhang Anbang hit the desk with his fist, overturning the teacup. He had been robbed of ten million even before he could retrieve one cent of the lost five million. He admitted to himself that he had underestimated Ding Meng. The complaints of those who worked under him, the joy of his opponents who gloated over his disaster, the discontent of his various connections — all these, like high tide, were coming to swamp him. There was no way out. The only thing to do was to fight back desperately and turn the tide.

First, he put pressure on Qian Gong. He had learned, from the operator of the switch board, of the content of the conversation between Ding Meng and the Bureau of Light Industry. "All right, then, I certainly would not be standing idly by," said Zhang Anbang to himself. He made a long telephone call to his wife at the Organization Department of the Provincial Government. What he said to Qian Gong several days ago about helping him to get permission for his transfer was in fact a pack of lies, all that talk about having received information from his wife that the department would soon give its approval. Now, indeed, he was asking his wife to do just that. Of course, his wife was only an ordinary officer in the department, but sometimes a petty officer or administrator in charge could influence the transfer of significant personnel. Zhang Anbang knew this very well. Naturally, he reiterated to his wife: he needed Qian Gong and so did the vinylon factory. Otherwise, the completion of the construction work would be a serious problem indeed.

After that, he spoke with Director Tan of the Ninth Department of the Provincial Construction Company, dropping all the necessary hints. In addition, he had many of his social connections alerted and then organized. All this was done quietly without betraying any sign of intrigue. Results? Suffice it to say that many of the cadres of the Bureau of Light Industry had the impression, within a few days, that "Qian Gong had gone too far". Of course, they meant that "Ding Meng had gone too far".

All the activities of Zhang Anbang were finally brought to bear upon Ding Meng. But he merely grinned with scorn as he realized he had to cope with more pressure. He had seen worse before. He had fought, for example, in the War of Resistance Against Japan. In 1966, when the "cultural revolution" began, he could not see right away that it would bring catastrophe to China. What upset him most at the time was that he had been unjustifiably branded as an anti-revolutionary. Also, because of his "important airs" he was denounced the most severely and his condemnation was known everywhere in the province. His only son was beaten to death and his wife, who had gone through thick and thin with him for years, was also tortured to death. He wept secretly; that was all he could do....

But he felt he had no time for any recollection of the past now. He did not believe China was finished, or that he himself was finished. Neither did he believe that the filty mess in society could not be sorted out. Of course, he had learned to cope with complications and that to put right the present ill practices he could rely only on practical strength. It was no use indulging in moaning and groaning. Obviously, what with the far-reaching power of Zhang Anbang, who was surrounded by many obsequious cadres of the vinylon factory, the apparent dispiritedness and feebleness of Qian Gong, the cynicism of Bai Sha, who believed that she had seen it all before, and the calculating opportunist Qian Xiaobo — he could see nothing but darkness everywhere. But having had a good go at sorting out things, he now understood the situation clearly. To change all that, he felt he still needed something. And that was work.

The dean of the office of the Light Industry Bureau, Ge Guangsheng, paid a special visit to the vinylon factory. He told Ding Meng that the deputy directors of the bureau were very worried.

"About what?" asked Ding Meng.

"Lao Ding, let me give you a bit of my opinion." Ge Guangsheng was a very shrewd Cantonese, short and dark, with a high forehead and deep eyesockets. His eyes were full of life and he spoke with a southern accent. "Now is not like more than ten years ago. In many cases, we have to be reasonably flexible and accommodating. Leave some leeway, as it were. Otherwise, the completion of the vinylon factory can't proceed accordingly."

"That's your personal opinion?"

"Yes."

"What about them, the deputy directors?"

"Also personal opinions, much the same as mine."

"That's fine. I've been given complete authority by the Party Committee to investigate the whole matter of the 'thirty million'. Please don't interfere in my business. Your personal opinion indeed!" Ge Guangsheng was very embarrassed as Ding Meng went on, "When you go back, please let all the comrades know that they have all been invited to express their views at the meeting of the Party Committee. As for you, now I have a little bit of my personal opinion. You are not what you used to be."

Nie Runde, the deputy Party secretary and director of the vinylon factory, came to inform Ding Meng that the Ninth Department of the Provincial Construction Company was about to move its main labour force to another, new construction site. A token number would remain here.

"What? You mean leaving the construction work half completed?" Ding Meng's eyes were wide open as he stared at Nie Runde.

This kind-looking old man, his eyes narrowed into a line, said steadily and firmly, "No, they don't say they're leaving." Ding Meng replied, "All right. If they want to quit, please themselves. They're not the only construction unit in China, you know." Nie Runde answered, unruffled, "This kind of winding-up work is demanding, I hope you understand. A great deal of work and not sufficient pay. All bones and no meat, as it were. The other construction units probably won't be willing to take it up. . . . Besides, they've already hooked up with other departments of the Provincial Construction Company. All for higher wages, you see."

"So this is our glorious Communist Party! Is that it?" Ding Meng was pacing the room hastily. After a few steps, he stopped and asked, "Are you sent by Zhang Anbang to tell me all this?"

"Yes. . . . Oh, I also wanted to come and tell you myself."

Ding Meng gave him a quick glance and said indignantly, "And we can still carry on with the work of modernization?"

"You're the only person taking things seriously. It won't work, Ding Meng." Nie Runde's words of advice came from his very heart.

"Why don't you join me then? If everybody takes things seriously, of course it will work! Now what?. . . Is it because the "cultural revolution" has taken away all your courage?"

"No, not that. It's the present situation."

"Then why don't you withdraw from the Party?" Ding Meng's awl-like eyes were piercing Nie Runde, who gradually lowered his head. Finally, Ding Meng said, "Give notice that the Party Committee will be calling a meeting."

At the meeting, Ding Meng came straight to the point and said, "On the whole matter of the 'thirty million', it seems to me that there is contention between two ways of thinking and two ways of doing things. One is: increase in work efficiency, meticulous calculation in preparing the budget, less spending and fast completion of the project. The other one is the pursuit of personal interests under the disguise of guarding those of the factory, thus impairing the earnings of the country. That is to say using the money of the state to increase one's political capital. Your Secretary Zhang Anbang is a classic example of that, I'm afraid."

A wave of shock went through the room. Silence reigned. Zhang Anbang forced an uneasy smile as he looked at everybody and shook his head in disagreement.

Ding Meng gave a full account of everything related to the "thirty million". He sharply criticized the Party Committee for its failure in holding on to principles firmly. Finally, he said, "Anyone who is not prepared to carry out his duties his post demands is welcome to resign."

After the meeting, he stayed behind to talk with Zhang Anbang privately. "Show your cards," he said bluntly.

"What can I show?" Zhang Anbang stretched out both his hands and forced another uneasy smile. He wanted to relax the tension and dispel Ding Meng's stern airs. "The present situation is this," he began speaking calmly. "If you don't stretch the budget a little wide for the construction unit, they won't work for you. Simple as that! Not that they don't want to help, you understand. If you assign funds to them strictly according to the fixed quota, they'll end up with deficit. That means they may not even be able to pay the salaries of their workers, let alone the monetary awards for outstanding performance. This is a common phenomenon throughout the country, you know. Or, take another example: the purchase of land. Let's say agricultural land for which you have to pay, according to custom, whatever they could get in three years. A few hundred yuan a mu, right? But add other costs to that such as that of agricultural equipments, and you'll need at least seven or eight thousand yuan per mu. That's a fact, I hope you understand. Lacking in equipment or without any transport arrangement, what can you do? You'll have to rely on whatever material you've got in the warehouse for exchange, to get things done, you know. Otherwise, all you can do is to follow the original plan and apply to the authorities for assistance. That will take a hundred years before anything is done. The 'thirty million' has not been worked out by myself alone, you know. Without the 'thirty million', I'm afraid any other secretary won't be able to see the completion of the factory through." Zhang Anbang was secretly pleased with his factual presentation. That was a very strong card indeed, and, as he saw it, the problem could not be solved otherwise. There was no need to mention the Ninth Department's transferring its labour force.

"I see. Your words are final. Let me ask you, though. According to the present situation you've mentioned, if I decided to work for you here as an over-all supervisor for a year, do you think I could complete the work with a budget of twenty-nine million?"

Zhang Anbang had a good look at the serious expression on Ding Meng's face and said, after some thinking, "Yes, I think it's possible."

"What about twenty-eight million?"

Zhang Anbang felt the conversation had turned sour. After that, it would certainly be twenty-seven, twenty-six and so on. He was thinking deeply and did not give any reply.

"Well, let's talk about the twenty-nine million first. Why do you insist on thirty million when twenty-nine is enough? Isn't that extra million put in by you yourself?" Ding Meng paused for a short while and then resumed, "The present situation is not wonderful, I know. But neither do I believe you're working in a communist society. Indeed, you are making capital of this 'present situation', seeking personal gain! . . . This is your share and that, mine. Simple enough! Only in China now do we find this 'present — situation —'!"

Zhang Anbang was secretly sneering at the seriousness of his old superior. However, he said, "I'm only trying to run the vinylon factory a little better. Not for myself, I hope you'll understand."

"Not for yourself?" There was a slight expression of sarcasm on Ding Meng's face. "You can wait and say that again after I've become deaf."

"All right. I won't give you any more explanations. All I can say is that it doesn't matter how much money you grant us as long as there's guarantee of the labour force to carry on with the work. Then I'll be able to see things through. I do hope the bureau will help to solve that problem as soon as possible. Apparently, the Ninth Department has decided not to work for us any more." Zhang Anbang knew that if the Ninth Department refused to carry on, it would be impossible to find a unit in the whole province, for at least half a year, to take up the work.

"Well, you'll have to solve that problem yourself," Ding Meng did not even look at him and said unconcernedly.

"Me?" Zhang Anbang was at a loss for words for a while. "I . . . can't possibly solve that!"

"Then you'll have to step aside. Whoever can solve that will be the chief commander. Simple enough, isn't it?" Ding Meng stood up and had a quick look out of the window, indicating that the conversation had come to an end.

Zhang Anbang felt that he was completely in Ding Meng's hands now. He dared not threaten to resign, by way of bargaining, for he knew full well how that would be received. For the first time he found himself driven into a corner and his heart was filled completely with anger and hate. He was gnashing his teeth with spite as he stared at the grey hair on the back of the head of Ding Meng, who was leaving the room. However, when the head moved as Ding Meng was about to turn round, his cordial smile immediately came back to his face and he said, "Well, I'll think of a way. Can't just sit and eat and let you down."

"Letting me down?" A slight, disdainful look swept over Ding Meng's face. "I'm now acting in the capacity of the secretary of the bureau's Party Committee. If I could speak my mind, representing only myself, I would be shouting at you, you scoundrel! Look at yourself now, and see how you've changed!"

Ding Meng's last words of rebuke carried somewhat the concern of an old superior, not unlike the care of an elder member of a family. But all that concern and care only aroused in Zhang Anbang more hate than any severe reprimand. He could not bear being put in his place. Scornfully, he smiled and said in his heart, "Just you wait! Don't be too pleased with yourself and too soon!"

VII

In the evening Zhang Anbang came home. He reclined on the sofa, thinking over everything thoroughly. He was determined not to see Ding Meng win in this personal battle; it had gone far beyond the bounds of the "thirty million". He hated people like Ding Meng. All he wanted now was revenge, a good fight, and the conclusion that he, only he, was the real master at the vinylon factory.

The telephone on the desk was ringing. He took up the receiver and made a few appropriate laughs. It was a call from the secretary of the Office of the Bureau of Materials about the extra job openings. The tone was very impatient: "Is it possible or not? If not, tell us and we won't bother you any more. We'll find a way out."

Zhang Anbang did not show any anguish. Neither did he dare mention one word about the scuttling of the "thirty million". Firmly, and acting well, he chuckled briskly, "No problem. There won't be any delay. Rest assured you can leave everything to me." He also wanted to ask after the directors of the bureau and went on, ingratiatingly, trying to make witty, small talk. But the caller hung up with a bang. He was very annoyed so much so that his face was turning pale and the corners of his mouth were twitching. He also put down the receiver with a bang. Then he thought of the dissatisfied faces which had been surrounding him for the past two days and their impatient, urgent requests. He thought of the very traitor by his side — entirely against his expectation, Bai Sha had submitted to Qian Gong all the accounts of the materials in the warehouse! He was consumed with extreme anger. Opportunists, all of them, full of self-seeking! After a long while and much effort, he cooled down.

Bai Sha came in. She put aside her scarf and sat down in the sofa as she handed Zhang Anbang a new budget report. "The supplementary budget asking for increased funding has been worked out afresh. Qian Gong has gone over it and given his approval. It's going to be fifteen million," she said.

"He?... Of course, he's the expert on such matters!" Zhang Anbang's face revealed a slight trace of cold sarcasm. "He has given me such good help. I'll have to do him a good turn, of course."

"What do you mean by this?"

"What do I mean?" Although Zhang Anbang still had enough sense left to remind him that he should not go too far, eventually he lost his control and vented his feelings. "If I can't get my 'thirty million', he'd better not dream of going back to Beijing. Well, let Ding Meng go and console him!"

Bai Sha could not help shuddering somewhat. She had never seen Zhang Anbang so spiteful before, and said sharply, "Don't you think you're going too far?"

"I needn't go that far. . . . Ding Meng, the Bureau of Light Industry, the National Construction Committee — they can't help him, can they?" Bai Sha's taking sides with Qian Gong further provoked Zhang Anbang. At the thought of her "betrayal", he was infuriated the more as he said, "All that babbling when somebody is so worried!"

Bai Sha instantly stood up, staring at Zhang Anbang coldly. Her anger and disapproval stung him, no doubt, and he quickly came back to his sences, regaining his self-control. He sighed, patting the handrest of the sofa and said, "All right, all right. I'm merely uttering some words of irritation. The work hasn't been to my liking, that's all. And I'm nursing a little wrath. Not cool enough. . . ."

"Don't you think all this is really a big shame?" asked Bai Sha.

Zhang Anbang was about to say something, but suddenly the door opened and his daughter Haiyan appeared. Her face was burning red. Pain, shame and disgust shone through the glittering tears in her eyes. Undoubtedly, she had overheard every word of the conversation.

"Haiyan, you. . . ." Zhang Anbang stood up, not knowing what to say.

She stood there, her lips trembling, not able to utter a word. Then she turned, biting her teeth and rushed through the room.

His daughter had gone.

Bai Sha had also left.

Zhang Anbang sank into the sofa, dispirited.

The telephone rang. He picked up the receiver. Upon hearing "Hallo", he thought it was from one of his subordinates, yet asking again about what was happening concerning the "thirty million". He answered, irritatingly, "It's all right. It's all right. Thirty million, thirty million. You'll get it and don't you worry! I couldn't be bothered any more!"

The voice at the other end sounded cold, deep, and severe. He recognized it at once. It was Ding Meng. He held on to the receiver listlessly and sat down in the sofa.

After the telephone call, the room appeared exceptionally quiet and desolate. Zhang Anbang felt lonely, tired and fed up. He felt: "To hell with all the ambitions! Forget about politics and just live the life of a proper man. That's it. Let it be a simple and quiet life. That's better than anything else."

But the temptations of personal gain were too strong. His eyes fell inadvertently on his desk, where lay several reports addressed to "Secretary Zhang" waiting for his instruction and approval. Lying beside these documents was a thick red-and-blue pencil, the very symbol of power itself.

More than an hour later, he got up from the sofa, put on his overcoat and, dragging his tired and listless body, went out.

At the bottom stairs of the dormitory, he looked up and saw Ding Meng standing before him above, quietly staring at him. His looks were more than solemn and stern. From his eyes also flowed the kindness and tenderness of an elder and, almost imperceptibly, some of his pity. All at once, Zhang Anbang was moved. More than ten years before, he recalled, in the first month after he had been promoted deputy manager of a factory he was negligent in work and that led to a great loss in production. The unanimous demand was that he should be sacked and disciplined. Then, standing before Ding Meng, he was met with the same eyes as those now set on him. At the time, Ding Meng bore the brunt and, against all opposition, allowed him to make self-criticism and continued his work in order to redeem himself through good service. With tears in his eyes, he worked for all he was worth and eventually got everything right, well making up for the loss in production. Now, Ding Meng was looking at him in the same old manner; only his hair had gone grey. . . .

Zhang Anbang's conscience came back as he recalled those other days — true, another kind of practical life but it was guided by the beliefs of his youth and the oath he had sworn before the flag of the scythe and hammer. . . . However, this light of innocence only flickered in his heart and it soon faded into his "awareness of the present" as he objectively sized up the situation. The sense of awakening and the shame flashed before his eyes and then it was all gone. And traces of scorn, callousness and his indomitable will to conquer remained on his face, intact. Ding Meng noticed all the emotional changes in Zhang Anbang and could not help admitting, with pain in his heart, "Aye, finished and done for. . . . total and complete!"

Zhang Anbang went up the stairs and passed by Ding Meng closely. Indifferently, they exchanged greetings. Then he came into Bai Sha's room on the third floor. She was sitting still, with no expression on her face whatsoever. Casually, he sat down, took the new budget report out from his pocket and put it on the desk.

"Fifteen million," he said. "I've gone over it. Let it stand as it is. Very good." He sounded tired, listless but warm. "Tomorrow, I'm going to the provincial hospital for a medical checkup. You'll look after the matters concerning the budget, won't you? If there's any serious problem, go and discuss it with Lao Nie." Most dutifully, he handed over the task to Bai Sha. The tone of his voice suggested somewhat that he was leaving the vinylon factory for ever. It was full of melancholy and carried with it the feeling of inevitability. After a short pause, he started mumbling, as if all to himself, amidst sighs and reflections: "I think I'm building up an enterprise, but it's far from being easy. I thought I could enjoy the privilege of uttering words freely, including angry ones. . . . But I end up doing harm to my comrades. . . . That's unpardonable." Slowly, he stood up, about to leave. "Fortunately, all the comrades understand me. Let me be criticized, if that's what I deserve. . . . In any case, the vinylon factory is in all our hearts. Among ourselves . . . we also have the feeling for each other."

Bai Sha looked at him coldly, unconcerned.

Zhang Anbang wanted to leave her with these subtle sentiments of loss and, appropriately, did not say anything more. Then he left.

VIII

The next day, Bai Sha put down before Ding Meng several sheets of paper which were filled with her calculations and explanations. That was her "answer" to Zhang Anbang after thinking over everything deeply for the whole sleepless night.

"What's this?" asked Ding Meng as he looked up.

In her usual, calm voice Bai Sha replied, "This is an account of Zhang Anbang's ingenious invention in cooking up the false budget."

Ding Meng nodded. "Oh, you've done it, haven't you? Please pass it on to Qian Gong."

Bai Sha was slightly taken aback. His simple, flat response

was not what she had expected. "Also. . . ." She paused for a while and intended to carry on.

"Give it to Qian Gong, too. That'll do," said Ding Meng kindly as he interrupted her, implying that there was no need for any elaboration.

The way Ding Meng handled the matter made Bai Sha feel that she had been slighted, after all her earnest efforts. Her eyelash trembled a little. "Ha," she said lightly, getting ready to leave.

"What? You're offended that I don't take this seriously?" Ding Meng fully realized how she felt and, patting the sheets of paper on his desk, went on in all earnestness. "I do. What I take even more seriously, however, is why Comrade Bai Sha has produced this only now." He paused for a while. "I've something to discuss with you, though. The bureau intends to run a budget-planners training class. We hope you'll join it and also act as an assistant to Qian Gong. After he's been trans-ferred to Beijing, you'll be with the bureau in charge of the work of budget examination. What do you think?"

"That's beyond my ability," replied Bai Sha.

"Haven't you studied budget planning before?"

". . . . No."

"One should have the courage to speak the truth, you know." Ding Meng was smiling. "You haven't studied that before? But what about Li Bei? Change the name, and one can then change the facts?"

Bai Sha trembled slightly, her face turning red at once. She stood up, consumed with anger.

"One should boldly face one's past and present. I hope you'll agree with me," said Ding Meng as he looked at her.

"I don't need that kind of talk!" retorted Bai Sha and she started walking out.

"You call that strength of character?" Ding Meng also stood up. "Afraid to face facts, that's your greatest weakness. . . . And You're weaker than anybody in that respect."

Bai Sha instantly stopped.

"You've gone through a lot of bitter experience, I know. But precisely because of that, you should be able to conduct yourself better in your work and in your life. . . . Otherwise, I'm afraid you're not worthy even of that experience. I hope you'll understand me."

Momentary silence ensued.

Finally, Ding Meng gently put on the tea-table beside Bai Sha a copy of "Plans for the Budget-Planners Training Class" and said, "Do take it and have a look. If you change your mind, please talk it over with Qian Gong. If not, return it to me."

IX

Like a whirlwind, Zhang Anbang swept through the provincial capital, gathering political force. His activities among the high-ranking officials over, he returned to the factory and played his trump card. The provincial government had asked him to attend a conference which would last half a month. He also announced that he had to stay in hospital for medical treatment. Then, on the same day, he left the factory.

The difficult problems remained. Nie Runde, the old manager of the factory, was sitting before Ding Meng. His stiffened face, all wrinkles, and his drooping eyelids showed all the worries. What was to be done? Clear enough, that was Zhang Anbang's tactics. He would disappear from the scene for several months. The lack of sufficient labour force alone would paralyse the construction of the vinylon factory. Then the stage would certainly be set for Zhang Anbang's mighty comeback. . . .

Ding Meng decided at once to go and consult the Provincial Construction Bureau in the capital.

"Lao Ding, you're still furious? Ha, ha! . . ." laughed Ma Bin, the secretary of the Party Committee of the Construction Bureau after listening to Ding Meng. A gaunt and talkative man, he and Ding Meng had gone through a lot together and he understood his friend well. He went on, shrouded in a cloud of cigarette smoke. "Well, just tell your old comrade-in-arms what to do."

"I want you to solve the problem."

"About the labour force? Haven't I just phoned the Provincial Construction Company? At the moment, only the Ninth Department is available. Well, about all the things you've told me. . . . Ha, ha." Ma Bin burst into another fit of laughter. "You're right, of course. But they also have their problems. Let's do this. I'll ask the company to put together the labour force of the Ninth Department and get on with the work. How's that? . . . As far as I can see, the approval will take two or three weeks at the most, after the case has been studied by various people." He noticed that Ding Meng was not pleased and immediately changed his mind. "Let's make it simple. I'll ask the company and the Ninth Department people to come here and sort things out with you. How's that? I hope you appreciate I'm making an exception for an old friend."

"A big favour indeed!"

Ma Bin was laughing heartily again. "You're not satisfied? . . . I'll tell you this. You've only just resumed work. After some time, you'll understand things better. The present situation is just like that!"

"Present situation again!" Ding Meng could not help knitting his brows.

In the afternoon, Lao Tan, head of the Ninth Department, and the others came to see Ding Meng. A man with ruddy cheeks, short and robust. He understood the special relation between Ding Meng and his top senior and did not put forth any argument, only awkwardly listing his difficulties. "All right, there's no need to go on with your moans," interrupted Ma Bin as he stretched out his arm, which looked like the thin, dry branch of a tree. "You'd better carry on with the work! . . . Director Ding insists on principles, you know, and you should support him. . . . That's it. Any comment from the company?" He pointed at Ding Meng again and said, "As to specific matters, you discuss them with Lao Ding and people from the vinylon factory later." Lao Tan nodded approval.

But when he was back in the vinylon factory for "detailed discussions", Lao Tan still refused to accept the new budget of fifteen million.

Ding Meng went to see Ma Bin again. All he could do was nodding and making another telephone call; nothing came of that. At last, Ding Meng understood. As leader of his bureau, Ma Bin could not make too strict demands on his subordinates; otherwise he would not be able to enjoy the "authority" to command. So, that was another "present situation"!

Now, Ding Meng was frankly criticizing his old friend, Ma Bin let him pour out his words, listening and nodding. From time to time he leaned back laughing heartily as if he had been listening to the naive views of a young man. Ding Meng was infuriated. His eyes were like red-hot iron being hammered on an anvil, its sparks flying in all directions. He was fuming, as he said, "You're totally apathetic and numb! You're a cheat!"

Ma Bin was not visibly shaken, but the smile on his face gradually disappeared. He said with a heavy heart, "Lao Ding, that's true. I've become apathetic and numb, as you said. . . . A pessimist." He paused for a while and then sighed, looking worried. "Lao Ding, like you, I've also fought. . . . The problem is. . . . Aye, let's not talk about it!" Instantly, he looked up and said vehemently, "It's not just the Ninth Department or just a construction bureau! It's the whole . . . all like that! What can you do?" He breathed a deep sigh. "Lao Ding, it's not easy if you want to get things done."

"That's why we have to make an even greater effort. Otherwise, what hope is there, you tell me?" Ding Meng sympathized with the feelings of his old friend and tried to console him. "You have a little quiet rest. Let me go and see Lao Tan and talk things over with him."

Nie Runde was very worried about Ding Meng, fearing that things would develop into a deadlock. He went to see Lao Tan for a chat. Purposely, he disclosed that Ding Meng had already contacted several district and city construction companies and he had decided that very soon he would sign the contract with one of them. He also mentioned that the Bureau of Light Industry had planned many new projects for the next few years, which would constitute a very large proportion of the provincial construction work. In a tone of apparent seriousness, he said, "Ding Meng's quarrel with your Ninth Department is not a small one, you know. He told me that from now on your department won't be given one single construction project by the Bureau of Light Industry. I agree with you, of course. Director Ding is really going too far. . . ." He sounded as if he were very displeased with Ding Meng. His words greatly upset Lao Tan and, although he did not say anything, he was forced to think seriously of all the implications. It would be ideal indeed if the Ninth Department was entrusted with some construction projects in its own district, for then they did not have to work far away from their base and the families of the workers would be particularly pleased.

Nie Runde told Ding Meng about the conversation with Tan. Knitting his brows a little, Ding Meng asked, "Which country's diplomatic game are you playing?" Nie Runde sighed and said that he did not like it either but, under the circumstances, that was the only thing to do. After this, Ding Meng asked Lao Tan to come and see him.

Lao Tan was very annoyed that Ding Meng had put pressure on him through the Construction Bureau. Right now, however, he did not show any sign of displeasure. He was prepared for some hard bargaining. Ding Meng saw through all his clever acts at once and said quite simply, "Lao Tan, you're trying to bargain with me, aren't you? I see it's going to be somewhat like the business negotiations with people from foreign countries." He pointed at Nie Runde beside him and said, "Lao Nie's words have softened you, obviously. Now you have to carry on with the vinylon factory's construction work. You haven't said it yet, but I know you want to get a high price."

The ruddy face of Lao Tan was puffed up, looking even redder.

"We'd better not play this kind of game," Ding Meng went

on. "We're all members of the Communist Party and can't get rid of its hallmark, can we? Let me tell you this. All Lao Nie has told you is mere bluffing. I haven't hooked up with any construction unit — I'd love to, but haven't done it yet. Our future work project may not necessarily be concentrated in this district, either."

Astonished, Lao Tan looked at Ding Meng with his eyes wide open. Ding Meng continued, "I do realize it's no use approaching your Construction Bureau. Neither can I give you orders. I understand this very well. Negotiations? You're in a very superior position and can dictate the terms, if you like. But let me remind you: more than twenty years ago you were the whole province's first captain of the Youth Brigade. Weren't you? Now you've become the model of fraud and deception.   Aren't you ashamed of yourself?"

Lao Tan's head was bending low. He was chain-smoking, failing to connect a few times. Nie Runde was sitting still, his pipe in his mouth and his head also lowered, not uttering a single word.

"Humbug! — you, me and the whole country! What can we do?" Tapping at the desk, Ding Meng sighed with a heavy heart.

Lao Tan went back to his office in the Ninth Department. He smoked for a solid half day, in low spirits. While he was in the midst of worry and confusion, Qian Gong appeared, sent by Ding Meng to help the Ninth Department to get on with the work following the budget of fifteen million. He was stunned. When had he expressed willingness to accept the new budget? Was Ding Meng not too authoritative?. . . Still, not knowing why he did it, he collected his men and the drafts and followed Qian Gong to the building site.

Qian Gong spread out "The Plan for Organizing Construction". The specific proposals therein, meticulously worked out based on his expertise, with all their money-saving measures, won the workers' great admiration. Lao Tan, too, was moved. He could no longer remain unruffled, particularly when he heard that Ding Meng had decided to run a budget-planners training class through the Bureau of Light Industry, so that the trainees from his department would be the future budget experts.

That night he went to see Ding Meng. He did not explicitly indicate that he had accepted the new budget of fifteen million. Instead, he frankly talked about some of the difficulties he had encountered. As he could not increase work efficiency, he had thought of relying on economic regulations in designing new ways of management. Indeed, he had submitted a report, which was then passed on to the Construction Bureau by the company. But several months had gone by and he had not heard a word how it was received. There was nothing he could do. After all, he could not bother them every day.

"You should have — everyday." Ding Meng very much appreciated Lao Tan's attempts as he gently patted his hands. "Be daring. The Construction Bureau will support you, I'm sure." He paused for a while and went on. "Tell me, apart from the bonus — Oh, I'm taking too simple a view of economic regulations — Do we have a way out?. . . The good, old tradition shouldn't be thrown out!"

He meant, of course, the work on political thinking. Some people, he was well aware, took a dim view of that.

X

The slicing of the vinylon factory's supplementary budget by half aroused the attention of the whole public. In the provincial capital, the talk about Ding Meng had gone well beyond the circles of the Bureau of Light Industry and the Construction Bureau. Everybody knew that the "fierce* director" had been absolutely uncompromising in dealing with the vinylon factory. It was also generally known that Ma Bin, the Party Secretary of the Provincial Construction Bureau, had been dragged to the factory so that he could see for himself how work efficiency

---

* Ding Meng's name, "Meng" means fierce. — *Trans.*

could be raised in building construction. In the present wind of sluggishness and half-heartedness, now stood a firm, eye-catching banner which inspired hope. It stirred people's hearts and they boisterously expressed their opinions.

Ding Meng called an extensive meeting of the Party Committee at the vinylon factory. He wanted to begin work on reorganizing the leadership.

Zhang Anbang felt a little uneasy as he watched, in the provincial capital, how things developed. When the Party Committee informed him that he should attend the meeting, he felt even more he had to counteract the threat with stronger measures.

Consequently, problems came to Ding Meng thick and fast. About the already purchased land, the production team again raised its objections all because it had not been given the lorry promised by Zhang Anbang. The transfer of several urgently needed technicians was blocked at the District Organization Department, where the officer in charge was one of Zhang Anbang's close friends. Because the railway trucks — even they were procured by Zhang Anbang through his connections — were suddenly withheld, the steel windows, desperately needed for the completion of the workshop, were stranded in Tianjin. There was problem over the construction of the special railway track for the transportation of coal for the boiler rooms because of a certain "agreement", unwritten in the budget of "thirty million", between Zhang Anbang and the railway bureau. Finally, even the iron covers for the sewage pipes were not available. The memo from the material-supplying unit simply said, "Owing to unforeseen difficulties, we regret that we can't deliver. . . ."

Ding Meng was knitting his brows as he listened to all this "emergence information". Each item, of course, was enough to wreck the one-year plan in the completion of the construction project. He was not caught unprepared, though, as he said to Nie Runde, "Ask some of the cadres to deal with these problems the best way they can. We must get on with reorganizing the leadership. After this, we can attend to all these problems one at a time."

Meanwhile, Ge Guangsheng brought him the news from the provincial capital that the Provincial Organization Department had not approved the transfer of Qian Gong to Beijing. That somewhat surprised Ding Meng. He came into Qian Gong's room and found him and Ge Guangsheng, Nie Runde shrouded in depressing cigarette smoke.

"It's no use being disheartened," said Ding Meng as he entered the room. They did not utter a word, only lifted their heads to give him a quick look and then turned their eyes in another direction. In truth, however, they were indignant and depressed mainly because rumour had it that the Provincial Organization Department had decided to remove Ding Meng from the Bureau of Light Industry. He did not know this, of course.

"Why don't they agree?" asked Ding Meng.

"I don't know. Qian Gong has probably offended Zhang Anbang. His wife works in the Organization Department, you know," said Ge Guangsheng angrily.

"That's violating the law and discipline!" Ding Meng was in a rage.

"What can we do when there's no evidence of that? They do it in the name of the Organization Department and say it's strictly according to the needs of the province. Perfectly justifiable!" added Ge Guangsheng.

"Absolute nonsense!"

"Director Ding, you'd better ... leave it alone," said Qian Gong at last. "Aye. ... Lao Ge is right. These days, who takes his work seriously will be in trouble. ..."

"So you don't insist on principles?" asked Ding Meng reproachfully.

"Me? I'm not talking about me. ... I don't care about them. They can do whatever they like. But I won't let them have one single cent more than needed." Qian Gong became indignant and, making gestures, went on. "Just let me do it. So that's that! ... I see things clearly now. Even if I'm back in Beijing, if I don't remain firm and meet force with force I won't be able to produce a good budget."

Fervent feelings swept over Ding Meng, but he did not show any sign of joy. Instead, he looked at Ge Guangsheng disapprovingly. "What have you been preaching? . . . You and your pessimism and negativeness!"

"Me being pessimistic? . . ." Ge Guangsheng was full of deep emotion today. "That's the present situation!"

Present situation! Upon hearing these words, Ding Meng was burning with anger. "Such grumbling over only one matter!. . ." After a pause, he regained his calm and said, "If everybody does his best, everything will be all right. Well, about Qian Gong's transfer, we'll study the case in a couple of days when we're back at the bureau. Then we'll contact the Organization Department."

"You contact the Organization Department?" Ge Guangsheng sounded even more harsh. "It will contact you first, I'm telling you, and 'promote' you immediately to be the vice-president of the Provincial Workers' Union! The eleventh vice-president, it seems."

"What?"

"Some 'kind-hearted' people have reported that you were persecuted severely during the "cultural revolution", your health is now not very good and therefore you shouldn't be doing the strenuous work at the Bureau of Light Industry. . . ." Ge Guangsheng wanted to carry on, but Ding Meng instantly stood up and chided him, "No more of that! It's merely hearsay."

"Hearsay nevertheless has better cause than official explanations." Ge Guangsheng was getting angry.

For a while, Ding Meng said nothing. His eyes showed slight signs of fatigue. He looked at Ge Guangsheng again, this time with forgiveness in his eyes, and repeated what he had just said, "No more of that. It's merely hearsay." He was gentle but firm. Ge Guangsheng remained silent. Ding Meng stood still for a few moments, staring into the distance out of the window. Then he turned round and said to Nie Runde.

"Tomorrow morning, we'll get on with the extensive meeting of the Party Committee."

XI

Meanwhile, the news of Ding Meng's transfer from the Bureau of Light Industry spread through the factory — it came from Zhang Anbang remote-control transmission. It first caused a tremor among the cadres. The whole afternoon people were fidgety. Some of them, disturbed no doubt, were talking excitedly and confidentially, preparing a fierce "counter-attack". They were going to "turn the tide" at the last extensive Party Committee meeting the next day. Many others, however, were watching the scene with worries on the minds. . . . In the evening, spread another piece of news: today, the Railway Bureau said to the people who had been sent by vinylon factory to sort out the problems concerning the construction of the special railway track, "Please ask your Ding Meng to come here himself!"

At night Nie Runde came to see Ding Meng. He pushed open the unlocked door and saw Ding Meng standing before the window gazing at the dark night dotted by a few scattered light. His face betrayed a few traces of worry and he seemed to have aged a little more. Struck by the feeling of shame and guilt, he stood hesitating at the door.

"Something serious?" asked Ding Meng gently as he turned and noted his presence.

Nie Runde hesitated somewhat and said, "Things aren't quite normal in the factory. Is the meeting tomorrow off?. . ."

"No," replied Ding Meng decisively. "It's on. Things are very normal, you know. . . . Any other business?"

Originally, Nie Runde wanted to report on the problems concerning the railway track, but now he merely said, "If there're still problems, we'll find ways of sorting them out ourselves."

"Good. . . . Please thank the comrades for me." Ding Meng nodded slightly. Of course he knew of the trouble over the railway track that day.

As if everybody realized Ding Meng would like to have a quiet evening, nobody came to bother him. His house, normally filled with laughter, now seemed empty. The night was deep and quiet. The room was kept warm by the fire from the stove. He opened the window a little to let in some cold air. He paced the room and then stopped unawares before the mirror. For the first time, he looked closely at himself in the mirror and noticed that his hair had turned all grey. He was getting old and there was not much time left!. . . But the things to be done were too many. So, too, the things that deserved his worries. Of course, he was not concerned whether or not he would still be the director. Neither was he worried about the outcome of the battle over the "thirty million". What he did worry about was the Party, the country! He could not believe that the country would be left in the hands of people like Zhang Anbang who could not care less about the Communist Party. But the practical problems inevitably increased his concern in that respect. . . . Gazing at the diminishing lights that decorated the night, he thought deeply. Very deeply.

The door opened. It was Ma Bin coming to see him at midnight. "Lao Ding," he said sincerely. "I should learn from you. Under any circumstances, one shouldn't lose confidence. One should remain optimistic."

"To tell you the truth, I'm pretty worried," replied Ding Meng.

"That the construction work can't be completed, based on the new budget of fifteen million?"

"No," Ding Meng picked the alarm clock on his desk, rather preoccupied. He tightened the spring a little and put it down. "A clock wound up will go on ticking. I needn't worry too much about the vinylon factory. Every section has been mobilized. Even if there are more difficulties, they won't so easily get in the way of the completion. What I worry about. . . . Aye, you know that." He tended his grey hair with his hand, unintentionally.

Ma Bin understood at once how his old friend felt. He, too, appeared dignified. After a while, he said, "However, Lao Ding, your worrying and mine are different. You worry, all right. But you're still optimistic and full of confidence. I worry and it leads to pessimism, despair and loss of confidence."

"My only fear is that your kind of worrying may turn out to be the ultimate truth!. . ."

Ma Bin remained speechless for a while. Then he hastily objected, passionately, "No, no, no! I disagree. My kind of pessimism and despair can never be the ultimate truth!. . . Lao Ding, that's it, how many people have been awakened once you're serious about the 'thirty million'? Qian Gong, budget planner Bai Sha, factory manager Nie, Lao Tan of the Ninth Department and there's also me. Yes, even your old friend, who is lagging so far behind, is now at least awakened!. . . I do agree with what you've said. To change the present situation, only one thing is lacking. And that is work!"

"So you think we still have hope, eh?. . . That's certainly good!" Ding Meng's eyes were carrying his worries and deep thoughts, but in their glitter was seen something of his old humour when making jesting remarks.

Translated by W. C. Chau
Illustrated by Zhao Ruichun

ZHANG XIANLIANG

(1936 —   )

Born in 1936 in Nanjing, Zhang Xianliang began work as a teacher in Gansu Provincial Cadre School after graduating from high school in Beijing in 1955. In 1958 he was sent to a farm in Ningxia, where he did manual labour. He was promoted to be the editor of the journal *Shuo Fang* in 1979. The following year, he joined the Union of Chinese Writers and was elected director of the Ningxia Writers' Council.

After writing over sixty short poems in the fifties, he went for a long period without producing anything. Since 1979, however, he has published a novelette, *Amorous Whispers Inside a Dungeon*, and ten short stories, one of which is entitled "The Story of Old Man Xin and His Dog".

The following work of fiction is the basis for the film *The Horse Herder*.

*   *   *

Body and Soul

He was the abandoned son of wealthy parents....
— Victor Hugo, *Les Miserables*

BODY AND SOUL

Zhang Xianliang

I

Xu Lingjun hadn't expected to see his father again.

The place was an elegantly furnished room on the seventh floor of a luxury hotel. Outside the window was nothing but an empty expanse of sky faintly streaked with the white strands of a few wispy clouds. . . . Beyond his farmhouse window on the remote loess plateau were the yellows and greens of the open country, expansive, yet close. Since his arrival in the city, he felt a sort of giddiness, as if he had been caught in a sudden burst of the high clouds. The bluish, fog-like smoke which came out from his father's pipe and floated through the room added to the unreal quality of everything before his eyes. And yet his father was still smoking the same brand of pipe tobacco from the pouch decorated by an Indian chief's portrait, and the fragrance of tobacco tinged with the sweet aroma of coffee which he had often caught wind of as a child offered proof to his senses that far from being a dream, this occasion was indeed real.

"Let bygones be bygones," said his father with a sweeping gesture of dismissal. Ever since he received a B.A. from Harvard in the thirties, he had preserved the dignified air acquired in his days in Cambridge. He sat on the sofa with his legs outstretched in a swank Western suit.

"As soon as I reached the Mainland, I fully understood the saying: 'Eyes straight ahead.' You'd better get moving on now and make preparations to leave the country."

The furnishings of the room and his father's clothes brought back memories and a strange feeling came over him. Let by-gones be bygones indeed! But how could he forget the past?

Thirty years ago, on a day in autumn like this, he was walking on Xiafei Road trying to find his father's abode. He had in his hand the address written by his mother. Eventually, he found the place: the same building, the same garden. The rain had stopped and the dripping leaves on the trees looked parched and lifeless. On top of the walls, he could see the barbed wire. He pressed the bell on the grey wall. After a long while, the small window on the iron door opened and the same man who used to take letters to his father let him in. They walked along the foot-path, which had trees on either side, and reached the two-storeyed building where his father lived.

Then, thirty years ago, his father looked much younger. He was wearing a beige sweater and his arm was resting on the mantel piece. Opposite him, sitting in the sofa, was that very woman Lingjun's mother had been cursing every day.

"So this is your child," she said. "He looks very much like you. Come over here, my dear child."

Lingjun did not move; instead, he glanced at her. He remembered seeing a pair of sparkling eyes and brightly rouged lips.

His father lifted his head. "What's the matter?"

"Mother's ill, and she asks you to come back."

"She's always ill, always. . . ." His father angrily strode from the fireplace and paced to and fro on the carpet. The carpet was green with a white pattern woven into it. Lingjun followed the trail of his father's footsteps, and only with difficulty held back his tears.

"Tell your mother that I'll come back after a while." His father was finally standing in front of him. Yet he knew that it was an empty promise and that his mother had heard this more than once on the phone.

In a soft, hesitant voice, Lingjun persisted: "She wants you to come home right away."

"I know, I know. . . ." With a hand on Lingjun's shoulder,

the father guided his son to the doorway. "Go on back first, and take my car there. If your mother is seriously ill, tell her to go straightaway to the hospital." His father saw him to the vestibule where he suddenly stroked his son's hair. He hesitated as he spoke. "If only you were a bit older, you could . . . could understand. . . . Your mother is . . . is hard to get along with. She's such a . . . such a. . . ." Lingjun looked up and saw that his father was rubbing his knitted brow. With one look at such a weak, anguished expression, he actually began to pity his father.

But as Lingjun rode in his father's Chrysler limousine through the yellow leaf-covered streets of the French concession, his eyes were filled with tears. He was overwhelmed by feelings of shame, self-pity, and loneliness. Why should he feel sorry for anyone else when he himself was so sad? He'd never received much in the way of maternal affection from a mother who spent much more time caressing her Mah-jong tiles than his hair. Nor had he got much in the way of paternal guidance from a father, who, on his return home from work, would turn glum, depressed and vexed and begin incessant quarrels with his mother. His father said that if only Lingjun were a bit older, he could understand. . . . Actually, with only eleven years behind him, he already understood quite a lot: what his mother needed most was tenderness from his father, and what his father needed most was to break away from an odd and capricious wife. But neither his mother nor his father had any use for him. He was nothing more than the product of an arranged marriage between a graduate returned from America and a landlord's daughter.

As it turned out, his father didn't return home. And when his mother soon afterwards found out that Lingjun's father had left the Mainland with his mistress, only a few more days passed before she died in a German-run hospital.

It was just at this time that the Liberation Army entered Shanghai. . . .

And now, after thirty long years, replete with more misfortune than any time before, his father had suddenly returned and wanted to take Lingjun with him out of the country. The whole business was so strange that Lingjun could not believe that the man sitting across from him was his father, nor that he was that man's son.

His father's secretary, Miss Song, opened a wardrobe to pick out some clothes for the old man, and inside Lingjun caught sight of large and small suitcases covered with colourful hotel stickers from Los Angeles, Tokyo, Bangkok, and Hong Kong, not to mention the oval airline tags printed with "Pan American Boeing 747". The small wardrobe revealed a wide world. Meanwhile for Lingjun, it had been only three days since the local authorities had relayed his travel notification from the China Travel Service. For two days and two nights he had endured many a jolt aboard bus and train before finally arriving.

Lingjun had placed his grey patent-leather suitcase on a corner of the sofa. Such a suitcase was considered "Western-style product" back at the farm, but as soon as it appeared in this room, it seemed to shrink back in shame. Hanging from the suitcase was a nylon-string bag with a toothbrush, toothpaste, and a few tea-boiled eggs left over from his trip. As he glanced at the tea eggs with their hairline cracks tossed together at the bottom of the bag, he recalled the eve of his departure when Xiuzhi, his wife, had urged him to give his father some of these eggs.

Two days earlier, Xiuzhi had insisted upon taking Qingqing along to the county seat's bus station to bid him farewell. Lingjun hadn't left the farm since getting married, so this long trip took on the aura of nothing less than an epoch-making event in their small family.

"Daddy, where's Beijing?"

"Beijing is northeast of the county seat."

"Is Beijing a whole lot bigger than the county seat?"

"Yes, a whole lot bigger."

"Does it have asters?"

"No."

"Does it have jujubes?"

"No."

"Oh —" Qingqing's drawn-out sigh was like that of an adult, and she looked extremely disappointed as she cradled her chin in one palm; to her way of thinking for a place to be good it had to have asters and jujubes.

"Silly girl, Beijing is a big place," Old Zhao, the coachman said and playfully added: "Your dad is really off to distant places this time around. You'll be leaving the country with your granddad before long. Isn't that right, Instructor Xu?"

Xiuzhi drew up her knees as she smiled mildly at Old Zhao from her seat right behind him. She didn't say anything but through her smile alone she expressed her trust and loyalty. She could no more imagine Lingjun going abroad than Qingqing could imagine how large Beijing was.

The country road with its crisscrossing ruts was rough and bumpy, and the draft horse pulling them lurched ahead with a choppy gait. Tidy rectangular farm fields stretched out to the north of the road, while in the murky and indistinct reaches to the south lay the grassland where he had once herded horses. It seemed the area had a sort of magnetic attraction. Each bush and tree had the power to evoke a continuous stream of memories, and Lingjun suddenly felt all the more sympathetic towards this country.

They reached a clump of three white poplars, which he recognized at a glance from the sturdy jujube tree right behind them. He got down from the carriage and broke off a branch of the jujube, and the three began eating the fruits after he returned to his seat. These wild fruits were a specialty of the northwest, mildly sweet despite their tartness. During the famine of 1960, he had once survived on wild fruits like these. Years had passed since he'd had any, and now that he was eating them the flavour enhanced his feeling of nostalgia. No wonder Qingqing asked whether or not there were jujubes in Beijing.

"Surely her grandpa has never eaten jujubes," said Xiuzhi with a smile as she spit pits out of the carriage. This was the broadest rein she had given her imagination in connection with her father-in-law's return from abroad.

She wouldn't have needed much imagination — the resemblance between father and son was that Xiuzhi could have recognized her father-in-law if she had met him on the street. Each man had long and narrow eyes, a straight nose and a full mouth. One could even say that they shared genetic traits as shown in their deportment and gestures.

The father did not come across as being very old. His skin was as dark as his son's, a tan clearly picked up — on the beaches of Los Angeles or Hong Kong. There was nothing wan or sallow about it. He was still quite particular about his appearance, very mindful of his clothes. However much his hair had greyed, he kept it immaculately groomed; though old age spots had appeared on the back of his hands, his fingernails were well manicured.

Scattered around a delicate set of china on the coffee table, there lay a "3-B" brand pipe, a tobacco pouch of Moroccan leather, a gold-plated cigarette lighter, and a tie pin set with diamonds.

How could he have ever eaten jujubes?

II

"Ah, even here you can listen to the latest hits," said Miss Song in fluent Chinese. A jasmine fragrance wafted from her tall and buxom figure. She had a violet silk ribbon tied around her long black hair, which hung down her back in black strands that looked like a horse tail when they swung to and fro. "Just look, Mr. Chairman, people in Beijing are getting into the swing of disco and they dance even better than those in Hong Kong. Modernization has arrived!"

"No one can withstand pleasure's enticement." Lingjun's father smiled in the manner of a philosopher who has long since seen through all human vanity. "They no longer consider themselves ascetics now."

After dinner, his father and Miss Song escorted him to the dance hall. He never knew that Beijing had such places. When he was a small boy, his parents had taken him along to night-clubs in Shanghai such as "The Gate to a Hundred Pleasures" and "The French Evening Club", and today he seemed to be revisiting their old haunts. However, he soon grew uneasy as he gazed at these effeminate-looking men and masculine-looking women roving around under the soft lighting like ghosts amid moonbeams. It was as if he had been ushered onstage to stand in for one of the actors, and were incapable of playing the role expected of him.

A moment before in the dining room, he had felt a shudder of disgust when he saw how many entrées were merely poked at before being carried back to the kitchen uneaten. In the state-run cafeteria back at his county seat, everyone brought an aluminum box for leftovers which would be finished off at home that night.

As each tune was struck up in the dance hall, several couples began to dance about in odd postures. Instead of holding each other close, they stood face to face and rocked back and forth, challenging each other like gamecocks. So *this* was how such people draned off their excess energy! He thought of the peo-ple who at this very moment were harvesting rice in steaming hot paddy-fields. Bent over at the waist, they swung their arms endlessly, now from right to left, now from left to right. They would occasionally raise their heads and call out to the water carriers in a hoarse voice, "Hey, some water over here!" If only he could lie down now in a patch of green shade by a canal gurgling with yellow water, and catch the scent of rice straw and alfalfa in the gentle breeze — how much better that would be. . . .

"Can you dance, Mr. Xu?" Lingjun suddenly heard the ques-tion from Miss Song, who was now sitting next to him. The mood he had just begun to enjoy evaporated. He lowered his head and glanced at her: she also had a pair of sparkling eyes and a mouth brightly rouged with lipstick.

"No, I can't." Lingjun gave her an apathetic smile. He

could graze horses, plough fields, harvest crops, and winnow rice . . . what use would it be to know how to dance — especially this kind of dancing?

"Don't embarrass him," said his father to Miss Song with a chuckle. "Look — Manager Wang's come over to ask you to dance."

A handsome man wearing a grey suit walked around the table up to Miss Song and beamed as he bent over her. The couple went off to the dance floor.

"What more is left for you to consider?" Lingjun's father relit the pipe. "You know better than I do that the policies of the Communist Party often change. At present, it's relatively easy to get a visa, but who can say how it will be later on?"

Lingjun turned around and faced his father. "There are also things here which I'm unwilling to part with."

"Including all the suffering?" His father's question was thought-provoking.

"The value of happiness can be increased only through suffering."

"What do you mean?" His father stared at him shifting his shoulders in puzzlement.

Lingjun's heart was swept by a wave of sadness. He remembered that his father also belonged to this strange, incomprehensible world; mere similarities of physique could not remove the cause of their spiritual estrangement. He looked at his father in much the same way as his father stared at him, but neither man's gaze could penetrate the others' eyes to see what lay deep beneath the surface.

"Are you still . . . still hurt?" At last his father asked.

"No, not in the least!" Lingjun's arm waved in a gesture of dismissal exactly like his father's. "It's just as you said: bygones are bygones. The present age is another matter altogether. . . ."

A different tune was now playing. This time it was low-key and relaxed, like water that flowed through long irrigation channels. The lights seemed a bit dimmer, for Lingjun could scarcely make out the figures swaying on the dance floor. His father hung down his head and rubbed his forehead back and forth, once again exuding an air of weakness and suffering. "All right, bygones are indeed bygones. But when you think back on it, there was all that suffering . . . at any rate, I've really missed you, and especially so now that . . . that. . . ."

Lingjun was somehow touched by his father's low murmur which harmonized with the relatively refined song. "Yes, I believe you," said Lingjun, all but lost in reverie. "I've also missed you."

"You have?" His father raised his head.

Yes. During an autumn night twenty years ago, moonlight shone through the latticework of a rain-torn paper window on a group of men lying in what looked like rag piles. A dozen or so slept in a low, one-room adobe hut. As Lingjun lay against the wall, he noticed that his clothes were soaked with the odour of humid soil. Shivering in the cold, Lingjun figured he might as well climb out from under the humid rice straw. Outdoors, the mud flats under the moonlight glittered like shards of broken glass. Mud puddles lay everywhere. A stench of decay filled the air.

Lingjun found a horse corral where piles of horse manure added to the warmth. Horses, mules, and donkeys snorted as they chewed the hay piled in their mangers. Seeing an empty manger, he crawled into it. He would sleep in a wooden manger just as the newborn Jesus had once done.

The moonlight shone in at an angle, dividing light from shadow in a diagonal line across the gables of the horse stable. Each animal's head hung down by its manger as if worshipping the moon. A feeling of extreme despondency came over him as the entire scene came together to underline his plight in a symbol of isolation: forsaken by the people, he was forced to join ranks with livestock!

He wept. The narrow manger pressed in on his body, just as life had constricted him from all quarters. First he'd been abandoned by his father. After his mother died, his uncle had made off with all of her possessions, taking every thing except Lingjun. Later he moved into a school dormitory, where he lived and studied on a public education grant. The Communist Party took him in, and the Communist Party had trained him. Despite the sensitive and taciturn personality his abnormal family had ingrained in him he slowly became involved in the collective spirit prevalent during the optimistic atmosphere of the fifties. Throughout most of that decade, all high school students shared the same beautiful dreams of the future. After graduation, his dream turned into reality. He entered the classroom wearing his blue twill Mao suit holding lecture notes and chalk in his hands. He had found his own path in life. However, because the school's Party branch secretary had to fulfil the quota of Rightists to be arrested, the official stuck Lingjun into the same political category as his father. Blood relationship, it seems, inevitably determines for ever the class to which one belongs. So he was again identified as a member of the capitalist class. In the past, the capitalist class had abandoned him, leaving him nothing but the word "capital" to appear on his *curriculum vitae.* Later on, the people had abandoned him and given him the added label to wear of bourgeois Rightist. Finally, he was abandoned by all and sent down to a remote farm for labour reform.

One horse, having finished eating its hay, sidled along the manger over to where Lingjun was lying. It came over as close to him as the rope tied around it allowed, and stretched out till its mouth was above his head. Lingjun felt a warm breath on his face. He saw the brown horse move its lips by his head in search of rice grains in the manger. A moment passed before the brown horse discovered his presence. Rather than being alarmed, it leaned over to sniff Lingjun's head and nuzzle his face. Deeply moved, he embraced the horse's long, gaunt head and, choked with noiseless sobs, wiped his tears dry on the horse's mane. Before long, he was on his knees scraping the grains at the bottom of the manger and pushed them over to within the horse's reach.

Father, where were you then?

III

And now his father had arrived.

It was no dream! His father was sleeping on the next bed, right beside him, and he was stretched out on a "Simmons" bed. He ran his hand along the mattress: how different from a rock-hard wooden manger! Moonlight shone through the gauze curtains, casting checkered patches on the carpet, the sofa, and the bed. The impressions Lingjun had received over the day now clearly emerged in the dim moonlight, and his overriding feeling was that he was totally unadapted and unaccustomed to all this. His father had returned, but as a complete stranger. His father's return had merely brought back memories of suffering and disturbed his peace of mind.

Although the season had already moved into autumn, the room seemed to be getting more and more hot and stuffy. There seemed to be no reason not to throw off his blankets, sit up in bed, turn on the bed-table light, and look around the room with indifference. His gaze rested on his own physique. He looked over the curves of his muscular arms, his calves lined with veins, his feet with toes splayed, and his palms and soles patched with yellowish calluses — and he recalled what his father had just told him during the afternoon.

After finishing their coffee that afternoon, his father sent Miss Song away. He then remarked on the development of his company abroad, the incompetence of Lingjun's various younger stepbrothers, and his yearnings for Lingjun and his native land.

"With you by my side, I could be consoled a bit," said Lingjun's father. "The more I thought about what happened thirty years ago, the more uneasy I felt. I realized that with the Mainland's recurring class-struggle compaigns, your bourgeois family background must have made life miserable for you. I even went so far as to imagine that you were no longer alive, and my concern for you constantly plagued my mind. The image of you as a boy often appeared in my thoughts. I recall especially clearly how you lay at your maid's bosom that day right after your birth: it seems only yesterday that at the Overseas Chinese Hotel next to the Nanjing Foreign Affairs Bureau, your grandfather held that banquet celebrating your birth. On that day, such leading families of industry and commerce as the Rongs, the Guos, the Lius, and the Zhengs all sent representatives from Shanghai to join in the celebration. I gather you know that you were our family's 'eldest son's eldest son'. . . ."

Now that Lingjun looked at his strong and wiry physique, defined and yet contained within the lamplight filtered by a light green lampshade, he was struck by a strange impression. Because his father had just told him, for the first time, about the circumstances of his childhood going beyond his earliest memories, a clear contrast formed in his mind between his two selves of the present and the past. He at last discovered what had been troubling his father: a fabulously wealthy family's eldest son's eldest son who had been wrapped in swaddling clothes of silken brocade and praised at a banquet with all the trimmings by port-city industrial magnates and their wives, had become a *bona fide* labourer! Yet along the course of his life from one extreme to the other how much suffering and joy he had experienced!

Lingjun had no home to which he could return after being released from labour reform. So it was agreed to keep him on the farm to herd horses, and he became known as a herdsman.

Early in the morning, when the sun's light had just poked above the treetops in the willow grove giving a sparkle to the silvery dewdrops on the prairie, Lingjun opened the gate to the corral. The animals inside jostled each other as each vied for the front ranks in the dash out to the prairie. With neighs of joy and cries of alarm they ran off through the thick grass. The horses cocked their tails high above their flanks at an angle which made them look like arrows shot towards the willow grove. Astride his horse, he felt as if he were throwing himself into Nature's embrace as he galloped over the prairie through which the horse herd had trodden path after dark-green path.

On the prairie was a marshland full of reeds. The animals spread out among clumps of reeds, lowering their heads to forage for grass. From his position outside the marsh, all he could hear of the horses' activities were their snorts and a continual splashing about. On the up-slope of a hill, he lay down and gazed at the sky where snow-white clouds were in the same state of continual flux as human life. As the wind brushed the blades of grass and marshy waters, it picked up a fresh moistness, the scent of horse sweat, and the very breath of nature; as it touched him all over from head to foot, it gave him a sort of consolation. Raising an arm and bending his head down towards his armpit, he caught the scent of his own sweat mingling with the scents of nature. These were wonderful feelings of spiritual refreshment which gave rise to boundless reveries wherein he believed himself merged with the winds of the wilderness. He was everywhere at once and had discarded his sense of singularity. His depression, outrage at fate, and sorrow all dissolved as an intense love for life and nature took over in their stead.

At noon, the horses made their way out of the reeds one by one, their bellies full and round, their manes bristling with spirit, and their tails swishing back and forth to drive off horseflies and gadflies. They gathered around him in a trusting and intimate manner, gazing at their herder with large, gentle eyes. Now and then, number seven horse which had white and mottled dark spots, circled around the leaner members of the herd and finally slipped alongside the lame number one hundred horse, nibbling and pestering away at it with its mouth fringed with a sparse growth of whiskers. Number one hundred wouldn't take this lying down, but would lower its rear end to kick backwards with the gusto it had prior to going lame. Number seven would draw back and raise its head high; then it would dash back and forth through the herd while kicking up a silvery spray just as a naughty child might try to divert attention from its mischief by pulling off a "disappearing act". At this juncture, Lingjun would raise his whip and shout fiercely a few times. Each horse would lift up its ears and direct a glare of rebuke at number seven which would quiet down like a schoolboy who had been scolded. It would stand knee-deep in the marsh, twitching its mouth and grinding its long front teeth in exasperation. At such times Lingjun felt that far from watching over a mere pack of animals, he was more like a prince in a fairy tale who was the companion of supernatural beings animated with human intelligence.

Under the high noon sun, the shadows of clouds along the mountain foothills were slowly moving. A flock of marsh waterfowl known locally as "water buffalo" appeared somewhat listless in the scorching heat and began chirping as they poked among the reeds.

This area had not only the majestic vastness of "winds rippling through the prairie grass to reveal cattle and sheep", but also the delicate beauty of purple hills and jasper streams. An abstract concept like "the motherland" could be distilled into the limited space of his experience and in the process revealed the magnificent form of its entirety. Lingjun felt content; life was fine after all. Nature and labour had given him many things that he could not have received in a classroom.

Sometimes rainstorms came. First, rain clouds like curtains of black silk gauze would touch down on distant mountain slopes. Brilliant rays of sunshine bathing the broad grasslands would become a pleasing golden colour. The rain clouds, pushed by the wind, would then move slowly down the mountain slopes. Before long, raindrops the size of beans would fall down at a slant, while layers of murky white mist hovered upward all over the prairie. Before the storm arrived in its full fury, Lingjun would have to drive the horse herd into a nearby grove of trees. Brandishing his whip, he rode his horse at a furious gallop in the face of gusts that blew open his tattered jacket like a pair of wings. Veering this way and that through the herd, he chased down the horses which had turned away from the herd, directing them back to the fold with shouts and gestures. At such times he felt his own body brimmed with fiery strength, and that he wasn't a useless nonentity; in the struggle with the wind, the rain, and a multitude of insect pests, he gradually regained his self-confidence.

Only in such adverse circumstances would the herders from each brigade be able to get together. The shack which had been built to shelter them from rain was like a narrow skiff anchored in a haze of fog and rain. The shed was somewhat cool and damp inside, permeated with blue smoke from cheap tobacco. Lingjun would listen to the herdsmen's jokes told in bawdy language, and he was startled to notice how rarely they expressed complex feelings about labouring or life which would be comparable to his own. They had been simple and down-to-earth from the very beginning; life may have been hard for them, but when all was said and done they were happy and content with their lot. Lingjun began to admire them.

One day an old herdsman over sixty came over to Lingjun with a question. "People say you're a Rightist. What do they mean by Rightist?"

He dropped his head in embarrassment, and slowly replied, "Rightists . . . well, Rightists are people who have made mistakes."

"Rightists are just people who came out with a little straight talk back around 1957," said a herdsman from the seventh brigade. "The scholars really got it that year." The seventh-brigade herdsman was a frank and outspoken fellow who was fond of cracking jokes. Everyone called him "Stiff-necked Guo."

"As for calling straight talk 'making mistakes' or what not, if nobody talks straight, everything will be out of whack." The old herdsman seemed lost in thought as he took a few puffs on his pipe. "On the other hand," he continued, "it's better to be a labourer, anyway, and not a cadre. I'm almost seventy, but my eyes aren't cloudy, my ears aren't deaf, my back isn't stooped, and when I eat I still chomp and crunch away. . . ."

"That means your kids and their kinfolk will have to be labourers too," interrupted Stiff-necked Guo with a smile.

"And what's wrong with them being labourers like me?" the old herdsman countered. "If you don't keep up with manual labour, you'll just make a mess of your life; you'll mess up as an official, or you'll mess up as a scholar. . . ."

This sort of random conversation could stir Lingjun to a joyous feeling close to that of seeing a rainbow after a thunderstorm. He longed to return to a state of ordinary simplicity, to attain his fellow workers' sense of contentment.

Through a long period of manual labour, and amid the physical fluctuations to which both man and nature are ever subject, Lingjun was gradually able to acquire a settled way of life. This new way of life molded him according to the strict daily patterns he had established on his own. In the course of time, his past faded into something like a vague dream, or a tale which he had once read about someone else. His settled way of life, so completely different from the life he had led as a youth, also divided away many of his youthful memories. His years in the city began to smack of illusoriness, and rural existence alone seemed a hard-and-fast reality.

At last, he not only had grown accustomed to life in this locale, but also would no longer be able to find life elsewhere satisfying: he was now a real herdsman.

By the time the "cultural revolution" broke out, local people had long since forgotten about Lingjun's past. It was only after the fervent political campaigns were well under way that a few people recalled his classification as a Rightist! Lingjun had to be dragged out before the public for a spell of pillorying. At this juncture, however, herdsmen from several brigades assembled inside the shed for a discussion and they firmly concluded that the glazing on the lower slopes would simply not do. After hailing the farm administrators with a perfunctory farewell, they gathered the livestock together with whistles and shouts, and began to drive the animals up into their summer pastures in the hill country. Of course, Lingjun had to accompany the horses, since not a single member of the revolutionary masses was willing to forsake the revolution to replace Lingjun at a post which precluded a return home for several months. A couple of herdsmen helped Lingjun hoist his light baggage onto a horse's back. The men swayed back and forth atop their mounts as they left that chaotic place where trouble was in the offing.

Once the herdsmen reached the main trail, a couple of them cheerfully shouted: "Let's go!   We're off for the hills — who cares what those faultfinders back there get up to!" A medley of piercing whistle echoed with a chorus of shouts as the thud of horse hooves kicked up billowing yellow clouds of dust. Far in the distance were the moist upland pastures, which shone with a crystalline sparkle like jadeite. . . . Lingjun had always had a special feeling for this day which was indelibly engraved in his memory.

This place contained his sufferings as well as his joys. Yet as his personal experience grew, his sense of joy gradually went beyond the realm of an emotion that could merely be balanced off against suffering. His sufferings consequently paled into insignificance.

In the spring of last year, Lingjun was suddenly recalled from the hillside pasture by the farm's administrative board. With a straw hat in hand, he apprehensively stepped into an office over whose door hung the sign, "Political Department". Assistant Director Dong first read through a formal document, and then told Lingjun that he had been mistakenly labelled a Rightist and was now exonerated and that preparations had been made to assign him to the farm school as a teacher.

Assistant Director Dong's countenance was solemn and wholly devoid of expression. A horsefly which had been in the office before Lingjun's arrival was buzzing back and forth, now alighting on the wall, now alighting on the filing cabinet. Assistant Director Dong followed the fly with his eyes, and his hand gripped a magazine in eager anticipation of attempting a swat or two.

"You may go to the secretary next door and pick up your transfer directive from Miss Pan.   Report to school tomorrow." The fly finally landed on the office desk. The magazine slapped down after it, but the fly had craftily flown off to one side. Assistant Director Dong sank back into his seat, dejected.

"You must do your job well from now on, and see to it that you don't make mistakes again. That's all!"

The suddeness of this event jarred Lingjun with the force of an electric shock. He felt in a stupor. In his situation he couldn't really grasp what his exoneration meant in the context of the nation's political life or what fundamental changes it would bring to his own life. He had never even dared imagine that such a day might dawn. Yet, intuitively, he felt continued good fortune was coming his way. Like a trace of pure alcohol in the bloodstream, a diluted feeling of happiness began to take him out of his stupor into a dizzying excitement. First, his throat went dry. Then his whole body began trembling slightly. Finally, he could not hold back a flood of tears, and from his chest came such deep sobs they sounded like echoes in a mountain valley. This scene even touched the solemn and expressionless Assistant Director Dong, who extended his hands to Lingjun. When Lingjun held Dong's hands in his own, he at last began to feel a vague hope for the future.

So, once again he entered the classroom wearing his blue twill Mao jacket and holding lecture notes and chalk his hands. He had renewed his dream of twenty-two years back.

None of the farm workers were well off. Their children wore tattered clothes, and the smell of sweat, dust, and a sort of sun-bleached aridity permeated the classroom. The children behind their simple and rough-hewn desks stared up at Lingjun with wide-open eyes, unaware that a man who formerly tended livestock had become their teacher. Yet it wasn't long before he earned the children's confidence. He didn't make any extraordinary contributions to speak of. He had not even dared imagine that he was serving socialism or the "four modernizations": he felt such glorious motives were for heroes. He did nothing but fulfil the responsibilities as a teacher. Yet in doing so, he received the children's respect. On the morning of his departure for Beijing, he saw that the children had lined up along the road in front of school to gaze after the horse cart which was taking him away. They, too, had probably heard of how he had finally made contact with his father from abroad, and was about to leave the country with that rich father. The children held back their tears and with sad expressions quietly watched him ride in the horse cart across the military reclamation bridge and through the white poplar forest until he disappeared from view out in the wasteland. . . .

Now and then some herdsmen still came from several miles away to visit Lingjun. The old herdsman was now around eighty, yet his stride was as vigorous as ever. Sitting on Lingjun's brick bed one day, he picked up and examined a modern Chinese dictionary. "I'm afraid it'd take a lifetime to read a book this thick, even for a fellow with some learning."

"That's a dictionary," countered Stiff-necked Guo. "Now really, aren't you getting a little mixed up in your old age?"

"Yes, and a lifetime it's been, too. I might as well have been blind for all the good my eyes have done me: when I go to see a movie, I can't even read the title. All I can do is watch the actors move about." The herdsman sighed, for this brand-new age had made schooling a necessity. "These days, whatever you do, you've got to have schooling. Last time I picked up medicine for my livestock, I was about to squeeze ointment down their throats before I realized what was what."

" 'Old Righty,' " said Stiff-necked Guo to Lingjun, "You've taken yourself off that dust heap we herders are stuck on. Folks like us are done for, and our kids are now counting on you. . . ."

"That's right," added the old herdsman, "if you can teach my grandchild how to read a book this thick, you'll be doing right by your old friends on the prairie."

These conversations may have lacked literary polish but they made clear the significance of his work and began to define even more clearly his hopes for the future. From the herdsmen's bodies Lingjun caught the odour of horse sweat, grass, and other intense natural smells. The intimacy he felt with the herdsmen was so utterly different from the stifling atmosphere he felt with his father and Miss Song.

Through the eyes of the herdsmen, his students, and his colleagues, he had been able to see his own worth. What could be more fortunate than to catch sight of the preciousness of one's own worth through the eyes of other people?

IV

In the morning Lingjun took a stroll along Wangfujing Boulevard with Miss Song and his father. He discovered that he was no longer used to city life. The cement and asphalt here was nothing at all like the countryside turf which was so soft and smooth underfoot. Along the boulevard flowed an unbroken stream of people who were strangers to one another; though a bustling scene, it nonetheless smacked of cold indifference. In addition, it wasn't long before the unending noise from voices on all sides made Lingjun tired from nervous exhaustion.

At a handicraft store, Lingjun's father ordered a blue-and-white dinner service of fine Jingdezhen porcelain, for which he wrote out a check amounting to 500 yuan. Lingjun went to a chinaware store, where he selected a pickle jar costing a little over two yuan. The small, exquisite jar was just like an artifact dug up from a Han Dynasty tomb, with its antique design consisting of curved lines of yellow and brown. Lingjun had never seen such a beautiful household utensil in any county seat of the Northwest. Xiuzhi, who always went on about how good the pickle jars were in her hometown, had long wanted a pickle jar like this. The jar they now had at home was an earthenware one which someone had brought in from Shaanxi Province; Xiuzhi had got it in return for several evenings' work of stitching soles onto five pairs of cloth shoes. The old jar's light blue glaze, long since faded to a shiny white interspersed with blue blotches, was remarkably ugly.

"Your wife must be very beautiful," said Miss Song with a coquettish smile shortly after their return to the hotel. "It really makes people jealous to see how much you love her." Miss Song was wearing a new outfit today: a light violet V-neck sweater over a red and black checkered silk shirt, with which she matched a sheer grey nylon skirt. A recent spell under the hot and steamy rays of the autumn sun added to the pungency of her jasmine perfume.

"Marriage has always been a kind of pledge and duty," sighed Lingjun's father. He sat to one side, slowly stirring the coffee in his cup. Perhaps this topic had brought personal associations to mind, for the old man seemed to be carefully choosing his words. "No matter whether a man feels affection for his wife or not, he must scrupulously abide by that pledge and duty to the very end. Otherwise, his conscience will become troubled, and he will feel remorse. My request that you go abroad with me does not include you alone: you must bring your wife and child with you."

"Well then, Mr. Xu, aren't you going to tell us about your romance?" inquired Miss Song. "Your love affair must have been a very moving experience. I can't believe that a man as handsome as you are wouldn't be chased by a woman."

"How could I have had such a romance?" Lingjun replied with an apologetic smile. "When my wife and I got married, we didn't even know each other . . . a 'romance' would have been even more out of the question."

"Oh — " Miss Song said in a sort of mock surprise, while the old man once again uncomfortably shifted his shoulders.

Lingjun wanted to tell them exactly how his marriage with Xiuzhi had come about, yet the social background of that abnormal form of marriage was a great calamity — a calamity that was also an insult to the Chinese people. He was afraid that his account would evoke derisive laughter at things which were sacred to him. As Lingjun hesitated, he quietly sipped his coffee. The bitter taste of coffee also contained a sweet taste; in fact, bitterness and sweetness were inseparable. Only when the two mingled did they produce that special flavour which so fires the enthusiasm of coffee drinkers. Lingjun's father and Miss Song could appreciate the subtle flavour of coffee, but were they capable of comprehending the complexity of life? During that chaotic era, marriage was just like other social institutions, completely robbed of its normally deserved dignity.

It was purely a matter of convenience. His father and Miss Song were able to see the absurdity, all right, but they did not know how to turn that kind of convenience into a blessing. Moreover, the more difficult his circumstances, the more precious seemed his unforeseen good fortune. Lingjun felt that it would be difficult for anyone to understand the sad and yet powerful emotions that come to mind each time when, along with Xiuzhi, he recalled the circumstances of their peculiar marriage.

It happened on a spring afternoon in 1972. That day had passed for the most part much like any other: Lingjun had returned to his hut after finishing his routine of getting water for the horses and corralling them. He had just set down his horsewhip when Stiff-necked Guo burst in.

"Hey, Old Righty, you want a wife?" asked Stiff-necked Guo, brimming with excitement. "If you do, your wish is my command, and I'll bring her over tonight."

"Then just bring her over," replied Lingjun with a smile to what he thought was a joke.

"Okay! 'One word is enough for a gentleman's agreement.' All you need to do is take care of your own personal preparations. The woman's papers are all in order. I've just been over to see your supervising Party secretary, and he says that as long as you're willing, he's ready to sign all the papers right away. Okay, I'll get the papers signed for you, and hand them over to the Political Department when I go by the Farm Administration Bureau on my way home. When I make it back here, I'll bring her along, and tonight will be your 'evening in the bridal chamber'!"

Night had just fallen, and he was sitting on a stool reading *The Liberation Army Literature Monthly*, when he heard a chorus of children's shouts outside: "Old Righty's wife has shown up! Old Righty's wife has shown up!" The door banged open, and Stiff-necked Guo again burst in just as before.

"All settled! I won't take as much as a sip of your wine, but shouldn't you give me at least a drink of water to show your gratitude? Don't need more than enough to choke on! All afternoon I've been running back and forth so fast that my feet hardly touched the ground — and for fifteen miles to boot." After gulping down a ladleful of well-water which he'd scooped out of Lingjun's bucket, he wiped his mouth dry with his sleeve and heaved a long sigh of satisfaction. Gazing out the door, he finally broke the silence with a shout: "Hey! Why haven't you come inside yet? Come on, come on in! This house is yours. Come on and get acquainted ... this is Old Righty, the one I told you about; his real name is Xu Lingjun. He's as good as they come, just a little bit poor; but the more poor, the more honorable, you know!"

Lingjun finally noticed that there was, in fact, a female stranger standing in front of a group of children. Wearing a wrinkled grey tunic and carrying a small white bundle, she was indifferently and yet carefully sizing up his sooty and dusty adobe hut, as if she were actually preparing to move in.

"This . . . this can't be done!" cried Lingjun in alarm. "You've carried this too far!"

"Why can't it be done? You're the one who'd better get serious." Out of his pocket Stiff-necked Guo pulled a sheaf of papers, which he slammed down onto the edge of the kang. "The papers have all been signed. This is the law . . . the law! Do you get it? Keep in mind that I told the Political Department you were off herding horses and had asked me to take care of the paperwork for you. If you back out now, that'd be about the most ungrateful thing I ever heard of! Do you hear me, Old Righty?"

"This can't *be*, can it? Can it?" Lingjun answered Stiff-necked Guo with the same question again and again, his arms outspread in consternation. The woman had already come inside and sat down on the stool where Lingjun had been a short while before. She was unperturbed, as if the two men's conversation bore no relation to her at all.

"It can't be? You're asking *me* about something that involves the two of you? Who do you want *me* to go ask?" Stiff-necked Guo replaced the "law" on the kang. "All right, now, take it easy! Just don't forget to invite me over for a drink next year when you celebrate the birth of your first kid." He walked straight to the doorway, where he paused with his arms akimbo and began shooing the children away as if they were chickens: "What are *you* looking at? So you never saw your own parents get married? Go on back home and ask *them* about it! Go on, scram!"

With that, Stiff-necked Guo walked away.

Under the dim lamplight Lingjun stealthily sized up the woman. She wasn't beautiful at all: freckles ringed her tiny, upturned nose; her hair was yellowish and lack luster, and there was a weary expression on her haggard face. Lingjun could not understand how she could have any feeling for him. He poured her a glass of water and put it down on the wooden chest, saying, "Have a drink; you've walked such a long way. . . ."

She raised her head and saw the cordial expression in his eyes. After silently finishing off the water, her energy seemed to revive a bit. She knelt down on the quilt folded over the edge of the kang, and reached for a pair of Lingjun's trousers which were frayed at the knee. Putting them in her lap, she opened the bundle she had brought, picked out some patches, needle, and thread, and with lowered head began mending away. Her movements were methodical, and one sensed a sort of suppressed vitality in them. This vitality seemed to be something she could not express directly or in a personal manner, but could only get across through arranging objects and putting the room in order. Despite her own drab appearance, she tidied up the adobe house so thoroughly that it soon became sparkling clean. As her nimble fingers ran over such things as the clothes, quilts, and mattresses, it was as if they were depressing the piano keys corresponding to various scales, and the adobe hut began to resound with music.

Lingjun suddenly remembered his long-ago encounter with the brown horse, and his heart at once felt a wave of sorrow. He felt they had known each other a long time and also that he had been waiting many years for her. With a feeling of

ecstasy unlike anything he had known before, he sat by her side. He covered his face with his hands, afraid to believe that good fortune had really arrived, afraid that this lucky event would leave new misfortunes in its trail. Looking into the darkness of his palms, he tried to take in this new emotion.

By this time the woman had put aside her needle and thread. Her intuition told her that he was a man whom she could depend on for a lifetime. She didn't have the slightest idea that he was a stranger and spontaneously put her arm lightly around his hunched shoulders. There, atop the gunny-sacking spread over the brick bed, the couple talked until dawn.

Xiuzhi was originally from Sichuan, the "land of plenty". But it had become so impoverished during those hard years that one couldn't find even enough sweet potatoes to eat, and large numbers of starving peasants had no choice but to wander away. Young women could manage relatively well by finding a marriage partner in the near-by provinces and setting up a household there. As long as a Sichuanese village could manage to marry off one of its young women in this way, the woman in question could be counted on to find similar connections for other eligible women in the village. In this way, batch after batch of young women would leave "the mountains and rivers of 'old' Sichuan" while taking along nothing more than a piti-fully small bundle of their possessions. They went over Yang-ping Pass, crossed the Qinling Mountains, and threaded their way through innumerable tunnels long and short as they hurri-ed towards the future which awaited them in Shaanxi, Gansu, Qinghai, Ningxia, or Xinjiang. Families capable of scraping up some money would buy their young women bus tickets, while women from poorer families would have to hop trains. Their bundles contained little more than some patched clothes, a round mirror, and a wooden comb. With the aid of this equipment, they offered their youthful beauty as the stake in the gambling den known as life. They might win a life of good fortune, and they might lose everything. . . .

This kind of discount-price marriage had been popular from the very start on the farms in Lingjun's region. Unable to afford the betrothal gifts required for marriage with a local girl, young and old bachelors alike sought out women from Sichuan. When such a woman got married, she often tried to make matches for several eligible women still back home. It was as if she had a personnel file which could be consulted whenever an eligible bachelor came into view; she would write a letter summoning another Sichuanese woman, who would get married directly upon her arrival.

Xiuzhi was one of the women summoned by such a letter of marriage brokering. She came in search of a young man who was a tractor operator in the Seventh Brigade. After a delay-ridden and tortuous journey, she arrived at the farm with her identification. However, three days before her arrival the man was crushed when his tractor overturned, and he died of in-juries shortly after. Xiuzhi did not even go to the crematorium to pay her final respects; owing nobody a debt of gratitude, she felt there was no need for her to go.

Xiuzhi was ill at ease while putting up at the house of an acquaintance from her hometown; she knew that her acquaint-ance was having a hard go of it: her husband was a cripple, and the couple already had a child to look after by their second year of marriage. All Xiuzhi could do was sit, dispirited, in front of the Seventh Brigade's horse corral, where, like a sun-dial, she watched her own shadow slowly move.

Stiff-necked Guo came to the corral each noon to bring the horses water. One day he learned what her situation was like, and promptly left the horses grazing in the pasture while he went from door to door in the hope of finding her a way out of her bind. There were only three single men in the Seventh Brigade at the time; though they went to the corral one by one to take a look at her, none of them could get interested in this woman's short and skinny body. Stiff-necked Guo finally thought of Lingjun, who was then in his mid-thirties.

That was precisely how Lingjun got married, and what his romance consisted of!

"Old Righty's gotten married!" The marriage became an event of great importance in his production brigade. Weary of

exhortations to "firmly grasp the revolution", these people were
glad to extricate themselves temporarily from factional squab-
bling, and all of them expressed sympathy for this "Rightist
element" who had never belonged to any faction, had never done
others any harm, and had all along held to the plain and matter-
of-fact imperative of "promote production". Humans have a
good nature after all, and in response to the warmth the others
showed Lingjun, his warmth for them quietly surfaced in turn.

Some of the local people gave him a cooking pot; others gave
him a few pounds of grain; and still others gave him some
ration tickets for cloth. In addition, a young veterinarian set
up a settling-in fund for Lingjun by collecting half a yuan from
each neighbouring household. It even happened that at the
Party branch meeting, a unanimous resolution was passed for
the first time since the outbreak of the "cultural revolution" —
Lingjun was formally granted the three days' vacation to
which newlyweds are legally entitled. People were fine after
all, even during that period of darkness!

The couple began to set up their own household, all the
while feeling deeply indebted to the sympathy expressed
through others' charity.

Xiuzhi had been an optimistic, diligent woman from the beginning. She had received only two years of primary schooling
at a market town near her home village, and was unable to describe her reactions to life in poetic terms. On the evening after
she moved to Lingjun's, the cinema brigade showed *Lenin in
1918* in the grain-drying enclosure. From that day on, one of
Vasily's lines became her pet phrase: "If we can have bread,
we can have milk, too." She always said that with a giggle.
With her thin eyebrows and small eyes, as soon as she started
laughing, her eyes looked like two crescent moons. When you
matched that with her dimples, you could see that she had some
particularly attractive features after all!

Since Lingjun herded horses, he wasn't at home during the
day. Every day she stood under the hot noon sun to mold
adobe bricks out of mud, letting them bake until firm. After
wheeling barrowfuls of bricks to three sides of the house and

stacking them up, she eventually had built a three-sided bound-
ary wall. Within a land surface of 9,600,000 square kilometres
of China, she had suddenly portioned off eighteen square
metres for her own use. "Back in my native place", she said,
"every house has some trees around it. If you walk out the
front door and see nothing but open sky all around, what kind
of a house does that add up to, anyway?" She later ventured
out into the woods and dug up two white poplars, each about
as big around as the rim of a rice bowl. She dragged them
home with a strength that was startling, and planted one on
each side of the house.

Now that the courtyard was fully enclosed, Xiuzhi began to
raise domestic animals. She raised chickens, ducks, geese, and
rabbits; and when she added pigeons to the fold, the local people began calling her "Commander-in-Chief of Armed Forces".
That this state-operated farm did not permit workers to raise
their own pigs was Xiuzhi's greatest regret in working out her
scheme of the way things ought to be. While lying alongside
Lingjun at night, she often told him of a dream she had just
had about how big and round their pig had grown.

The remote farm where they lived was like a pond of
stagnant water, where the leadership neither exerted themselves
in carrying out correct policies nor accomplished anything positive in their implementation of incorrect policies. With all of
the pressure they put on people to "cut off the tail (remnants)
of capitalism", Xiuzhi still was able to stand up to them like
a stubborn weed whose green stalk extends upward from a
crack between flagstones. The small animals which she raised
bred as rapidly as if they had sprung from a magician's foot-
locker. "If we can have bread, we can have milk, too." Sure
enough, by the time a year had elapsed their life had changed
greatly. Although they still took in miniscule wages, they were
already able to live a life of plenty. Xiuzhi had a true ability to
go against the current of society. While others shouted about
the transition to communism, in her own courtyard she imple-
mented a commodity economy's restoration to a natural economy. Xiuzhi had produced everything with her own hands.

On her way home from work, she was followed by her chickens, ducks, geese, and pigeons. Qingqing was strapped to her back, the larger fowl waddled at her feet, and the pigeons perched on her shoulders. Firewood and grain stalks kept the stove blazing, and water bubbled in the iron pot. Xiuzhi may have never studied "operations research", but she could do her many tasks in an orderly and unrushed fashion, rather like a thousand-arm Guanyin Bodhisattva.

The woman who had once lived on sweet potatoes now brought Lingjun a warmth which he had never before enjoyed. Her warmth made the roots of his life take hold even more deeply in this land, and what gave those roots nourishment was none other than their own labour. The couple's marriage intensified Lingjun's feelings for this land, and made him understand even more clearly the basic simplicity, purity, and appropriateness of a life of manual labour. He had acquired the happiness and contentment for which had been searching all these years.

On the day that Assistant Director Dong announced Lingjun's exoneration and signed the necessary papers, Lingjun took home a grant of five hundred yuan issued by the Finance Section in accordance with new policy directives. When he told Xiuzhi what had happened from beginning to end, her face shone with an expression of surprise. After wiping her hands clean on her skirt, she counted the brand-new banknotes, one by one.

"Hey, Xiuzhi, from now on we'll be just like other people!" While cleaning up in the wash basin, Lingjun noticed that Xiuzhi was still hovering over the kitchen table with a look of joy on her face. "Hey, Xiuzhi, why don't you say something? Cat got your tongue?"

"How'd you get a hold of all this?" exclaimed Xiuzhi with a smile. "There's too much to count! I've been counting and counting it; it's so much money!"

"For heaven's sake! You're really just. . . . Well, what does money amount to, anyway? What's really worth getting happy over is how I've been given a clean political slate. . . ."

" 'Clean politically slate,' my foot! As far as I can tell, you're still the same old you! They used to call you a right-winger, then half a lifetime later they admit they've made a mistake; once they admit their mistake, they tell *you* not to make any more mistakes from now on! In the past we were blamed, and in the future there'll still be blame to be-dished out! Now that we've got money, we can enjoy some extra comforts. Don't nag me so . . . just let me get this money all counted."

Yes, the wife who was fifteen years his junior had never considered him to be different from other people, for she had always preserved the simplicity and wisdom of country folk. The quibble over whether or not he was a Rightist involved a concept that had simply not entered her small brain. She only knew that he was a good man and an honest man — and that was enough for her. While at work, she would often raise the topic with her female colleagues: "My little daughter's father behaves himself — always rolls with the punches thrown at him. . . . Give him three kicks and he won't even fart back at you. And even wolves closing in on his ass won't cause him to get worried. If a fellow like this gets taken advantage of, that's a real sin which will mean a curse on the next generation for sure!"

Yes, Xiuzhi was fond of money, and was often down in the mouth about not being able to spend a penny in two places. Even a trifling sum of five hundred yuan could make her so immensely satisfied that her fingers trembled and her eyes glistened with tears of joy. However, when she found out that Lingjun's father was a wealthy "foreign capitalist", she did not mention the word "money". All she did was to urge Lingjun to take a few more "five-spice" tea-boiled eggs for his father. She would often raise the topic when instructing Qing-qing, who was barely seven years old by that time: "The only time money's fun to spend is when you've struggled to earn it yourself; then your conscience can be at ease. When I buy salt, I know that I'm paying for it out of the money I got from selling eggs; when I buy pepper, I know that I'm paying for it

out of the money I got from harvesting grain; and when I buy
your schoolbooks, I know I'm paying for them out of the money
I got from doing overtime farmwork. . . ." Xiuzhi managed
to do without abstract ethical precepts, high-flown philosophical concepts, and such. Nevertheless, this simple and clear
advice had already made the youngest member of their family
realize many things: manual labour was a noble endeavour;
only remuneration for manual labour could allow one to enjoy
pleasure; and wealth deriving from exploitation or dependency
was a disgrace.

Xiuzhi could not sing. When Qingqing had turned one
month old, the family of three took a bus into the county seat,
where they had a family portrait taken at the county's only
photographic studio. Popsickle vendors were walking the streets,
and hawking their wares with drawn-out shouts: "Pop —
sickles!" Later on, the chant of "Pop — sickles" became the
only lullaby Xiuzhi ever mastered. While cuddling Qingqing,
she would lightly sing the word in as close semblance to the
Northwestern dialect as she could muster. The sound of
Xiuzhi's singing voice was monotonous, distant; not only did
it induce Qingqing to fall asleep, but it also made Lingjun, who
was off reading to the side, feel a sense of well-being so rustic
as to border on the primitive. At such times he would enter a
region of what seemed to be pure beauty.

There were also popsickle sellers on Wangfujing Boulevard
in Beijing, but they didn't shout their wares. They merely sat
with vacant expressions in their stores. How dull in comparison! Lingjun missed that lullaby as sweet as a dream, and
he missed the optimistic and dimpled smile. "If we can have
bread, we can have milk, too."

No, he wouldn't be able to stay here in the city. He wanted
to go right back. The people who had helped him during times
of distress were there, and they were now counting on his
help. The land into which his sweat had seeped was there,
and at this moment his sweat was sparkling and glistening on
the harvested fields back there. The wife who had helped

him to go through the trying circumstances was there, and so was his daughter. Everything he had was there. The roots of his life were there.

Lingjun had returned at last. He'd finally arrived at the small county seat he knew so well. In front of the bus station ran the county's sole asphalt road, which was nevertheless partly obscured by a thin layer of yellow dust. When the wind blew, dust would begin whirling around the entrances to the retail store, the banks, and the post office. The cotton-fluffer machine on the other side of the road still ran with a monotonous hum, as if it had not stopped since his departure for the city. Peasants selling glutinous rice, fried cakes, and melon seeds were still crowded together in front of the entrance to the bus station. On both sides of the road meandering from east to west were adobe houses, some of which had old-style carved lintels above their doorways. The newly-built theatres was caught in the midst of a scaffold, a large group of workers were bustling around on all sides.

All afternoon he had felt as if, having hung from a parachute floating to earth, his feet were once again treading on solid ground. He loved everything about this place, blemishes and all — just as he loved his own life, including the sufferings in his past.

At dusk, the horse cart which carried him passed by the production brigade where he used to live. The setting sun's rays were just then slanting over from the western hills, and the villages as well as their inhabitants were all shrouded in a blurry, rose-coloured layout. All he could make out of his homestead from afar were the two white poplar trees that Xiuzhi had planted, and which now towered high over the adobe house's flat roof; the pair were so motionless that not even the slightest fluttering was in evidence, as if they were staring at him with rapt attention.

The yard fowl were returning for their nightly roost, and they seemed to recognize Lingjun as they spread out to both sides of the road and stood dully staring at him with wide eyes. Only after the horse cart had retreated far into the distance did they lower their heads and lazily head back to their pens.

A current of warmth filled Lingjun's heart. He recalled the conversation with his father on the brink of his departure. On that evening, father and son sat facing each other on a sofa. Clothed in silk pajames, his father's back was hunched over and his face was heavy with a mournful expression as he smoked his pipe.

"You're leaving so soon?" asked his father.

"Yes, the school is getting ready for mid-term exams."

His father was silent for a while before he continued. "It's been a happy occasion for me to return here and see you." Although he tried to remain calm, his lower lip trembled slightly. "I've discovered how very, very mature you are. Perhaps the reason for this is the resolute faith you have. And more power to you for it. Faith is precisely what people seek. Honestly speaking, in the past I've also done my share of seeking, but religion can't actually give a person any. . . ." Having reached this point of his conversation, he dropped his arm downwards in a tired gesture. When he continued with his monologue, he changed to a different topic. "When I was in Paris last year, I read an anthology of Manupassant short stories in English translation. There was one story about a reunion between a member of the National Assembly and the son he had conceived during his youth. The son later turned into an idiot. The first time I read the story, I couldn't sleep a wink that night. Afterwards, I often seemed to see a troubled vision of you standing in front of me. Now that I've seen what you really look like, I can stop worrying. You've really caught me by surprise; it's as if you had become a . . . as if you had become a. . . ."

His father didn't come up with any definition of what Lingjun seemed to have become. However, Lingjun noticed a look of consolation in his father's eyes. He felt that father and son alike were satisfied with their reunion and parting. Each of them had got what he needed. His father's troubled conscience had been mitigated. Lingjun had reviewed half of his life in a critical moment of decision and had gone on to learn a significant lesson about life in general.

The sun was hidden behind the western hills. The final sunbeams of the day shone with a faded yellowish colour on the multi-coloured clouds just above the hills. The clouds in turn reflected diffused sunlight back down onto the prairie below the foothills and the villages dotting the wilderness, where the light's colour finally darkened into the deepening shades of a gentle twilight. As Lingjun came nearer and nearer to the school, he was able to catch sight of its playground from quite a distance. It looked like a clear lake set amidst a stand of pink-blossomed trees bathed in yellow light. This tender emotions flowed into the evening breeze to form a warm current that revolved around his whole body.

He felt that when his father had mentioned his faith, his father had not really understood his present spiritual state. Rational knowledge alone without a foundation in perception was hollow. In certain aspects and at certain times, feeling was much more important than doctrine. And the most precious thing he had acquired in these twenty-odd years of life experience was his feeling for manual labour. As his thoughts reached this point, tears came to his eyes. He was moved by the very image of himself: he had not walked that hard two-decade path in vain.

He finally arrived at the school. At that moment there were a few people standing outside his front door and gazing out towards the horse cart on the road. Xiuzhi was wearing a white cotton skirt, which in the gentle shades of deepening twilight looked like a spot of bright and clear starlight. More and more people gathered together there until they finally recognized him, at which point the entire group began running along the road towards him. At the very front of the group was his little daughter in her red dress, which looked like a bright ember shooting towards him. She was running closer and closer, closer and closer, closer and closer. . . .

Translated by Philip F. C. Williams
Illustrated by Zhou Jianfu

MA FENG

(1922 —   )

Born into a poor peasant family in Xiaoyi County, Shanxi Province, in 1922, Ma Feng joined the Eighth Route Army in 1938. He went to Yan'an in 1940 to study at a branch school of the Lu Xun Art Academy. In 1943 he returned to the Shanxi-Suiyuan Border Area to work with a cultural brigade there. He has been a correspondent and editor for various newspapers including the *Liberation Daily,* and editor-in-chief of the Shanxi-Suiyuan Publishing House.

In 1949 he was elected a member of the All-China Federation of Literary and Art Circles and council member of the Union of Chinese Writers. He studied in 1951 at the Central Research Institute for Literature. In 1956 he acted as the vice-chairman and then chairman of the Shanxi Provincial Federation of Literature and Art Circles and the provincial branch of the Union of Chinese Writers.

He began publishing when he was twenty and in 1945 co-authored a novel with Xi Rong, *The Heroes of Lüliang,* which brought him public acclaim. In 1950 he published a collection of short stories, *The Enemy Village,* followed by "A Wedding", "Han Meimei", and "Old News", which were included in his *My First Leader* and *Sunrise Over the Mountains.* In the 1960's his novel *Biography of Liu Hulan* and his movie script, *The Young People in Our Village,* were well received.

93

THE "ON-THE-SPOT" WEDDING

Ma Feng

Those who have worked in the countryside probably have taken part in various kinds of "on-the-spot" meetings,* but have any of them attended an "on-the-spot" wedding? Probably not. I, on the other hand, have. It was in late January of this year, a few days before the Spring Festival. One morning as I was reading the newly released "Bulletin of the Third Plenary Session of the Central Committee", the county head of the Women's League, Wu Aiying, came rushing in looking for me.

"Secretary Zhou, tomorrow the Xiling Brigade is having an 'on-the-spot' wedding. We all hope you'll be able to come," she said with excitement.

Noting the questioning look on my face, she quickly explained: for the past few years mercenary wedding in the Xishan District had been causing serious problems. To take a wife the family of the bridegroom-to-be had to come up with at least five hundred to six hundred yuan, in some cases as much as one thousand yuan, for the girl's family as a betrothal gift. Not too long ago in the Xiling Brigade a pair of young lovers had waited three years and still could not get married because the young man's family had not been able to find the money. Finally the two of them, hand in hand, jumped off a cliff to their death. After this incident, Wu Aiying took some people with her to Xiling to investigate the matter first hand and to do some grassroots work, trying to mobilize the masses to criticize the harmful custom of mercenary marriages. Recently, in the mid-

---

* A meeting meant to demonstrate a particular point, held at the site of the situation to be discussed. — *Trans.*

94

dle of her work, she discovered that three couples had decided to get married without bothering about betrothal gifts. She and her colleagues felt that these couples should be held up as a good example for the community. So, after consulting each family, they organized a collective wedding ceremony, and invited all the neighbouring peasant families and local leaders. She hoped I could also attend this "on-the-spot wedding" in order to strengthen the influence it would have on the villagers.

As I had been transferred only recently to this county, I did not know Wu Aiying well. She struck me, however, as an extremely capable leader. The Women's League here worked enthusiastically, and I felt I really should show my support. Also, I wanted to have a look at the Xiling Brigade, now that the opportunity had presented itself. So, after lunch, we set off by car for the countryside.

The county seat was a little more than fifty li from Xiling, by a road that twisted and turned its way through the mountains. At times the jeep could just barely squeeze through. On the hill side were thick bushes and trees, and midway up the slopes were row after row of terraced fields. The village of about 110 families lay at the foot of a steep cliff. The houses looked dilapidated; only occasionally could you see a couple of newly built tile-roofed houses. In the village, the walls on either side of the street were pasted with colourful posters, urging men and women to choose their own spouses and do away with mercenary marriages.

As the car entered the centre of the village, a man driving two cows blocked the road in front of us. I could not see what he looked like; I only caught a glimpse of a large patch on the back of his cotton-padded jacket. The driver blew the horn repeatedly, but, as the man did not pay the slightest attention or show any intention of driving the cows to the side of the road, we were forced to slow down. It was then that I noticed a poster on red paper stuck on the wall to my right. The thin paste was still dripping down between the cracks in the bricks. The poster read: "A warm welcome to Secretary Zhou for coming to attend the 'on-the-spot' wedding ceremony organized by our brigade." I guessed that Wu Aiying had telephoned them to say that I was coming, and they had hurriedly posted this slogan.

At last, the man had driven the cows round the corner, and the jeep soon arrived at the door of the brigade office. A group of cadres approached us as soon as the car stopped, and, smiling, led me into the courtyard. Ten or so young men and women were in the process of making decorations for the wedding ceremony. Some were busy with large red paper flowers; others were cutting the character "double-happiness" out of paper; still others sat pasting paper lanterns or making ornaments from strips of silk. The large courtyard was alive with the exciting atmosphere of preparation for a wedding. The young people smiled at me, then turned to whisper among themselves, but before I had a chance to say hello to them, I was ushered into the brigade office.

In the office, Wu Aiying quickly introduced me to each of the cadres, while someone brought in water in a basin for me to wash my face, and someone else got tea for all of us. Everyone was very excited, and could not wait to tell me the news. The young men of the village were especially delighted to hear that I was coming, for they all hoped that through this "on-the-spot" wedding the custom of mercenary marriages could be completely eradicated. I was also told that the families of the young people to be married felt particularly honoured. This might very well be true, since the coming of the county secretary specifically to take part in the wedding of common peasants in this sort of out-of-the-way mountain village was, after all, rather an important occasion. Then wedding presents arrived from nearby brigade: sheets of silk expressing congratulations and framed pictures. . . . The room was buzzing with high-spirited conversation, when the cotton curtain at the door was lifted and a young woman poked her head in, saying in a low voice to the branch secretary, Zheng Guyu, "Uncle Zheng, can I see you for a minute? I need to talk to you." Wu Aiying called out warmly: "Erlan, if you have something to talk about, come on in!"

The young woman had no choice but to come in, and, following her, a strong, rough-looking young man. Wu Aiying introduced them, explaining that this was one of the three couples to be married the next day. The girl's name was Wang Erlan, and the boy's, Zheng Yunshan.

"So, is everything ready?" Wu Aiying asked, giggling. "You see! Even the county secretary will be at the wedding."

Wang Erlan sighed softly, lowering her head. "Comrade Wu, our wedding . . . is off. . . ."

"What? What happened?" Wu Aiying asked hastily. Wang Erlan, her face crimson with embarrassment, was unable to say a word. Her boyfriend, Zheng Yunshan, said gloomily, "What's happened? Her father's changed his mind. He's just given me an ultimatum. He wants five hundred yuan from me. If I can produce it, we'll be married tomorrow. If not, we're through."

"Really!" the leaders exclaimed in surprise.

The news was totally unexpected, and everyone in the room sat for a moment in stunned silence. The young people who had been in the courtyard making decorations for the wedding now crowded into the office, and, upon hearing that this demand for money had been made at the last minute, they too were stupefied. I asked them whether or not they had done propaganda work in individual families. Everyone began answering at once, interrupting each other in their efforts to tell the story, and filling the room with the clamour of voices. From the general hubbub I managed to learn that Wang Erlan's father, Wang Shuanniu, had at first personally agreed not to ask for a betrothal gift. Erlan and Zheng Yunshan testified this was the case. Furthermore, it was quite clear that these two were very much in love and had chosen each other of their own accord. Their houses were diagonally opposite each other, and from childhood they had worked and played together. Besides, the parents on both sides were entirely satisfied with the match. Who could have imagined that there would be this last-minute hitch? Wu Aiying was almost crying with anger. The league branch secretary, Zhou Tiewa, in a fury, exclaimed: "This Wang Shuanniu is obviously making trouble on purpose just to pull the rug out from under our feet! We absolutely have to do something about correcting this sort of old-fashioned thinking!"

"I think we'd better get a clearer idea of the situation first, and see why he's suddenly changed his mind," I said at once.

"Right. I'll go and have a talk with him," said Branch Secretary Zheng Guyu, who had not spoken a word until now. He got up and left with Wang Erlan and Zheng Yunshan.

Zheng Guyu was over fifty, and during the period of advanced agricultural producers' cooperatives he had been the branch secretary for this village. Overthrown during the "cultural revolution", he had only recently been reinstated. Everyone present agreed that he was the only one who would be able to speak to Wang Erlan's father. What kind of person was this Wang Shuanniu, I asked. Apparently, this old man was nearly sixty, of poor peasant class background. During the War of Resistance Against Japan he was a militiaman and during the land reform period in the 1950s he was extremely active. His family background was good, he worked hard, and he was honest. However, he was a little stubborn, and had earned himself the nickname "Old Ox". He was by habit a man of few words, but the few things he did say could knock you over. If you asked him to go east, he would pigheadedly head west. Sometimes he was even at odds with himself. One time, as he was scooping out nightsoil, he carelessly splashed some on his pants. Furious, he picked up his scoop and began fiercely jabbing at the latrine pit, yelling over and over: "Splash, will you? Splash, will you?" Of course, soon he had covered himself from head to foot. They told me a number of these stories, possibly with some exaggeration, but nonetheless one could see in these accounts the eccentricities of this old man.

As we were discussing the problem Zheng Guyu returned alone. He reported that Wang Shuanniu insisted on that five hundred yuan and no matter how much one begged and reasoned with him he simply would not change his mind. Furthermore, all this pleading only sent him into a fury, and he had taken off for the mountains outside the village.

Zhou Tiewa spoke up, "He can leave the village, but he can't escape the problem. The monk has gone but the temple remains, so to speak. We'll sort him out tonight when he comes back!"

Some of the young men spoke up in agreement.

Wu Aiying turned to me and asked, "Secretary Zhou, do you think we could expose 'Old Ox' at the 'on-the-spot' wedding as an upholder of undesirable customs and educate the masses through comparison?"

Most of the people present expressed their approval, in particular the young men, who were by this time quite adamant. They claimed "Old Ox" was flagrantly resisting the marriage law. If we did not take the necessary steps to criticize his behaviour, they said, how could we put an end to this malignant practice. The old branch secretary, Zheng Guyu, his head lowered, seemingly absorbed in smoking his cigarettes, sat silent, waiting for everybody to calm down. Finally he began, "Turn a wedding ceremony into a criticism session? It just doesn't seem right. I mean, it's as if 'Old Ox' had sprained a muscle and we haven't even bothered about taking his pulse accurately. If you stretch a string too tight, it'll snap."

Obviously, Zheng Guyu's experience had made him cautious, and I agreed with him. According to what I knew about the countryside, cases like this stubborn 'Old Ox' were most usefully handled through individual discussion. Perhaps it would be best for me to use my capacity as a leader to try to persuade 'Old Ox', and with luck we could avoid a deadlock. I asked them to arrange for me to have supper at his house, and Zheng Guyu immediately sent someone to notify the family.

"How about the other two couples?" I asked. "Are there any problems with them?"

Everyone assured me that nothing would go wrong, and Wu Aiying suggested that I go to the other two households myself just to make sure. They led me first to Wang Shunxi's house.

The courtyard of the house was old and crumbling, but they had swept it spotlessly clean. On each side of the door they had pasted a red paper scroll with appropriate wedding congratulations and, on the windows, the characters for "double-happiness". With friends and relatives coming and going, the atmosphere was clearly one of preparation for a wedding. Wang Shunxi was a very friendly and polite old man. He expressed his gratitude to me a number of times, saying that a county leader coming to attend his family's wedding was an honour which none of them had ever dreamed possible. He was greatly in favour of collective wedding ceremonies, which, he said, provided all the pleasure of extravagance with none of the cost. His family tried again and again to make me stay for supper, but I had to refuse as politely as I could. Originally I had planned to visit the other family, but on coming out of Wang's front door, I saw Erlan standing waiting for me anxiously. I asked if her father had come back yet, and she nodded quickly. Saying goodbye to the others, we set off directly for Erlan's house. On the way Erlan informed me:

"My father has just come back from cutting firewood in the hills. When he heard Secretary Zhou had arranged to have dinner at our house he said, 'So, he doesn't want to eat well at the brigade headquarters. He decides to come to a common peasant's house to eat . . . hmm. . . . Just like the old cadres.' He wouldn't let my mother prepare anything extra, you know. . . ."

I said at once, "He's right not to."

Erlan sighed and said: "Secretary Zhou, my father has a bad temper. If he says anything unpleasant, I hope you'll try to bear with him."

I laughed and reassured her, "Don't worry. I won't get in an argument with him."

Following Erlan, I went into the courtyard of their house. Straight ahead on the northern side were three run-down rooms, and on the western side, a row of cowsheds. A hefty old man was standing in front of the food trough, sifting hay, his head lowered. Erlan yelled to him, "Father, Secretary Zhou is here."

The old man raised his head and glanced at me. Then, with a curt "go in and sit down", he turned and dumped the remaining hay in the sifter into the trough. As he turned, I suddenly noticed a large patch on the back of his cotton-padded jacket; so this was the man driving the cows who would not make way for our jeep!

Erlan lifted the old curtain over the front door and I went in. An old woman, clearly Erlan's mother, was in the middle of preparing dinner, and a fourteen or fifteen-year-old boy, who I later learned was Erlan's younger brother, was pumping the bellows. They greeted me warmly, inviting me to come in and sit on the brick bed. Just as Erlan had the small table all set, "Old Ox" came in and sat down opposite me without saying a word, giving me a chance to examine him carefully for the first time: a rectangular face, a full beard, a forehead covered with deep wrinkles. His two eyes steadily met my gaze, as if waiting for my questions, but he answered at most one sentence for every three of mine. I asked him how many working days he could earn a year, how many points he got for a work day in bonuses, and how he was doing in general. But instead of answering me directly, he said, "All I can say is we aren't starving to death." Then he shut up like a clam.

His wife, on the other hand, kept trying to pick up the thread of my conversation to ease the oppressive atmosphere a little. After a while, "Old Ox" suddenly spoke up, "If you have something to say, why don't you just come out with it! I want five hundred yuan as a betrothal gift and that's that! What are you going to do about it? Will there be a criticism session? I'm ready."

"This isn't a matter for criticism," I replied promptly. "I just want to ask you why this afternoon you suddenly wanted a betrothal gift when at first you had said you didn't."

"The state changes its policies all the time, you know. Why can't an ordinary peasant change his mind?"

Erlan, probably afraid her father would get angry and say

something which would leave me in an awkward position, hurriedly broke in, "Father. Supper is ready. Why don't you eat first, and talk later?"

"Old Ox" grunted in agreement and in an instant our food appeared on the table: a large plate of sour cabbage mixed with green peppers and five bowls of mixed corn and sorghum porridge cooked with a few slices of yam. "Old Ox" did not pick up his chopsticks. Instead, he sat smoking and watching me take bits of the sour cabbage to eat with my porridge. Suddenly, he asked, "How's the food?"

This was a very simple question, but to tell the truth I was not at all sure how to answer him. Should I say it was good when clearly I was having a little trouble getting it down? Or should I say it was bad, which would undoubtedly upset him. Finally, I said to him quite frankly: "In fact, this food is not very good, but I'll manage." Then, suddenly filled with emotion, I added, "Thirty years after liberation and the peasants are still living on the edge of poverty! This is no better than during the land reform!"

"Old Ox" nodded his head and asked, "Which side were you on during the 'cultural revolution'?"

"I was labelled a capitalist-roader. I was stuck in jail for three years, and then sent to a cadres' school for seven."

Hearing this, "Old Ox" seemed suddenly to cheer up a bit. He put out his cigarette and told his wife to heat up a pot of spirits and slice a plate of pork. I began to make signs of protest, but Erlan's mother said, "Originally this wine was for the wedding, so it's no trouble." Then she and Erlan sliced the meat and heated up the liquor.

"Old Ox" grabbed hold of my bowl and said, "If you don't want to insult us, you'd better drink. If you think you'd rather not, then just eat and I'll drink alone."

This being the case, I really could not refuse. Then in the midst of this drinking, "Old Ox" said to me, "Okay, let's start talking."

"Talking about what?" I asked.

"The evil of mercenary weddings, how reactionary it is to

demand a betrothal gift, how backward the peasants are, and so on and so forth."

I laughed, "How do you know I want to talk about all that?"

"Show me one cadre who doesn't want to talk about all that crap," "Old Ox" replied. "Why else would you have arranged to have supper at my house?"

"Okay, then," I answered, "let's lay all our cards on the table and clear some things up, shall we? I only want to ask you one question: Why are you so stuck on this five hundred yuan betrothal gift?"

"Old Ox" sat sullenly drinking his spirits without speaking. After a while, he broke the silence. "I haven't arranged a meal for a cadre for quite a few years. Don't know if you're supposed to pay for a meal like today's."

"Of course I am," I answered. "It's national regulation. No matter how good or bad the food is, it's thirty cents a day, plus one and one-fifth catty's worth of grain coupons."

"Old Ox" said, "I've been supporting Erlan for twenty-three years. If we figure on twenty cents a day, how much should I get?"

He stopped, waiting for my reply, but before I had time to open my mouth Erlan broke in, "So I just sit here and eat the family's food? I earn at the very least two hundred work days a year!"

"She's right, isn't she?" I asked "Old Ox".

"Yes, she's right. But, if I marry her out, those two hundred days in work points will go with her."

"So according to you, betrothal gifts for marriage should be perfectly reasonable and legal?" I laughed.

But, "Old Ox" answered me with a question. "If I marry my daughter out without a bride's price, where will I get the money to help her little brother take a wife."

Hearing this, Erlan's brother turned bright red and raced out of the room carrying his rice bowl with him.

"Old Ox" continued to eat while he said, "It's all very well for you to say, 'The child is still young, and if we carry out the new marriage law thoroughly there won't be any bride's prices in the future.' Ha! If you think I can count on you to carry out the new marriage law. . . ."

Erlan's mother cut in, "You should stop talking nonsense immediately!"

"Nonsense? In the past few years when *haven't* we 'thoroughly carried out' the marriage law? But, name me one family who doesn't want a bride's price for their daughter! show me one family who didn't pay for the bride! If they don't do it openly, they do it under the table."

"Do you mean to say that Wang Shunxi's family paid money under the table?" I asked, startled.

"Well, maybe they didn't, I don't know," replied "Old Ox". "So their family didn't pay anything. But they're just exchanging mutton for pork."

I had no idea what he was talking about, but Erlan's mother explained: The girl Wang Shunxi's son planned to marry was the daughter of Wang's younger aunt, and, coincidentally, Wang's daughter had been given to that same aunt's son. It was called exchanging one relative for another, and of course neither family demanded a bride's price.

"How about the other family?" I asked.

"The other family?" "Old Ox" looked blank for a moment. "Umm. . . . You mean Wu Chengyou's family? Their family has even less reason to spend money."

"Also an in-marriage?"

"Not quite," replied "Old Ox". "His son is a 'reversible son-in-law' ".*

"Since today men and women are equal, isn't it just as good for the man to go and live with the woman's family?"

"You have to look at the situation to see whether it's good or not." "Old Ox" took another drink and explained. When Wu Chengyou was middle-aged he lost his wife, and had only this son, to whom he was both father and mother. Father and son were strong labourers, but they just could not accumulate

---

* It is traditional for the girl to go to the boy's family to live with her in-laws. A "reversible son-in law" goes to his wife's family to live. — *Trans.*

enough money for the son to take a wife. The son was going on twenty-eight or nine and still single. He got involved with a widow a few years older than himself, but because the woman had a child, she absolutely refused to go to the father-in-law's house, and suggested that the man come to live at hers. Wu Chengyou pondered this for quite a while, but in the end he had no option but to agree. The other day, the old fellow even came crying to "Old Ox" and said, "I just have this one son, and it's really worrying me to death! I can't see my son living his whole life as a bachelor."

"Old Ox" sighed as he finished speaking. "We peasants have no way out. We just have to make do as best we can."

As he spoke he started to pour himself some more spirits, but the pot was empty. Giving the pot to Erlan he said, "Bring me another pot."

"Father, our guest stopped drinking long ago. You should. . . ."

"Old Ox" gave her a quick look. "I have hands of my own, you know," he said, and started to get down from the brick bed. Erlan's mother quickly took the pot from him and filled another half a pot, even pouring him a glass. Then she said, "You like that boy, Yunshan, and said from the beginning you didn't want a bride's price. Yesterday you even said: 'Even if it makes us so poor that we have to beg, we won't sell our daughter out.' And now this afternoon, you began making such a fuss that no one in the family has had a moment's peace. And all the leaders in the village are upset. . . ."

"Enough of that!" "Old Ox" interrupted his wife. "I'm not marrying my daughter out to make some leader happy."

I smiled and replied, "As far as I can tell, this move of yours is all because I came."

"Old Ox" did not deny it, but instead took another drink and said, "So even the county secretary has driven out here for this trivial affair. Do you mean to tell me that after this 'on-the-spot' wedding the custom of mercenary marriages will disappear?"

"Even if we can't get rid of it, isn't it still better than encouraging it?" I answered.

"Old Ox" did not reply for some time. Finally, he said, "There's nothing strange about selling one's daughters. In old China selling your daughters was nothing. People often sold their sons and even their wives! Why? I'll tell you. *Poverty!*"

By this time, his face was red to the base of his neck and small beads of sweat had appeared on his nose. He poured himself yet another cup, at which Erlan's mother could not help frowning a little, but immediately the frown vanished as she said with a smile to her husband, "Here, give me the pot, I'll get you some more."

"Old Ox" exclaimed, "So you want to get me drunk, do you? I'll be damned if I drink another drop." And with this he poured his full cup back into the pot, then picked up his bowl to finish his porridge. Erlan's mother turned her back to him to give me a wink. "Old Ox" went on, "Ever since the movement of Land Reform and cooperatives there's been less and less of this kind of thing. I married my eldest daughter out in 1965 without asking for a penny. I even threw in some clothes and a pair of bamboo baskets. Ask her mother if you don't believe me!"

Erlan's mother nodded in agreement. "Yes, it's true. At that time we all had some grain stored up and deposits in the credit cooperative. What family would risk disappointment and loss of face by asking for a bride's price?"

"Old Ox" continued, "But in these last few years, what with 'cutting off the capitalist tail' all the time, cutting off private plots, cutting off supplementary work — the next thing they'll be cutting off will be people's heads!"

I asked him how much he had received for his income before the "cultural revolution". Erlan's mother answered bluntly, "For the few years Zheng Guyu was running things we got at least 450 catties in grain rations, plus a bonus of one yuan; in good years our bonus was one yuan twenty. But recently we've been getting 280 catties of rationed grain, and a bonus of twenty-five cents. . . ."

"Old Ox" interrupted, "If you're such a big leader, *you* tell me: how are we supposed to manage these days? If things go on like this, never mind the wife and children, we'll be wearing signs selling ourselves!"

I began, "All this was caused by Lin Biao and the Gang of Four. . . ."

But "Old Ox" interrupted me: "The overthrow of the Gang of Four was a good two years ago, and our village is still exactly the same as before! It's as if you're treating a broken bone not by setting it but by rubbing a little mercurochrome on the skin. Ha! An 'on-the-spot' wedding! Do we get an 'on-the-spot meeting' when we have a baby girl? Production just won't increase. You can take your fancy meeting and shove it!"

Though I had only had two cups of liquor, I suddenly felt as red as a beet. Erlan's mother undoubtedly felt embarrassed as well, because she directed her next comment at "Old Ox", "Why don't you just go to the brigade office, and shoot your mouth off there. That's great! Giving Secretary Zhou a scolding."

"Humph," "Old Ox" said apologetically, "Old Zhou, I didn't mean you. You're just a newcomer; it's not your fault. Ai! All this talk and I've got off the point."

"No!" I said, "You're right on the mark. Your criticisms are correct, and it's good that you make them."

I spoke in all sincerity. He was speaking the truth. Furthermore, until I came to Xiling I really had not considered these problems. To be sure, mercenary weddings were despicable, but was it principally up to the peasants to change that? If we did not get to the root of the peasants' difficulties, if we did not think of ways of ensuring the peasants a better life, if we just depended on propagandizing the new marriage law, how could we expect to solve any real problems? As I was thinking all this, I suddenly noticed Erlan giving me a steady and meaningful look. I understood and said quickly, "Old Wang, let's get to the point. What do you plan to do about Erlan's wedding?"

"Quite simple," he replied. "Give me five hundred yuan and there'll be a wedding tomorrow. Or, if you prefer, you can haul me to court tonight and they can get married tomorrow."

As far as I could see, more talk was just so much wasted breath. All I could do was make a bit more small talk and leave. Erlan showed me to the door without a word, clearly extremely disappointed. I tried to comfort her, "I think your father's being especially stubborn on purpose, but I suspect if you two really love each other you'll be able to marry sooner or later."

Erlan just nodded.

I got back to the brigade office to find the room already filled up with people eager to hear the news. When they learned that I had got nowhere with Old Wang they turned ugly. They said "Old Ox" did not know a good thing when he saw one, and was too stubborn to accept it even if he did. Some more people suggested a criticism session, but I urged them against it. If "Old Ox" would not come round immediately, we should give him some more time to think it over. Enforcing orders, criticism and struggle sessions — these were not solutions. The young people, seeing I was not going to come up with any clever manoeuvres, slowly wandered home, eventually leaving only Zheng Guyu. I took the opportunity to learn some more from him about the situation in Xiling during the past few years. From what he said it was easy to see that the analysis of "Old Ox" was accurate. In the past few years production had indeed been seriously set back, and the people had really reached their limit. As Zheng Guyu continued, I could see he himself was on the point of tears. Pausing for a moment, he said, "I think the best step we can take now is backwards. Backwards to the original route. For example, in this area we simply have to depend on the mountains for food; we should first of all raise our winter production level. . . ."

The next day the "on-the-spot" wedding proceeded as planned, with more than a little pomp and circumstance. I noticed "Old Ox" had come to have a look at the excitement. I did not read the words of congratulations which Wu Aiying had written for me. Instead, I talked about the things "Old Ox" had said, the things I knew in my heart were most important: to eliminate mercenary weddings altogether, mustn't we first put all our efforts into improving production, raising the average income, and helping the commune members to prosper? Finally, based on the spirit of the Bulletin of the Third Plenary Session, I agreed with Zheng Guyu's suggestions for future planning. As soon as I had finished, the courtyard filled with prolonged applause. Zhou Tiewa pushed her way through the crowd, and grasped my hand, saying excitedly:

"Secretary Zhou, you have finally got to the root of the problem of mercenary weddings. As long as the policies from above are in accord with what you've just said, we'll promise to work all out to improve life in this mountain area."

Then everyone began making suggestions for improving winter production: digging for the ingredients for Chinese medicines; collecting mountain peach and almond pits; chopping wood for spade handles; weaving bamboo baskets. . . . The wedding ceremony had virtually become a production mobilization meeting, something I had not expected at all. A few words according to the spirit of the Third Plenary Session, and, to my surprise, I had stirred up this much energy!

Just then, a path opened in the crowd, and I saw Wang Erlan and Zheng Yunshan approaching, both with big red flowers in their hair. They were coming to take part in a belated wedding ceremony.

"So, your father agreed?" I asked Erlan.

Erlan simply smiled and nodded, and Zheng Yunshan said, "Her father let me write him an I.O.U. for 500 yuan."

"Write an I.O.U.?" yelled Wu Aiying. "That's ridiculous!"

Zheng Yunshan laughed and said, "He had me write — 'To be paid in your next life.' "

The entire crowd, including Wu Aiying, burst out laughing.

"Only 'Old Ox' could pull a stunt like that," said Zheng Guyu. "He must have been born under the sign of the duck. No matter how well you cook him, his bill stays tough."

Translated by Ellen Hertz
Illustrated by Zheng Shufang

GU HUA

(1942 —   )

Born in 1942, in the countryside of Jiahe County, Hunan Province, Gu Hua's real name is Luo Hongyu. In 1961 he began his studies at Chenzhou Regional Agriculture School. Later he became an agricultural worker at the Agricultural Science Institute. In 1975 he joined the Regional Song and Dance Troupe, where he worked as a writer. He was later transferred to the Regional Cultural Union. In 1980 he joined the Union of Chinese Writers. That same year he was elected a member of the Federation of Literary and Art Circles in Hunan Province.

Gu Hua published his first piece of writing in 1962. In 1978 he published *Mang River Songs*, a collection of short stories. By the end of 1981 he had published four novelettes, among which was *Golden-Leafed Forest Lotus*, as well as more than thirty short stories including "An Orchid for You". His novel *Lotus Town* came out in the same year and was warmly received.

THE IVIED CABIN

Gu Hua

For many years now, the story of "Naogelao Yulang" has been circulating in the Misty Border Mountain District. "Naogelao Yulang", in Yao* dialect, means "the young woman of Yao". The story goes that in Green Feather Hollow, in the heart of these ancient and secluded hills, lived a young Yao woman named Pan Qingqing, whose job it was to guard the forests. She was born, raised, and married in the hills. She seldom left her abode and had been to the Forest Department only once — granted. That was not quite far away. No wonder the young men of the department had never had a glimpse of her, however much they had heard that she was some sort of a mountain fairy.

Her ancestors lived in Green Feather Hollow in the ivied cabins which were built with trunks of fir so strong that no axe could ever break them and they could stand up to any attack by the wild boar. Layer upon layer of white fan-shaped fungus had grown on the trunks, which now looked black just above the ground. Behind the cabin, was a clear mountain stream which flowed quietly all year long.

The cabin's only contact with the outside world, apart from a narrow foot-path, was a telephone line put up before the "cultural revolution" for reporting fires. One winter, however, the snowfall was particularly heavy and the line snapped. During the turbulent times of the "cultural revolution" the leaders of the forest district were replaced whenever those contending for power moved up and down on the political seesaw; na-

---

* Yao: a minority people mainly distributed in Guangxi and other southern provinces.

turally no one had been sent to fix the fallen telephone line. And so this steel thread, the symbol of modern civilization, never did make its way back to the secluded forest hollow. In the midst of these thousands of acres of forest, the day alternated with the night and nothing much happened.   But for the occasional crowing of a cock, the barking of a dog, the cry of a child coming from the cabin, or the pale blue thread of smoke rising from the chimney, the valley of Green Feather Hollow would have appeared, still and quiet, as if it had been sleeping. Neither the chirping of birds nor the blossoming of flowers and the falling of their petals could ever have waked it up.

Pan Qingqing's parents had passed away early.   Her husband, Wang Mutong, was a tall and strong Han.* He was so powerfully built that he looked as though he could kill a tiger with his bare hands. Both husband and wife were employed as forest guards.   Before every meal it was Wang Mutong's habit to drink a glass or two of the corn liquor which Pan Qingqing brewed.   Except for an occasional drunken fury, when he would beat Qingqing till she was bruised in places with marks of purple and blue, he was not a bad husband after all. Generally, he took good care of his wife.   He never made her climb the hills herself to gather firewood, which was always stacked neatly in piles beside the cabin door. He never sent Qingqing out to clear the firelanes as there had not been a fire at Green Feather Hollow for over ten years. He never made Qingqing tend the garden or grow vegetables, yet all the year round the large plot beside the bank of the stream was always loaded with onions, fresh melons and vegetables, more than they could eat.   All Pan Qingqing had to do was to feed the pigs, nurse the baby, wash and mend the clothes, and attend to the other household chores, so that at the age of 26 or 27 she still maintained the look of freshness and tenderness of a young girl not yet married.   Though completely illiterate, Wang Mutong believed that he knew all he needed to know. He felt that he was really the lord of Green Feather Hollow: the woman was

---

* Han: the majority nationality of China.

his; the children, the cabin and the mountains were all his. Of course, the leaders in the Forest Centre had sent him here to guard the forest and he was, in truth, merely their subordinate.

Before Pan Qingqing had given birth to the children, she asked him several times for permission to travel the 90 kilometres out to the Forest Department to have a good look around. That permission was each time denied. Instead, she was severely beaten and forced to kneel as punishment for asking. Wang was afraid once his pretty and charming wife had got to that worldly and exciting place she would be attracted by a new kind of life. More than that, he feared she might be lured away by the flashy, smooth-talking youth there.

Not until Pan Qingqing had given birth to a son and then later a daughter did he begin to rest assured about her. It was as if Qingqing had now become tied fast to his belt, and had truly become his woman. He maintained his rule in the family with beatings and forced kneelings and rigidly arranged the daily schedule. Father, wife, children: everyone in Green Feather Hollow knew his or her place. Theirs was a small society with its hierarchy all right.

Wang Mutong and Pan Qingqing were cut off from the world as they spent their days. Although husband and wife were not always in agreement on everything, they were accustomed to their life in the forest and things generally went fairly smoothly.

Wang Mutong went to the Forest Department once a month to pick up his and his wife's salary and came back with the family's ration of rice, oil, and salt. Each time he returned, he would tell Pan Qingqing everything that had happened and all the gossip he had heard in the department. Pan Qingqing would sit in wonder with her big black eyes wide open listening as if her husband had brought home tales of distant lands. These past few years he had been telling her mainly of students outside rebelling and making trouble, of old, bespectacled intellectuals being paraded like monkeys through the countryside with labels hanging from their necks, or of forestry technicians who, after half a lifetime studying, now attempted suicide by drowning in buffalo wallows which were so shallow that he was dragged out with his back still dry. Later on, came the criticism of a certain kind of "deer",* which of course was not the ordinary sort of wild swift-running animal that could be hunted with a gun. That term was used to denigrate the learned scholars. . . . "Ah, we are much better off here in Green Feather Hollow you know. The soil is so rich almost anything you put in it will grow. We've had no schooling, true; but no one will ever come here to bother us. . . ."

Pan Qingqing understood only some of her husband's accounts; some of it of course made no sense to her at all. With childlike innocence she shared the fears of those learned men out there. Surely, she felt, it was a calamity to be able to read and write! She could not help secretly rejoicing for herself and her husband. "It is better to live in Green Feather Hollow." She had heard this said often enough and truly believed it. She did not want even to think of the Forest Department, that place filled with open strife and invisible intrigue. She did not expect too much of her husband; she wished only that he would not strike her too hard when he was angry. Every night as soon as it grew dark they would go to bed. A mere half litre of kerosene was enough to last them through half a year to keep the lamp lit themsleves warm. Only the moon and the stars peeping through their window saw what was going on during the night.

"Qingqing, we should have some more babies!"

"We've already got Little Tong and Little Qing. Haven't you said the leaders nowadays forbid everyone to have too many kids and that all the women should go and get themselves fixed?"

"No matter, we could have another five and it wouldn't be too many!"

"You enjoy making me suffer, don't you?"

---

* Wang confused two words which sound similar: scholar and deer.

"Suffer? What suffering is there when a woman raises children?"

"There's nothing to be afraid of! At most they won't issue grain rations for the kids. We've soil and water here at Green Feather Hollow. Look at my hands. They're as thick as oak planks. Do you really think we couldn't raise a few more children? After winter I'll have the soil ready for cotton-plants. Next year you bring the spinning wheel and loom your mother left you, and scrub them clean."

"Oh, look at you! You treat me like a hen that you can just keep well fed and penned up in the hills."

"You are mine!"

Pan Qingqing said nothing as he hugged her tightly and his armpits were giving out a strong smell. She was meek and docile. She was her man's woman and fully accepted that it was her lot to be reprimanded and beaten. She felt that in the full blossom of her youth, to give birth to more children was as natural as a tree bearing fruit. When she nursed her baby the white milk from her breasts flowed as endlessly as the sap of the trees. Her man was virile; he was not afraid of tigers or wild boar. He embraced her with arms as strong as iron, and then they did what other couples outside the forest most likely also do. But he did it with the strength of someone who felt as if his energy could not have been directed into another channel.

In the summer of 1975 "Ace Hand" came to Green Feather Hollow. Don't get me wrong. This "Ace Hand" doesn't mean some "high-level" cadre. He was a city youth who had come to settle down in the Forest District in 1964. His real name was Li Xingfu, meaning happiness and referring to the fact that he was born in the year of Liberation. He was a tall and lanky youth, almost elegant in appearance, and revealed an engaging wit when speaking with the local workers and cadres. During the "cultural revolution", when the Red Guards put out the call to "establish ties" with the masses, he was swept along by the current of revolutionary fervour. He tried to hop on a train, but fell instead on the track and lost his arm as a result.

From that time on, one shirt sleeve hung empty by his side. He stayed in the city for a few years, and then returned to the Forest District where the local workers gave him the nickname "Ace Hand". The leaders there didn't know what to do with him. They telephoned every logging camp, and every tree-farming brigade in the district but no one was willing to take him. They all said that not only was "Ace Hand" unable to perform physical labour but worse, he was a "Little Revolutionary General". His efforts to "establish ties" with the workers ended up somewhat like dropping ashes on beancurd: you could not blow them off or brush it clean and there was no way to get rid of that kind of contamination.

One day while collecting his family's ration of rice, Wang Mutong happened to run into the chairman of the District's Political Affairs Section. Chairman Wang put his hand on his forehead and said to himself, "Right! Why not send Li Xingfu to Green Feather Hollow to help Wang Mutong and his wife in guarding the forest? This isn't just a convenient arrangement; it is perfect! It will add another guard to a post where besides the hard-working Wang and his wife there isn't another soul for 100 kilometres around. In a place like this Li Xingfu, if he is to establish ties at all, he will have to do it with the monkeys and pheasants."

When Wang Mutong heard another hand was to be added to Green Feather Hollow, he was very happy, but when he heard Li Xingfu had only one hand he expressed reluctance. "Lao Wang, haven't you been asking to join the Party for years? This is nothing more than a test which has been arranged for you," said Chairman Wang as he slapped him on the arm. "Just because Li Xingfu has only one arm, he's easy to deal with. It doesn't mean he won't be able to do what you want him to do. I'll talk to him personally about his duties working under you. I'll make it clear that while he's at Green Feather Hollow he's to follow your orders in all matters, report to you on everything, and ask for permission whenever he wants to leave the hollow. But what about you? You should widen your horizon, as it were. Take this young intellectual who has been somewhat misguided. Educate him and reform him, if you can." Nodding his head, Wang Mutong decided to accept this trial, this weighty responsibility of educating and reforming a young man.

So "Ace Hand" came to Green Feather Hollow and the community headed by Wang Mutong now had an important new member. Wang Mutong and Pan Qingqing built a hut for Li Xingfu only twenty or thirty steps from their own cabin right beside the clear green mountain stream. They used tree trunks to erect the walls and fir planks for the roof. Thus the two cabins, one big one small, one old one new, formed a pristine neighbourhood. In the beginning Wang Mutong had no hard feelings for "Ace Hand". On the contrary he rather enjoyed hearing Li Xingfu calling him "Brother Wang".

Li Xingfu was soon enraptured by the beautiful scenery and peaceful atmosphere of Green Feather Hollow. Wang sent him out on fire patrol every day. Each morning he climbed the narrow path that looped and twisted its way like a snake up the mountain and into the forest fog. It was like walking into a dream world. The thick milk-white fog which filled the valley gave him the feeling that it might take him away from this world. At about 9 or 10 o'clock in the morning, when the sun first broke through the dispersing mist, he would sit in the doorway of his lookout post as the trees above burst forth in emerald green while the boundless sea of fog remained below. Then all he could see was one towering cluster of hemlock and pine floating above the billowing mist. At a time like this, he almost believed that this was fairyland, like the jade forest of Peng Lai,* beyond the reach of human beings.

Of course, Li Xingfu did not believe he was living in this forest fairyland. Even though Wang Mutong and Pan Qingqing were also young, he knew that he must behave properly and maintain an appropriate distance from lovely "Sister Qing-

---

* The fabled abode of immortals. — *Trans.*

qing", whose big black eyes seemed to be full of songs. But young people could not do without company. Would he really be able to make friends only with the golden-haired monkeys, thrushes and grouse of this green valley?

Wang had two children, a seven-year-old boy named Tong and a girl named Qing, who was five. At first the two children were a little afraid of "Ace Hand". But "Ace Hand" caught a couple of red sparrows for Little Tong, and picked a bunch of wild flowers for Little Qing to wear in her hair and then let her see her reflection in a small round mirror. That changed everything! The brother and sister began to call him "Uncle Li" or "Elder Brother Li". After a few days Tong began to stay the night at his hut. Pan Qingqing had to come to call him home but he refused to leave.

These children of the hills were lovable in their wild way. One day a snake slithered into the hut scaring "Ace Hand", who was shaking all over. Tong calmly informed him, "Snakes won't bite unless you step on them first." Then he went on speaking with an air of authority, "There are mainly three kinds of snakes in Green Hollow. The green bamboo snake is the laziest. Usually he just lies coiled up on a bamboo stalk and doesn't move at all." Little Tong looked up, closed his eyes, puckered up his cheeks and said, "Like this, fu, fu, fu, he spurts out his venom to catch the birds. When a bird is near, he strikes at it with lightning speed and then holds it in his mouth. After this he lazily coils back up around the bamboo stalk again and eats it slowly. Now the howler snake is not like that at all. His scales are mud coloured but he's fierce looking that when he crawls along the ground even the grass parts to make way for him. He can grow to half the length of a man. He looks like this." Little Tong opened his mouth and stared without blinking, stretching his neck out so that his head stuck out as far as it could. "Hoo, hoo, hoo, oh it's frightening! Then there's the snake that's as thick as an axe handle and as long as a shoulder pole. Father calls him 'Forty-eight Lengths'. When he moves he sways his head so far back and forth you'd think he's crazy!" "Ace Hand" immediately took hold of Little

Tong's head so he wouldn't get carried away imitating this too. He asked, "How do you know all this?"

"I've seen the green bamboo snake myself. Father told me about the howler snake and forty-eight pieces although I've never seen them. He catches snakes and sells them in the Forest Department." "Ace Hand" looked at the boy, who, he thought, ought to be in school rather than studying the ways of snakes. Then he thought of that frightful snake which had already slithered away from his hut and he could not help shivering again.

As he observed the children, the children observed him too. Every morning "Ace Hand" brushed his teeth and rinsed his mouth by the stream bank. Little Qing would always stick her head half way through the cabin door to stare at him, out of curiosity. One morning Little Qing timidly approached him and asked, "Uncle, is your mouth dirty?"

"Ace Hand" looked at her not quite understanding what she meant. His mouth was filled with tooth-paste.

"If your mouth isn't dirty then why do you rinse it every day?"

"Ace Hand" burst out laughing. He rinsed his mouth, wiped his face, and then said to Little Qing, "Later I'll ask your mother to buy you and Little Tong each a brush. Then every morning when you wake up you can brush your teeth, too, and your teeth will be as white as snow and very pretty."

Little Qing remained unconvinced. "Mum never uses a brush and her teeth are snow white."

To convince her, "Ace Hand" asked, "But does your mother's mouth smell?"

"When she kisses me her mouth always smells sweet. If you don't believe me, kiss her yourself. . . ."

"Little Qing, you devil, what are you doing out there? You come right back here!" her mother yelled from the cabin.

"Ace Hand" blushed. His heart pounded as though he'd been caught doing something he should not have done. He went back to his cabin at once.

It was only a trivial matter, but Wang Mutong heard about

it. He made Little Qing kneel as punishment just outside the cabin door. Obviously, this was for "Ace Hand"'s eyes! Though no other warning signs were given, "Ace Hand" knew he had to be more cautious. Though there was no cause for suspicion he felt that he had to keep his eyes on things.

Life for the inhabitants of Green Feather Hollow flowed on as smoothly as the clear green stream which ran behind the cabins. At its deepest, the water reached one's calf; in the shallow areas it came only to the top of one's feet. Yet the shallow stream reflected the dancing trees, the clear blue sky, the freely drifting white clouds. And now it reflected one more thing, too. "Ace Hand" had erected a tall slender pole beside his cabin to support a radio antenna.

This was bound to stir up trouble. The small black box in "Ace Hand"'s cabin talked and sang, breaking the hitherto silence of the night in the forest. At first only Little Tong and Little Qing dared come into his cabin, once evening fell, to listen to it. Gradually, armed with the excuse that she had to call the kids home, Pan Qingqing would go in herself to listen for a while. Naturally, this resulted in Wang Mutong's going over to bring his wife and children back to their cabin when it was time for bed. Sometimes, when Wang's voice was too gruff, Pan Qingqing would answer somewhat in the tone of a spoiled child, "It's early! When it's all dark we'll go to bed. It's such an awfully long time till it's light again!" Then she would go on, "When it's all dark we'll go to bed." The woman now thought the night was "awfully long". Wang Mutong was perturbed. This big forest guard who could eat an entire jin of rice at a single meal never went to listen to the magical songs and voices which came out of that bewitched black box. He maintained the dignity of a man who would not tolerate offence, while he solemnly observed how the situation develop.

Not long after, "Ace Hand" helped Pan Qingqing and the two children clear away the refuse from the vacant plot between the two cabins. They neatly stacked the firewood by the doorway, levelled the ground and removed the pig and dog manure. Soon the whole place was looking neat and tidy. "Ace Hand" said they should grow some flowers on the lot. He also promised to teach Pan Qingqing and the children how to read and how to do exercises following the radio programmes. This made Qingqing so happy that she was all smiles. After that the children tagged along behind "Ace Hand" from morning to night. They talked incessantly of what "Uncle Li says . . ." and what "Uncle Li forbids. . . ." They had grown closer to him than to their own father. This made Wang Mutong all the more uncomfortable and irritable. Although Li Xingfu had only one hand, he had unwittingly altered the life at Green Feather Hollow as completely as earthworms had silently turned over the whole fields.

"Woman, he's come to this hollow just to show that he's a cultured type and to show up your old man!" said Wang Mutong to his wife. Sure enough, "Ace Hand" eventually put forward four proposals. One was that they should ask the District Headquarters to send someone immediately to repair the telephone line which had lain broken for many years, and that a wired-broadcasting system should be installed on the plot between the two cabins. Secondly, he proposed they post painted wooden signs at every mountain pass around Green Feather Hollow displaying all ordinances concerning forest preservation. The third proposal was that they set up a firewatch patrol schedule. He and Wang would carry on two shifts between them: a morning shift and an afternoon shift, each one eight hours long. While on duty it would be impermissible to gather firewood, dig for valuable roots or attend to any private matters. The fourth proposal was that they set up a small study group to discuss politics and culture in which Little Tong and Little Qing could also take part. When Pan Qingqing heard the proposals her face lit up. She gave Wang a sidelong glance which expressed what she wanted to say without using words, "You see, this young man has culture; he doesn't think as we do and he speaks so beautifully!"

Wang had expected something like this for quite a while. His face stretched taut, his mouth clamped tight as an iron vice, and his eyes were full of fire as he stared at his woman ferociously. "A newly-built outhouse smells great the first few days. Watch yourself!" Then he said brusquely to "Ace Hand", "We've got a saying around here something like this, 'When city boys come to the country they ought to act as the locals do.' In other words, the guest ought to follow the host's lead. Of course, you're not a guest here, but you don't rate as the host either. There hasn't been a forest fire at Green Feather Hollow for twenty years. Is there a leader in this whole district who wouldn't find that commendable? Has there ever been a time when I didn't act as a model guard? I've never had to rely on a telephone line, or wooden signs, or two shifts of patrol or any study group. You'd be better off keeping your axe sharp and your body strong. The district put me in charge of what goes on in this hollow a long time ago. Don't forget those three conditions given you by Chairman Wang from the political section."

With a severe look Wang Mutong crossed his arms behind his back, his eyes flashing. "Ace Hand" stared blankly, his mouth agape, his face pale. Pan Qingqing looked apologetic, but she dared not utter a word of reproach to her husband for his rude and unreasonable behaviour. She said to "Ace Hand", "Brother Li, he's not a cultured person and these are only the words of a. . . ." But when she saw her husband was on the verge of flaring up again, she said no more.

Wang Mutong laughed coldly and then said, "Yes, I'm just a hick and he is cultured, but these are times when the cultured are led by the hicks. We hicks are in charge now! Don't you forget, Li Xingfu, that the leaders sent you here to Green Feather Hollow to be educated! To be reformed!" Having said that, he swung his massive body around and left. His footsteps were ringing with a booming sound that made one think he was leaving craters in the ground at each step.

"Ace Hand"'s proposals were up against the stone wall of Wang Mutong's stubbornness, and there was not going to be any break-through. His heart sank. What Wang said was true, though. He had been sent out to this hollow to be educated

and reformed. Indeed, nowadays it was a matter of hick educating the educated. This was the fashion. So be it. He could
not help fearing Wang Mutong, somehow. He knew as well
that he could not change the present unfortunate situation himself. Still, he was energetic and full of vigour. He did not let
himself fall into idleness, for when he was idle he would fell
lonely. Then he would ponder the meaning of life and even
wonder if throwing himself off a cliff might not make more
sense. He had brought with him two books printed before the
"cultural revolution". One was *A Survey of Tree Species* and
the other, *Common Facts About Forest Fires*. Every day as he
patrolled the mountains he would bring along *A Survey of Tree
Species*. By studying the illustrations he learned to distinguish
the several hundred different kinds of broadleaf evergreens in
that area. He planned to carry out his own study of the natural
resources in Green Feather Hollow, both to prepare the first
data of that sort for later logging operations and to ensure that
his stay here was not completely fruitless. He thought Pan
Qingqing might understand so he told her of his plans. Sure
enough, she advised him as kindly and gently as she would be
advising her own brother, "Silly! Go ahead and do what you
want. You don't need anyone's permission."

"You don't think Brother Wang will mind?"

"Is there anything wrong with what you want to do? Oh
you. . . ." As Qingqing said this her voice lingered on the last
word. Her shining black eyes pierced him as she spoke directly
to his heart. Without knowing why, "Ace Hand" was afraid
to look into those eyes. Qingqing's admonition sounded like
music, and like a mountain stream it turned and twisted its way
and found into his heart.

Autumn had arrived. "Ace Hand" collected the seeds of
cliff fir, golden forest lotus and ginger trees. He kept the seeds
in an old envelope. He thought he would set up a small nursery
in which to plant the seedlings so that later he could take the
saplings down to the Forest Department, where he could hand
them over to the technicians for proper care. In order to prepare the nursery he had to burn out a clearing in the wild shrub

first. He knew Wang Mutong had not the slightest interest in this kind of endeavour, so he asked Qingqing to lend him a hand.

That day Wang was gathering firewood up on the mountain slope. As it turned out, the patch beside the garden which "Ace Hand" and Qingqing chose to clear, happened to be just the spot on which Wang had decided to plant his cotton. They set the plot ablaze. As a brisk wind was blowing, in no time thick smoke was billowing from a roaring fire. The two of them were just like brother and sister talking and laughing, happy and cheerful. Suddenly, Wang came racing down from the mountainside. With cold glare he snatched his axe from behind his back and levelled a pine sapling. Then wielding the young tree with both hands he beat out the fire. "Ace Hand" explained the situation at once. Enraged, Wang shouted back, "Don't ever do anything like this without my permission. I've got other plans for this spot! Li Xingfu, you should have asked me first, instead of torching down this patch on your own. Tonight I want you to write an account of self-criticism!"

"Whom should I give it to?"

"Whom should you give it to? Do you think I'm not in charge around here just because I can't read? Let's get one thing straight as long as you're working under me. We'll stick to the rules." Qingqing looked at her husband and wanted to cry. Wang ferociously instructed her, "You go back and feed the pigs! Then get some water over here for the ashes."

"Ace Hand" stole a cowering glance at Qingqing. Not daring to answer back to her husband, she turned around and walked away. She wiped the tears from her eyes with the back of her hand.

Everybody had a certain degree of self-confidence, and self-respect. But if a small rip in it was left unattended it could become a hole, too wide to be papered over. Even the earth was rent in places. Wang felt the challenge from "Ace Hand". At the same time he thought his own woman had turned wild; she was no longer as obedient or as docile.

When Wang went on his next trip to District Headquarters to pick up his family's ration of grain, he felt an unexplainable anxiousness as he left the cabin early in the morning. There was something bothering him which he could not put aside. He was a rugged man with plenty of stamina. Though it was a 180-kilometre round trip on mountain paths, as night approach-ed he started his journey back, carrying 125 jin of grain! By the time he got back to his home he was reeking with sweat. The door to his cabin was unlocked and the light was shining bright within. "Strange," he thought, "the woman had not yet gone to bed." He walked into the room. No one was there. Then he heard laughter and music coming from "Ace Hand"'s cabin. He felt the oven and the stove; they were both cold. He rushed out and ran to "Ace Hand"'s cabin. There he could see everything clearly. His wife was sitting, her chin cupped in her hands. Little Tong was leaning against her knee, listening to the sound of a woman singing enticingly. "Ace Hand" was holding Little Qing on his lap, his cheek pressed tight against hers! Wang Mutong recognized the song coming from the black box. It was a love song of the Yao people, "Boyfriend and Girlfriend with Lovers' Hearts."

"Oh how pretty, when my Mum was alive she loved to sing these songs," she said. Wang watched as his wife looked at "Ace Hand" with disturbing intimacy.

"The Yao people have always loved to sing and dance. . . ." "Ace Hand" too was returning his look with improper famil-iarity. Wang Mutong could bear no more. He repressed the rage in his heart enough not to let out a torrent of filthy lan-guage and merely said, "Little Tong! Little Qing! are you two little devils planning to listen to love songs all night? Do you see any light up in that sky?" When Qingqing realized her husband had returned, she hastily grabbed Little Qing in one hand and Little Tong in the other and hurried them outside. She said, "Ai ya! You devil, why didn't you stay the night in the headquarters? Look how tired and sweaty you are!" Wang Mutong didn't answer. He was grinning his teeth and then muttered uneasily, "I was afraid if I spent the night away, you'd spend it at his place."

When they got back to their cabin, Qingqing lit a fire at once to boil some water and warm up some food. She did not prepare any liquor though, afraid her husband might use it as an excuse to beat her. That night Wang showed an unusual coolness, a reticence that made Qingqing shudder. The atmosphere within the shack was tense. He used the hot water to wipe his body and wash his feet. Then paying no attention to the supper his wife had laid out upon the table, he solemnly and silently got into bed. Qingqing massaged his feet and back several times in a conciliatory way knowing the anger that was bottled up inside of him. But he lay as frighteningly still as a heavy powder keg.

Wang Mutong was not just a powerful man, he was also calculating and self-centred. He felt his status in Green Feather Hollow was at stake. It seemed to him now that not just Qingqing but Little Tong and Little Qing might also forsake him. He was a simple, honest, exemplary forest guard suffering from the acts of others. Was he supposed to sit back and watch "Ace Hand" step by step steal his wife and children away from him? Could he let himself be defeated by an amputee, a carefree intellectual youth sent out to the countryside? Hell, no! To begin with he would have to re-establish his standing within his own household. Early the next day with a lively expression and eyes opened round he announced with a voice that boomed like muffled thunder, "Little Tong, Little Qing, kneel for me! Kneel! Now listen! Starting from today both of you and your mother are forbidden to enter "Ace Hand"'s hut. If any of you go in there, your old man will gouge out your eyes and break your feet!" Qingqing turned pale as she listened to all this. Little Tong and Little Qing kneeled behind her, their teeth rattling in fear, trembling like two slender saplings in a winter storm.

Then, since "Ace Hand" had not yet left for work, Wang went over to his cabin to ask for the self-criticism he had assigned a few days before. "Ace Hand" confessed that he had not written it yet. "You haven't written it? So you think I was talking only for my own good? Listen, Li Xingfu, the district leaders have put you under me. From now on you're not allowed to do or say whatever you please. You must behave yourself properly. I'll give you one more day. Hand in your self-criticism tomorrow morning." Glaring at him and with fists swinging like iron hammers, Wang Mutong laid down three more rules, "From now on, every night you are to give me a report on your whole day's activities. We'll do it right here in this cabin. If you ever want to take time off you have to ask me first. You are not to come to my cabin unless you have a damned good reason! And one last thing, if you ever use that radio of yours to lure my family over again, you'd better watch out for these hands! One of my fingers could pull down that fir pole with all its wires and throw it right back beyond the mountains where it came from!"

In order to increase the effectiveness of his prohibition, Wang Mutong took one concrete measure too. Normally, when he left his cabin to go east by the narrow foot-path to the Forest Department, or west by crossing the stream to head for the hills on fire patrol, he had to walk past "Ace Hand"'s cabin. Brandishing a shovel and rake Wang cleared out another foot-path for himself and his family, a roundabout route of an extra hundred steps or so.

Clearly this was the way things were going to be; "Ace Hand" had no choice but to accept it. Wang's status in Green Feather Hollow had now become unassailable, somewhat like that of an intrepid forest warlord of ancient times and he was equally intolerant of disobedience. Formerly Wang had seldom gone to "Ace Hand"'s cabin, but now that his wife and two children dared not go there, he went every night to listen to "Ace Hand"'s report on his day's activities. Obviously, he enjoyed the taste of power in making "Ace Hand" as submissive as one of the "Five Bad Elements". *

---

* Landlords, rich peasants, reactionaries, bad elements, and Rightists. — *Trans.*

The inhabitant of the small cabin now resembled a snail drawn into its shell. Even the music which the black box played was now just barely heard. "Ace Hand" bowed the neck to this new grim reality and admitted defeat. Life at Green Feather Hollow returned to its previous sleepy, lonely existence.

The weather that winter was unusual. While there was heavy frost, it never snowed. The old people of the region said that this kind of dry winter would mean a dry spring. Every morning the innumerable acres of forest surrounding Green Feather Hollow were coated in frost. The broadleafed ever-greens looked as though they had silver strands draped over them. It was a white, snowy world before it dissolved each day with the noon-day sun. In the valley of the hollow the two cabins, one tall, one short, wore a crown of white jade every morning. The stream behind the cabins was lying frozen and gone was its past babbling sound.

On these dry, cold, frost-laden days, Qingqing would feed the pigs twice a day and cook two meals for the family. But as there were no chores for her to do outside, she got the old clothes out and did the mending work. Nowadays, it was her husband instead who took the children to the hills to play. Qingqing often sat at home beside the fireplace with a strip of cloth in her hand, sometimes as though in a trance for half the morning. Everyday Wang brought back a wild rabbit or badger. He would skin it first and nail it on the cabin wall. The meat dripping with fat would then be stewed in a large pot and its lovely smell would go for miles. Strangely, like a pregnant woman, Qingqing took only a tiny portion of the stewing meat and turned her head, nauseated. She felt as though a boulder had been weighing her down and below that rock were all the things of her life. Her husband beat her more often now. Her body was bruised black and purple. At night she would study her husband's expressions, watch his eyes, afraid even to breathe too loudly. During the beatings she would look on as his hands delivered their blows on her legs and her back, wherever the bruises would not show. Her eyes would change from moist to dry, dry to moist, and she wept at the bitterness of her life. She hated her husband's viciousness. She believed "Ace Hand" was the only one in the world who respected her, the only one who treated her like a human being. Her heavy-handed man treated her as if she were a criminal. "Ace Hand" and she were equally pitiful, she felt. But sometimes, too, she hated all that had happened. Why had he not gone anywhere else except Green Feather Hollow, only to disrupt her family life?

Qingqing was terrified every night when she crawled into bed and smelled the odour of her husband's sweat. Often she wept to herself silently in the pitch-dark, but little by little her despair turned to a desire to resist. Night after night when she came to bed she would stubbornly press her face against the wall as though it had been glued there. Even if her husband pulled and tugged she would not budge. Wang ground his teeth with hate and curse, as he said, "I'd like to see you dead."

"Then let me die."

"Don't count on your luck. All you're thinking of is that young man."

"If you beat me, I'll shout. I'll shout."

"You slut!"

Unlike before, Qingqing now dared to fight back. She did not know why, but she realized somehow that he was very afraid "Ace Hand" would find out about her nightly abuse.

Life is lopsided; emotions defy logic. Qingqing knew she was changing though she was not sure whether it was for better or worse. One thing that was different this dry cold winter was that she now enjoyed dressing up. She loved to wear the silver Venetian head scarf and the rose coloured felt jacket which in the past was lying on the bottom of the wooden chest. She kept her clothes fresh and clean, as though ready at any time to leave the hills for some visit. She also enjoyed filling the brass washbasin, which her mother had left her with clear stream water so that she could admire the reflection of her face. Several years ago she had asked her husband to buy her a mirror while he was on one of his trips to the Forest Department. Yet every time he came back empty handed, and merely said that he had forgotten. It occurred to her now that he had done this on purpose, afraid that she would see how her face shone like moonlight, how her eyes sparkled, how her lips glistened like red lotus petals freshly laden with dew, how lovely her dimples were when she laughed, and how lovely they disappeared when she did not. Who would not be attracted to such beauty? Was "Ace Hand" attracted to her? Oh! How scandalous! Her heart was beating fast and her mind reeling. She pressed her hands to her burning cheeks and bowed her head. It was as though she had done something so horrible and shameful that she felt she could no longer face another soul. Actually, of late she had often found herself gazing out towards "Ace Hand"'s radio, soap, and cream for the skin still seemed as miraculous as anything in the world. It seemed in fact as if a completely new world were enticing her. . . . Li Xingfu! Ah what a lovely name, "Xingfu" (means happiness). But was that pale lanky young man really happy? Each day he used his only hand to chop firewood, wash his clothes, cook his food, afraid even to look at me. When he meets Wang Mutong he acts as if he were confronted with a tiger. How pitiful! Though she acted with the charming shyness of young Yao women, she did feel a gentle and soft compassion for "Ace Hand".

At one time, "Ace Hand" came back from a trip to the Forest Department and brought with him two sweets wrapped in gold and silver foil for Little Tong and Little Qing. Little Qing thoughtfully broke off a piece and stuck it in her mother's mouth. Qingqing hugged the little girl tightly and kissed her on the lips again and again. She asked crazily, "Little Qing, does Mum's mouth smell funny?"

"No! No!"

"Does it smell sweet?"

"Sweet. Mum, your breath is always sweet!"

How silly! Just listen to what you were asking your daughter. She thought back to half a year ago when "Ace

Hand" had just come to Green Feather Hollow, and his talk with Little Qing as he brushed his teeth early that one morning. Her face flushed. The sweet slowly melting in her mouth seemed to drip down straight into her heart. She looked again at her daughter's pink delicate face and saw her own sweet lips reflected there. This was something his powerful husband could not control or even notice, for if he could, surely he would beat her for it too.

One day while Wang was in the hills collecting firewood Qingqing took a bucket to the stream to fetch some water. "Ace Hand" was there washing his clothes in the bone-chilling water. His hands were frozen stiff and red. She put down her bucket, rolled up her sleeves, walked up to him, took the clothes from him and began to wash them herself. Flustered, he straightened up and then stepped back.

"Qingqing, you shouldn't have done this! If Wang Mutong saw. . . ."

Qingqing replied without raising her head, "What's the matter? We're not doing anything wrong."

"I know that, but Wang might beat you."

Her hands stopped. She said nothing.

"Look, your arms are all bruised."

"Be quiet! Stupid, my hands are bruised from the pigs running up against them in the pen." Her eyes were now filled with tears, but she stoically held them back. There was nowhere she could go to cry out loud, to feel better afterwards. She dunked the clothes two or three times, scrubbed them, and then got them out of the water, wrung them and dropped them into his galvanized steel pail. Without turning back her head she scooped up her own bucket and walked away, forgetting to fetch her water.

Back in the cabin, she fell against the back of the door. Her hands and feet were like jelly and her whole body seemed to be sapped of energy. Her heart, however, was thumping wildly as though it wanted to leap from her breast. She did not cry; in fact she almost felt like laughing. This was the first time in her life she had ever done anything with a young man behind her husband's back. Qingqing felt pleased long after her racing heart had subsided. When her husband came back from the mountains he was not suspicious. She had won her first battle.

The frost-laden drought continued into the new year. Many of the broadleafed evergreens around Green Feather Hollow stood bare-limbed like starving old men with thin bony arms stretched towards heaven. A thick blanket of dry leaves lay on the mountain slope. Each time the frosty winds blew, fallen leaves of every shape and hue, like scraps of goldfoil and jade pieces, filled the air with a rasping sound. Then they scattered pell-mell in their beautiful colours.

The long drought prevented "Ace Hand" from staying in his shell. Every morning he got out of bed before daybreak. Then with a hatchet hanging from his hip and the book *Common Facts About Forest Fires* tucked under his arm, he would go off to the hills on patrol. Several times he worked up enough courage to suggest to Wang Mutong that they ought to rake the dry leaves from the fire lanes. Wang paid no attention, of course, because he disliked him and so ignored all his proposals. He said that only he, Wang Mutong, was in charge at Green Feather Hollow, and so everyone else could just keep his suggestions to himself. But this time "Ace Hand" showed a certain stubbornness. As though he had had a premonition, he adopted a rigorous schedule of fire-watch patrols. He persuaded Qingqing to take Little Tong and Little Qing out to clear the dry scrub from around the cabins. He also read *Common Facts About Forest Fires* over and over again to Little Tong and Little Qing, actually, he read it to Qingqing and Wang Mutong.

One morning Wang Mutong heard Little Tong ask: "Uncle Li, what does it mean to run into the headwind?"

"That means if a forest fire is coming, you must head for where it has already burned and run to that place for safety."

"Uncle Li, what if our cabins burn up too?"

"Then we'll run to the stream and stay in the water near the bank where there're no tall trees around."

"Bullshit! Such talk of nonsense!" Wang Mutong refused to listen to any more of this. He cursed viciously, scaring away Little Tong, and then asked "Ace Hand", "Li Xingfu, what are you up to anyway? Are you planning to set a forest fire here at Green Feather Hollow? Why else are you plotting how to escape from one?" "Ace Hand" was left speechless by the question.

"Lao Wang, floods and fires show mercy to no one," he replied.

"Are you telling me then we are going to have a forest fire here this winter?" Wang disdainfully snatched *Common Facts About Forest Fires* from out of his hand. Although he could not read a single word, he flipped through it as if he were doing something beneath his dignity. Then he flung it back to "Ace Hand", and said, "This is probably one of the books by those fortune tellers who try to predict the future."

"Lao Wang, this drought has lasted an awfully long time. The whole mountain is covered with dry leaves now, and every night the radio broadcasts. . . ." He didn't know why but "Ace Hand" always felt ashamed when he stood in front of Wang Mutong, looking like a pale weakling.

On hearing him mention the radio broadcast, Wang began to chuckle coldly. He interrupted to ask, "Has that black box of yours been singing any more of those moaning love songs lately?"

"Ace Hand" did not know how to take his remark. But he kept a straight face and said, "Lao Wang, I have a suggestion. I'd like you to report to the District Headquarters for me. Ask them to send someone out to repair the telephone line immediately. If by any chance something did happen, some sort of emergency, we need a way of contacting the outside world."

"If you want to make a report, just go to the headquarters yourself and do it there. I'll give you two days' leave! While you're there why don't you find out if they can send a whole fire brigade to stay up here too!" Wang Mutong gave "Ace Hand" a deriding sidelong glance and casually yawned. "I'm not bragging, but I've been living at Green Feather Hollow over twenty years. I guess I know something about forest fires!"

That night, as usual, Wang Mutong went to "Ace Hand"'s cabin after dinner. What was surprising was that while in the past Wang always assumed a chiding manner as though he were lecturing one of the "Five Bad Elements", tonight he acted differently. He was unusually amiable. "Comrade Li, when you're at the headquarters, will you do me a favour?" He took out a piece of white paper which he had brought along and asked "Ace Hand" to write for him a request to join the Party. "Ace Hand" was astonished. Wang Mutong put one of his fingers between his teeth and bit it till it began to bleed. Then he held his finger as though it were the pole of a banner. It was dripping with blood. "Quick write this out for me: 'Esteemed and beloved Forest District Leader, I am writing you in my own blood this request to join the Party. . . . I'm not educated. I am a country hick, but my heart is red. I will always do whatever the Party says. . . .'" "Ace Hand" was terribly frightened. He quickly found a writing brush and dipped it in the blood on Wang's finger as he wrote. He finished the request as fast as he could. Oh dear! He dared not look at that blood, and his whole body trembled, his clothes soaked through with sweat. Once the blood letter was written, Wang carefully folded it and stuck it into a pocket in the inner layer of his clothes. He did not trust "Ace Hand" after all. He would not let this politically unreliable person submit his sacred request to the District Headquarters.

The next morning, without even having bandaged his finger, Wang set fire to a new patch of land beside his garden because he wanted to clear another section of his private plot. He was a hard worker, and had already cleared about two thirds of an acre of land for vegetables. The district required only that he raise three pigs, cure the meat at the end of the year and turn it in. Whatever else he raised beyond that belonged to him. He paid no attention to any philosophy or "ism"; his belief in the Party was a belief in himself. He thought the Party should be composed of people just like him. He raked the dead branches and fallen leaves into big piles and then set them

ablaze. Every year after winter he burned the area in this way
to fertilize the fields; even though there was a drought this
winter he would not think of breaking with tradition.

"Ace Hand" was petrified of Wang Mutong's burning of the
brush during such a dry spell, yet he dared not say anything
against his doing it. He could not sleep well at night, and he
often had nightmares of a monstrous and bright conflagration,
as magnificent as the clouds at sunset, racing along as swiftly
as a river. For two nights he secretly climbed the mountain to
cut a branch of a fir sapling. Then he stood on watch beside
the heaps of ashes left by Wang Mutong's daytime burnings.
He would stand there for most of the night. The winter wind
assaulted his hands, feet and face and they were stinging with
pain. Why did he guard these ashes? He had not written a
blood letter requesting to join the Party. Even if he had, no one
would believe what he was going to say about what he had
seen. In the ashes he could see flames and sparks. All that
was needed to start a forest fire was a few such small sparks
falling on the leaf-covered mountain slope. Once started it
would spread, consuming everything in its path. He should go
back to the headquarters to make a report. First, ask them to
send someone to repair the telephone line; second, request they
send someone here to check up on the work being done at
Green Feather Hollow and convince Wang Mutong that he had
to change his ways. He told his plans secretly to Pan Qingqing.
These past few days her eyes were swollen and filled with tears,
and she faced him with a bent head. She felt tender love, resentment and hate towards this pitiful young man. She always
felt as if she had a world of things to say to him.

That afternoon as "Ace Hand" stood hunched over his oven
preparing some food for his journey, Qingqing suddenly dashed
into his small cabin! This was an open violation of her husband's severe month-old probihition. "Ace Hand", bewildered,
stood up. Qingqing appeared to have just come back from
work outside. She was wearing only a flimsy blouse, which
was too tight. The button beneath her collar had come open,

half revealing a portion of her enticingly full, well-rounded breasts.

"Qingqing, what are you. . . ." "Ace Hand" lowered his head. He was so alarmed he could not even finish his question.

"Idiot. Sometimes you're smart but sometimes you're so stupid. I'm not a mountain demon!" She said, because "Ace Hand" indeed looked utterly scared, as though he had just seen a ghost. Pan Qingqing felt more than ever a mother's tenderness towards him.

"Qingqing . . . you . . . you. . . ."

"I've come to ask you to do me a favour when you go down to the headquarters."

"Ace Hand" pulled himself together, raised his head and looked at Pan Qingqing.

"Here's 100 yuan. Please buy a radio just like yours for my family. Buy a mirror too, some soap and some of that skin cream. Also buy Little Tong and Little Qing those brushes that you brush your teeth with every morning. We'll set up a pole at our place too, to put up an antenna."

"Ace Hand" gazed at Qingqing in amazement. This forest woman was really like a goddess of beauty. Her breasts were full, her limbs were well proportioned, and her body were healthy and strong. She was gentle and sweet, her body radiating an irrepressible youthful energy.

"Hey, what are you looking at me like that for? I'm as miserable as you are." Pan Qingqing piquedly turned sideways, her face blushing and her eyes lowered.

"Oh, yes, yes, Qingqing, I was ah. . . . I ah. . . ." "Ace Hand" temporarily lost his train of thought, as though he had discovered something glowing from Qingqing's body. In no time he awoke from his trance and said with a blushing face, "If you spend all this money at once, aren't you afraid that Wang Mutong. . . ."

Qingqing had been looking at him with an expression filled with joy. But when she heard him ask if she was "afraid of Wang Mutong", she felt as though he had sprinkled salt on the honeyed sugar in her heart. "Afraid? I've been afraid for over

ten years now. Every winter he catches animals, every spring he sells the skins, and all that money is added to a salary which neither one of us ever spends. Our cashbox is filled with ten yuan notes. He can't bring himself to spend it. He doesn't even know what to spend it on. . . . No! I'm not afraid! The worst thing that could happen to me is that I might die." As Pan Qingqing said this, her eyes were filled with tears.

"Qingqing, give me the money. I'll buy these things for you," said "Ace Hand", his eyes now brimming with tears too. "Don't cry. You've been wronged. I am worthless. I hate myself! Qingqing, please don't cry. If Wang Mutong came down from the mountain and saw us now he'd beat you and curse me. . . ."

"Oh you, you are not a human being. The ivy which clings to my cabin has more strength than you!" Qingqing glared at "Ace Hand" with resentment and hate. She turned and left.

"Qingqing, Qingqing. . . ." "Ace Hand" ran to the doorway; he meant, unconsciously, to lift his arms to embrace what he desired, but his left empty shirt sleeve remained dangling at his side.

When "Ace Hand" reached the Forest Department, he found that people everywhere were writing slogans in large characters: "Oppose the Rightist Deviationists!" "Criticize the Capitalist Elements Within the Party!" The cadres and workers in the tall office building of the headquarters were all shouting in confusion, running in and out of their offices. "Ace Hand" thought it would be most appropriate to make his report to Chairman Wang of the Political Section. After all, it was Wang who had sent him to Green Feather Hollow in the first place. He waited almost all morning beside the office door. When it was almost time for lunch he leaned in through the doorway.

"Eh? Li Xingfu? What are you doing back here?" Chairman Wang, who had been preparing to leave, was standing before his desk. He patted his forehead and then placed his hands on his hips, but his attitude seemed pleasant enough. As best he could, "Ace Hand" hurriedly reported his suggestion that someone be sent to repair the telephone line.

"Fix the line that's been down these last 10 years!" Wang exclaimed, astonished at the very suggestion. "Is this Wang Mutong's proposal? Ah, so it is yours, after all! Li Xingfu, we rely on Wang Mutong to take care of things at Green Feather Hollow. Although he's not educated he is very reliable politically. He's been an exemplary forest guard for over ten years. It's not like we can just snap our fingers and have that telephone line fixed. That sort of thing requires money and materials, you know. Very soon now another political campaign will be underway. We've got to call on everyone in the country to oppose the Rightist deviationists. This is our most important task at the moment. Do you understand?"

"Ace Hand" then proposed that the headquarters send someone to Green Feather Hollow to investigate the fire prevention work there. He reported, too, how Wang Mutong had been burning fields during the dry season. He began to fear that Wang was impatient because he wanted to go to lunch.

"Hm, Li Xingfu, it seems you've made some improvement since I saw you last." Again, Wang appeared to be surprised, but as he went on his expression turned severe. "However, let me make this clear: we here at the headquarters have complete trust in Wang Mutong! While you are stationed at Green Feather Hollow, you are to follow his orders, learn from him and be reformed by him. Don't try any more of these tricks. I understand that Wang's wife is young and pretty; don't do anything you shouldn't or you might lose your other arm too. You're still young, and you've got a future ahead of you. Behave accordingly!"

So that was that. Not only was "Ace Hand" unable to make a full report, but he was also given a stern reprimand. Obviously, the leaders did not trust him. He felt as though all that talk had gone for naught. He was like a sore-ridden mongrel, driven from place to place, kicked and beaten by everyone along the way. He spent the next two days walking by himself along the main street between the supplies cooperative and the plant nursery. He hated his parents for having urged him to be schooled; he hated the fact that he could not be transformed back into an illiterate, foolish hick so he might join the ranks of Wang Mutong and that sort. These days no one felt that education was worth it; on the contrary, nowadays wherever you went people believed that knowledge was the cause of reactionary tendencies, and that only people like Wang Mutong could carry on the revolution.

Eventually, he thought of Green Feather Hollow, of Qingqing, Little Tong and Little Qing. At least there, in that little secluded place, cut off from all the world, were three people who did not look down on him, who believed in him. At the thought of this, "Ace Hand" seemed to come back to his senses. He bought two months' supply of oil, salt and rice at the grain store. Then he went to the cooperative and bought Qingqing a transistor radio, soap, skin cream, toothbrushes and a big round mirror with a loop on the back. Finally, he went to the grocery store and bought two jin of steamed buns. Early the next morning, carrying the load with a bamboo pole slung across his shoulder, he started off for Green Feather Hollow.

When he got to Black Mountain Valley, the sun was already setting in the west. Just one more ridge and he would be at the hollow. He would be safe and sound in his cabin before it was completely dark. Then he saw some black smoke wafted over from the hollow by the breeze. Was Wang Mutong still burning clear some fields? Why was there so much smoke? . . . He was already exhausted but he did not stop to rest. He wanted to get to the mountain pass quickly to have a clear view. As he became more anxious his legs became heavier. A horrifying thought was creeping into his mind. Just before he reached the pass, he could smell the smoke carried over from the other side of the mountain and hear the cracking and roaring sounds of fire! Good heavens, Green Feather Hollow was not burning, was it? But where else could this smoke and roaring sound have been from? The sky, slowly darkening now, glowed red above the mountains; was it the setting sun? The evening clouds? Or was it the raging flames of a forest fire?

He raced up the mountain, his entire body dripping with hot sweat. Beads of perspiration the size of finger tips clung to his forehead. It was as if some spirit had been pulling him towards the mountain pass. Soon a raging fire, which filled the valley with its incarnading light dazzled his eyes. He nearly fainted. Green Feather Hollow! Heavens! Green Feather Hollow was a sea of flames! The mountain winds stoked the fire, whose tongues of flames resembled thousands of giant centipedes stretching out and up along the mountain ridge, cruelly, wantonly leaping upward. The valley was filled with wave after wave of billowing smoke; the roaring fire surged ahead. Trees centuries old were burned entirely, their trunks looking like giant torches. The scorched cliff crumbled with booms like land mines. From out of the clouds of smoke shot flaming red arrowheads, which flew like dancing crimson snakes in the scorching blasts of air.

"Qingqing! Little Tong . . . Little Qing!" "Ace Hand" dropped his bamboo pole at the pass. Shouting, he ran down into the flame-engulfed valley. Though faced with imminent danger he could not leave behind Qingqing, nor the children. They were the only three friends he had. He ran ahead recklessly. Amazingly he did not stumble. Soon he ran into the clouds of chokingly thick smoke, where he saw a raggedly dressed woman with dishevelled hair and dirty face climbing towards him.

"Qingqing! What's happened! Are you all right?" "Ace Hand" called to her ecstatically when he realized it was Pan Qingqing. When she saw him her two hands reached out in a plea for help before she collapsed to the ground. He dashed to her side. Half kneeling, half squatting he embraced her. "Qingqing, Qingqing. . . . It's me, Li Xingfu." "Ace Hand"'s throat was dry, his voice hoarse; he cried as he spoke to her. It took almost ten minutes before she regained consciousness. When she opened her eyes she murmured, "You, you. I always thought I'd see you. . . ." Then she laid her head on his chest and sobbed.

"Qingqing, don't cry, don't cry. Tell me how the fire started."

"Let's go. Help me up. . . ." Pan Qingqing said as she struggled to her feet, and then tried to stagger up the mountain slope. "Ace Hand" jumped to help her, only to hear her say, "That damned heartless bastard! That same day you left for the headquarters he discovered our cashbox was 100 yuan short. He accused me of stealing the money to give it to you. No matter what I said he wouldn't believe me. He beat me about the head and chest. He beat me till there wasn't a part of me that wasn't black and blue. Damn him! Then he locked me up in your little cabin. For three days and nights he gave me not so much as a sip of water. I spent all last night using my fingers to scratch and twist free one of the boards. Then I ran to the stream to drink and saw the forest was burning . . . those fires he started . . . burning . . . burning all the wild things of the mountain."

"And Little Qing, Little Tong?"

"That bastard! After the fire started, he took the cashbox and led Little Qing and Little Tong along the stream and out of the valley. That is the way you told him. . . ." Pan Qingqing's body sank weakly against his shoulder, but she did not cry any more. Instead, she began to comb her hair, and even reached out to brush back a sweat-drenched lock of hair from his forehead.

"Ace Hand" was terribly frightened by this immense disaster. They climbed up to the pass to find the bamboo pole he had dropped earlier. Once there, he remembered that he still had two jin of buns in his pocket and a flask of cold water. He quickly brought them out and gave them to Qingqing to eat. Qingqing was starving. She devoured each bun in only three or four bites. After consuming four of them "Ace Hand" gave her some water. Qingqing leaned against his chest again and rested.

"Ace Hand" hugged her tight as he stared blankly into the raging fire below. He suddenly remembered that behind the mountain opposite was Lovers' Hollow. There in that hollow was a beautiful stand of cliff fir and golden forest lotus. He had heard the nursery specialists talk of it. The age of these two kinds of trees dated back to the time of the ice ages. They were living fossils that existed on the brink of extinction. His heart brightened, he said to her, "Qingqing, the fire has only burned part way up the mountain slope. Let's circle around to the opposite side, to the fire lane that protects that mountain ridge. If we can save the trees at Lovers' Hollow, someday, if we're ever able to make our way back to the headquarters, we'll have something to say for ourselves." Yet having said this "Ace Hand" looked back upon the narrow foot-path that led to the headquarters with eyes that clearly said this was his final farewell.

"I'll go with you. No matter where you go, I'll follow." The food and short nap had revived this strong young Yao woman.

The forest fire at Green Feather Hollow was spotted by a P.L.A. radar post 100 kilometres away. The post immediately telephoned the Misty Border Mountain District Headquarters. The Forest Department leaders ordered a brigade of men with horses to go into the mountains to fight the fire. Unfortunately most of the valley's evergreens had already burned, leaving behind naked black charred trees which looked like gangs of demon prisoners who had managed to escape from Hell.

Seven days later Wang Mutong returned to the headquarters with his two children and carrying a wooden box. No one knew where or how they had survived the catastrophe. He did not know what had happened to Pan Qingqing or Li Xingfu. With tears streaming down his face, he confirmed that the fire had been set by Pan Qingqing and her adulterous lover, "Ace Hand". It had nothing to do with the fires he had set to clear the fields. For over ten years he had been a model forest guard. To vindicate himself further he presented to the Headquarters' Party Committee his blood written request to join the Party. Naturally the district leaders believed his sobbing report. They sent some civilian militia to Green Feather Hollow to track down and arrest the two lovers. During their few days in the ash-covered mountain spot the militia found only the charred remains of some wild animals. No one knew if Pan Qingqing and Li Xingfu were still alive.

Meanwhile the district, as everywhere else, was caught up in a class struggle that was to decide the fate of the nation. In order not to impede the progress of the "Oppose the Rightist Deviationists" Movement the civilian militia filed a report according to the custom of that time which announced, "The fire started by class enemies was extinguished in time by the revolutionary cadres and masses. . . ." And that was that.

Wang Mutong refused to go back to Green Feather Hollow under any circumstances. Fortunately, the headquarters had just received an urgent message from Heaven's Gate Cave, a forest area on the border of Guangdong and Guangxi provinces, that an old forest guard had died of illness. The district leaders sent Wang Mutong and his two children there to take up the post and continue his difficult, wild, self-reliant way of life. It is said that that year Wang Mutong married a Guangxi widow. He resumed his old habits of going to bed at sundown, and working arduously. As luck would have it, she also had two children, one boy and one girl. Both of them hoped that they would make perfect future partners for Little Qing and Little Tong. So a new generation was reared at the old cabin of Heaven's Gate Cave.

After the fall of the treacherous Gang of Four, many people in the District Headquarters maintained that Pan Qingqing and Li Xingfu might still be alive somewhere deep in the forest, leading a very different sort of life. Other people surmised that once the nation had redressed all the wrongs suffered by those who had been unfairly treated, perhaps Pan Qingqing and Li Xingfu might suddenly walk hand in hand into the headquarters to ask for their just pardons.

Impossible? Even the naked black-charred trees which were not completely burned that year in the fire of Green Feather Hollow, have now put forth buds these past two years and their branches have been covered with new leaves.

Translated by Richard Belsky
Illustrated by Zheng Shufang

ZHAO BENFU

(1947 —   )

Zhao Benfu was born in 1947 in the countryside of Fengxian County, Jiangsu. After graduating from Fengxian County Middle School in 1967, he returned to the countryside to work as a cadre in a production brigade. In 1971 he joined the Communications Office in the county seat to work as a reporter for the County Party Committee's Propaganda Department. In 1980 he was transferred to the county broadcasting station, where he is currently working as an editor.

"Old Sun Sells His Donkey" is his first work. "On the Sands of the Yellow River", a novelette, came out in January 1982.

OLD SUN SELLS HIS DONKEY
Zhao Benfu

Nothing in this vast world of ours is so strange that it does not occur somewhere, sometime. It was just such an unexpected event which finally made up Old Sun's mind: "I'm going to sell that donkey!"

It happened one day when Old Sun had gone to the county town to deliver some goods for the purchasing station. By the time he had delivered the goods and picked up something for someone in the village, it was getting late, and with sixty li ahead of him he hurried his donkey out of town and was on the same road whence they had come.

Old Sun was getting on in years. That morning he was out of bed at four o'clock, on the road by five, and had to climb quite a few stairs in the department store. No wonder he was feeling drowsy even before his cart left the town. Walking alongside the cart, already half asleep, he noticed that once out of the town there were very few people on the road. "I still have quite a long way to go," he thought to himself. "The cart is empty, and the donkey knows this road; why don't I just take a quick nap." No sooner said than done. He hopped on the cart, and, holding his whip in one hand, fully clad, he fell asleep to the "clump, clump" of the big black donkey's hooves as it made its way along the road.

As it happened, not far ahead was a small grey donkey pulling a flat-bed cart. A corpse was lying on the cart and on either side walked the sobbing relatives of the deceased.

Seeing a fellow donkey of the opposite sex, our big, black donkey was struck with a sudden and unreasoning passion, and, putting all other considerations aside, stepped up his pace to

145

keep up with his mate, who was heading straight for the crematorium. Meanwhile, Old Sun had fallen sound asleep and was dreaming peacefully.

A number of corpses were lined up in the courtyard in beds, stretchers, carts and the like, waiting quietly. The gloomy relatives were scattered about, squatting or standing, and they looked up blankly at the new arrivals.

The big, black donkey, following close at the tail of his little grey friend, pulled up and got in line in the most well-behaved of manners.

Perhaps because these two carts arrived together, everybody assumed that two people from the same household had died. The two carts were immediately surrounded by a group of sympathetic and, curious onlookers, whose questioning stares soon turned into direct inquiries:

"Are they from the same family?"

The relatives shook their heads and said, "It started following us a while back."

This was odd, especially as the other cart was accompanied by neither driver nor relatives. A few plucked up their courage and silently crowded around Old Sun, stretching their necks to have a better look into the cart: his face was ruddy, his expression serene; in fact, he did not look at all like a dead man. And, listen! The sound of breathing! ... For one dreadful moment, the crowd stood stockstill as if they had seen a ghost. The sight made their flesh creep and their hair stand on end. Then suddenly they drew back in a confused mass. What was going on?

The donkey, perhaps frightened by the crowds, or perhaps because it suspected they were going to take advantage of its master, threw back its head and began to bray loudly. This sent the other donkeys present into an accompanying chorus of "hee-haws". The hitherto solemn atmosphere of the crematorium had suddenly become that of a lively donkey market.

Old Sun woke up in alarm and sat up to see what was going on. He rubbed his eyes. Where was he? Why was he surrounded by all these people, each wearing a different expression of horror or surprise, and some looking as if they were about to flee in terror. He steadied himself and looked around again. What was he doing in the crematorium? He was shivering all over. My God! What a lovely place to wake up in! And, these people think I am a ghost come back to life.

Old Sun was furious. He leapt from his cart as if to beat his donkey, then reconsidered. No, this was not the place. He had better wait until he had left this inauspicious crematorium. Without so much as raising his head, he turned the donkey around and whipped him out the gate.

To anyone else, this incident would have been a joke, but to Old Sun it was a matter of great significance. He maintained that this omen of ill-fortune only confirmed a premonition that he had been feeling for quite a few days.

Most of the people in the village would not have believed that Old Sun had something on his mind. Everyone knew that he had made a small fortune transporting goods for the purchasing station. Furthermore, with the new responsibility system, his wife could stay at home, while his son and daughter worked. However, all these changes in the last couple of years made him uncomfortable. Surely, there was a hitch and he was not sure if the recent wealth of his family was a sign of good luck or coming misfortune! True, it was good money for the family, but it was money hard-earned. In fact, his job working as "the legs" of the purchasing station involved more hardships than most people would ever realize.

Old Sun's home was not far from the Yellow River, in a poverty-stricken and out-of-the-way corner where three provinces met and which the authorities had paid little attention to. The land was poor, but there was a certain kind of cogongrass which flourished in and along the old course of the Yellow River, stretching as far as the eye could see, and it was as if, like this grass, the people of the area had learned to make do on this barren terrain. In addition to farming, most families raised livestock, and under the blue skies of summer and autumn, with the sheep and cattle grazing among the blowing grass, one had the feeling of being in the vast grasslands north of the Great Wall. The raising of livestock had become an important source of livelihood for these peasants.

The county heads had set up a purchasing station. When enough sideline products such as sheepskin and wool had accumulated, a truck would be sent to take all the goods to the county town. However, livestock could not be left to accumulate, and, since the county found it could not afford to send in a truck every few days, "leg power" became absolutely essential for taking these animals into town as soon as they were ready to sell. This was considered a supplementary form of state-financed transportation.

Although the pay for "leg power" was relatively high, it was not easy to find people willing to do the job. A trip to the county town and back involved one hundred li in travelling time, which meant getting up at five, only to return late at night. Very few people were prepared to put up with such trying conditions, and, furthermore, few families could escape their household chores long enough to leave the village. The most tiring aspect of the job, however, was that because it was difficult to get anything in this out-of-the-way place, people were always requesting things from the county town: one family wanted some cloth, another needed some sugar, the production brigade was buying a water pump or fertilizer and would like to have it carted back, and so on. With more than one hundred families in the village, there were always some such requests. No one wanted to take on this much responsibility even though the job would bring home extra money. What was more, several years ago during the movement to "let mass criticism inspire great efforts", Old Sun, "the legs" of the purchasing station, had been publicly criticized and labelled a "self-interested" element, making the position even less appealing. Those who had the energy for the job felt that they could put it to better use elsewhere.

Old Sun had faced more than half a year of public criticism. Now, as a result of his constant running back and forth, his old case of rheumatism flared up. His left leg was permanently paralysed by the long illness, and trembled when he tried to

walk. Once a talkative and fun-loving man, he had now become silent, almost dull-witted. It was enough to bring tears to
anyone's eyes.

In the fields a half-disabled worker like Old Sun could do
very little to improve production, while, on the other hand, the
purchasing station felt his absence sorely. If the sheep were not
taken to the county town in time, they often became thin, sick
or even died and the once-profitable purchasing station was now
running at a loss. When the people of the village wanted to
buy things, they could no longer ask Old Sun to pick them up
on his way back home. Instead, they had to make a special trip
themselves, wasting a good many labour hours. As time went
on, everyone hoped someone would come forward to take on
the job, but nobody volunteered. Before long, the people's
thoughts began to turn to Old Sun again, but no one dared say
anything for fear of reopening past wounds.

Old Sun was by nature happiest when he was helping others.
When he saw the looks of appeal on the faces of his fellow
villagers, he realized once again the trust they had in him. His
feeling of abandonment began to disappear and his old enthusiasm returned. To everyone's delight, as soon as the government
policies began to loosen up two years ago in the spring, he immediately borrowed money and bought himself a big, black
donkey to start his second term as "the legs" of the village.

Yes, Old Sun had taken up his old job again, but not without
careful consideration. He had suffered greatly in the last few
years, barely escaping death, and who could be sure that the
new government's policies would not take a turn for the worse
any minute. He considered and reconsidered, but finally decided that not only he would benefit from the job, the villagers and
the country would benefit as well. This should be nothing to be
ashamed of! And so, for the last two years, throughout the
sweltering heat of summer and the bitter cold of winter, this
old man of sixty with a half-disabled leg had been working
harder than most people do in a lifetime. His thirty-year-old son
had got himself a wife, and the daughter he had originally planned to marry off in exchange for his son's wife had found her-

self a husband she liked. He even had plans to pull down his old house and build himself a new one.

Now, just as he was beginning to feel pleased with himself, as if he could again provide for his family, he began to hear rumours that the government's policies were going to tighten up again. Every night a small crowd would gather outside Old Sun's house to discuss one topic: when would things ever settle down and leave them to get on with production, a question which nobody could answer. All of this, of course, was only based on hearsay and what these words "tighten" or "control" really meant, whether or not transportation would be forbidden, Old Sun had not the slightest idea nor the ability to think clearly about the question. The government's policies over the last few years had been constantly changing, so that something permissible one day might well be forbidden the next, and the very word "change" now struck terror into his heart.

A few days after the rumour had begun, the brigade leader notified everyone that the commune was to have a new secretary. This new secretary happened to be the same Vice-Section Head Han of the county standing committee, who had been responsible for labelling him a "self-interested" element only a few years before. Old Sun felt he had no small cause for alarm, for he had no way of knowing whether this leader named Han still wanted to "let mass criticism inspire great efforts". He remembered one criticism session at which someone had accused him of forgetting the basic principles of communism. Old Sun had disagreed with him, at which point Vice-Section Head Han had frightened him nearly to death by announcing over the megaphone for all to hear: "You are taking the capitalist road, and if you continue, that road can lead to only one place: death!" From that day forth, it was as if he had been placed under a spell, and he muttered the words "road to death" to himself for the next half a year. Even today the memory made his hair stand on end. The more he thought about it, the more nervous he became, until finally he worked himself into a state of absolute terror.

It was in the midst of this terror, of constant apprehensions and suspicions, that this omen of ill fortune appeared. Where had the big, black donkey taken him — and nearly succeeded in getting him "cremated alive" — if not down the "road to death"! Man is most likely to revive discarded beliefs in superstition when he feels his own life is out of his control: at this point, Old Sun was so jumpy that the slightest hint of trouble left him quivering with fear.

Having driven the cart out of the crematorium and back onto the proper road, Old Sun's fury came to a head. He yanked the cart to a stop by the side of the road, and standing in front of the donkey, began to whip him head-on. All of Old Sun's pent-up ire came raining down on the back of the poor beast, who reared wildly in the air and had soon got himself tangled in his harness. Covered in sweat and gasping for breath, Old Sun stopped and went around to the donkey's buttocks, tapping at its hoof with the other end of his whip. "Lift your foot up!" he yelled. But, the donkey had no way of understanding that Old Sun simply meant to untangle the harness, and, fearing another beating, lifted his leg and gave Old Sun a swift kick in the forehead. He cried out in pain, pressing his hand against the wound to stop the blood which was already seeping between his fingers and down his arm. It seemed Old Sun's troubles would never end. Another flick of the whip to the donkey's head sent it galloping off, pulling the cart behind. It did not take more than one hundred steps for the cart to go careening into a ditch with a great crash, but it took a good deal of effort, and the help of a good many men to get it out again. By that time the donkey had thrown its hip out of joint.

Returning home, Old Sun went straight to bed, where he lay, tossing and turning, for three days. He thought about every detail of what had happened from beginning to end. He was troubled by the thought that fate was simply playing tricks on him. Eventually, he came to the antiquated conclusion that life and death were decided by fate, wealth and poverty by the gods and there was nothing he could do about it. He began to feel that the black donkey was a kind of godsend warning him that misfortune lay ahead.   If he gave up his job now mightn't he avoid catastrophe?

Old Sun had already hardened his heart to the idea of selling his donkey, but in its present condition he would have to accept a large cut in price, and he did not like that. As soon as the wound in his forehead had healed sufficiently, he led the limping donkey to the commune veterinarian.

Dr. Liu of the veterinary station was as eager as he could be to help, but unfortunately his skill did not match his eagerness. Ten years ago the excellent doctor Wang Laoshang had lost his job simply because he had once served as a horse doctor under the warlord Zhang Zuolin. If only he were here now, he would certainly be able to do something for this poor donkey!

Dr. Liu circled around the donkey, and then asked Old Sun to tie it into the sling. Grabbing hold of its disjointed right leg, he tried to lift it a couple of times, panting and puffing with the effort, but he could not fit it back into position. Finally, wiping the sweat off his forehead, he said, "It's no good! You'd better slaughter it."

"Slaughter it?" Old Sun would not allow that! He suddenly remembered all the things he liked about this donkey. After all that time together, wasn't it natural to feel some compassion for the poor beast.   No, he was not going to have it slaughtered! "Let me try my luck at the Liuzhen Fair," he thought.   Perhaps someone would buy it, and if the donkey was properly taken care of Old Sun could rightfully say that he had saved a life. As for taking a cut in price, he was determined not to let it bother him.

Up at four o'clock, Old Sun fed the animal, made himself a little something to eat, and then led the donkey slowly to the street. By the time he had travelled ten li, some people were already on their way back home having finished their business in town.

Old Sun entered the town, and half-heartedly led the donkey to the north in the direction of the animal market. This market was located in a thickly-shaded willow grove. Every kind of livestock imaginable was for sale here: oxen, horses, donkeys, mules. The market was comparatively quiet, except for the occasional whinny or bray of the animals. The buyers circled around looking over the livestock and each other in silence, quite different from the deafening atmosphere of a street market. In this kind of animal market both buyer and seller are experienced peasants, silent and calculating. According to the tradition of the market, all bargaining is done by means of eye contact and hand signals, and all prices are counted off on the hands.

Old Sun selected a crooked willow tree and tied his donkey to it.   Then he brought out his tobacco, and squatted down to wait.

The peasants here thought of livestock just as they thought of the land, that is, with a special intimacy and tenderness. Ever since raising and selling private livestock was permitted, the animal market of the Liuzhen Fair had become a big attraction. One look around was enough to convince anybody that few people were buying animals for purposes of transportation; instead, most people were buying for domestic use. Any money these peasants had saved would be spent first on a horse or donkey, and not on a bicycle, for bicycles were of limited use, and they depreciated in value with wear and tear. A donkey, on the other hand, had many uses: you could ride it if you needed to go somewhere — and on the sandy soil of the Yellow River valley it was no slower than riding a bicycle. But, of course, its main use was in farm work. The villages in this part of the country were scattered, and sometimes as much as ten li separated house from field.   For carrying nightsoil or collecting crops, a donkey was as convenient as a boat in a region with many rivers or lakes. Furthermore, livestock produced nightsoil and after you had raised a baby donkey or calf for two years its price doubled.   In comparison, the bicycle had virtually nothing to offer.   Indeed, a first-class economist could hardly have analyzed the situation more thoroughly!

Old Sun took a look around him: today the buyers outnumbered the sellers.   He felt extremely optimistic.

It was not long before a man who seemed nothing but skin

and bones walked over to Old Sun's donkey: "Hey! Is this donkey for sale?"

Though Old Sun had seen this man coming from afar, he pretended not to have noticed him. He sat quietly smoking his pipe. Hearing this old man's question, he looked up at him for the first time and casually nodded his head. He planned to drive a hard bargain. Knowing that the buyer and the seller are engaged in a contest of will and of the ability to size up their opponent, too much eagerness to sell would certainly look bad. He was applying the old military tactic of leaving someone space, the better to trap him in later. Who could be sure: perhaps Old Sun was a descendant of the brilliant military tactician of ancient times, Sun Wuzi!

However, Old Sun's opponent was no amateur. He opened the donkey's mouth, then snorted, "Hmm. Four years old," but from his tone of voice it was clear that he had taken a liking to this donkey. It was not until he stood silently stroking his long, mountain goat's beard and examining the donkey's frame that he noticed the slightly hanging back leg. "Hmm? Is it lame?"

"Disjointed. It's nothing. It'll heal good as new." Old Sun had managed to squeeze three sentences out of only eight words. Perhaps, the less he said the more likely the old man was to believe that the problem was a small one. But when Old Sun turned around, he found the old man had already gone. He stood up with a sigh, and yelled after the old man, "Are you blind? This donkey can outwork ten horses. I'm not kidding!" The old man did not even look back.

Just as Old Sun was beginning to feel discouraged, he felt a heavy tap on his shoulder, and turning around, recognized Hu Er from the local butchery. Hu Er gave him a nasty grin and said, "What are you shouting about? Why don't you sell me your old lame donkey and I'll make it into soup!"

Old Sun would have preferred not to pay any attention to him, but he knew this fellow was hard to deal with and so, turning to him he asked coldly, "What's your offer?"

"Heh, heh." Hu Er began to chuckle. "Would I cheat an old neighbour?"

Hu Er pulled out a cigarette and threw it in Old Sun's direction, but Old Sun threw it promptly back, pulling out his own bag of tobacco. "I'll smoke my own," he said. He had a suspicion that the cigarette had its price.

Apparently deciding not to bother with formalities, Hu Er lit his own cigarette, then cocked his head, one hand arrogantly clutching his lapel, and said to Old Sun, "How about fifty yuan?"

Old Sun blinked with irritation: a nice-sized donkey like this . . . for only fifty yuan! A complete rip-off! He gave Hu Er a menacing look and turned his back on him without a word.

"Fifty-one." Hu Er maliciously upped his offer by one yuan.

"You can up the price ten yuan if you want, but you're not going to buy yourself an animal from me," said Old Sun with a shrug. He thought to himself: "You little twerp. You should be careful who you try to cheat. Old Sun's been around, you know."

Seeing the situation was beyond negotiation, Hu Er gave a "Hmph!" and left.

One by one people came over to have a look at the big black donkey, but one by one they left as soon as they noticed it was lame. For these peasants, buying an animal was like being blessed with a son: who needed one who ate more of the family grain than he could ever earn back in labour?

It was almost noon, and the marketers had for the most part entered the bargaining stage. Buyers had selected the animals they wanted and were no longer looking for new possibilities. The managing personnel were busy helping the two sides strike a bargain, usually after several prices had been indicated by hand, back and forth, with the middlemen's commission growing steadily at each exchange. Already, satisfied buyers were leading their livestock out of the market for home.

Old Sun's casual calm of earlier that morning had turned to uneasiness as he watched for potential buyers. He waited, but still no one approached him. Leaving a nearby acquaintance to keep an eye on things for him, Old Sun walked off to survey the scene for himself. He reckoned there were about seven hundred heads for sale that day, and at least four hundred had already been sold. Donkeys and oxen were the most popular, though to Old Sun's surprise, some people were buying mules or horses as well. Apparently, the local peasants were fully confident that the government policies would not change for the worse, or at least the rumours of tightening up had not discouraged them from buying.

The trust and confidence of these peasants came as a shock to Old Sun, and for the first time he wondered whether the torment he had put himself through during these last few days was warranted.

As Old Sun wandered about in this half-daze, he suddenly heard the sound of cheering. He followed the noise to where a crowd of people were gathered around a black mule, all oohing and ahing in admiration. A short, pudgy fellow was pulling the mule through the crowd, his face flushed with self-importance. Hey! Wasn't that his son's uncle on his wife's side? He felt a surge of irritation: this little rat had bought himself a mule? When Old Sun was facing public criticisms during the "cultural revolution", this coward had come to see him only once, and in the evening too, probably afraid to be seen! Old Sun had always held him in utmost disdain, but today, suddenly, he felt far inferior to this brother-in-law of his. With all those people crowding around clucking in admiration, no wonder Old Sun felt jealous. Suppressing his mixed feelings of disgust and admiration, he turned his back on the crowd and wandered away. He was certainly not going to exchange greetings with his relative under these circumstances.

It was in this state of turmoil that Old Sun returned to find his donkey surrounded by a small crowd. Was there a buyer? Excited, he elbowed his way through the crowd, sizing them up as he said, "Who's interested? I'm the owner."

All eyes were now on him as he tried his best to collect himself, wondering with irritation why he could not control his heavy breathing. A man of about seventy pressed forward. He had a clear, humane look about his face, with a black mole on his left cheek and a flowing white beard. On his right shoulder, rested a long, bamboo-joint pipe. Old Sun was filled with a feeling of great respect for this kind old man. Somehow he felt that he had seen this face somewhere before, but he could not remember where.

This man had apparently already looked the donkey over thoroughly, for he approached Old Sun immediately and asked politely, "How much are you asking?"

"How much are you offering?"

"Hmm. — I can't give you a counter-offer if you don't give me an offer." The man answered, smiling.

"I'll consider this much." Old Sun stuck out first one finger, and then five more.

"Such a fine donkey; I wonder why you are selling it." The old man seemed in no hurry to set a price. He acted as if he were simply chatting with a friend.

This comment struck Old Sun right where he was the most vulnerable, but doing his best to hide his uneasiness, he bluffed, "This donkey . . . aah . . . this donkey is too hard to handle." He rubbed the scar on his forehead as if providing some sort of proof, at which the crowd burst out laughing. He added earnestly, "but, when it comes to work, this animal can't be beat."

"That's right!" the old man nodded in agreement. "Animals with strange temperaments are always good workers." Then walking around the donkey's hindquarters, he said casually, "Leg out of joint?"

"Easily fixed. The donkey man can fix it in a minute," Old Sun explained, a bit too hastily. Some people in the crowd laughed again, and the old man smiled as he stroked his beard. Then he went on, "It's hard to say. With a dislocated joint, if it is the kind that can be fixed all it needs is one switch of the whip, but if it is the kind that can't be fixed, all the yelling in the world won't help."

A strange diagnosis! This man must be an expert. A thought flashed through Old Sun's mind, and he asked abruptly, "May I ask, your name is —."

"Wang Laoshang."

"Ahha!" Old Sun's guess had been correct. This was the

same miracle docter whom the veterinary station had got rid
of ten years ago. No wonder he looked so familiar! Then, thinking of the comment about "the donkey man" which he had just
made in front of all these people, he felt utterly embarrassed. He
hurried over to shake Wang Laoshang's hand, saying distractedly: "Excuse my poor memory. I haven't seen you for ten years.
Mr. Wang . . . have things been going well for you?"

Wang Laoshang lost his job ten years ago, and had been sitting at home with nothing to do until just last year, when he was
rehabilitated. As he was already getting on in years, the only
convenient thing to do was to advise him to retire. His health
and spirits had improved a great deal recently, and he had
opened a small clinic in his house. It occurred to him, however,
that anytime an animal outside the village was seriously ill he
would have to pay a house call, and so, having made up his
mind to buy himself a donkey, he had come to the market today.
He added that it would not be bad for business to put in an appearance at the livestock market. After buying a nice little donkey for himself, he had agreed to help some of his acquaintances
to select livestock of their own. That was how he and his group
of friends had come to consider this donkey.

With this introduction, Wang Laoshang pointed to the small
group of old men and said politely to Old Sun, "They are the
people I'm helping. Why don't you suggest a price?"

Old Sun was deeply perplexed. Seeing so many peasants
buying their own draft animals weakened his determination to
sell the donkey. Giving up the animal now seemed very rash
indeed. And now, hearing that Wang Laoshang had started his
own private practice, he grew even more excited. Now, at last,
this man could fully exercise his talents. As for himself, wasn't
working for the four modernizations the same as fighting the
Japanese had been in his day? "And I have almost nothing to
offer — just a whip and six legs, me and my donkey, to help the
country and my fellow villagers as best I can! How selfish to
always be worrying that a change in government policies will
bring me misfortunes! If the policies had not changed in the last
two years, would I have dared buy a donkey in the first place?

Haven't I been able to find a wife for my son? Why was I so ready to believe any rumour that I heard? And, so what if there are changes! Things can only change according to what the people want."

Old Sun's mind was made up: he would be damned if he would sell this donkey! However, it was going to be difficult to back out now; having said he wanted to sell, how could he change his mind at the last minute?

He stood muttering to himself. Ahha! He had an idea. He had originally aimed to sell the donkey for one hundred yuan, but he had changed his strategy. Holding out two fingers he said to Wang Laoshang, "Here's my price," he thought to himself. "This will scare them away."

"Two hundred!" A few onlooker gasped in amazement. This old man was not playing fair.

Just then, a rough voice was heard from outside the circle of people, as a man elbowed his way to the centre: "How much? Two hundred for this rotten animal? It's an out and out crime!" It was the furious voice of the butcher, Hu Er.

"Fine! If you're not interested, that's your business," retorted Old Sun coolly. So saying, he untied the donkey and made as if to leave.

"Wait a minute! We're interested." Wang Laoshang stepped forward, blocking his way. He grabbed the rope from Old Sun and turned to his friends, "Who wants to buy?"

. . . .

They stood nudging one another, nobody daring to open his mouth, each doing his best to retreat quickly and quietly. It was clear that they had not the slightest interest in buying the donkey. Old Sun chuckled to himself.

Knowing perfectly well what was going through everyone's head Wang Laoshang laughed. "I see everybody thinks the price is too high, but if the leg were healthy, I'd say it was too low, I think it's worth about. . . ." He held out three fingers.

"Three hundred!" The onlookers gasped again. The group of old men still hesitated.

Wang Laoshang's smile suddenly disappeared, and he began

rolling up his sleeves, warning those gathered around to see the fun: "Everyone back up a few steps, please. Make room, please make room." Taking the whip from out of poor confused Old Sun's hand, he hid it behind his back. He told Old Sun to support the donkey's dangling right leg, while he walked slowly to the donkey's left front side. The crowd of onlookers was growing, all curious to see what sort of magic Wang Laoshang was about to perform, and they stepped back in silence to give him room. One could have heard a pin drop.

For about thirty seconds, Wang Laoshang stood quietly facing the donkey's left side. His eyes seemed kind, as he waited for the animal's apprehensions to disappear. Then, suddenly, with a great "Hey!" he gave the donkey's left ear a sharp thrash with the whip. Taken completely off guard, the donkey reared up, thereby placing the entire weight of its body on its left hindquarters, which made a slight crunching sound. When it had calmed down and placed all four feet firmly on the ground, the left hind leg had been forced back into its socket and was now the same length as the other three.

This technique, called "the magic whip", was well known but rarely seen. It simply used the animal's own body weight to force the bone back into the joint, and had proven far more effective than the usual rubbing technique.

Returning the whip and taking the rope from the hands of Old Sun, Wang Laoshang led the donkey twice around the ring formed by the onlookers. It limped only slightly from the pain, which had not yet had a chance to subside, but in every other respect the leg was as good as new. The onlookers sent up a cheer and broke into a round of applause.

At this point the people who had asked Wang Laoshang to help them buy a donkey came rushing forward, jostling one another for position. "I'm buying!"

"I asked Mr. Wang first!"

"No, *I'm* buying!"

. . . .

The buyers were arguing heatedly when Old Sun suddenly shouted out: "I'm not selling!"

Silence fell upon the crowd. All eyes were fixed on this old man with his donkey. Old Sun looked as red as a chicken which has just laid an egg. In one swift movement he snatched the rope from Wang Laoshang's hands and turned to leave.

So, the seller had gone back on his word! The crowd's mood changed abruptly. They looked from the face of the seller to the faces of the buyers and back again. What was going to happen?

One of the prospective buyers was an extremely thin old fellow, the same man, in fact, who had approached Old Sun initially. With a look of determination, he yelled to Old Sun:

"You've already set a price, and now you're not selling? Why the hell did you offer in the first place?"

A few others shouted in agreement, "You've got to sell now! What do you people say?" someone yelled to the crowd of onlookers.

"He'll sell after a good knock on the head!"

"Take the donkey first!"

And, with a cry, the small group of men rushed forward to wrestle the rope from Old Sun's hands.

Just in the nick of time, Wang Laoshang stepped up to the small crowd of buyers to call a truce and try to reason with them: "Don't be ridiculous! There're plenty of donkeys for sale; go look for another one." He gave them a conciliatory smile, while the crowd joined in his efforts to calm everybody down.

As for Old Sun, having got what he wanted, he decided the best thing to do was to slip out of the mess as quickly as possible. Pushing through the crowd, as if deaf to the quarrel he was leaving behind, he threw himself onto the donkey's back, and with a loud "Gee-up! Go!" he was gone.

Translated by Ellen Hertz

CHEN JIANGONG

(1949 —   )

Chen Jiangong was born in 1949 at Beihai, Guangxi Province. He moved with his family to Beijing in 1957, and graduated from the middle school attached to the Chinese People's University in 1968. After that he became a miner for ten years at the Jingxi (West Beijing) Coal Mine. In 1977 he matriculated at the Department of Chinese Literature at Beijing University, and graduated in 1982. At present, he is on the board of directors of the Union of Beijing Writers doing professional writing and assisting in editorial work. He became a member of the Union of Chinese Writers in 1982.

Chen Jiangong began to write in 1973. He has published poetry, prose, short stories, and other works. Since 1979, his works "The Meandering River", "There's a Wise Fool at Jingxi", "Judgement After Death", and "No. 9 Pulley-Handle Alley" have received great acclaim among his readers. His "Phoenix Eyes" and "The Fluttering Flowered Scarf" were selected as the best short stories of 1980 and 1981. In 1981, a collection of short stories, *The Enchanting Starry Sky,* was published.

PHOENIX EYES

Chen Jiangong

It is common knowledge that women in Beijing outnumber the men, but young men in Jingxi have indescribable difficulty finding girl-friends.

What could be the reason for this? Are they that hideous? Cripples? Mutants? Or are they bums, or good-for-nothings? No! And, if you don't believe me, go and see for yourself. Past Sanjiadian,* the streets are swarming with handsome young men of all shapes and sizes — muscular, fine-featured, take your pick! Would you be interested in a model worker? Or an innovative young technician? Or do you like the sensitive type, a music lover, for example? Were they in Beijing proper, they would have girls running madly after them. But they are in Jingxi, and that makes all the difference: they are miners in the underground coal-mines. Most girls, when they hear this, simply frown and turn away, and no matter how attractive the young man standing before them, the answer will always be: "Sorry, I'm busy."

And so it was that the young men of the mines had quite a hard time of it. As this continued, some of them began to hate their work clothes, and tried their best to erase the printed words "X mines" from their breast pocket — they were afraid of being laughed at as they walked down the street. Some of them even came to some conclusions about "the art of love": "First of all, you should never let her know you are a miner until you have her completely at your feet." One young man took this advice a step further, and when asked by a girl he met

---

* A suburb of Beijing. — *Trans.*

163

at a party what he did for a living, he answered that he worked
at "a certain institute producing black metallurgic powder." Ha!
Jingxi is full of such tales, but I dare not go on, for the young
men of the mines may protest that I am making fun of them.

Are all the miners so ashamed of themselves and their position? Certainly not: there are many dignified and self-respecting
young men among them. "Just because others look down on us,
it doesn't mean we have to look down on ourselves! Are we
somehow less worthy simply because we are miners? If there
is ever an energy crisis, they'll find out how valuable we miners
are!" The young speaker was a miner named Xin Xiaoliang
from the Yannan Mines. He had absolutely no patience for
those people who looked down upon his job. It is said that
once when several girls came down the shafts to visit, the secretary of the Workers' Union, who was showing them around,
began apologizing for how bad the conditions were underground, begging them to be careful. Xin Xiaoliang happened
to overhear them and burst out irritably, "Don't worry! This
isn't the Hill of Longevity,* but our little Empresses Dowager
won't twist their ankles." The secretary turned crimson, but
Xin's fellow workers were delighted. "You'll never win a
girl's heart that way," they joked. "We're afraid you'll have
to spend your whole life with electric drills and jackhammers."

Some concerned souls had taken it upon themselves to introduce girls to him, but the girls had always given him the cold
shoulder after the first meeting, and there were innumerable
others who had not even bothered to meet him once they learned that he was a miner. All this, however, only made Xin — a
handsome young specimen of a metre, eighty — so stuck-up and
stubborn that he barely gave girls a second glance. There wasn't
a girl in the dining-hall or the mining-lamp room who was not
slightly afraid of him; his remarks were simply too cutting. At
mealtime he would beat his bowl with his spoon outside the
kitchen window if the attendants were even a second late in

---

* A hill in the Summer Palace, built entirely for the pleasure of the
Empress Dowager. — *Trans.*

opening: "Let's go! Open up! You lazy bums! This mine isn't feeding you for nothing, you know; if you can't do your job go home and take care of the kids." When he came up from the shaft, the girls taking his lamp would sometimes give him a quick smile, but he would just stare back as if to say, "Who the hell smiled at you! Do you think it improves your looks?" He had reduced many girls to tears in this way, but he did not stop there. The worst, by far, were his "pet-names". He was imaginative, and his inventions rang true: for one girl working in the dining hall who always squinted, as if disgusted by something, he had chosen the name "Yuck"! The great, swirling permanent on the girl selling steamed bread had been the inspiration for the name "Breakfast Roll". The worker in charge of the fourth window happened to be a very beautiful girl. Her eyes, which were bright and slightly turned-up at the corners, were a charming example of what have been called "phoenix eyes". But, Xin Xiaoliang preferred to call her "cat eyes" behind her back.

When the girls in the dining hall heard their "pet-names", they were furious, swearing that they hoped he would be stuck with a horribly ugly girl-friend when he did eventually get one. Their curses made absolutely no difference, however, as Xin had long ago determined to remain a bachelor all his life. In fact, with his clear-skinned face and twinkling eyes perfectly set off by charmingly dishevelled hair, he was as attractive as he was rude. When he worked he worked hard, and everything he picked up he was immediately good at. If he had not been so stubborn he would not have had much trouble finding a girl-friend, but to everybody's surprise he would simply not go to meet the girls introduced to him.

His attitude was a perpetual source of worry to his mother, who was beginning to wonder if their family was ever to have a grandson. She wept to see Xiaoliang chase away one match-maker after another. On one occasion, impatient with her grumbling, her son said, "Mom, please! Don't talk about it any more, you're making my ears ache. I'll go meet the next one."

"If you had only said so earlier, I could have begun preparing for a beautiful wedding long ago," she complained.

"But I'm going to be honest with her," he announced somewhat threateningly.

His mother was fully prepared, "Did you think I wanted you to cheat the girl?"

As it turned out, this word "honest" meant something very special to Xiaoliang. At their first meeting, the girl said, "So, I hear you're working in the mines."

"Yup."

"Underground?"

"Of course!"

"Then . . ." the girl put out a feeler, "the safety precautions underground must be pretty good."

"No!" Xin Xiaoliang exclaimed, with his special brand of honesty, "Not at all! Miners often die in accidents. In fact, our mines are a breeding ground for widows." This was pure nonsense of course, but as a strategy it worked exceptionally well, getting rid of not only the girl but also the match-maker in one fell swoop. What mother wouldn't be worried? In desperation, Xin's mother poured out her anger on her retired husband: "All you can do is drink tea — drink tea or play cards with that group of doddering old friends of yours. You never say a single word about your own son's marriage. . . . And you call yourself a father!" Old Xin had also been a miner, and, like his son, had quite a sense of humour. "So what do you suggest I do? I'll go and get a rope, you pick out the girl, and I'll drag her home by afternoon!"

Xin's mother was getting more and more impatient. Whenever she met the other mothers of the neighbourhood, she would grumble endlessly about her son's "marriage problems". One evening, the warm-hearted Grandma Qiao dropped by.

Grandma Qiao lived in Willow Leaf Residential Area, several miles away from New Workers Village where Xin Xiaoliang's family lived, so it was really quite a feat for her to hobble such a distance. Seeing Grandma Qiao in her new clothes, Xin's mother guessed the purpose of her visit immediately, and hurriedly invited her in for a cup of tea. These two old women sat whispering for quite a while before calling Xin Xiaoliang in. "Xiaoliang, Grandma Qiao has come here especially to see you. I hear the girl's very nice looking. . . ."

Xiaoliang slowly raised his hands and stood rubbing first his eyes, then his entire face, as if trying to keep himself awake. Then, turning to Grandma Qiao with a polite smile, he asked, "Where does she work?"

"She used to work in the Number Three Cotton Mill. Recently she was transferred to the mines so that she can look after her old mother, her only remaining family. She works in one of the dining halls. . . ."

"Hmm. Quite near here." He was still pretending to be sleepy and his mother, looking savagely at him, wanted nothing more than to give him a good, swift whap with her broom.

Grandma Qiao smiled. "She is not only near here, she is also quite a catch. I hear she's considered the most beautiful girl in the dining-hall — double eyelids, delicate skin. . . ."

"Thank you very much." He closed his eyes, motioning her to stop. "But there's really no need to go on. It's very kind of you to take the trouble to come all this way, and I'm sorry to disappoint you. I'll tell you what: you find me a girl so ugly even her grandmother can't bring herself to love her and I'll consider the matter settled. This girl you have picked out is not for me. She is reserved for section chiefs, Party secretaries, or their sons. I'm not so lucky. . . ."

"How can you turn her down before you even know who she is!" His mother was furious.

"There's no need. She will certainly look down on me, and I'm not going to cultivate any powerful connections to make up to her. I wouldn't get past the first date. Anyway, I don't have the heart to trouble Grandma Qiao further." So saying, he stood up, flashed Grandma Qiao a smile of apology and left the room.

"Can you believe that boy! Can you believe him!" His mother was trembling with rage, and, for the first time, completely at a loss for words.

"It doesn't matter, don't worry. Looking for a girl-friend is his own business. If you really want him to find someone he's in love with, forcing things will get you nowhere." Grandma Qiao was an open-minded woman, and with no hard feelings she soon tottered off home. But, things were not so simple. On the way home she began to worry about what she should tell the girl's mother.

Meng Bei was the daughter of her old nextdoor neighbour, and had just turned twenty-four years old. Several days before, Meng Bei's mother had asked Grandma Qiao to help find a suitable young man for her daughter, and she had agreed right away to do her best. "Don't worry, my dear. I can't make any promises about other people's daughters, but certainly your daughter won't be a problem." Imagine her surprise, then, when this stubborn Xin Xiaoliang expressed not the slightest interest in the match. How was she to explain this to Old Lady Meng? Could she tell her that Xin Xiaoliang had refused flat out, even before knowing the girl's name? That would be sure to hurt her friend's feelings. Furthermore, the girl was indeed very beautiful, and it was said that beautiful girls were hyper-sensitive.

Though Grandma Qiao had done the best she could, she felt distinctly uncomfortable as she entered Meng's house. This young man, she told Old Lady Meng, would never do for Meng Bei. He was short and his face was nothing much; just think of the contrast! "Tomorrow I'll find her a better one. It would really be a sin if our Meng Bei were stuck with that Xin Xiao-liang for a husband. She'd absolutely faint if she saw him!" Grandma Qiao certainly had a way with words — these casual comments delighted Old Lady Meng, and when her daughter came back from work she reported the whole story to her as a joke. To her surprise, instead of laughing, her daughter began to pout, her lower lip trembling dangerously. "It's all your fault!" she complained, slamming her cup down heavily on the table. "Why don't you mind your own business!" Old Lady Meng was puzzled. She had often interferred in her daughter's private matters before, and though her daughter had never been very pleased, she had never become so angry either. Meng Bei stomped off to her room, wondering, likewise, why she had flown into such a rage. Could it be that she was angry with Xin Xiaoliang? There was an old saying that girls with "phoenix eyes" were the toughest to deal with, and though it was not particularly flattering, it did have a ring of truth to it. One should think twice before getting on the wrong side of the phoenix-eyed Meng Bei. She had recognized the lie in Grandmother Qiao's report instantly; she knew Xin Xiaoliang too well — perfect height, powerful build, charming face. He must have said something offensive which Grandma Qiao had been too embarrassed to report, and so had invented this lie instead. What Grandma Qiao did not know was that Meng Bei had met Xin Xiaoliang even before her transfer to the mines. She even knew the size of the chip on his shoulder, and exactly which sex he held responsible for it.

It was just before Spring Festival of last year. She was on her way home from the city by train to spend the holidays with her mother. As the train pulled out from Yongding Station, she noticed two young men chattering away animatedly. The young man sitting just behind her and sharing her seat-back was a well-built fellow with a loud voice. He was apparently quite restless, for each time he got excited he would pound her seat-back with his shoulders as if his whole body was filled with energy for which he had no outlet. Sometimes, laughing, he threw his head so far back that his thick hair came tumbling over the top of the seat and brushed against hers, but all she could do was to move away in annoyance. The friend sitting opposite him, whose nickname seemed to be "Joker", looked a little younger, and seemed to make it his duty to make fun of his friend on every possible occasion. At first, Meng Bei paid no attention to their conversation, only overhearing bits and pieces, something about "going fishing" in Beijing . . . "caught nothing but a belly-ache. . . ." Wondering to herself how they could catch fish in winter in Beijing, she suddenly began to giggle. "Going fishing" in miners' jargon means looking for a girl-friend! Meng Bei had been brought up in a mining area, but this was the first time she had ever heard this rather unusual expression and she listened with interest as the bigger of the two began his "fishing" tale. The "Joker" cut in constantly with wisecracks, and several times she thought she was going to burst out laughing herself. One time, unable to hold back any longer, she got up quickly, as if to look for some hot water, and disappeared into the area between the two cars to laugh quietly to herself.

"You see how my mother ran around all day for this stupid affair. First, she forced me to wear this suit, and then she began pestering me: 'When you go to Beijing, don't let him see that you're nervous . . . and don't behave like a hick, either. Remember, the girl's father is a cadre in the Coal Ministry. . . . And be respectful; call him Uncle'."

His imitation of his mother's nervous tone of voice must have been superb, for "Joker" burst out laughing.

"So what happened? I bet you were completely tongue-tied the minute you walked in the house."

"What do you mean? Just because others look down on us. . . . It's not as if we're completely incompetent! I was just as proud and dignified as I could be."

"Cut the boasting! Your head's swollen enough as it is. Anyway, if you're so 'proud and dignified' how come you're coming back empty-handed?"

"Empty-handed? Listen, no matter how good-looking she is, I'm not interested. And this one was no beauty."

"Sour grapes, sour grapes!"

"Rotten grapes! Do you know how many nightmares this meeting will produce, how many years it has chopped off my life! I bet she hasn't been able to find someone from the city, so her parents thought they'd offer her to me . . . at a discount! And her father has the nerve to call himself a cadre in the Coal Ministry! I'll tell you, he didn't have very nice things to say about us miners. 'There's no problem with you, young man; it's your job that's the problem!' He even boasted that he could manage to have me transferred from underground work. Boy, did he make me angry! 'There's no problem with you, old man; it's just your heart that's rotten to the core!' If it hadn't been just an introduction, I would have given him a piece of my mind!"

"It's disgusting!" "Joker", too, was filled with indignation. "Old buddy, I'm going to get you a girl-friend or die trying. Then we'll send them a wedding invitation. . . . See how they like that!"

"Forget it! Don't get me angry again. I'd rather be a bachelor all my life. All girls are snobs."

"So, pal, you've thrown in the towel, eh? A yellow-belly? A chicken?"

"A chicken! I showed them, don't worry. As I was about to leave, seeing there was nobody in the room, I turned off their radiators, then took the taps and threw them into their mailbox. He may work in the Coal Ministry, but his family is going to pass one hell of a cold night tonight!"

"Yah, ha, ha. . . ."

The two young men began laughing hysterically, setting the seat-back into violent motion.

And so they chattered on like this all the way home, as if performing a cross-talk,* with Meng Bei eavesdropping in the next seat. The more she listened, the more she wanted to hear. Many times she thought she would die with the effort of stifling her laughter, but like many others she was also outraged by their prejudice — there was no need to malign the entire sex on the basis of a few bad experiences, and besides, they were only talking in stereotypes. If she had been among people she were familiar with, as in the cotton mill, she would have had a thing or two of her own to say. Were all young men the acme of perfection? It would be the easiest thing in the world to come up with several cases of arrogant young men looking down on women textile workers. Such were her thoughts, as she listened on in silence — and even when her seat was hardest hit, not a word of protest did she utter.

Meng Bei got off at Yannan Mines, and was surprised to see the two young men get off as well. Overhearing someone come

---

* A kind of quick-paced comic dialogue famous in Beijing. — *Trans.*

up to greet them, she learned and still remembered their names: that big fellow with a chip on his shoulder was Xin Xiaoliang; the "Joker" was named Zhao Tao.

It was not long after this incident that Meng Bei was transferred to the mines. Xin Xiaoliang was well known here: his name was constantly being announced over the morning loudspeaker for breaking records, or for overcoming some danger or other. He was even the hero in a wrestling competition organized by the Workers' Union. And how could she not know the person who shouted "Lazy bums!" outside the dining-hall window everyday.

Meng Bei had a great deal of respect for herself. The moment she laid eyes on Xin Xiaoliang, remembering their chance encounter on the train, she had felt a surge of pent-up irritation. What arrogance! He had no respect whatsoever for women! Nevertheless, she thought, it was true that there were girls as snobby as the ones he had described, and her heart softened somewhat. After only a short time in the mines, she had already heard story after story of miners looking for girl-friends, and among these stories was the history of Xin Xiaoliang. She thought of him now with a feeling almost of awe, and even when she heard the pet-name he had chosen for her she dismissed it with a smile, saying to herself: "Hmph! And you call yourself a man? All you can do is think up these ridiculous nicknames to let off steam! You don't even bother looking for a girl who might be able to really get to know you. . . ." By this time, sitting on her bed, leaning against her neatly folded quilt, Meng Bei was piping mad. She tried to imagine exactly what had happened when Grandma Qiao was in his house, and just what sarcastic remarks he had made. She could even visualize the movements of his eyelids! . . .

Meanwhile, at Xin's house that same night, a happy Xiaoliang had fallen fast asleep as usual, never imagining, not even curious to know, that the girl he had so flatly refused was none other than the girl he had labelled "cat eyes"! Such questions as "Was she really that beautiful?" "What was her name?" never even occurred to him. At ten o'clock, back from watching television, he had crawled contentedly under his quilt and was soon dreaming. How inconceivable he thought that several miles away in Willow Leaf Residential Area a girl did not get to sleep until midnight . . . all on his account. Don't be fooled by the upward tilt to her eyes, the half-smile hovering about the corners of her mouth! Lying in bed, biting her lips with a motion which sent her dimples dancing, Meng Bei was very angry indeed!

She was not a girl to be trifled with, and she was eminently equal to all of Xin Xiaoliang's thoughtless bluster. She began to keep close watch on him. Before long she found a chance to beat him at his own game. One might even find it remarkable to watch how obedient he soon became.

The day after Meng Bei's sleepless night, at lunchtime, Xin lined up in front of the fourth window to buy his rice porridge and fried cakes, and who should be there to serve him but Meng Bei.

"Two ounces of rice porridge, four fried cakes." He put his gigantic enamel bowl through the window.

"Clank, clank." The big spoon hit the bottom of the bowl. She filled the enamel bowl with two ounces of porridge. Then, thumping down the bowl on the window-sill so the porridge nearly spilt over, she commanded:

"Take them!" She stretched out her hand holding the four fried cakes.

Xin Xiaoliang had brought only one bowl which was now filled with porridge. If he took the fried cakes, he would not have a spare hand to give her his food tickets. "Put them here!" He balanced his chopsticks on the bowl.

With a long hard stare she put the fried cakes down forcefully on the chopsticks. The chopsticks immediately rolled off the bowl and the fried cakes fell into the porridge. He thrust his head in through the window to slurp up the porridge brimming over the edge of the bowl. "Well, well! Look what you've done!" Then, still clicking his burnt tongue to try to relieve the pain, he flew into a rage:

"What the hell do you think you're doing? I don't want

them! Do you call these fried cakes? They're soup fried cakes now! I don't want them!"

But, seeing his predicament, she only burst out laughing, her eyes flashing with victory. "Calm down, will you? I guess you'll just have to make do today. Next time, bring another bowl."

"You little idiot! Don't you even know how to handle a fried cake? I don't want them!" He was shouting quite loudly by this time.

Meng Bei, on the other hand, was all smiles, saying in gentle voice, "If you had square chopsticks instead of round ones this would not have happened. Calm down and eat them. What's the difference once they're in your stomach."

It was useless to continue shouting. He swallowed hard and took the "porridge fried cakes" to his table.

There were only a few windows and few assistants in the dining hall, so it was nearly impossible for him not to run into her, especially as, unbeknownst to him, she was still seeking revenge. This first rout was by no means adequate and a series of deliberate punishments followed. If it wasn't too much gravy in his beancurd it was filling his bowl, as if by mistake, with the tomato dish when he had clearly asked for cabbage. For his part he would sometimes stand as if struck dumb by irritation he could hardly express, but at other times he stayed by the window for some time, fuming with anger. The most infuriating thing, however, was Meng Bei's constant smile, just as in the "Fried Cake Affair", as if she would never dream of losing her temper the way he did. Under such cheerful attacks, what could Xin Xiaoliang do but retreat.

Xin Xiaoliang had never been treated this way in his life, and after several of these mysterious battles he began to have misgivings. "When have I offened her? Why is she so hard on me? he wondered.

Zhao Tao was eating lunch with him. "After you call her 'lazy bum' and 'cat eyes', why are you surprised that she wants to take revenge?" "Joker" gave him a wink.

"But things were fine a couple of days ago. Why now?" Xin was completely puzzled.

"Okay, leave this to me.   Your 'chief of intelligence' will investigate the matter for you." Young as he was, Zhao Tao deserved his self-proclaimed title "chief of intelligence". He was a smart fellow, and in the miles of territory which made up the mines there was no place he had not gone, no one he did not know.

Two days later Zhao Tao was back with his "intelligence".

"You have offended her," he said seriously, pulling a long face.

"Horseshit! I've never paid her the slightest attention."

"Ha, ha! That's the key. Old Yang in the club told me that you had given her the cold shoulder."

Good God! Xin suddenly saw the light. Old Yang was Grandma Qiao's husband. Grandma Qiao's "most beautiful girl in the dining hall" was Meng Bei! If only he had asked her name at the time! Striking his forehead with the palm of his hand, he began to laugh, poking Zhao Tao in the ribs, but his laughter was short-lived as he began to wonder what he had said that could have offended her so. He was not stupid, but he could not figure it out for the life of him. All he had said was that she was reserved for section chiefs, Party secretaries or their sons — was she angry about this? No, Grandma Qiao would not have reported this to her. Was she offended by his remarks that "she'll certainly look down on me and I'm not going to cultivate any powerful connections to make up to her?" He simply could not understand: "If these things have offended her, what can I do to avoid offending her again?" There appeared before his eyes the first scene at the window, and he remembered the way her somewhat sullen look had suddenly changed to glee at his distress. There was something fishy going on, but he could not quite put it into words.

Young men, think carefully before you boast of your ability to resist the force of a young woman in love. Look at your courageous representative, Xin Xiaoliang. Awakened to his folly, it was as if all his long-harboured prejudices against the gentle sex vanished from his consciousness. He began to recall every detail of their interactions since the first punishment, and though there was really not much to ponder, he pondered nonetheless, and scolded himself more than once, "I have no future! I am a good-for-nothing."

The next day, going to the fourth window to buy dumpling soup, the sight of Meng Bei set his heart beating madly though there were still five or six people in front of him in line. He bought two ounces of dumpling soup, pretending to be as indifferent as before, but unable to resist a sidelong glance at her. Her white working clothes suited her, highlighting the outline of her rounded shoulders. Her loose, sleek hair waved gently in the wind of an electric fan nearby, and a lock fell into her eye. In one elegant, sweeping gesture, she raised her right arm to brush the lock of hair away, pouring the dumpling soup into the bowl with her left.

"Two ounces, twenty-five cents." As usual, she put the bowl down heavily on the window-sill, looking directly into his eyes with her delicate mouth closed tight, her lower lip twitching gently. Flustered, Xin brought out thirty cents. She took it, but as she threw the five one-cent tickets back in change, a puff from the fan blew three tickets into his bowl. "Whoops!" She shrugged her shoulders and wrinkled her nose wryly, then burst out laughing. Blushing, she stuck two fingers into the porridge and pulled out the tickets. "They're clean, don't worry," she said, her eyes still staring boldly into his, as if to say, "Scold me, if you dare!" and then, triumphantly, "You don't dare, do you!"

Had this been the day before, Xin Xiaoliang would surely have been screaming at the top of his lungs by now, but today.
. . .

"Well, if it were any other girl. . . ." He stared at her with a sad, helpless smile. Then he took the new tickets she handed him and left with his dumpling soup.

Over his shoulder, he heard the girl's laugh — a laugh from the bottom of her heart. Lifting the spoon to his nose he muttered quietly to himself, "I'm a good-for-nothing."

And, true to his word, that was just what he became. He did not shout or make trouble in the dining hall anymore, but stood, quiet as a mouse, waiting for the window to open. Seeing her on duty would make him blush even before he lined up. All this may have escaped others' eyes, but it could not escape Zhao Tao's. "Why are you so well-behaved today, Xiaoliang? Why aren't you shouting 'lazy bums'? You haven't had a drop of liquor, and yet your face is all red." Neither could Xin Xiao-liang escape "Joker's" jests. At the lunch table, when Xin raised his bowl to his lips, Zhao asked him whether the food tasted especially delicious today. If Xin took off his hat, Zhao asked him whether he felt a little bit hot, somehow. When Xin finished eating, Zhao would point to the bottom of the bowl: "Scrape up every last bit! Such delicious corn porridge is hard to come by!" Xin pushed him aside saying, "Shut up and leave me alone!" But Zhao had not played his trump card yet. "Why do you insist on burning your bridges behind you, old pal? You will need your 'chief of intelligence' again before long."

He was right. One morning as the siren was about to sound, an excited Zhao Tao came leaping onto the train to the shafts. He told Xin proudly that he had gotten the latest intelligence, hitting Xin's work helmet with his pick and chuckling to himself, "Wonderful! . . . Just wonderful . . . 'cat eyes' . . . ha, ha. Marvellous!" Usually, when he had a bit of intelligence, Zhao liked to keep Xin waiting until Xin was hopping up and down with impatience, but this time he was not in the mood for suspense. "This is first-class intelligence."

"Okay, enough. The refreshments lounge is not open to-night." Usually, taking advantage of his position of superiority, Zhao Tao would drag Xin to the refreshments lounge every night to give him the latest report on Meng Bei's every smile, every frown.

"My treat tonight." Zhao promised with a snap of his fingers. "Meng Bei gave Hu Lianguo the brush off!. . . Don't think this is only a victory for you, my dear friend. No! This is a victory for all miners."

Hu Lianguo was the son of the chief of the Labour and Capital Section, Hu Yutong. He had started out as an underground miner in the Yannan Mines, but his father had soon sent him to

the Yanbei Mines as an "assistant", simultaneously transform-
ing him into a cadre. The two mines were closely connected,
and so, it seemed, were their section leaders.

Hu Lianguo had been after Meng Bei? This was news to
Xiaoliang.

"He asked a deputy chief of the Food Section to be the
match-maker. He also said that in the office of the managers of
his mines one of the typists had gone off to college and there
was an empty place. . . . You catch the drift, anyway. You'll
never guess what Meng Bei said in reply."

"I'm sure she's bursting with happiness."

"You wretch! You couldn't be more wrong!" Zhao dismissed
Xin with a wave of his hand and went on. "She simply asked,
'And, what should I do if his father kicks the bucket tomor-
row?' Ha, ha. . . ."

The siren hooted and the train clanked off. Zhao put his
mouth to Xin's ear and shouted over the rumble, "She also said
she would never dare agree to a match with him, as he was a
section chief's son. She added that if he were a miner she might
give it some thought! This is really an important signal, Xiaoliang. An important signal!" And kicking his legs up in the air,
he began to laugh.

"What a fool! Does she prefer beancurd to a typewriter, a
dusty, black face to a clean white one?" Xin laughed coldly,
doing his best to appear indifferent.

Zhao knew Xin too well. "Don't try to fool me." He gave
Xin a poke and began singing over and over in a loud voice the
first line of the People's Liberation Army Military March:
"Advance, advance, advance!" his body swaying with the rock-
ing of the train.

Usually after work, around Xin's eyes and on either side of
his nose were big, black spots, the signs of his "quick scuffle"
with soap and water in the bathroom. Today, however, he
spent more than half an hour under the shower in a "protracted
battle" with the accumulated dirt of the day. He came home in
the afternoon, but instead of staying for supper at home as usual, he asked his neighbour to pass on a message to his mother

that he had "some business in the mines" and left. What was his "business in the mines"? It seemed merely to involve eating dinner in the dining hall, but, of course, Meng Bei was at the fourth window. After dinner he hung around the vicinity absent-mindedly until ten o'clock, when he went back to the dining hall to have some refreshments. Four meals in one day, and had the dining hall not closed, he might have stayed for a fifth! And that day of all days, when his poor mother had spent the whole afternoon at the store shopping for his birthday!

As Zhao pointed out, Xin had changed greatly since he received that "most important signal". For one thing, he had not used the nickname "cat eyes" since that day; secondly, he now had his supper in the dining hall; third, he always bought his meals at the fourth window; fourth, during meals he would sit lost in thought, staring off into space; fifth, he avoided the words "bachelor all my life"; sixth. . . . Zhao was clearly up to his job as "chief of intelligence", and he read Xin's thoughts as if they were written all over his face. "You're so dashing, usually, old pal. What are you waiting for now? If you haven't the courage, your good friend would be delighted to put aside all considerations of face to ask her whether she loves you!" Zhao's comments were right on the mark, as usual; Xin's characteristic arrogance had deserted him just when he needed it most. Zhao was more anxious than Xin about the whole affair, "We miners must make collective efforts if we are going to hook any girl-friends at all. It is not easy to find a girl with good judgement." And, rolling up his sleeves, as if itching to have a go, he added, "There's no hope for me, with my looks and my job put together. I'm destined to be a bachelor all my life. But you, my friend, should find yourself a good wife. You're as handsome as they come, and a girl would have to be blind not to see it." Zhao had been a miner for only a few years, but he was imitating the tone of the old miners, speaking as if from extensive experience. He was indeed willing to go all out for his closest friend, with no thought for himself.

Several days later, it happened that Xin and Zhao had the same day off. At lunch time, Zhao arrived late and there was no one left buying food at any of the windows. Heading straight for the fourth window, his head cocked to one side, "May I offer a suggestion?" he said to Meng Bei.

"Hmph!" thought Meng, looking him up and down. "As if you could have anything worth suggesting. It's sure to be a trick!" But all she said was: "Take your suggestions to the section leader."

"No, this is a personal suggestion. Listen, I hear you have a nice-sized bonus, and Xin Xiaoliang has been ill for several days and has had nothing tasty to eat. Haven't you noticed the way he comes to the dining hall several times a day?"

"Get out of here!" she said, blushing. "I'd be happy to go out of my way for anyone but him. It serves him right if he's sick."

"Do you really mean that?"

"Of course, I mean that!" she answered quickly, but sweetly. "Go and tell him that he deserves it."

Picking up his bowl with a sigh, Zhao Tao did his best to look dejected, all the while laughing to himself. He finished his lunch in a hurry and went to see Xin Xiaoliang.

"Don't as much as put your little toe out the door, do you hear? Something important is going to happen this afternoon."

"What, what is it?"

"The Party secretary is coming to have a talk with you."

"With me? What have I done?"

"Nothing wrong. You're in luck, old boy. You'll find out in a little while."

Then, stripping to only a T-shirt, his shirt flapping madly in his hand, he rushed off to a bar nearby and ordered a litre of beer and a dish of sausage, saying to himself. "Hmph! If he didn't have to stay at home this afternoon it would be his turn to treat me!"

And, in the meantime, what was Meng Bei doing? After she drove Zhao away she stood for a long while staring distractedly out her window. All girls are hypersensitive — they can guess the meaning behind a boy's every glance — and Meng Bei was no exception. The smallest stir of Xin's heart could not escape her notice. At first she was delighted to think that she had conquered such an arrogant young man and that she had revenged herself so fully. It was fantastic! But, now, it occurred to her for the first time: "My God! Who has really conquered whom?" Why do I always hope he will stand in front of my window? Why, after each exchange with him, do I feel I've been too harsh? Why do I always find myself wondering whether or not he likes me? . . ." Love works in mysterious ways, and no one, poet or psychologist, can write a definition of love as subtle as the thing itself. Meng Bei had fallen deeply in love with Xiaoliang, but she had no idea when it had begun. Maybe it was the first time she heard him, heard his hilarious conversation with Zhao Tao on the train. And, speaking of Zhao Tao, what was he up to? Meng Bei knew that he was Xin's closest friend, but who could tell if Xin was really ill or not. If he were really sick, why would he come to me? "Go home if you want to eat delicacies, don't come to the dining hall three or four times a day." No doubt about it, she thought, something was troubling him. Her face was flushed red and a smile hovered over her lips: "You don't look much like a hero now, sending messages through your friend. I'd be delighted to go and cure you of this 'illness' of yours!"

That afternoon, exactly as Zhao had told him, Xin stayed at home, waiting for the Party secretary. Hearing a knock, he opened the door to find . . . Meng Bei? He had been duped, and he guessed immediately by whom. Of course, the girl at the door made him feel quite a bit happier than the Party secretary, but it was so unexpected! He was thrown into confusion, his tongue did not seem to be his own.

"Well, it's you. . . . What are you doing here?" He regretted the question before it was out of his mouth — much too impolite.

Meng Bei looked at him with a smile, said nothing, but instead sat herself down in a chair in the living-room and began to look around. "I heard you were ill and couldn't eat or sleep. Is it true?"

"Nonsense!" He was damned if he would admit it to her,

but he really had no appetite anymore. "I sleep like a baby; eat like a horse; everything's fine with me."

She sniffed in disbelief, her bright eyes looking him over quickly. "It was your friend, Zhao Tao, who told me you were sick. He even placed the blame on the dining hall. He said the food there just didn't satisfy you . . . and that's why you go there five or six times a day. . . ." She could not help laughing.

"Do you believe that guy? He can. . . ." He swallowed the rest of his sentence. He wanted to say, "He can talk the happiest couple in the world into a divorce," but he felt it might be somewhat inappropriate.

"So, you're really not sick?" Meng Bei felt like hitting him.

"I have never felt so carefree in my life."

Damn him! Meng Bei did not know whether to laugh or cry. She, too, had picked up some tricks from the girls in the cotton mill: at this point, even the most obstinate young man should have given a hint of encouragement by saying "I haven't been sleeping well," or "I can't eat these days," but he. . . . There seemed to be no way to make him submit. She was about to leave. "Hmph! Carefree! To be single all your life? A bachelor? I. . . ." However, in the end girls' hearts are softer than boys'. Meng Bei did not leave. Her face red with embarrassment, she asked question after question, completely at random, thinking to herself: "I'll give him ten more minutes. If he continues to play the fool, I'll leave and never speak to him again. Hmph! What will he do then?" But, ten minutes passed, and she thought to herself again: "I'll give him five minutes more."

While Xin and Meng Bei were sitting there in uncomfortable silence, two people hiding in the kitchen were feeling equally uncomfortable. Not long before Meng had arrived. Xin's mother had come back from the market with a friend, our old friend, Grandma Qiao. On the way home, Xin's mother had helped the old woman along, thanking her and apologizing in one breath, as she poured out a stream of curses on her stubborn son's head. She hoped Grandma Qiao would not take offence, but could she try to find another girl for him. The two old women helped each other to the door, and were about to

enter the house when they heard a girl's voice. Peering through the window, Grandma Qiao said quickly to Xin' mother, "Good God! We have gone out of our way for nothing. I see your son can take care of himself."

"He can? With whom?"

"The Meng's daughter, the one I mentioned to you last time. Interesting. . . . It seems they have got in touch on their own somehow." Grandma Qiao started to giggle, clutching her waist for fear she would hurt herself laughing.

Xin's mother moved closed to the window, wanting to have a careful look, but Grandma Qiao pulled her into the kitchen. "Don't make trouble! We old women should make ourselves scarce."

And, so, the two old women hid in the kitchen until they could bear it no longer. Though it was summer, the stove was still burning and the room was smothering. However, much more intolerable to Xin's mother was the silence that had come after the girl's initial burst of laughter. She begged Grandma Qiao to come out and investigate with her: "You don't know how pig-headed my son can be. We can't hide here and leave him to bully that girl. . . ." Finally, after the endless pleading and the sweltering heat of the kitchen became too much for her, Grandma Qiao was persuaded to emerge from hiding.

The two old women, entering the room, broke the uncomfortable silence. After a moment's small talk, Grandma Qiao came straight to the point, making the young people blush. "Xiaoliang. Last time you were so puffed up with pride you swore you would be a bachelor all your life, but you have been keeping a secret from me. Wasn't it you who wanted a girl so ugly even her grandmother couldn't love her? Do you think a beauty like Meng Bei will give you a second glance? . . ."

"What are you talking about, Grandma Qiao?" Xiaoliang made a face for her to stop.

"It's no use making faces at me, I'm determined to clear all this up." Grandma Qiao then turned to Meng Bei and said, "To tell you the truth, if Xiaoliang weren't so stubborn, he would be next to perfect. You see, I didn't lie after all. He's tall and handsome! You two are meant for each other. . . ."

Meng Bei stared angrily at Xiaoliang for a moment; then turned away smiling. Could she help it if she had been born with a smile on her face?

While Grandma Qiao was breaking the ice for the young couple, Xin's mother had been busy sizing up the girl, overwhelmed with joy.

"This sweltering room is no place for a pair of young lovers, especially on a nice day like today, and with a film playing at the club. . . ." Grandma Qiao began in an authoritative tone, "Go to the club and tell my husband that I've sent you and tell him to give you two seats."

Was it because Grandma Qiao's order was too powerful to disobey, or was it that the two young people themselves had thoughts of leaving? At any rate, blushing scarlet, each carrying an umbrella, they left. Qiao was really quite a talker — the "nice day like today" was drizzing stubbornly.

The wave of self-satisfaction that had carried Grandma Qiao thus far had not yet exhausted itself. "Party Secretary Li saw me yesterday and said: 'I hear you are a busy match-maker these days, Old Qiao.' I was afraid he was going to criticize me, so I asked timidly: 'Have I done something wrong, Secretary Li?' He laughed: 'Wrong? All those fine young men of ours, working hard for the four modernizations, and no girls paying any attention to them! You should do something for them. These young men have hearts of gold. . . .' Aah, how I do go on! Last night I told my husband, 'You should use your club in a joint effort with me. Make sure every couple I send your way gets a chance to see the film.' Who would have thought that Xiaoliang and Meng Bei would be the first couple?"

Grandma Qiao, chuckling as she spoke, turned to find Xin's mother weeping with joy. "What's wrong with you?"

"I thought Xiaoliang would be a bachelor all his life because of his job. This girl is really a find."

While the two old women were chattering away, Meng Bei and Xin Xiaoliang were walking down the road by the Yongding River.

"Can't we do anything about Grandma Qiao?" Xin laughed, stealing a glance at Meng Bei, who only stared back:

"It's you that's the problem!"

"Me? What's wrong with me?"

"What about the way you misbehaved?"

"Misbehaved?"

"Just think about it for a minute. . . ."

He scratched his head for a while, seemingly unable to remember. Meng Bei stopped, and said, "Come here!"

Obediently, Xin came a step closer, holding his umbrella up over both of them. "What tricks are you up to this time?" he asked. "What are you going to do to me?"

"You should just thank your lucky stars I haven't made you beg forgiveness."

"What in the world have I done?"

"What was that nasty thing you said about me? Come clean!"

"Nothing nasty."

"Don't lie to me!"

"Okay, what did I say? Give me a hint."

"About my eyes. . . ."

"Your eyes, your eyes. . . ." Xin tucked his head slightly, narrowing his own eyes, and beginning to laugh mischievously. He looked sidelong at her beautiful, up-turned eyes. "I said you had 'phoenix eyes'. Otherwise, how could they have found me attractive?"

"Ha, that's too much! You, attractive? With that face? You're about as gawky as a giraffe." It seemed all the unpleasant words in the world could barely pay him back for the insult his first "cat eyes" had caused. Then laughing suddenly, she said, "But still, there is one thing that redeems you. . . ."

"What's that?"

She moved closer to him and whispered gently in his ear, "You're just the kind of man I like."

Translated by Ellen Hertz
Illustrated by Zhou Jianfu

THE FLUTTERING FLOWERED SCARF

Chen Jiangong

I

Qin Jiang was a very strange man. Although he had written many novels which, everybody agreed, abounded in deep feelings, the way he treated people in ordinary life seemed to suggest that he did not have the least human understanding. Recently, I had twice tried to arrange an interview with him for a feature article, but each time he flatly refused my request. Last Saturday evening, I caught a glimpse of him before I got off the number 103 bus. Naturally, I called him but he ignored me completely. He was standing there holding on to the handrail, cold and aloof, wearing a grave look. Was he out of his mind? He did not look like it. On the contrary, he appeared to be a simple and honest man. His works were profound but not difficult to read and they were certainly not written by a shallow-minded person. But why all this strange behaviour?

As chance would have it, I was assigned to cover the occasion of the Best Novels Award sponsored by the literary magazine *Blue Clouds*, and we happened to be put in the same hotel room. His short story "The Tow-Hand" had won him an award for its penetrating theme, its delineation of rugged, unsophisticated characters, and its robust style. He did not show up, however, not even after the ceremony was over. Was it because he was very busy at S. University at the time, or was it because he wanted to avoid the blinding magnesium lights and the ensuing interviews?

But that evening he came in. A thin figure, of medium height, he had a longish square face with sharp, angular features. The eyebrows were straight and thick, the eye-sockets were slightly sunken and I could also see a high straight nose. His lips were compressed forming a straight line, while his chin was a bit tilted. Here was the same man I had seen a few days before: fatigue was written all over his face, and his dry eyes kept blinking all the time. Although he gave me a nod and smiled slightly, I could see that there was still something weighing on his mind. He went to the sofa and sat down.

"How come you're so late? Were you working on something for the editors?"

"No."

"You look tired."

"Do I?" He did not deny the fact, neither did he seem to be interested in carrying on the conversation.

We kept silent.

I could not bear embarrassing situations like this, so I said, "You didn't show up at the awards ceremony and that was quite a disappointment to everybody. Comrade Ma Zhenyuan came over and gave some instructions. He even said he hoped he could meet you someday."

"Hm." He knit his brows and said, "I phoned to say for I couldn't make it. There were a few things at school that I had to attend to. And that's why I couldn't come."

"Comrade Ma asked me, on leaving, to invite you to his home when I did see you," I said. "He'd love to have a chat with you. He says you're a very promising writer."

He said nothing.

After the lights were out and he had lain down, he suddenly asked, "Could you find an excuse to let me off? I — I don't want to see him right now."

"Why?"

Silence again.

This really was carrying things too far. Comrade Ma Zhenyuan, now over seventy, was a leading figure in the literary circles. The young man should have known better, I thought.

I said, "We don't know each other very long, this is the first time I've met you, so naturally I don't know you well enough. But I should think, at least, for courtesy's sake, you ought not to —"

"Oh." He struck a match, lit a cigarette, and began to smoke in silence. After a very long pause, he said, "Hm, yes, I *do* want to see him. I did expect he'd come, but — "

"What's that? Do you —" From what he said, I had the feeling there was some subtle relationship between him and Ma Zhenyuan.

"Well, it seems I'll have to tell you, after all, because I need your help to get me out of trouble. But can you keep a secret, at least for a while?" There was a bitter smile on his face as he said, "You'd never dream of it. I'm his son!"

"What? Does Comrade Ma Zhenyuan know? Doesn't he know about it yet?"

"Don't shout like that. Lie down, won't you? No, he doesn't know yet. Qin Jiang's my pseudonym. All he knows is that his son Ma Ming's working on a Changjiang River steamer in Sichuan Province. He doesn't know I'm now studying at university, or that I've written novels. I'm simply Qin Jiang."

"How did all this come about?"

"Well, actually it's quite simple. I was the black sheep of the family." He puffed at his cigarette, threw me a glance, and exhaled the smoke slowly. "You'd never imagine what I was like in those days. Some seven or eight years ago, I used to dawdle away my time all day long with my friends at the 'Old Mos'. You know the 'Old Mos', don't you?"

" 'Old Mos'?" Oh, yes. I remembered the Moscow Restaurant of course, now called the Beijing Exhibition Hall Restaurant. "Old Mos" was what children of high-ranking cadres called it, then.

"The 'Old Mos' had just reopened, as you know. It had silver dinner service. Every time we went there we would filch a spoon or a fork — not to sell it for money afterwards, mind you, but to show that we'd been to the 'Old Mos' again. It was something worth showing off, rather like a medal awarded for distinguished military service. We often went to Kangle, too. It was in Wangfujing Street then; it's moved now. We caroused and caused a lot of trouble at the place. It was certainly a dissipated life. One of their waitresses was very beautiful. I remember once asking her to bring me a bottle of soft drink, and I gave her a ten-yuan bill for it. She came back with the bottle and dumped all the small change on the table, which seemed too small for it. In my drunkenness I swept it all on the floor, and the coins were clinking and rolling everywhere. All my friends loved talking about that afterwards.

"In those days we used to take turns treating each other. After we'd eaten and drunk to our hearts' content, we'd all end up in someone's home. There we'd jabber away — we dared not dance in those days, nor did we have videos. So we just chatted all day long and played cards. Of course, we would curse the "Empress of the Red Capital",* too, sometimes. We never went home before three in the morning.

"You don't believe what I'm telling you, do you? I'm not surprised. You see, I grew up in a boarding school for cadres' children. I knew what the stripes and dots on officers' uniforms meant, and I could easily tell the difference between cars like Red Flag, Benz, and even Volga and Babieda. Yet I was totally unprepared for life. Then, its waves came, soon enough. One day, I was hailed as a hero and everybody was saying, 'Of course, the son should carry on with his father's work, and he was a tough young man.' Then, the very next day, I was branded as an undesirable element, a son of a bitch of the condemned gang. I rode on the crest of fortune or sank in the political current, depending on my father's luck or misfortunes at the time. So I often got dead drunk and cursed heaven and earth. I couldn't find the right niche for myself and I didn't know what I should do. Father began complaining more and more. Perhaps he felt his career was coming to an end, and couldn't find people to boss around or find fault with. He told me I was a 'parasite'. He would open my door

---

* I.e., Jiang Qing. — *Trans.*

in the mornings and yelled, 'Hey, get up, old Ob!' Later, I realized he meant I was Oberomov. I had my own kind of sarcasm for him, too, in return. I addressed him 'Old Bol' — short for 'Bolshevik'. I said, 'You're up early, Old Bol. Better go and read your Marxist Bible; it'll do you a lot of good, you know!' That made him so furious he shook each time —"

Qin Jiang was now laughing heartily. I could not help laughing, too.

"So that's how the unworthy son got kicked out in a rage, huh?"

"No, I left myself." Qin Jiang stopped laughing. A moment later, he said, pondering, "Do you think I was happy with that kind of life? My mind was a blank when I lay in bed at night. I'd accomplished nothing so far and the fear of wasting my youth coiled round me like a python. But then, very soon I would fall asleep. The next day by sunset I got on my Phoenix bike to join my friends in revelry again for another drinking bout. I soaked myself in all sorts of drinks.

"Heaven knows why I suddenly decided to get out of Beijing. Maybe it was the result of the incessant grumbling of 'Old Bol', or it might have been due to one little incident. Somehow, I suddenly had an idea one day and took some friends of mine to the Victory Restaurant. I ordered a seventy-yuan meal. Mother had passed away, consequent upon the severe political attacks she had suffered. That was before I went to the countryside in 1967, when father was still in prison. So I went to the Victory Restaurant to get myself enough food for the train journey the next day. Here, I had been once accused of theft and grossly insulted. So now I wanted to give myself airs! Just as we were in a state of drunken ecstasy, with all the food and drinks on the table, I spotted an old waitress of over fifty. She was the one who had saved me from a thrashing on that day of humiliation after accepting my explanations. I went over to her, half drunk, and, with cup in hand, addressed her as "my saviour". I beckoned my friends to come over to give her a toast. She pushed me aside saying she didn't know who we were. Then, giving me a stern look, she disappeared. I'll never forget that look of hers as long as I live. It'll remind me of those days when I stood among the old peasants in the countryside, and cast exactly the same kind of look at the nouveaux riches staggering drunkenly out of the commune office. I was afraid of such looks.

"It was the end of 1976. Everyone showed his true colours: those who had sacrificed everything for the sake of truth; those who had been very industrious; the loafers and even those obsequious time-servers. Me? I felt I was just a smart good-for-nothing; no good in the past and would be no good in the future! Suddenly, I was terrified by the thought of being eliminated in the race. I realized that I had been plunged into abyss of misery.

"So, I decided to get out of Beijing, to be away from all the 'small Sanyos' and 'big Sonys', away from the innumerable family dance parties — when I left Beijing, these parties were in full swing and very popular among my friends: tangos, rumbas, discos, etc. Damn them! 'Old Bol' didn't believe I'd go to Sichuan as a worker; he thought I was tired of playing around in Beijing, or perhaps I'd got myself into some trouble. He asked me tremblingly, 'Why?' I said, 'Gosh, you ask why this and why that about everything, don't you? Why should there be a why? There isn't any why! No sense in living here, that's all. Going to try another way!' So that's how I left —"

The trees were rustling in the night wind outside; it lifted the silk window curtains, and brought into the room a delicate fragrance of lilac.

Strange how Qin Jiang had become so lively and talkative! Gone were the stiffness and worried looks. In truth, what he had just told me was enough material for a perfect write-up of an interview: "Life Reforms People". After a few years, this same Qin Jiang, who found "no sense in living" and who had left Beijing to find "another way", eventually turned himself into an engineer of men's souls. A talented young author had now come home. His father did not know yet that the promising youth he had praised so highly was in fact his own good-fornothing son, but —

"I certainly congratulate you, Qin Jiang. Because of that first step you took, you're what you are today. Still, I don't understand why you don't want to go and see your father. He'd be awfully glad to see you, I'm sure."

Maybe my words were too abrupt and they had hurt him. He was silent once more. After a long while, he said, "I *would* like to see him. I used to imagine with great pride what the scene would be like when I appeared before him suddenly with the school badge of S. University pinned on my shirt. The news of my book *The Tow-Hand* having won an award and our meeting each other at the awards ceremony would have given him even a greater shock. But then I thought I'd better wait. I'm not in the right frame of mind for the moment. . . ."

"Why?"

"Because of something else." There was a sad note in his voice. Although I could not see his face now, his voice had made me recall that worried and fatigued expression I had seen before.

"What's happened?"

He sighed. "It's something that happened recently. But then, it's a long story. Let's go to bed. We'd better get to sleep."

"I'm not a bit sleepy. Why don't you get it off your chest?"

He did not pay any attention to me. In the dim light, I saw his cigarette butt burning.

II

For the next two days, we had group discussions. In the evening, reporters and correspondents flocked to our room. He could not leave the place, nor did he show interest in talking after the lights were put out. After dinner on the fourth day, I dragged him out of the hotel to a tiny flower garden in the midst of the streets.

"Honestly, why should you go back to our rooms to be pestered by those guys?"

We chatted about various things. As dusk fell gently, we sat down upon a terrazzo platform.

"I can see you've got something on your mind. What is it?"

He smiled. "Talk about others pestering me! You're a hard one to get rid of, aren't you?"

I said, "Let's not talk about it, to save you the pain."

He did not answer. After a pause he said, as if to himself, "It's rather unbearable to keep things pent up inside, you know."

The moon was gliding through the clouds and crickets were chirping in the rustling breeze. An occasional car passed by, casting its headlights on us through the trees. He pulled a blade of grass from under his feet and began chewing it.

"To tell the truth, I owe a great deal to literature. It has turned life into a textbook for me. I would have been extremely miserable, even disillusioned. But now, I look upon life only as a man's tragic journey. Literature has made me so aware and determined."

"Are you referring to the recent event?"

"Yes."

"Well, what is it?"

"It's a long story." He spit out the blade of grass.

"I've told you that at the end of 1976 I went to Chongqing, through the help of my buddies, and worked on a steamer. I'd played with boat models when I was a kid. And since I yearned to see the sights along the Changjiang River, I had a sudden whim and ambition to start out properly on a new voyage of life. Laugh at me if you like. There wasn't one single bit of tenacity left in me and I wasn't prepared for such a voyage. Whisky and brandy had taken every bit of strength out of me. To be expected to do calculations, designing, or burn the midnight oil? How could I stand such rigours? I was used to dancing all night under blazing pendant lamps. And now to study these boring volumes as one of the demands of my work. Unthinkable! I was used to relaxing in a comfortable sofa, with my legs crossed, listening to chamber music. Even the easiest job used to irritate me.

"I put up with the ten or twelve impossible days before the steamboat sailed from Chongqing to Shanghai, and then from Shanghai back to Chongqing. I couldn't stand it. Oh, I realized I was done for. I'd never accomplish anything. I started a diary several times, each time resolving to keep it to the end of my days, to record my struggles when I bestirred myself to do something. But I never completed the diary. I also resolved to study English. I bought some books and a transistor radio, but all I learned was ABCD. It all seemed so utterly vague to me, not quite as easy as Japanese because you can at least understand a lot of the Japanese words in their looks — they have so many Chinese characters in their language. So I gave up studying English half way. I began to recall with relish my 'little circle' in Beijing, the 'Old Mos', and 'Kangle', the 'discos' and 'big Sanyos', wondering what they saw in the fashionable videos. . . . I dare say, if it hadn't been for her intrusion upon my life, I would have easily gone back, and continued to live a satiated, comfortable but pointless life. It was just at this crisis in my life that I met her —"

"Who is she?"

"Her name's Shen Ping. We met on the boat." He paused, and then forced a bitter smile. "We didn't really 'know' each other. It was only — I remember everything about her. It was one day early in the spring three years ago. Oh, yes, it was February twenty-sixth. That's right, because I insist I began my present diary on that day. That morning, our boat, the *Red Star 215,* was anchored in the light fog. Have you ever been on a boat in Chongqing? If so, you'll certainly know what I mean. Not only didn't the fog disperse, but it got denser and denser, and the sun was completely lost in it, emitting only weak greyish rays. Boats couldn't sail in such low visibility. There was no choice but to anchor in the middle of the river. The engines stopped. I came out of the engine-room to get a breath of fresh air and saw a girl standing on the fourth-class deck. Unlike the other passengers who were either asking all sorts of awkward questions or swearing, or who were putting their hands over their eyes as they stared at the sky, she was leaning against the railing reading. She was so different! How I envied her! She was completely absorbed in her book. Her eyes were sparkling, the corners of her mouth curled up slightly, and her lips quivered from time to time. I didn't know what it was that had moved her. She looked simple: her hair was tied up at the back of her head in two short braids. She was wearing a blue jacket and blue trousers with no ornaments. However, the embroidered blouse collar peeping out from her jacket betrayed a young girl's instinctive love of beauty. She was tall and healthy, with fine features. I didn't know why the combination of her simple attire and her poise had attracted me so much. . . .

"I was already twenty-five then. I'd know quite a number of girls in my circle in Beijing. Some of them had chased after me, too; but I was never in love with any of them."

"So it was love at first sight, wasn't it?"

"No, not quite. I simply felt she was a bit of a mystery with a certain pride or arrogance that I hadn't known before. How shall I describe it? The way she held that book in her hand completely unaware of her surroundings. Somehow, it made you feel she was superior to or above everybody else. If I wanted to, I could easily carry on a conversation about Austerlitz and Waterloo to impress some shallow girls. But this girl made me feel I was rather deprived. Yet I had my doubts. I wasn't sure she wasn't a fake, putting on sophisticated airs deliberately. . . .

"Towards noon, the fog dispersed. Our boat went forward at full speed. The sun was shining brightly; the river flashed back its rays. She wasn't reading now; instead, she took out an azure-coloured nylon scarf and tied one end of it to the post. The wind was raging. It flapped the scarf, and the two red phoenixes on it seemed to be dancing together. She caught hold of the other end of it and leaned on the railings, staring into the foggy distance.

"My shift done, I went to the dining-room for lunch. As I walked past behind her, I noticed the knot she made on the post at the end of her scarf had become loose. I leaned against the cabin door and watched her for a moment with locked arms. I couldn't help saying, 'Hey, there. Stop being so romantic. That thing's going to be blown into the river any minute, and the River God will be wearing it soon! Upon hearing this, she turned round, gave me a grateful look and tightened the knot in the scarf. There seemed to be tears in her eyes. I was now quite pleased with myself. 'What's this for? Some kind of signal for somebody?' I said casually. She blushed and replied, 'It's for my mother.' 'Your mother? Where's she?' I asked, surprised. She pointed towards the riverbank ahead and said, 'Over there!' There, by the riverbank and in the midst of the bamboo, I saw smoke curling upwards slowly. Her mother, she told me, was teaching in a primary school. Over there, was their home, too. She had tied the scarf on to the railing to make it easier for her mother to spot her. 'Sad, isn't it, this separation?' I said jestingly. She shook her head. 'No, it's not separation. But . . . it's certainly sad!' Goodness, such conceitedness!

"She was on her way to Wuhan; from there she would get a train to Beijing, for she had enrolled in the Chinese Department of S. University. She really had done extremely well. With only a junior middlle school education, she nevertheless got the hightest marks in the university entrance examination in her district. Of course, she was very pleased with that. Well, who wouldn't be? 'You didn't sit for the college exams?' she asked me. 'Me?' I rubbed my greasy hands with a wad of cotton and could only smiled bitterly as I threw the cotton ball into the river. 'A man of real worth doesn't need that!' She stared at me, with a mischievous glint in her eyes. I looked blankly at her, and said nonchalantly. 'Perhaps I'm not all that worthy.' She chuckled and said, 'Do you mean what you say? If you truly despise these exams, you can jump into the river and don't swim. I've proved my worth through these exams. My mother's a Rightist — she says she isn't and father has abandoned us to 'make revolution'. In my childhood mother taught me and I learned that Xibo of the Zhou Dynasty compiled *The Book of Changes* when he was placed in confinement

and that Confucius wrote *Spring and Autumn Annals* when he was out of favour at court. H'm! A college education for me? I was never recommended, no chance whatsoever! But look at me now!' She kept pressing her fingers against the flowered scarf which was fluttering and curling round her face. She seemed to be admiring it as a banner of victory.

"I don't know whether you ever had this feeling when you were young: a chance meeting with a young girl, a glance of the eye, or a faint smile will remain with you for ever. That was how I felt when she suddenly became everything in my heart. Now, don't misunderstand me. What she left with me was not merely a kind of simple, sweet memory. No, much more than that. I didn't have the courage to see her again after that conversation. All I dared do was look out constantly from the engine-room and watch her reading in the dying rays of the setting sun undisturbed by the sad, shrill cries of apes and monkeys in the hills. There she sat perfectly still: her feet upon the railings, her head resting against the back of her deck-chair. The water was rushing by, the hills seemed to have been split as we cut through them hastily downstream. It was impossible for me to know how hard she must have struggled. She might have already begun to experience the hardships of life when she was in swaddling-clothes! Who knows? But look how pleased and proud she was now! As for me, well, I'd been through four or five years of suffering, too, and, I was still cursing things occasionally. But apart from all that cursing and ranting and, oh yes, my knowledge of Chinese and Western food, what else had I got to be proud of?

"From that day I declared war upon myself. I began to study hard; I resorted to all sorts of methods to keep myself awake. I arose with the cock's crow, and made my vows again. It hadn't been easy to turn over a new leaf. If it hadn't been for her, I would've given up long ago as I had done before. But this time I succeeded, because her figure, her bearing, even her flowered scarf were constantly in my eyes; her words were constantly in my ears. You would have laughed at the vows I made then — I swore I would get into S. University to study

Chinese. Then I could see her again. That put me on the literary path, so to speak. Of course, it was also because I'd always liked literature in the past; but perhaps more so on her account. Life is full of such accidents. The funny part of it was that I didn't even know her name! Later on, things which had seemed vague to me gradually became clear — you know, things like talent, tenacity, passion, etc. Hard work, writing, physical labour, nature, society, and people — everything began to display its charm. I didn't need to have her to goad me on. Yet she constantly appeared in my mind. She was the first one to throw me a rope when I appeared to be drowning. Maybe she hadn't realized that. A kind of yearning also began to fill up my heart. Maybe it was what you'd call love? At any rate, I waited. Some day, I said to myself, I would surprise her by standing before her and aunounce proudly, 'It is all because I once met you!' "

"Toot toot —" Truck after truck passed by on the road, shattering the silence of the little flower garden. The iron rods in the trucks clanged noisily while sounds of the engine pierced the night air. Damn it all! For when the noises died down, Qin Jiang did not say any more.

I glanced at him. His lips were drawn tightly; there was a cold grim look, and the rest of his face was hidden by the shadows of the trees.

It seemed I had touched him on a painful spot in his heart. I sighed, and then said sympathetically, "I understand now. You're in love with her. When you enrolled at the Chinese Department of S. University and saw her, she was already —"

He did not say anything.

"Listen, you can always find another girl somewhere. Leave it to time and you'll get over this."

He shook his head. "You've misunderstood me."

"How?"

"If things were as you guessed, it wouldn't have mattered so much. Of course, I'll suffer, but I can get over it. Trouble is, things aren't so simple."

"What in the world is the matter?"

"That girl I met on the *Red Star 215* — maybe I'll never see her again."

"Cancer?" I cried in alarm.

He started, and shook his head, the corners of his mouth letting out a painful smile.

III

"As soon as I arrived at S. University, I was anxious to find her. I didn't know her name, and felt embarrassed to ask. I often watched every girl closely as he went past me. I was sure I'd recognize her the moment I saw her because she had appeared so many times in my dreams and in my mind these past two years. . . ."

"Did you see her or not?"

"When I did see her again, I'd already been at the university for over twenty days. All the students in the department had been gathering together to celebrate the thirty-first national anniversary. After all the performances were over, we formed many circles. While some of the students were beating the drums, paper flowers were being passed around. The sound of the drums made it all very exciting. Whenever the little paper flower was passed on to someone, he would at once throw it over to the person next to him as if he had received an electric shock. The auditorium was filled with laughter and gay conversation.

"To tell you the truth, how could I be in a mood for such silly games? I knew she was somewhere among the several hundred students gathered there. But how could I ever find her?

"I hadn't hoped in vain though. At last, shouts rose from a circle near me. The beating of the drums stopped. A girl was pushed out of the circle. It was she! I recognized her at once. She wasn't wearing her hair in braids. Instead, it was in a loose bunch and thrown back on her shoulders. She seemed to appear even more charming than she had been on the steamer.

No wonder I hadn't been able to spot her in the crowds. She was still very sure of herself, natural and composed. She didn't argue with the girls beside her, but tightened her lips slightly and walked to the centre of the circle to draw a lot. She had to solve the riddle, written on the paper, within two minutes. She couldn't and had to draw, as punishment, from a multi-coloured bamboo basket a lot which gave a description of her future husband.

"Everyone was shouting loudly. She had the bad luck to be caught, whoever the schemer was. Whatever name was written on the paper, the person would be declared her 'future husband. Although it was all a joke she bit her lower lip and reached into the bamboo basket. One could tell from the look in her eyes that she was nervous. The ridiculous part of it was that I was even more nervous than she was, although she hadn't noticed it, of course. Somehow I felt that the lot she drew would have something to do with me one way or the other.

"She took out the slip and was about to read out what was written on it. I didn't know why, but my heart was beating fast. What was on it? She blushed and stood on tiptoe as if about to jump any second. Then she struck her hands together and cried out in spite of herself, 'Goodness! What kind of kidding is this!' Everyone laughed. Some shouted, 'Why get so excited? Hurry up and read it out loud!' Others said, 'I bet it's exactly according to her wishes!' At this she understood their hints. She blushed and stamped the ground, saying, 'I didn't mean that! Of course I didn't mean that!' This made everybody laugh even louder. At last, someone snatched the slip from her hand and read it: 'He has a dignified appearance. He is handsome and attractive, young and promising. Boundless prospects await him.' In the midst of laughter the young man who read from the slip went up to her very solemnly and, extending his hand, whole-heartedly congratulated her. She withdrew her right hand and kept it behind her. That caused even more laughter in the room.

"Granted, she had drawn the best lot and had provided everybody with much amusement. But I was a bit put off somehow. When the party was over, I didn't come anywhere near her, much as I had imagined myself doing hitherto. Even when she went past me, dragging her chair, I remained calm and collected. Her face was still flushed. Of course, she hadn't noticed me.

"For this I cursed myself endlessly. I couldn't understand why I had been put off by a harmless game like that. Was it the resentment on account of my selfish love or something else? Several days later, I went to her dormitory in the evening. 'Do you remember me?' I asked. She seemed to have been upset about something, for there were tears in the corners of her eyes. Upon seeing me, she was surprised, and shook her head. I said, 'Well, so your handsome and charming lover with boundless prospects has put everything else out of your mind!' I could see she wasn't in the mood for jokes. She lowered her lash and said, 'What kind of joke is this and who are you, anyway?' 'A defeated worker on the steam-boat who almost jumped into the Changjiang River.' I replied. 'You?' She stared at me, as she had done before; clapping her hands, she laughed, and said, 'Ah, now I remember!' After asking me to come in, she seemed to be preoccupied again. She forced a smile, but couldn't find anything to say. I fixed my eyes on her and jested as I had done on the steamer. 'What's up? Is it a matter of life and death again? Who is it? Is it really something sad again? Where's your flowered scarf?' She didn't answer but sat listlessly on her bed. The scarf with the phoenixes was lying on it. She gazed out of the window absent-mindedly. Outside, the autumn rain was drizzing. How I wished she would ask me how I had come to study there too, and what had happened to me in the past two years! But she seemed to be miles away. After a long silence, I said, 'Has everything been going well with you these past two years?' She drew figures on the bed-spread with her fingers. 'What difference will it make? People like us who aren't from good families or don't have any connections in literary circles should be content to go back and teach in a little riverside town after another year or so.' They were cold words. She added, with a wry smile, 'A bit better than a professional teacher like my mother. She teaches in primary school; I'll teach in high school.' I was quite startled, for suddenly, she had become a stranger to me. I asked her what had gone wrong, but she didn't answer immediately. Gradually, tears filled her eyes.

Actually, it was nothing serious. Her classmates hadn't invited her to join them on their autumn excursion. Maybe they'd forgotten. With so many in the same class, it was understandable that someone would be left out. Yet, who could understand what this meant to a sensitive, young girl from a remote small town? She said she had been made to feel she was not worthy of thin company. Of course, she'd never heard a mazurka or polka, and didn't know who Delacroix was; nor did she have a friend or relative who was a scholar, or generally well known. So, of course, she didn't dare knock on any professor's door. She feared they would think she was uncultured and in any case she wouldn't have been able to put in a word in the elegant conversation. Even if she managed to say a few words, she would be only making a fool of herself. She was so earnest. One could sense the unfairness and indignation she must have felt. Was it contempt? Was it reluctance to accept her place? Or was it another expression of 'you just wait and see'? It was all three. She sounded exactly the same as she had done when she was telling me about herself on the river boat.

Strange, not only was I devoid of the previous emotion, but a feeling of loss and sadness also came over me. It was as if I had been dreaming in the golden autumn light and then suddenly discovered some dead leaves. If everything she had said were true, was it all that uncommon? Beside our Pomegranate Lake were many fir trees which had sprung up from among the thorns and brambles. Of course, there were shoots which were lucky enough to have their roots in rich soil. Same with human beings. There were those who belonged to study groups of the so-called 'Death-Defying Committee' and youths who had their book with them even in the dead hours of the night in the dormitory washrooms. Of course there were also the romantic types, or those who obtained high positions through their connections. And, inevitably, there were those who, in Kissinger style, engaged in 'shuttle diplomacy' among publication circles and academic organizations. There's nothing new in all this. What's strange, though, was that she should have been so upset by a petty incident such as having been left out of a fall excursion or felt awkward at that party. No wonder her little bookstand was stacked full of books on Chopin and Beethoven! At first I had thought she was studying the history of art. Now I discovered it was for the sake of understanding the mazurka or polka. So it was nothing but vanity in her heart.

"I must say that I really knew very little about her in the past. I don't know whether it was self-respect or vanity that got her through those days of hardship and struggle. No matter what it was, it was understandable. But, are those the only things that give us strength in our battle of life?

"That's why I became disappointed. What she had been yearning for day and night was merely the envy of others. I discovered she memorized names like Monet, Van Gogh, Matisse, and Picasso. She had also learned to utter 'uh — ug' from her throat or through her nose. And that superior response often cut short other people's conversations. What did that sound mean? Approval, indifference or disapproval? The devil knows! At any rate, it's come into fashion now. I think it might have come from the foreign graduate students. Once, she told me in great excitement that she had located one of her mother's former students, that he was working at an institute for literary research, and that she was going to call on him to ask him to recommend her manuscripts, with the hope that she would be introduced to the celebrities.

"I met her one day in mid-morning. She told me how she had put to shame some people who had looked down on her. It seemed that they had taken letters of recommendation from somebody important to Professor Gao Tang at the literature research institute. Little did they dream of finding her in Professor Gao's room, much less of seeing her engaged in a lively,

fascinating conversation with Professor Gao. They were dumbfounded! One schoolmate after another kept asking her after
this, 'How come you know Professor Gao so well?' She described everything to me most vividly. This time she got her
genuine satisfaction. She had won. Maybe those schoolmates
would think she was somebody now and she would be accepted
into their clique? Hearing her talking with such relish, I really had nothing to say. I interrupted her with a cold remark,
'You really should be congratulated,' and left.

"I sat on a bench by Pomegranate Lake all afternoon. The
early spring breeze was swirling the sand back and forth. Her
image kept appearing before me — the girl I now saw in
college, and the one I had seen on *Red Star 215* reading in the
fading sunlight. Maybe, I have no right to interfere with anybody's life. Or I'm destined to suffer the pains of discourage-
ment in my heart of hearts. I wondered. Was all that hardship
and struggling she had been through only meant to get herself
into that small coterie? And, by the same token, was I to
struggle and fight to get myself back into my former coterie,
too? It was a quagmire and one would sink in spite of one's
fervour, perseverance and talent. Thank god, by sheer force
I got myself out of it! Ah, the strain and struggle! I was suddenly filled with courage and strength. A street lamp was
shining through the dusk. For a moment I became restless.
Why shouldn't I go and see her? Why not?

"She was about to go out to attend to some business. What
was it, I didn't know. Her hair was coiled up on top of her
head. A faint aroma of sandal-wood clung about her. It
seemed that my parting remark of the afternoon had not meant
anything to her. She looked gentler than ever, and as she
looked at me, her eyes shone. I had a feeling all this was not
meant for me, and that she was getting ready to meet somebody
else. She smiled apologetically and said she was a little busy
at the time, but she said that she could guess why I had come.
Of course, she ought to introduce her old friends to certain
celebrities, but she was too busy, and she couldn't help it.
Never mind, she would do it another time. What's more, I was

given to understand, we're both from the hills of Sichuan, and therefore unimportant here. I blushed. A sense of insult made my blood boil. The lights in the opposite dormitory went up and they troubled my eyes. I squinted, and took a deep breath. I told her I had come for a different reason. She then asked me if there was any other business. I said 'no' and left.

"That was March 20. You know what happened at S. University. Our men's national volley-ball team had won over South Korea in the world cup preliminary round, and everybody was excited by the news. The students were shouting with joy beating their bowls and basins in exultation. Thousands of them poured out of their dormitories. They lit torches, and a trumpet sounded somewhere with the tune of *The March of the Volunteers*.* Everyone shouted, 'Unite and revitalize China!' We paraded around Pomegranate Lake; we celebrated the whole night long. As I marched on, in their midst, tears rushed to my eyes. I suddenly realized many of them had been fighters in the past and they were still fighters today. Some might have fought against unjust personal treatment, but now they had found a new goal and that was the rebuilding of our country. It was noble. I could see here countless passionate youths making invaluable contribution in every sphere of our national life.

Yet, what was Shen Ping doing? Would she be excited by all this? Would she? I recalled 'Arbour Day' when the entire department went to the suburbs of Beijing. She happened to be on the same school-bus with me. The bus drove along the dry river-bed leading into the hills. Sometimes we could catch a glimpse of small and poorly-built huts on the hillside, or a few children tending sheep. Suddenly, as if moved by something, she said, 'How difficult it is to fathom one's fate! What can one say? How would you like to be born and raised in these barren hills and live here the rest of your life?' I looked at her casually and replied, 'You're congratulating yourself, aren't you?' She nodded slightly, and said, 'Of course, we have

---

* This song has been designated as the Chinese national song.

to live and do something. If we're happy just whiling our time away, we wouldn't have to suffer any pain. But somehow, I'm really a bit scared if I were one of them.' What she said was true. She wanted to forget her past. She couldn't help feeling that she was lucky not to have been swept away by the swirling currents of fate. Now she had found a new life in a new world. She wouldn't spare a thought for this wild mountain, this isolated village, or the young sheep-tenders. What had they to do with her anyway? Perhaps there would be things in life to make her indignant or goad her into a fight such as a cold eye or a cold shoulder, but certainly not things like these; no, not these. Ah, fighters aren't always such great people after all, are they?

"That same evening, I wrote her a long letter, more than ten pages. I asked her whether she had ever felt the danger of being swept away by life's miry currents. People were bustling about, appearing to be very busy with their concerns. And what were these? Money and self-interests! At present, the whole society was being submerged in such stinking water. Sad, but how true! Well, I said, go on and cultivate influential people, all listed in *Who's Who* no doubt, which one could get hold of easily. I expressed my anxiety and feared that she was on the path of destruction in her mad pursuit of fame and recognition. Naturally, I was carried away by my own emotions. I confided to her the feelings which had been gradually growing inside me since I last saw her on the *Red Star 215*. I admitted it was love. I told her it was this very unquestionable and indestructible love that had driven me to voice my hopes and anxieties.

"I was a bit too irrational then. Later on, I heard she already had a boy-friend — a student at Qinghua University and son of a well-known scholar (forgive me for not mentioning his name). The prophecy at that silly party game had come true after all. He was young and promising, with boundless prospects. As for me, I was only a very common person in her eyes. What's more, I had said all those unkind words to her. Even a fool wouldn't have written such love letter.

"After that, whenever we met, we'd only nod and say 'hello'. But I heard from other schoolmates of her thought of me: jealous, seemingly serious, and sentimental."

Qin Jiang raised his hands up to his chest. He pressed his fingers till the joints cracked. He stopped. He was looking ghastly. Under the mercury lights our shadows continued to grow shorter and shorter first and then longer and longer.

"Is that all?"

"It should be." He paused and then said, "And yet it doesn't seem finished. Or else, why should I get myself into trouble interfering with other people's lives?"

IV

We were back at the hotel. After going through the revolving doors, we entered the large lounge. We sat down in the long sofa.

"I seem to remember now you called me on the bus last Saturday and I didn't answer you, did I?"

I nodded and smiled.

"I was very upset then. That was why."

"I could see you had something on your mind," I said.

"I'd been to the Capital Theater and there I met a friend of mine. Oh, yes; he was one of the 'Old Mos' and 'Kangle' gang. His father's work was foreign affairs."

"Did this old friend of yours have anything to do with Shen Ping?"

"No. He came to Beijing on some business. But I found out accidentally that his younger sister — a girl I used to know — was in love. Her boy-friend's father was this particular scholar I had told you about. I was quite surprised and naturally questioned him. It turned out that this very boy-friend of hers was no other than Shen Ping's young man!"

"Really?"

"I was shocked, of course. I asked him very cautiously whether he knew about the love affair between Shen Ping and the young man. He went on talking as if it weren't worth any discussion. 'Of course I know!' he said. 'A Sichuan girl from your university. She clings tenaciously to him. He has told my sister he is sick and tired of her! I suppose he's only playing around with the girl. Naturally he'd be after my sister because he wants to go abroad. He's got some letters of recommendation from some professors. He wants to get a scholarship for MIT, so he wants the old man to pull some strings for him. That's why.' I didn't listen to what he was saying afterwards. I was suddenly in a spasm of pain. I thought of Shen Ping. It was that miry current again, the miry current of society, the miry current of life! And what was Shen Ping but a small blade of grass trying to stay up against its flow. The sad thing was that she knew nothing about it at all. Yes, completely ignorant! Hadn't she proudly announced that her boy-friend's going abroad? Oh, she's proud, all right. She's going to hang up her flowered scarf once more for him to see thousands of miles away. But did she ever realize the new boat was towards the reefs?

"On the bus back to school, I didn't feel like saying anything, not even when I bought my ticket. So naturally I didn't bother answering your call. I kept asking myself over and over again, 'Shall I tell her?' If I did, would she believe me? Would she say again that I was jealous? Furthermore, how much could one trust the accounts of that friend I met at the theater? Should I keep silent and say nothing? Then, of course, my conscience would suffer and the pain would remain deep in my heart. I realized then that love, especially first love, would come back to one's memory, however hard one might try to forget. You could burn up the wild grass, you know, but come the spring breeze and it would be given life again. I've won a literary award, true. But I'm still thinking of those distant villages, the wide river, and her fluttering scarf. Especially now, yes, now!

"By the time I got back to the dormitory, the lights were already out. I lay down quietly. My roommates were chatting about this person or that as usual: how somebody had found a

Bao Chai* type of girl-friend, how a lovely, innocent girl had made a fool of herself getting involved with some careerist or fortune seeker, how so and so had refined the art of arranging jobs through social ties, or how others had been busily engaged in 'secret diplomacy' in matters concerned with studying abroad, etc. Such talk irritated me. It was the same miry stream all over again; I could see very vividly. In a fury, I roared, 'OK! Let's quit talking and go to sleep!' I scared them all into silence, but I didn't sleep one wink myself that night.

"After I got up in the morning, I decided to tell her everthing. I didn't care whether she believed me or not.

"I saw her at breakfast. She was sitting at the next table. I took my bowl along and sat down beside her. She was quite taken aback and nodded not entirely trusting me. I munched a few mouthfuls of steamed bread in silence, and then began. 'Shen Ping, you — how's life been treating you?' Heavens! What kind of conversation was this? Even I myself began to suspect there was some 'evil intent' behind such words. 'I'm fine.' she said. In her glance I detected suspicion and mistrust. I said, 'I heard that your boy-friend — is going abroad?' She answered, 'Not yet. He's passed his TOEFL, but he's waiting for his passport. That may take a month or so.' How sophisticated she appeared now! Satisfaction and pride were hidden in her indifference. 'TOEFL', 'passport'. . . . Do you know, these are the most fashionable words now. The more casually you utter them, the more superior you appear. What else could I have said to her then? I knew what would happen if I said all that I really wanted to say. I hesitated, tonguetied.

"It looked as if I would have to do the most irrational thing. Lucky I didn't; it would have been too ridiculous. At any rate, that decision might have had something to do with the accidental return, gone for many years, of my inborn moral strength as a cadre's son. You see, I had found out her boy-friend's address and decided to talk with him and ask him whether he

---

* A female character in the classical Chinese novel *A Dream of Red Mansions*, who is plump and pretty and familiar with the ways of the world.

was just playing with this simple country girl. If so, I would lecture him until he admitted he was wrong. What a splendid idea! How romantic! How like a knight! I don't know how such an idea got into my head. Several days later, I went to see him in the evening.

"He wasn't at home. His mother said he was very busy. He'd got his passport long ago and would be leaving for America the day after tomorrow. This news convinced all the more that the stage had been set for Shen Ping's tragedy. Apparently, she didn't even know he was leaving so soon.

"All I could do was linger about outside the door for a while and left. Just as I was coming out of the building. I saw Shen Ping and a young man in the distance hand in hand. They were coming in my direction, and I got out of their way quickly She was wearing a fashionable light grey silk blouse with a silk belt around her waist, which showed off her shapely figure well. The tassel of her belt swung as she walked. She looked natural and poised, free and easy, without any trace of a country girl. Surely, she considered herself fortunate; she was happy today and no doubt, she thought she would also be happy in the future. Little did she know what was in store for her. As for me, all I could do was watch her enter that dismal-looking building with him.

"It soon became dark. The building was now lit up. Raindrops were falling on me. I didn't leave but instead wandered back and forth in front of the building.

"On the third floor, two huge shadows were silhouetted against the milk-white curtains of the window on the eastern side. There they were. Perhaps he was telling the final truth now. Very soon, I imagined, Shen Ping would be rushing down the stairs in tears and stumble into the evening drizzle. It was very dark outside. I might be of some help if I stayed on. At least, I could follow her again at a distance and watch her enter the women's dormitory. Still, how I dreaded the sight of her rushing out. No, I changed my mind. Let her rush out. . . .

"It was ten o'clock. The shadows on the curtains were still moving. I could see she was combing her hair. I stared at that familiar posture. Three years ago, when the *Red Star 215* went past Goddess Peak at dawn, she was standing on the deck, looking up, and the wind was dallying with her hair. She was combing her hair.... At the time, I was standing at the door of the engine-room watching her graceful figure. But now my heart suddenly ached because the light in the window upstairs went out. I splashed through the puddle and, in a few strides, got to the stairs of the eastern end of the building.

"Good thing I was in my right senses at the last minute. When I got to the second floor, I stopped and asked myself, 'What on earth are you going up there for?' I retraced my steps and came downstairs. I closed my eyes and let the rain fall on my face for a while. Then, picking my steps on the shadowy road, I walked on slowly. After several dozen steps, I turned round to look at the dark window again. My heart ached. It ached for Shen Ping, for her mother and for myself. I wished all I had heard at the Capital Theatre was pure nonsense, a pack of lies. Heaven grant it so! If it had been true, would she be happy now and for how long? Waiting for him to come back in one year, or two years? Would she be happy afterwards? I kept wondering. Maybe she's done for in her pursuit of all these shallow things. Who knows? It might give her some deep thoughts of what life was all about! If that was so, I'd forget what I'd seen tonight. If possible, I might even tell her I still loved her. . . ."

Qin Jiang stopped talking. He leaned against the sofa with his eyes closed, as if trying hard to calm down his surging emotions. He drew deep on his cigarette, and then blew hard at the smoke around us.

"What happened to Shen Ping afterwards?"

"Don't know. All this happened only the day before yesterday."

I sighed heavily.

He glanced at me, pushed away the smoke and said, "What are you sighing for? I've told you already that it's one of life's tragedies. It'll teach us to think a little more, to be a little more careful."

"That's right," I nodded. "But you haven't told me yet how all this has anything to do with your not turning up at the award ceremony and see your father again."

"Oh, that." he laughed, "I almost forgot." After a pause he added, "Maybe, in the first place, I'm not in the mood for that sort of thing. To appear in front of my father with a university badge on me and an award in my hands — well, shouldn't I have been proud of that? Yes, of course. But I don't see much sense in it. It would have reminded me of the flowered scarf on the *Red Star 215*. Life is long. I'd feel ashamed of such a glorious scene, actually. In the second place, I don't know if you understand it or not, but once people realize who Qin Jiang is, I'll be in the limelight and a lot of old friends will want to drag me off to the 'Old Mos' and 'Kangle' again. I'm not sure whether I have enough moral strength to withstand such things now. To tell you the truth, I really have to thank Shen Ping. She's made me think about a lot of things, and about the struggles in life."

"Aren't you going to see your father then at some point?" It might have been my professional habit, but I felt it such a pity to miss a dramatic scene.

Qin Jiang laughed once more. "Why be so persistent? When I feel better and if I'm in the right mood, I can go home at any time. But it won't have any news value, since it'll just be a son going home to see his father."

While we were waiting for the elevator, I asked, "Why don't you write all this down? There's so much material here for another masterpiece."

"Write about all this? No, not when all my schoolmates are still with me in college. If it were published, it would cause a lot of embarrassment." He shook his head. Suddenly, he looked at me and smiled. "Why don't you write it then, if you're interested?"

"You mean it?"

"What's the difference who's writing it? I don't have any 'copyright' on all that, you know." After a little thinking, he added, "On second thoughts, this might even be the best way of saying what I want to Shen Ping. And you're the most appropriate person to do that."

I understood what he meant.

And that is how I have written this novelette type of reportage, only changing the names of people and places!

Translated by Li Meiyu
Illustrated by Zhou Jianfu

LIU FUDAO

(1940 —   )

Born in 1940 in Hanyang County, Hubei Province, Liu Fudao taught in primary and middle schools soon after his graduation from a senior middle school in 1959. After working as a reporter for an army newspaper for some years, he took up cultural work in 1971. In 1979, Liu became a full-time writer and joined the Union of Chinese Writers in the same year.

Since 1972, he has published more than ten short stories and prose pieces such as "The Critical Moment" and "The Blue Dabie Mountains." The story "Spectacles", which he published in 1978, won the national best short stories prize.

THE MOON ON THE SOUTH LAKE
Liu Fudao

I

Some years ago, there was only one state-operated factory on the strip of land which skirted the curve of the South Lake. That was the Wuhan Third Pharmaceutical Factory. Over the last few years, however, the chemical plants in the city had been moved here one after another, consequent upon the vociferous protests of the residents against pollution. This strip of land had now become a chemical industry centre.

What factories were these? On the eastern side of the winding asphalt road, a row of signboards pointed out to the passers-by the location of these factories: the Central-South Chemical Factory, the Red Flag Chemical Plant, the Spark Chemical Factory and so on. Their names were all quite imposing and well chosen. But, in truth, they were what one would call "street-operated" workshops, which had only a hundred or so workers each. Some people naturally looked down on them and refused to call them factories; no, they were not worthy of such a designation! Nevertheless, they flourished defiantly and many of their products had no rivals in central and south China.

Take the Spark Chemical Factory for example. It had a pathetic look indeed, and nobody would think much of it. But it turned out a wide variety of products, such as anti-aging tincture, ferric chloride, ferrous chloride as well as small rubber caps for soya-bean sauce bottles with an annual output value of over a million yuan. Its ferric chloride alone was indispensable as a water-purifying agent for the whole Wuhan triple city.

215

The full name of this small "street factory" was the Spark Chemical Factory of Lion Street, Wuchang District, Wuhan city, but on its official seal the characters "Lion Street" were deliberately left out. In order to get approval, the factory's Party Secretary Wan had had to do some explaining to her superiors. She said, "The young men in our factory are all quite worried that the girls they want to make friends with will turn away upon hearing the words 'street factory'. Besides, these two words won't help in business matters. Once people notice them in our letters, they will not take their content seriously." All this sounded rather absurd, but the explanations, given in earnest by Secretary Wan, seemed quite reasonable and convincing. In view of the seriousness of the young workers' romantic interests and, more important of course, the future of the factory, the authorities concerned, being reasonable, gave their tacit consent. However, had the elevation of status, at least as shown on the factory's official seal, turned out to be a help? Whenever the factory wanted to buy some material, it still had to go through the whole process of imploring people for their understanding of its needs, as if asking for a favour. It also had to do with the fact that the products of this small "street factory", however good, were not for any domestic use; neither were they any good as playthings. And, what's more, whenever people heard the names of its products, they would be nervous and frightened: What the hell were these products? Some poisonous stuff? If so, surely nobody should help in its production.

That was how things stood. Now the fifty-year-old woman Secretary Wan had another problem. The factory's principal source of profit, ferric chloride, had to be changed from a liquid into a solid product. A two-storeyed workshop had been built for that purpose and all the necessary equipment installed. But the factory had not been able to get a boiler. In the words of Secretary Wan, "The fire is singeing our eyebrows!" It was indeed a desperate situation.

How should one describe Secretary Wan? It was not wrong to see her as a Party cadre, but it was also quite correct to look upon her as a housewife. Her ways and methods of work did not seem to proceed from any well-founded theory, but everybody had to do as she said. When the factory needed something, she would strike the "bell", a piece of steel, two feet long, and summoned all the workers. She then put the problem before them, asking them to suggest a solution. The workers would go home and consult the members of their family. They would, if necessary, call upon their relatives and friends, or go out of their way to ask their acquaintances in certain organizations or larger factories to help. After a verbal promise had been obtained, a formal letter would be issued, with the factory's seal on it. Usually, in order to get as soon as possible the materials of equipment the factory needed, Secretary Wan would have to go and see various people herself. But this time, in spite of all the usual efforts, there was still no boiler to be obtained. Eventually, some workers got hold of an important piece of information: the Jiangnan New Waterworks had recently purchased a large boiler. Their original small one was left in the courtyard of their living quarters. Immediately, a messenger was sent to make inquiries about the boiler, but the waterworks refused to sell it. They merely replied that the old boiler was still needed for their own use. Shortly after this, the workers of the "street factory" learned that if Assistant Manager Yuan, who was in charge of supplies at the waterworks, would agree to sign an order, the boiler could be obtained with or without a letter of introduction. The strategy was worked out: obviously, somebody had to go and see Assistant Manager Yuan. However, since he was rather difficult to approach, no one offered to take up the mission.

Dong, dong, dong. . . . Secretary Wan again struck the steel bar. She asked if anyone was willing to accept the assignment but no one responded. The workers were all looking at her in silence.

"It's no use staring at me like this! What are we going to do?"

"Let me try!" suddenly someone said in a muffled voice. Under normal circumstances, no one would take any notice of this speaker. But now, caught in this awkward predicament, Secretary Wan and the workers were as anxious for help as starving people waiting for the provision of rice. Whoever accepted the task would appear a saviour to them. However, when they looked at the speaker, both the leader and the workers had doubts and their hearts sank.

The volunteer was a young man named Ke Ting. Now that all eyes were set on him, his pale face at once turned a deep red. He was tall, about 1.85 metres, and certainly appeared conspicuous.

"Well, you may go and have a try. Anyhow ... anyhow ... you must get the boiler for us." Secretary Wan looked at him with half-closed eyes, not really impressed. She had almost wanted to say, "Well, since no one else volunteers to do it, go ahead, but, I don't expect miracles from you. . . ." Finally, she thought it best to give him a positive order.

Though Ke Ting held no respectable position or title, he was a well-qualified technician, and, as far as work was concerned, he had a good reputation in the factory. The solid ferric chloride workshop which would soon be put into operation was a large and somewhat modernized one. The blueprints and technological processes for setting it up had all been worked out by this young man, who had never taken any courses in a technical college. Indeed, the road he had taken was very much the same as those followed by most of the Chinese urban youths: soon after graduating from senior middle school he was sent to the countryside for two years and then he entered a street-operated factory after having been brought back. That seemed to be the pattern for the educated youths these days, and he had had no other choice. Yet, not long after his arrival, Ke Ting was able to solve the factory's numerous technical problems. Whenever some new technology was to be adopted, one could rely on him. As a rule, he would study both the new equipment and the directions carefully, and carry out repeated experiments till he understood exactly how things worked. He never let his colleagues down. All the youngsters in this factory admired him and even the old workers thought he was an extraordinary person. However, what was regrettable was that, though honest by nature, Ke Ting was far too shy. He had many ideas in his mind and wanted to be sociable, but words always failed him. No wonder the older workers were all greatly surprised when such a shy young man, who had never before done any public relations work for the factory, suddenly offered to go and see Assistant Manager Yuan and try to get the required boiler.

Indeed, even Ke Ting himself doubted whether he would succeed.

II

Now let us talk about something else. In the flourishing shopping centre of Wuchang, two rather attractive girls could sometimes be seen, dressed alike, with similar bobbed hair, and they were about the same height, roughly 1.72 metres. No matter how crowded the streets and how numerous the pedestrians on the pavements, they would always walk together, arm in arm. Because they were tall and had well-balanced figures, these two attractive girls used to catch people's attention. Even the arrogant youths had to make way for them, admiring them as the two of them went by. The girl with a round face was called Li Lu, while the other, who had an oval face, was Yuan Xia. The two of them had gone to the same school, but they were in different grades. However, their similar build, common inclinations and interests somehow had brought them together. As close friends, they had a lot to talk about whenever they got together. They also advised each other in their love affairs. Their fundamental requirement was: the young man should not be less than 1.85 metres tall. Good heavens! That was a tall order! At present, when the percentage of tall people in the whole country is not too high, it was certainly not easy to find a young man of 1.85 metres who was about their age and residing in the same city, let alone the other considerations such as family background, occupation and monthly salary! They also agreed that they would listen only to each other and not to any of the advice or orders of their parents or match-makers. For example, if anyone introduced a boyfriend to Li Lu, Yuan Xia would have a good look at him. If her dignified nose twitched, signifying disgust, as she pronounced, "Oh, what an ugly dwarf!" Li Lu's expression would change at once. And that was the end of the poor young man.

I mentioned above that the two friends frequently went out for a stroll in the flourishing district. That was half a year ago. And now, Li Lu had found a boyfriend, approved by Yuan Xia. On Fridays, their day off, Yuan Xia could no longer be with Li Lu as she used to before. True, Li Lu would come to see her with her boyfriend, but Yuan Xia understood that they did so out of consideration for her feelings, that they did not want her to feel neglected. Yet whenever Yuan Xia saw them off she could not help feeling enchanted by the sight of the two of them cycling joyfully, shoulder to shoulder.

Yuan Xia's mother advised her time and again not to stick so stubbornly to her terms. Why not consider a young man who was of the same height, or even a bit shorter? But her sugges-tion was usually greeted with strong opposition from both Yuan Xia and Li Lu. For example, Yuan Xia's mother said at one time, "Look at your father. He's shorter than I, but that doesn't bother me." Yuan Xia looked at her mother coldly, saying, "You want everybody to be like you!" Then, in a single phrase she summed up what she would be looking for in her future husband: a tall, honest young man. She openly an-nounced this at home: she wouldn't settle for less. Father be-came angry and demanded, "Don't you think you ought to put political standards first?" Yuan Xia replied stubbornly, "All right, then. I'll say an honest, tall young man. Any more objec-tions?"

Yuan Xia worked in the state-operated Third Pharmaceutical Factory, and she went there and back every day on her bicycle. One fine spring day in March, she thought of calling upon Li Lu on her way home for a heart-to-heart talk. The road lay along an embankment of the South Lake. The evening sun was shining obliquely on the lake, gilding its ripples, and a circular range of green mountains was reflected in the water. Yuan Xia now and then glanced at the scene far and near, as she complacently rode past several "ugly dwarfs". To her surprise, a rider on a "Phoenix 12" bicycle swept past her. She speeded up and soon got ahead of him again. Looking back, she noticed that the cyclist was a tall young man, about the same height as Li Lu's boyfriend. That was certainly interesting. After riding a bit farther, she looked back again to see if he was trying to catch up. This in a way was an insult to the young man, who was none other than Ke Ting going home after work. Now, we know that he was an honest man. But an honest person sometimes may also behave in a peculiar manner. When he realized that the girl was challenging him, he too speeded up and passed her again. But Yuan Xia didn't like that. Bending both her arms backwards and lowering her body almost parallel to the ground, like a cyclist in a race, she rode with all her might, and soon got ahead of Ke Ting. Without having time to straighten up, she suddenly heard a clanking noise and the pedals suddenly gave way. She glided on scores of metres more and then her bike stopped. She got off and saw Ke Ting riding past her. The "ugly dwarfs" behind also caught up and hurried past her, talking and laughing loudly at her misfortune.

On hearing their laughs, Ke Ting looked back and saw the girl was in terrible trouble, not knowing what to do. He felt sorry for her. Turning back, he did a half circle with his bike and stopped beside her.

"Let me have a look," he said, as he took out a test pencil on which was attached a small screw-driver. Then, he got a small spanner out from his key-ring and started working on the "Phoenix 18" without waiting for any word from Yuan Xia.

He tried the pedals and found that the chain was broken.

Helplessly, Yuan Xia stared at the young man and could not do anything while he was repairing her bicycle. She sighed, "What a mess!"

Night was approaching. A chilly gust of wind was blowing across the lake, which changed in colour from green to light blue and then to bluish black, appearing as mysterious as the evening sky. Although Yuan Xia was tall she was after all a girl. In the company of a stranger and in this desolate place, she could not help gradually feeling uneasy.

Imperceptibly, the slowly rising moon lifted the veil of darkness off the South Lake, and the evening sky was clearly reflected in the water. In this quite spring night, the moon and a few street lamps shone on the young man and girl who had met by chance. Yuan Xia was worried about her bicycle and she was also a bit scared. Her heart was full of gratitude and she kept wondering how she could thank him properly. Then she reflected: was it not better to let herself suffer alone for what she had done? Why should she involve other people in her trouble? But what would happen if he gave up and went away? Push her bike all the way home or carry it on her shoulder? She was genuinely confused. After considering the question once more, she decided that she had no choice but to rely completely on this stranger, who was working hard to repair her bicycle and whose name she did not yet know.

"Look, let's do it this way," Ke Ting said at last. "If you trust me, you can go home on my bike, so that your family won't be worried about you. I'll be able to fix your bike, but it will still take some time. Tomorrow we'll get our own bike back." He decided to wheel the girl's bike back home if he failed to have it repaired on the spot.

"But I don't like leaving you behind here," Yuan Xia said sincerely.

"You don't trust me, do you? You're afraid that I may play a trick on you and exchange your fashionable bike for my old one. Don't worry. There is a licence plate on my bike. You can go to the police and easily find out my name and address."

"No, I absolutely don't mean that!" Yuan Xia hurried to explain.

"Then why stay here? There's no need. I'll get up earlier tomorrow and bring your bike to the gate of your unit. Are you from the Central China Agricultural College or the Third Pharmaceutical Factory?"

Yuan Xia replied that she was from the latter. But she was

still reluctant to go. Apart from her sense of obligation to keep him company until he had finished repairing her bike, she could not think of any other reason for not going home. Ke Ting repeatedly urged her to leave him, and even threatened to stop repairing if she didn't, until she was finally convinced that there was really no need for her to stay. Then she rode away on his bicycle; her brain was in a whirl.

Early the next morning, Ke Ting arrived and waited in front of the gate of the pharmaceutical factory. The exchange ceremony was very simple. There was no handshaking and no signing of names. It was all over after a few brief remarks. In joyful surprise, she asked, "You've fixed it?" He replied, "Yes." Yuan Xia was full of gratitude and was wondering how she could reward him. She was about to ask his name and address but the young man smiled, got on his bike and rode away. Yuan Xia ran after him and called out loudly, "If you need my help, you can find me at the New Waterworks' living quarters."

Having heard the above romantic story, Li Lu, acting as Yuan Xia's adviser, slapped the table and expressed her surprise. She thought Yuan Xia was too negligent. If she had taken down his licence number she would have been able to find out his name and then it was quite possible that the two could meet again.

However, Yuan Xia defended herself, "If you had been in my shoes, you'd have been just as careless as I was. I was rather confused." That was what she said, but she had her regrets.

III

All practical Chinese people are well familiar with the ways of the world. In order to survive, they know they must depend on one another. "To help one another" is the spirit in all their daily affairs. Ke Ting had helped Yuan Xia by repairing her bicycle, but he had never dreamed that he would soon need the help of this girl whom he had met by chance. Of course, he had no ulterior motive in helping her. It was only when Secretary Wan spoke about the boiler in the New Waterworks' living quarters that he recalled what the girl had said to him.

On coming off duty, he rode directly to the New Waterworks' living quarters. In the courtyard he saw three blocks of new four-storeyed buildings and some old houses. Not knowing her name at all, how could he find her? He could not simply say he was looking for the girl whose bicycle broke down one evening while she was on her way home along the embankment of the South Lake. Ke Ting was at a loss. Suddenly, he realized it was a ridiculous idea, offering to try and get the boiler for his factory. Still, he was not going to give up. He watched every window, hoping to see that oval face he faintly remembered. Eventually, it grew dark and he left the place in dejection.

The next day, when Secretary Wan saw him she asked at once, "Young Ke what's happened to that boiler you were going to get?"

"I tried, but I failed," he replied.

"Did you see anybody?" she asked again.

"No, I didn't," replied Ke Ting.

Secretary Wan became impatient. "Then go and try again!" she said. "Whom did you ask for last time? Perhaps I can give you some help. If you don't know what to say, I'll tell you."

The young man dared not tell her the truth. He could only say, "I'll go and try again when my shift is over."

Upon hearing the word "try", Secretary Wan became even more impatient. "I'm telling you, my boy," she said. "This is no joking matter. If you have any difficulty, or if you must give them something, tell me. Anyway, take a packet of cigarettes with you."

"Leave me alone! She . . . doesn't smoke!"

Strange how Secretary Wan could tell Ke Ting had a girl in mind. Had he given himself away somehow? She laughed and began to see a ray of hope.

"Young man, how can you hide that from an old woman like

me? Of course, I'll support you if you fancy her. Talk about love and the boiler together. Surely, you can ask her to help you!"

Ke Ting said gravely, "Secretary Wan, you shouldn't be making fun of me."

Displeased, she asked, "And why not?"

Embarrassed, Ke Ting ran away. He worked quietly that day and left half an hour early to find her.

After a short wait outside her factory, he heard the whistle. A couple of reckless young workers rushed out first and hurried to the bus station trying to occupy a vantage point. Then, a host of cyclists emerged, gliding down the slope and were soon some distance away. Because of his special mission, Ke Ting looked only at the female workers. He saw many of them, but not "her", He wondered if she was decking herself out after work. Then, suddenly, she appeared, very neatly dressed, yet not in the current fashion. She was pushing her "Phoenix 18", surrounded by her girl friends, who were all at least a full head shorter than she. Yes, there she was! Tall and slender, with an oval face and very conspicuous! She was wheeling her bike and when she came to the gate, Ke Ting hesitated for a moment. He plucked up courage, and was about to call her, but she had already got on her bike, ready to go. At this "crucial" moment, Ke Ting's courage took over and he yelled, "Hello, comrade!"

The girls had noticed this young stranger and they smiled at each other, wondering which of them he was addressing.

Yuan Xia was taken aback for a moment, but she recognized him at once. Yes, it was he, whom she had been thinking of night and day, wanting to repay his kindness. "Ah, Young. . . . Is it really you?" She was both surprised and happy, her face fully flushed.

Her companions all got off from their bikes. Looking at this tall couple, they all had the same thought. One of the girls started making faces and called to Yuan Xia, "Hello, comrade! Do you still want us to wait for you?"

Of course, she didn't want them to wait! Yet Yuan Xia said, "As you please."

The girls' teasing, however, went on. "Come on! Why not tell us to leave you alone?" Then, they "flew" away like a swarm of bees.

Ke Ting said awkwardly to Yuan Xia, "I've come to see you about something."

Such a declaration under such circumstances would hardly mean anything, yet the girl, finding him so embarrassed, giggled and said, "Don't worry about them, let's go that way."

They got on their bicycles and set off in the opposite direction. They talked as they rode along.

"I went to the New Waterworks' living quarters to look for you."

"When?"

"Yesterday, after I finished work."

"I was at home the whole evening."

"There're so many apartment blocks in that courtyard."

"My home is in the second building, second entrance, on the second floor. It is very easy to remember and find. Just ask for Yuan Xia. They all know me."

This time, Yuan Xia's reply was quite positive and definite.

"Your father and mother are both old workers in the waterworks?"

"You can say father is an old worker in the waterworks. Mother was formerly in a street-operated factory. Later she was transferred to the waterworks."

At the mention of the word "street-operated", Ke Ting felt his most sensitive nerve had been touched. If he were not in a street-operated factory, he wouldn't have to come here to ask for help. Feeling uncomfortable, he continued with some reluctance, "Oh! Your father's an old worker. What's he in charge of?"

"Everything and nothing!" Yuan Xia replied mischievously.

Ke Ting caught on. "You mean he's a cadre, not a worker."

At this Yuan Xia was somewhat displeased. She retorted, "What if my father is a cadre and what if he is a worker?"

The girl's words were so abrupt and sharp that the young man could only say honestly, "I guessed you were from a cadre's family and your father is in a leading position. I didn't mean that an old worker could not be. . . ."

On hearing this, Yuan Xia thought, "So, like all the rest, you are nothing but a snob!" She lost interest in him and bent down her head, pedalling hard all at once. In a second or so, she was well ahead of the young man. When Ke Ting caught up and was about to say something, she made a gesture to him as if meaning to say "see you again" (or "not see you any more") and rode away even faster.

"I've been blind . . ." the girl, upset, thought to herself, looking sad and perplexed. Since she accidentally met Ke Ting in the spring, she had kept firmly in her mind Li Lu's criticism of her "tactlessness", and the young man had found a place in her heart. On her way home after work, whenever she could get away from her companions, she would come to that memorable spot on the embankment road. How she hoped that she could find him there again and recognize him at once! She would then be able say to him in a low voice, "See, how sharp-eyed I am!" But, that had remained only a hope. However, the repeated disappointment had only increased the fascination of her first love. With a somewhat guilty conscience she often felt that other people might have noticed the secret yearning in her heart, and she reasoned with herself by saying that she would like to see him again simply because she wanted to repay his kindness. But the unexpected meeting today had made her betray her secret joy, and all the excuses she had given herself for lingering on that memorable place were not to be taken seriously after all!

Yuan Xia pedalled away carelessly. Before long, the memorable place suddenly came into view. It broke her heart as she thought to herself, "When you were repairing my bike then, you looked so simple and sincere, but now you have become so vulgar. . . . Was I really blind?"

Left far behind, Ke Ting wondered why the girl was so offended. Had he said something which annoyed her? However, the boiler was on his mind, and he was not going to give up. He speeded up, shouting as he was getting near her, "Stop for a moment, please! . . . I've something to say to you. . . ."

To appeal to a girl was, after all, much easier than appealing to God. It was probably because of the young man's sincerity fully revealed in his anxious call, or because of her fresh memory of their first meeting which had since made her heart throb with excitement, or because of her own excuse of repaying his kindness — whatever it was, when the two of them got to the place where they first met, Yuan Xia stopped and got off her bike. Ke Ting did the same.

Realizing he had offended her, Ke Ting changed the topic and spoke to her about the boiler.

The heavy burden in her heart gone, she was rather amused by the thought that the young man did not know she was Assistant Manager Yuan's daughter. So she said to him gently, "Don't worry! Leave everything to me!"

"Leave it to you? Are you sure? I heard that Assistant Manager Yuan is rather difficult to approach. Does your father know him well?"

Annoyed and amused at the same time, Yuan Xia replied, "I've told you to leave it to me. What more do you want?"

Ke Ting added, "Well, if an arrangement can be worked out, I'll bring you a letter of introduction."

"Don't be so fussy! Let's talk about something else!" Yuan Xia stopped him. She felt that it was spoiling their fun being together, all that talk about the boiler.

IV

After he entered the living quarters of the New Waterworks, Ke Ting suddenly saw the desired boiler lying in the corner. He took out his steel tape to take its measurements. Yuan Xia, however, was getting impatient and said, "Even if the boiler is exactly what you need, you don't know if they're going to give it to you." Ke Ting then hastily followed her into one of the apartment blocks.

They reached the second unit, and went up to the second floor. Ke Ting, however, was oblivious of his surroundings. He was still trying to calculate in his mind the volume of steam the boiler could produce. Yuan Xia pushed open the door, grinned mischievously and announced, "This is Assistant Manager Yuan's home." This Ke Ting had not expected at all. His heart sank and he asked doubtfully, "Didn't you say that we should talk it over with your father first?" The oval-faced girl gave an equivocal reply in the manner of an experienced actress, "It's all the same."

Inside the small drawing-room three or four people were shrouded in dense cigarette smoke. They looked up and stared at Yuan Xia and Ke Ting. Tightly knitting her eyebrows, Yuan Xia fanned off the smoke with her hand, exclaiming, "Abominable!" She was tired of all these uninvited guests who frequently came to her home. A middle-aged guest was about to leave. He said, "Manager Yuan, I'll do as you've just suggested. When the time comes, I hope you will personally put in a good word for me." The two others also rose and said, "Manager Yuan, without you help, our problem can never be solved. We may have to come back and trouble you again." By now, Ke Ting had already taken a good look at Assistant Manager Yuan. He was a small man, not even of medium height, but his bald-head and shining forehead somehow gave him a certain dignity.

After all the guests had left, Yuan Xia said to Ke Ting, "Why don't you stay here and make yourself at home? I've something else to attend to for the moment, but I'll be back very soon." Then she closed the door and went out.

Now that Yuan Xia was gone, Ke Ting felt even more uneasy. He didn't know what trick the girl was playing on him. Was it because Assistant Manager Yuan was such a difficult man to talk to that she had deliberately left after the first introduction?

"Assistant Manager Yuan — Manager Yuan, I'm sorry to trouble you. . . ."

"No trouble at all! Do sit down, and let's talk it over."

Assistant Manager Yuan took the tall young man seriously. He smiled faintly and asked Ke Ting to sit down on the rattan chair beside the tea-table and gave him a cup of tea. Ke Ting felt that the manager was not so unapproachable as people said. Manager Yuan leaned against the desk in front of the window and sat back. He began chatting with the young man.

"You and Yuan Xia have known each other for a long time. Right?"

"No, we didn't know each other before."

"Well, how did you become acquainted?" Manager Yuan saw that the young man was clearly eligible as far as his height was concerned.

Ke Ting replied shyly and respectfully, "It was by chance."

The manager did not probe further. He picked up a small bottle on the desk, took out some pills and swallowed them with a little water. Then he ran his fingers through his sparse hair and said kindly, "You didn't know each other before, I see, but you are going to see more of each other from now on, and understand each other better, eh?"

Ke Ting felt something was wrong; he flushed and his heart was beating fast. He recalled that when they were talking about the boiler on their way here, the girl had insisted several times, "Leave it to me!" And on entering the house she was completely at ease, as if it were her own home. Could she be the daughter of Assistant Manager Yuan? Well, she certainly had the same surname. But when he looked at the dwarfish manager, he was again in doubt and could not be sure. However, he hoped that genetics might have played tricks in the present instance and the problem of getting the boiler would be solved. What luck if Yuan Xia turned out to be the daughter of Assistant Manager Yuan!

Nevertheless, the young man held on to his views regarding heredity. He turned the subject of their talk to the business he had in mind. "Manager Yuan," he said, "it is this. Our factory wants a boiler . . . the one in your courtyard. I've seen the brand and measured its size. It's exactly what we need. Yuan Xia brought me here. Will you please help us by giving your consent?"

That had done it! Till then Assistant Manager Yuan had been dreaming of being a future father-in-law, but now he had to resume the status of manager. He was disgusted. "About that boiler again!" And he kept silent for a long while.

Ke Ting begged again, "Our small factory needs your help, Manager Yuan."

After a long pause the manager asked, "What does your factory produce?"

"Our first product is called 'anti-aging tincture',"

" 'Anti-aging . . . tincture'? Ah! So you're making this! Is it really as good as it says?" The manager got interested, as he toyed with the bottle of pills on his desk.

"It's not bad. Customers in other cities and the armed forces have placed orders with us."

"Oh! That's proof enough. But I don't believe it can really prevent aging. I don't think it's really all that effective."

"It's been tested and approved by the chemical research institute. Besides, our customers are also satisfied."

The manager took up the bottle from the desk, and asked, "How does it compare with these life-prolonging pills?"

"That's something completely different," Ke Ting replied.

The manager laughed heartily, tilting his head backwards and resting his weight on the two rear legs of his chair. He said, "I think they're all the same, really. I've taken many bottles of these life-prolonging pills produced by Yuan Xia's pharmaceutical factory, yet I'm still going bald!" Then, as if to prove his point, he again ran his fingers through his hair backwards. " 'Life-prolonging pills', 'anti-aging tincture', they're lovely names, all right. They won't do you any harm. Don't you agree?"

After a little while, the manager sat up and both his head and the legs of the chair resumed their normal position. He said candidly, "Now here's what we'll do. You go back and talk it over with your Party secretary and factory director to see whether you can provide us with some of your product; then I can discuss your request with our other heads."

It suddenly dawned on Ke Ting that the manager had mistaken the prevention of the aging of rubber for a tonic which would prolong life. He wanted to laugh, but he dared not. He thought that if he told him the truth it would make the manager look a fool. So he could only say tactfully, "So far we haven't sold it to any private customers, because its price is too high. Moreover, it can't. . . ."

Manager Yuan, irritated by his roundabout reply, frowned and said, "Yes, nowadays we all do everything according to the rules. Which factory is yours?"

"The Spark Chemical Factory of Wuchang District," the young man replied.

The manager queried, knitting his brows, "Has Wuchang District such a factory?"

Ke Ting replied, "Its full name is 'The Spark Chemical Factory of Lion Street, Wuchang District'."

"Oh, I see, a street-operated factory!" The manager didn't bother to hide his contempt. "Now, we must act according to the rules. I'm not the only one in charge here, so it's not just what I say that counts. . . . Isn't that right? Moreover, we may still need that boiler ourselves. . . . Anything else?"

This sounded like the end of their discussion. Ke Ting at once felt chilled all over; he shivered as if he had caught malaria. Humiliated, he thought that he shouldn't have attempted to play the hero for his factory.

"Young man, you need experience. Perhaps you haven't often been out on business before. From now on, when you try to make contacts, you must bring a letter of introduction." The manager stood up, with a forced smile on his face.

This short man with his bald head! Ignorant! Foolish! Greedy! Snobbish! Ke Ting almost spat the words out. He was nursing his anger: a street-operated factory. . . . So what? Haven't street-operated factories created millions of dollars' worth of wealth for the country without any financial backing from the government? In truth, he himself at first had also been prejudiced against them. After work, he studied for the college entrance examinations and begged Secretary Wan to give him a chance. To him that was the only way to get out of the street-operated factory. Secretary Wan, however, said to him, "Our old master-workers have treated you well nursing you as old birds would nurse the young. Now your wings are strong and you want to fly away. Don't you feel sad at all leaving us?" With a sigh she continued, "Of course, if you insist, I couldn't stop you even if I wanted to. It would be selfish to consider only our interests and not those of the country as a whole. In short, I wouldn't do anything to harm your future. But I hope you'll wait until I've found someone to replace you." The young man's heart was softened; he wept, touched by her passionate words. Emotions and his personal future were in conflict, and eventually the former won. He could not let down the old masters and Secretary Wan. He felt sorry for his leaders. Secretary Wan should have been at home taking care of her grandson, but instead she was up at half past four every morning, and had to take three buses from north to south to get to work. Why was she working so hard? As for the sixty-five-year-old factory director, he had to ride on a ramshackle bike a hundred-odd li back and forth each day. Why was he so hard on himself? Having seen Manager Yuan and, comparing him with Secretary Wan and his factory director, Ke Ting appreciated their dedication all the more. Their stature grew all at once taller than ever before in his mind. They were so good, so kind to their workers!

Ke Ting stood up as if he himself, too had become taller. In this small room he had learned a great deal, only to value his integrity the more. He wanted to ask, "Mr. Manager! Is that boiler your private property, or is it the property of the People's Republic of China?"

Ke Ting looked at the manager in disgust and said, emphasizing each word as he uttered, "Thank you, manager, for your instructions!" Then he left.

He went down the stairs hastily. He was about to unlock his bicycle when someone grasped his hand. He turned round and found a woman carrying a basket of food.

"Hey! Why are you running away?"

Ke Ting was baffled.

"Look, I've just bought some food for you. When Yuan Xia told me you're here, I ran to the market as quickly as I could. Don't go yet; she'll be back very soon. She's been gone such a long time! Why don't you go up and wait a little longer with her father?"

In this tall, warm-hearted, frank woman, Ke Ting could easily recognize Yuan Xia. But he had been insulted, so he thought that the three of them were all the same; they were all making a fool of him. He replied glibly, "No, I haven't brought the thing required."

Not knowing what he was trying to say, Mrs. Yuan asked hurriedly, "What do you mean? What is it that you need to bring with you? I'm happy you've come just as you are. You haven't had a bite and now you want to go. That won't do! Yuan Xia will blame me when she comes back. If you hadn't kindly helped her repair her bike that evening, I really don't know what would have happened to her."

Ke Ting, however, freed himself from the grip of her hand, saying, "I'm too young and don't know anything. I didn't bring a letter of introduction!" He got on his bike and rode away.

Mrs. Yuan gazed at his back, not quite knowing how she felt. He struck her as a decent young man. The old man must have said something which had upset him! A letter of introduction! Nonsense! Such airs! Did he know what he was talking about? . . .

V

Yuan Xia was serious — she went straight to Li Lu's home without having first called her on the phone. Having learned that her "man" turned up, Li Lu was most curious to meet him. She grabbed her bike and hurried off with Yuan Xia.

The two "phoenixes" flew side by side; the two girls were talking and laughing merrily, leaving the street lights, trees, pedestrians and streams of traffic quickly behind them. It seemed that they were the tallest and happiest girls in the whole world. Good fortune was beckoning them on.

As usual, Li Lu gave a warning signal before she entered the flat. She shouted, "Uncle Yuan, Aunty Yuan, it's me again. Am I welcome?"

However, no one came out to welcome her, so she went in quietly. Oh, no! The small drawing-room had the look of a battleground. Uncle Yuan was, obviously, the wounded captive, bending awkwardly over the desk. Aunty Yuan was standing before him in full glory of victory.

"Where's the young man? Gone?"

Aunty said angrily, "Ask him!"

The manager begged for mercy. "He has helped us, so of course I'm going to help him! What more do you want me to do?"

Mrs. Yuan, seeing that reinforcements had arrived, launched at once a greater attack, "I don't care about your boiler, what I want now is that young man!"

Her husband pleaded, "Where can I find him now? Tomorrow you can ring up his street-operated factory and say that I've agreed."

Upon hearing the words "street-operated", Li Lu's heart sank. She wanted to ask Yuan Xia privately about it. She therefore tried her best to persuade Mrs. Yuan to go and prepare the meal. The old woman, however, was not so easily pacified. Taking Li Lu by the hand, she harangued the old man for his insensitivity as well as his disgusting airs. How could he have asked the young man for a letter of introduction? She declared she was not going to cook for him. She would rather "let the old devil starve to death". At this juncture, fearing that any further quarrelling might upset Li Lu, the manager decided to keep silent and admit defeat. Of the three, he was the shortest and the most unfortunate. But his wife did not stop giving him a long lecture until she was exhausted.

As soon as she entered Yuan Xia's room, Li Lu asked, "Tell me. Is he from a street-operated factory?"

Yuan Xia answered reprovingly, "What's wrong with that? Does it mean we think the less of him simply because he is a worker in a street-operated factory? A second-class citizen?"

Li Lu said, "No! Of course not. Don't get mad at me! I only fear that your parents may have objections."

Of course, Yuan Xia was not venting her anger upon Li Lu. Neither did she think it necessary to explain everything to her good friend. She said, "With his iron rice-bowl in his hand, my dear father has long forgotten the broken basket he once used when begging for food in the past. Indeed, if he had any respect for street-operated factories at all, he wouldn't have pulled every string to get my mother transferred to a state-run factory. So, whenever I hear others criticize bureaucracy and the privileges of high-ranking officials, I always feel both glad and sad at the same time. Sad because I've been deprived of my right to make such criticisms!"

Then Yuan Xia went on to make her stand clear to Li Lu. She held that if a man had a good character, there was no need to worry about his lack of status. Li Lu, out of concern, wanted to know more about the Spark Factory. Yuan Xia told her all she knew and what Ke Ting had explained to her. She said that the ferric chloride produced by the Spark Factory was needed by the Wuhan Steel and Iron Company in a big project. A specialist from West Germany had once suggested if they couldn't produce it, they could import it from his country. But, somehow, this small street-operated factory finally succeeded in producing it. Li Lu, finding Yuan Xia so passionate, could no longer remain indifferent. The two girls quickly agreed that he was the right man. They worked out a plan for action at once.

VI

The next morning, Yuan Xia and Li Lu arrived very early at the Spark Chemical Factory. There was really nothing much to be said of its appearance. Of course, if you looked at it from another viewpoint, bearing in mind that they had been struggling against numerous difficulties, it would appear quite different. Standing before the gate of the factory, Li Lu could see everything at a glance. She remembered the numerous products, including the ferric chloride needed by the modern steel plant that Yuan Xia had told her about the night before. Now, having seen with her own eyes the practical condition of this small factory, she couldn't help exclaiming in admiration, "Who would have thought it could do so much!"

"He's coming," Yuan Xia whispered.

Li Lu looked up. The young man was pushing his bicycle up the road in front of the factory. He was good-looking and tall. Her first impression was quite favourable; he wasn't in any way inferior to her own boyfriend. Then, came another exclamation of hers, "Who would have thought it possible!" She admired Yuan Xia's choice. Her round face became even rounder. She quietly urged Yuan Xia, "Be more assertive, more encouraging and more enthusiastic."

Her three suggestions did not seem very effective, though. Yuan Xia had come to apologize, and also she had something on her mind. She usually carried herself with ease and confidence, but now she had become rather tense.

Ke Ting had also changed. After his baptism of fire in Manager Yuan's small drawing-room, he now appeared cool, his eyes steady, and behaved like a crusader determined to fight against all evil. He was surprised to see Yuan Xia. Why had she come here, and what's more, with a companion? He racked his brains to search for the most sarcastic words and the most offensive phrases to irritate both of them. He was going to ask her where on earth she could find the time to come here. What were her instructions for him now? If she wanted to purchase some anti-aging tincture so that her respectable father could prolong his life, he would be only too happy to comply with her wishes.

"You've come very early," Yuan Xia went forward to greet him.

"You . . . you are earlier than me," Ke Ting stuttered. He was not used to fighting verbal battles. Moreover, he did not have the heart to ruffle the calmness reflected in her beauty and shyness. All the harsh and offensive words he had prepared in his mind at once vanished.

Silence and deadlock followed. In international discussions, it is not unusual to have a long lapse of time, say a few years, as a result of the postponement of further meetings. But on an occasion like this, the silence of even a few seconds could increase the tension. Silence was now more terrible than open war.

Secretary Wan came out, chewing half of a fried dough cake. She called when she was still some distance away, "Young Ke, have you got that boiler?"

"They want a letter of introduction!" Ke Ting replied. That remark was aimed at Yuan Xia of course.

"If you have already made arrangements, writing a letter of introduction won't cause me any trouble." Secretary Wan, not aware of the circumstances, was pleased. On coming nearer, she asked with great admiration, "Who are these two girls?"

Li Lu quickly said, "Assistant Manager Yuan told us to come here. Yesterday, after Comrade Ke left, Assistant Manager Yuan said, 'Don't let him waste time coming back and forth again. We are all very busy with our work for the four modernizations.' So he personally wrote an order and told us to bring it here as soon as possible."

Yuan Xia very much admired Li Lu's ability to gloss over her father's faults. She did not know what to say. The fact was, the girls were afraid that the matter would not be dealt with at once, and that the boiler might be assigned elsewhere. Li Lu also wanted to see Yuan Xia's young man herself so that she could better play the role of her friend's personal adviser.

So, the two of them had forced Assistant Manager Yuan to write the order himself!

Secretary Wan was full of gratitude. She wanted to invite the two girls to come in for a chat in her office, but was afraid that her oily hand might spoil their clothes. Li Lu, however, said she didn't mind and she followed her to her office. She told the secretary something about what had happened. At the same time, she learned from the secretary some particulars about Ke Ting. The secretary was so pleased that she gazed at Yuan Xia outside for a long time with her smiling eyes. Among their girl workers, some had married young workers of Third Pharmaceutical Factory. Now, such a pretty young girl worker of that pharmaceutical factory, and moreover, the daughter of Manager Yuan, had come over herself to their street-run factory! This would certainly add prestige to its secretary too! She felt grateful to Assistant Manager Yuan for his generosity: he had not only given her factory a boiler, but had added a pretty young daughter in the bargain! "Don't look down upon our small street-run foctory; even Assistant Manager Yuan himself has a good opinion of us!" she thought to herself with a sigh of satisfaction.

Yuan Xia sincerely apologized to Ke Ting. But Ke Ting was still in a bad mood. He didn't say anything. Then the steel "bell" sounded again and he had to go on shift. Yuan Xia did not know whether or not he had forgiven her.

That same evening, on the embankment of the South Lake, on the same spot where Ke Ting had repaired her "Phoenix 18" bicycle, Yuan Xia was waiting. She saw many bicycles pass quickly by. She wondered, looking a little melancholy, "Will the moon be enchanting tonight? Will Ke Ting turn up as he promised? Or, will he avoid her by taking a roundabout route home? He ought to see the difference between her and her father. . . ."

Translated by Zheng Aifang
Illustrated by Zhao Ruichun

WANG ZENGQI

(1920 —   )

Wang Zengqi, born in 1920 in Gaoyou County, Jiangsu Province, taught in a middle school after graduating from the Department of Chinese Literature of the Southwest China United University in 1943. He joined the Southward Drive Task Force in 1949. Later he went north to work as an editor, first at the Beijing Federation of Literary and Art Circles, and then at the Folk Literature and Art Research Institute in Beijing, until he was sent to the countryside in the vicinity of Zhangjiakou in 1957. Since 1962, he has been a playwright with the Beijing Opera Troupe of Beijing. He became a member of the Union of Chinese Dramatists in 1980.

He began publishing short stories in 1940, and his first collection of short stories appeared under the title of *An Unexpected Encounter and Other Stories* in 1948. His other publications include *Night in the Sheepfold and Other Stories* (1963), Beijing Opera librettos *Fan Jin Passes the Civil Examination in His Old Age* and *Shajiabang* (during the 50's and 70's) and *Short Stories of Wang Zengqi* (1981), which is a collection of his short stories written since 1979.

A TALE OF BIG NUR

Wang Zengqi

It is an odd name for a place, Big Nur, and very few people in the county know what it means. Indeed, it is a strange name, not to be found anywhere in the region. Some people say it is of Mongolian origin, perhaps dated back to the Yuan Dynasty (1271-1368). However, it cannot be ascertained whether the place had a name then or what people called it before that time.

A *nur* is a large expanse of water, not as broad as a lake but much broader than a pond. Big Nur looks limitless when it is swollen high in spring and summer. The source of two rivers, it has a narrow sandbank in the centre covered with cogongrass and reeds. In early spring when the water gets warmer, the purplish red shoots of the reeds and the greyish green wormwood on the sandbank soon turn emerald. In summer, the snow-white ears of the cogongrass and the reeds sway in the breeze. When they turn yellow in autumn, they are cut and used for thatch. The sandbank is always the first to turn white when it snows in winter and the last to thaw. The snow remains there glittering, while the ice melts into blue waters in the river.

The sandbank forms the watershed between the two rivers that rise in Big Nur. Going northward in a boat along its western side in the old days, one could see a cluster of buildings amidst clumps of willows on a small mound by the *nur*. Through the green willow branches could be seen, on a whitewashed wall, four conspicuous words in black painting: "Chicken and Duckling Breeders". In front was a small clearing, which was characteristic of all breeders, where some people sat on tree stumps chatting in the sun. Now and then someone would come out carrying two bamboo baskets, covered with nets, full of cheeping yellow fluffy chicks and ducklings.

East of the sandbank was a shop which made and sold starch. People liked to have their clothes and the covers of their quilts starched, because it made them feel fresh and clean. Made from Gorgon fruit by grinding, dissolving, caking and drying, starch was very cheap. A few copper coins would be enough for the starching of a whole tub of clothes and quilt covers. But, being the only supplier of starch throughout the county, this shop was by no means a small one, and it had four or five workers as well as two donkeys which drove the mill by turns. Outside the shop dazzling white lumps of starch were dried in the sun. Close to the shop was a store selling whatever they could get from the river such as water chestnuts, arrowheads, water caltrops and lotus roots. There was a fish market collecting and distributing fish and crabs, and also a depot for the purchase of grass. Beyond these were fields, cattle sheds and waterwheels. Big pats of cow dung were neatly pasted on cottages' walls to dry — to be used as fuel. It was a truly rural scene. To the north were the villages in Beixiang, while to the east the neighbouring county of Xinghua could be reached by passing through Yigou, Ergou and Sandou.

On the southern shore of Big Nur stood a green wooden house, formerly the office of a boat company. It had a waiting room at one side, and at the waterside was a quay. A small steamer had plied between this spot and Xinghua, leaving on odd-numbered days and returning on even-numbered days. Brightly painted and hung with colourful bunting, the boat had been a thrilling sight with its chugging engine and black smoke coming out of its funnel. This had once been a place seething with activity, with porters loading and unloading goods, passengers embarking or disembarking, pedlars selling beef, sorghum liquor, peanuts, melon seeds and candy covered with sesame seeds. After some heavy losses, however, the shareholders sold the boat and closed down the company, but the wooden build-

ing remained intact. It was empty now. Only some mischievous boys living in the vicinity played in the waiting room,
imitating acrobatic fighting in Chinese operas, or competed
with each other in peeing from the quay. Standing seven or
eight in a row, they pissed into the water to see who could
reach the farthest.

Big Nur was also the name of the land around the water,
where the town and the countryside met. There was a long
alley south of the wooden house of the boat company leading
to a street outside the north gate of the town. Big Nur was
so close to the town that even the hubbub of the town was faintly audible, but they were as different as chalk from cheese.
Without a single shop, Big Nur had its own colours, noises and
odours. Even the residents were different. Their lives,
customs and morals were unlike those of the town dwellers,
who wore long gowns and studied the Confucian classics.

II

Not far to the east and west of the boat company were two
small settlements, which were dissimilar in life style and
custom.

The one to the west was formed by some scattered low
houses with tiled roofs. Most of the inhabitants were pedlars
from places along the Lixia River. They sold radishes, dried
water chestnuts, Chinese hawthorns and boiled lotus roots with
their holes filled with glutinous rice. One man from Baoying
sold spectacles while another from Hangzhou sold bamboo
chopsticks. Like migrating birds, they would come regularly,
and renting a room from an acquaintance, stay for a period of
time, some longer, some shorter, and then they would leave
after they had sold their goods. They began business at sunrise and stopped work after sunset. After breakfast they went
out carrying their wares on their backs, on their shoulders, on
their arms or in their hands, hawking and crying out for
customers in a variety of accents and chants. At dusk, they

returned like birds to their nests. Before long smoke from damp fuel, a sweet yet pungent odour wafted through the eaves. They were merely hawkers who tried to make a little bit of money. Away from their native places, they did their best to be amiable and patient. Their settlement was always peaceful, and seldom had there been any bickering or scuffle.

Among the residents were also some twenty tinsmiths from Xinghua. Tin articles were widely used in this area, and every household had tin incense burners, candlesticks, spittoons, canisters, kettles, teapots and wine pots. Even chamberpots were made of tin. When marrying off a daughter, the parents would give her tin utensils for her dowry: at least two big tin containers which could hold four to five kilos of rice to put on top of a chest. When a woman gave birth to a baby, her parents would traditionally provide as presents, apart from two hens and one hundred eggs, two pots of glutinous rice porridge in the tin containers from her mother's chest. So even twenty tinsmiths could do very good business.

The work of a tinsmith did not require great skill; and their tools were simple: a shoulder pole with a bellow and some tin plates on one end, and on the other end, a charcoal stove and two bricks two feet square with several layers of paper pasted on one side. Tin articles were forged instead of being cast into shape directly. The material — some wornout tin utensils to be made over — was usually provided by the customers. A tinsmith usually set his load on the porch of a customer's house or on the open ground by the roadside. There he worked the bellows, put the old tin in to melt in the pot, while he placed the two bricks side by side with the papered sides facing each other and between them a rope coiled roughly in the needed shape. Then he poured the liquid in between the two bricks to press it into a plate, which he cut with a pair of metal shears and then beat with a wooden mallet on his anvil. As tin is very malleable, to make tin articles is not so difficult as it is to make copper ones, nor is it as noisy. In about the time it takes to eat a meal, the article would be hammered into shape ready to be handed over to the customer for use. If it needed to be given a proper finish, he would scrape it, polish it with sandpaper and finally rub it with a certain kind of grass till it shone.

These tinsmiths were very loyal and helpful to each other; they looked after their sick companions and never competed for customers. If they went into partnership, they made a point of sharing the profits fairly. Their leader was an old man whom they all obeyed. An upright man, he was very strict with all the other tinsmiths, who were either his juniors or his apprentices. He forbade them to gamble, drink or fool around with women and he wanted them to be honest and not to cheat. He insisted that they should never make trouble, nor should they be cowardly in face of bullying. Except when on business, they were not allowed to wander about the streets.

The old tinsmith was good at Chinese boxing and taught the others martial arts. He kept several rods and three-section cudgels in his room. When they were not at work, he would take them out to practise in pairs, claiming this was a good way of passing the time as well as useful for self-defence. For amusement, they also sang famous local operas. Whenever it rained and they could not go out, they would sing all day — sometimes even putting on make-up and stage costumes. Although the tunes were simple, the stories were interesting. Girls and women nearby would crowd round to watch and listen.

One of the apprentices was the old tinsmith's nephew, whose pet name was Eleventh Boy, as he was the eleventh child in his family. He was usually known as the Young Tinsmith. Very intelligent and handsome, he was a worry to his uncle. Tall, broad-shouldered, with a slender waist, he was well proportioned. Beneath his bushy brows shone a pair of large eyes. He wore a straw hat, with neat, well-fitting clothes and black shoes. In hot weather, he unbuttoned his shirt, revealing his broad chest and his spotless white cummerbund, five inches wide, wound tightly round his waist. He walked with a spring in his step. Such a fine young man was as rare in a group of tinsmiths as a phoenix in a chicken coop. The old tinsmith was well aware that when the girls and women gathered to hear them sing, they had really come to admire his nephew.

He constantly warned Eleventh Boy to keep away from the local women and girls, especially those living at the east end. "They're different from us," the old man told him.

III

To the east of the boat company were houses with adobe walls and thatched roofs. Some fragments of jars were placed at each end of most roofs to keep the thatch from being blown off. The residents there had been porters for generations. Men and women, old and young, with strong shoulders, which they indeed needed to make a living.

They mostly carried rice from the boats which landed at Big Nur. The rice was then taken away by these porters to the rice shops or the granaries of rich families, or to other big boats, moored at Loquat Sluice outside the south gate of the town, to be transported along the canal to other places. Sometimes they had to carry their loads to wharfs as far away as Cheluo or Mapeng Bay, about one to three miles away. Without stopping for a rest, they walked with quick, even steps, singing all the way. In a line of ten or twenty, each carried a load weighing at least one hundred and fifty catties. They shifted their loads from shoulder to shoulder in unison following the move of the man at the front. For each load they were given a bamboo tag, one and a half feet long and one inch wide, with one end painted red, the other white. At dusk they were paid according to the number of tags they had accumulated.

Apart from rice they also carried bricks, tiles, lime, bamboo poles, tung oil. . . . They had work to do all year round and never went hungry.

When their children were about thirteen or fourteen, they began carrying half a load in two willow baskets. After one or two years, they were strong enough to bear the whole load and earned as much as the adults.

The porters led a very simple life: earning their living by their strength, eating three meals of rice a day cooked on the top of an earthenware jar which had a hole in its side, for they had no real stove. No money was spent on fuel because villagers carrying reeds to sell at the market always dropped some on the road and the children, too young to work as porters, would collect these with a bamboo rake. They were nicknamed "Raking Devils". Sometimes to save themselves a lot of trouble, they simply snatched a bundle of reeds from a villager and took to their heels. By the time the villager had laid down his load and shouted his curses, they were nowhere to be seen. Since there was no proper outlet in the jar for the smoke when they were cooking, it would come out from wherever it could. Then it poured out from the windows or doors, drifting to the surface of Big Nur and lingering there. These households never stored grain. They bought enough food only for each day. The rice they ate was unpolished. At meal times the men squatted outside their homes, holding big bowls of rice with vegetables, small fish, preserved bean-curd or pickled hot peppers. They wolfed down their food with such relish that nothing in the world seemed more appetizing.

They celebrated New Year's Day and other festivals by changing into clean clothes, feasting and gambling. Each gambler put ten or twenty coins on the ground which were all piled into a high stack. Then they threw in turn another coin at the stake, and picked up as their gains the coins that fell down. Another game was rolling the coins. A brick was propped up at one end to form a slope and piles of coins were placed on the ground. The gambler rolled a coin down the brick. If it stopped at a spot five inches from a pile, he could take the money; if seven inches, he had to forfeit the same amount as the stack. The porters enjoyed themselves, while onlookers cheered loudly, adding to the fun.

The girls and women were as strong as the men. They were

able to carry as much as the men, walking just as fast. They concentrated on carrying fresh water products, perhaps because the men considered it beneath their dignity to carry dripping loads. They had slender figures and put pomade on their thick black hair, so that it was "too sleek for flies to rest on", as the local folk would say. The buns at the back of their heads were large and tied with red wool visible from far away. At one side of their buns they liked to wear a decoration. At the Qingming Festival it would be a willow ball which they made by picking a small willow twig, putting one end between their lips and rolling the bark down towards the other end to form the ball; at the Dragon Boat Festival it would be some mugwort leaves. At other times it would be a gardenia or an oleander in season, or a big red velvet flower when they could not get a fresh one. Because they carried their loads with a shoulder pole all the year round, nearly all the shoulders of their blouses were patched. An old blouse, with new patches in different colours, was the distinctive dress of the women at Big Nur. What a wonderful sight to see twenty women walking in a single file, like willow branches swaying in the wind, while carrying loads of purple water chestnuts, green water caltrops and snow-white lotus roots!

The women earned as much as the men and like the men they walked with great strides and sat with their legs wide apart. They also wore straw sandals as the men did, but they dyed their toenails red with garden balsam. There were no taboo words for them. They talked and cursed like men, using the same obscene language as the men used. They even sang the same rude songs. . . .

Unmarried women were more reticent, but once married they behaved as boorishly as they liked. There was an old bachelor called Huang Hailong, who had been a porter when young. Later he hurt his leg and was assigned to the wharf to look after the rice boats and collect the bamboo tags. Old as he was, he loved to touch this woman's breast or pinch that one's bottom. According to his seniority in the clan, the women ought to address him politely as grand-uncle, but all of them called him "Dirty Old Beard". One day before he played his old tricks again, several women had made a plan. Following a signal, they took immediate action and in the twinkling of an eye, the old man's trousers were thrown onto a tree-top. Another time, when the old man heard the bamboo clappers for selling noodles with dumplings, he got some fancy ideas again.

"Who dare take a bath in the *nur*?" he challenged. "I bet you each two bowls of noodles with dumplings that you daren't!"

"Really?"

"Sure!"

"OK!"

The women stripped and slashed in the water. A moment later, climbing ashore they cried, "Boil the noodles!"

People here seldom married in the customary way, so sedan carriers and trumpeters could hardly earn any money from them. Women came to the men of their own accord; the girls generally chose their spouses themselves. They were rather casual in their sexual relations and it was nothing strange about a girl giving birth to an illegitimate child at her mother's home. A married woman could have a lover, if she wanted to. How a woman got along with a man depended solely on whether she liked him or not. Most girls or women who fell in love with a man would naturally ask him for money to spend. But some not only did not want their lovers' money, they gave them money instead.

The townsfolk looked down on their morals and manners, but were theirs any better? It was difficult to say.

IV

At the east end of Big Nur, there was a household of only two members — a father and his daughter. Huang Haijiao, the father, was Huang Hailong's cousin. He had been a fine porter, capable of going up steep gang-planks with his load.

The grain bins of the big grain shops here were thirty to forty feet high with the planks sloping very steeply. One had to ascend them at one go. Whenever an older man or a woman hesitated at the foot, Huang would take their hundred-and-fifty-catty load and shoot to the top like an arrow. Raising his hands, he would pour the two baskets of rice into the bin and then stride down with only a few steps to the ground. Honest and simple, he did not get married until he was twenty-five. That year, when he carried grain to Cheluo, he met a girl who asked him the way. She had a long fringe and a bun in the popular Suzhou style on the back of her head, and wore a little rouge on her face. She was so flurried and anxious that she could not give the exact name of any place. Huang saw at a glance that she was a maid-servant running away from some rich and influential family. He talked with her for a while, and finally she agreed to live with him. She called herself Lianzi, a common name for maid-servants in the region.

A year later she gave birth to a girl. It was July. When the child was born, the sky was filled with rosy clouds, so they named her July Cloud.

Lianzi was deft and hard-working, but she liked to wear silk trousers, eat melon seeds and nibble between meals. She also liked singing ballads such as "The cold moon rises and sheds light on my chamber. Giving a yawn, I stretch myself and feel sleepy. Aiyo, aiyo, I'm sleepy...." All this was quite different from the local customs.

When July Cloud was three years old, Lianzi eloped with an actor in a theatrical troupe which was passing through the village. That day Huang had gone to Mapeng Bay. Lianzi washed and starched all her husband's clothes, gathered together her daughter's, cooked a pot of rice and purchased half a catty of wine for her husband. Saying that she had something to do, she entrusted the little girl to her neighbour. She locked the door, went away, and was never seen again.

Huang did not feel too sad, however, for things like that were not unusual. Even a caged bird sometimes flies away. But he adored the little creature she had left behind. Unwilling to see the child suffer at the hands of a cruel stepmother, he was determined not to marry again. Shouldering the responsibilities of both father and mother, he brought her up by himself. He taught her how to make fishing nets and weave reed mats when she was fourteen, because he did not want to see her working as a porter.

At fifteen she was as beautiful as a flower, her figure and face just like her mother's. Her face had an oval shape with long dark eyebrows and a dimple in one cheek. The corners of her eyes tilted slightly upwards and their long lashes made them look narrow. But when she suddenly looked round, they opened wide with a somewhat surprised and absorbed expression. When she made a net or wove a mat by the waterside, some youths would hang around, pretending to be busy with some jobs about the place. If she went to the market to buy meat, vegetables, oil, wine, washing soda, starch, cloth or cosmetics, she would be given better-quality or better-measure stuff than others for the same price. The women caught on to this, and asked her to purchase things for them. Whenever she went to the market, she had to carry several bamboo baskets and returned home with aching arms. If there was a theatrical performance in front of the Taishan Temple, people had to carry a bench or a stool to sit on, but not July Cloud. She went there empty-handed and was always offered a good seat. Few people applauded the wonderful performance, because most of them had their eyes fixed on her.

Soon she reached sixteen, the age at which she should consider marriage. But who would win such a beauty? The eldest son of the owner of the chicken and duckling breeders? The second son of the starch shop owner? Or the third son of the fresh water food shop owner? Both Huang and his daughter knew they desired it; otherwise what was the point of hanging around July Cloud all the time? But the girl did not take them seriously.

At the age of seventeen, July Cloud's life had a sudden change for the worse. Her father fell from a plank thirty feet high when he was carrying a heavy load up to the top of a bin, and injured his spine. At first he did not think it was serious. But the large quantities of medicinal wine and plasters did not produce the desired result. Eventually he was even paralysed from below the waist. Sometimes he got up from his bed and, taking hold of a high stool, shuffled some steps forward. Most of the time, he lay propped up against a pile of quilts in bed. He could no longer earn money to buy his daughter new clothes or velvet flowers. Instead, he had to depend on her to support him. Though still under fifty, he could do some light work, such as preparing bundles of string for his daughter to make nets. The girl would not abandon her poor invalid father. If anybody was willing to marry her, he must live with her and provide for the sick man. Who was prepared to do that? The only property they had was their thatched three-roomed house. The girl and her father each occupied a side room. The one in the middle was a small hall. The eldest son, the second son and the third son came from time to time, glancing at the slender figure behind the fishing net or sitting on the snowwhite mat. Their eyes were still filled with admiration, but their enthusiasm was dampened.

In spite of the old tinsmith's warning, Eleventh Boy still went to the east side of the *nur* frequently. Middle-aged women, young married women and girls liked to call him over there to repair their old tin kettles. On the way from Big Nur to town, there was a shady spot under the willows in front of July Cloud's house, a nice place to seek customers. While she wove mats, he melted tin, keeping each other company. Sometimes July Cloud stopped to help the young tinsmith work his bellows. When she went indoors to check on her father to see if he wanted to have a smoke or a drink of water, Eleventh Boy would cover the stove and take her place weaving. Once, when her finger was cut by a sharp reed, he sucked the wound for her. Through their exchanges she knew that he had no sisters or brothers and that his mother had been a widow for many years, doing needlework for others, straining her eyes. Eleventh Boy feared she would become blind some day. . . .

Kind people who saw them together would think that they were an ideal pair, but how could they marry? The girl's father needed a son-in-law to support him, while the boy's mother needed a daughter-in-law to look after her — how could the young couple satisfy both sides? As for the two, they loved to sit side by side talking. They were old enough to fall in love, and there were some tender feelings between them, but nothing seemed definite; everything was just like the clouds floating back and forth in the sky, unable to form rain.

One moonlit night July Cloud went to wash some clothes on a boat. As she crouched down on the bow to rinse a jacket, a naughty audacious boy crept stealthily up and tickled her from behind. Caught off her guard, she fell into the water. She could swim a little, but since she was scared and the current swift, she struggled, and then shouted for help. After swallowing a lot of water, she was washed away by the current. It happened that Eleventh Boy was practising Chinese boxing on the level ground outside the chicken and duckling breeders. He saw someone being carried along, her hair floating on the surface of the water. Quickly throwing off his shoes, he jumped into the *nur* and rescued her.

He managed to make her cough up the water she had swallowed but she was still unconscious. He had no choice but to lift her in his arms and carry her home. She was dripping wet, but soft and warm. His heart throbbed as he felt her body nestling closer and closer to him.

In her room she came to. (She had in fact been conscious long before.) He lay her on the bed. The moonlight shone on her as she changed her wet clothes. He snatched up a bundle of dried reeds and boiled her half a pot of sugary ginger soup. After she had eaten it, he left.

She got up, bolted the door and lay down again. She seemed to sense how she looked, lying in bed. The moon was exceptionally fine.

"You're an idiot!" she thought to herself.

Then she repeated it aloud. Before long she was sound asleep. That same night a man prized open her door.

V

West of a street near an alley opposite the boat company was situated a Taoist temple, named Lianyang Temple, in which was stationed a local armed force under the jurisdiction of the county government, but paid by the local trade association. Bandits were rampant in the region. They kidnapped people by hiding their boats amid the reeds in the *nur*, from which they could easily escape when chased. The merchants felt that they needed the protection of a special armed force. The force was well equipped, and it had boats with armour on three sides made of bullet-proof iron plates chest high, which were moored impressively on the *nur*. Before setting out on a mission, the soldiers could be seen shouldering two machine-guns and carrying more than half a crate of bullets aboard the boats.

A week or a fortnight later they would return triumphantly with few casualties, for the armoured boats and machine-guns gave them a decided superiority over the bandits. Once ashore, in a column four abreast, they marched through the long alley led by a dozen trumpeters, heading for the main street leading to the county government. When they reached the main street, the trumpeters began to blow. Behind them were the soldiers with loaded rifles. Their captives were sandwiched in the middle, sometimes three or five, sometimes only one, with their hands bound behind their backs. What was amazing was that the captives also marched boldly and spiritedly in step with the music. They even followed the officer of the day, shouting loudly, "One, two, three, four!" All the shops and stores were informed beforehand to withdraw their bird-cages of mynas or grey thrushes, because it might make the bandits unhappy when they saw them. As the captives would be thrown into prison after they arrived at the county government, if they saw the caged birds, they would feel depressed. The glittering brass trumpets and bayonets and the militant column, with some legendary bandit heroes, made a fascinating spectacle for the residents living along this street. It was as wonderful as watching lion dances, dragon lanterns, performances on stilts, children in fancy dress on high frames or a big funeral procession with all the required Taoist and Buddhist monks.

Getting rid of the bandits in the countryside was the soldiers' sole duty. They seldom drilled, except for taking the two machine-guns to the waterside and firing several rounds of ammunition. What made others aware of their existence were the twelve trumpeters practising at the edge of the *nur* from eight to nine in the morning and four to five in the afternoon. They would first blow a long note to warm up, then after a bit of individual practice they would join together to play marches and ceremonial music. (They played the ceremonial music for fun, because up to then, they had never taken part in a review.) After that they were free to do whatever they liked. Some slipped away to the doors of certain households and with a cough, stepped inside, closing the doors behind them.

Most of the trumpeters liked to dress well. They had plenty of free time. Their pay did not amount to very much, but each time they returned from the countryside they got a reward. Sometimes they held secret talks with the bandits and made a deal with them. That was why they could spend lavishly. Because they protected the local gentry and merchants, they had strong backers, so even when they caused trouble, nobody would make a fuss. They thought that it would be a shame both to themselves and their backers not to seek pleasures.

Their leader, Liu, known as Chief Trumpeter, was familiar with the women of several households. He was the man who had prized open July Cloud's door!

He left ten dollars when he left.

It was not the first time such a thing had happened at Big Nur. July Cloud's father learned about it that very night. Holding the money in his hand, he heaved a long sigh. When their neighbours heard about it, they did not say much. "That dirty beast!" the girls and women cursed.

July Cloud was thus virgin no more, but she did not shed tears or try to drown herself in the *nur*. A girl had to lose her virginity sooner or later, she thought philosophically. But why him? It should not have been him! What was to be done? Get a kitchen knife and kill him? Burn down Lianyang Temple? No! She had her invalid father to look after. She sat on the bed woodenly, utterly confused. Then it dawned on her that it was time to get up and prepare breakfast. She had to make nets, weave mats and go to the market. She thought of her childhood when she had watched a bride wearing a pair of pink embroidered silk shoes. She missed her mother, who was now somewhere far away. She did not remember what her mother looked like, but recalled that she had once dipped a chopstick in some rouge to make a red dot between her brows. She picked up the mirror and stared at her reflection. It seemed that she saw herself for the first time. She reflected how Eleventh Boy had sucked her wound in the finger — it must have tasted salty. She felt unworthy of him now as if she had done something wrong. Overcome with regret, she sighed, "Why didn't I give myself to him?"

This idea grew in her mind after each visit of the Chief Trumpeter.

Then the troop went off on a mission again.

One day she went to see Eleventh Boy and said, "Come to the east bank this evening. I've something to tell you."

When Eleventh Boy arrived at the appointed spot, she stepped aboard a sampan used for tending the ducks. (It was tied to a stump on the bank for public use. Local people could all use it to cut reeds or grass or gather wild duck eggs on the sandbank. It was too small for more than one person.) She punted the sampan towards the sandbank, shouting over her shoulder, "Follow me!"

In no time Eleventh Boy swam to where she was waiting.

There they stayed in the grass until the moon was high in the sky.

What a beautiful moon!

VI

The older apprentices knew about the affair but kept it secret from the old tinsmith. They left the door unlatched for Eleventh Boy and watered its hinges to muffle the squeaks. Eleventh Boy often did not come back until dawn. One day he pushed the door open at the usual time and was about to slip into bed, when the old tinsmith boomed, "Are you courting death?"

Affairs of this kind could not be concealed. The news finally reached Chief Trumpeter's ears. In fact, nobody had to tell him. He knew it himself, for July Cloud was cold towards him and detested the very sight of him. He refused to swallow the insult. True, they were not married, so it was nothing to him if they broke up. But it was a loss of face to let a young tinsmith steal her away from him. The young pip-squeak had dared to beard the lion in his den! That was unprecedented! Even his colleagues felt disgraced. They liked to bully others; their logic was that they could steal a horse but others were not allowed even to look over the hedge. If they ignored this insult, what would happen next?

One day before dawn, Liu with several men kicked open July Cloud's door, dragged the young tinsmith out from under her quilt and bound him up. They also tied up the girl and her father in case they summoned people to the rescue.

They dragged Eleventh Boy to the graveyard at the back of Taishan Temple and beat him up, demanding that he pack up, leave Big Nur at once and go back to his home in Xinghua.

The young tinsmith remained silent.

They ordered him to promise not to enter Huang's house or lay a finger on July Cloud again.

He still refused to say a word.

They tried to make him beg for mercy and apologize.

He gritted his teeth.

His toughness enraged these arrogant bullies all the more. "See how stubborn he is!" one of them said. "Beat him to death!" Seven or eight sticks rained down on him again.

He was almost reduced to a pulp as a result of the heavy beating.

Hearing that Eleventh Boy had been kidnapped by the trumpeters, the other tinsmiths searched everywhere for him until they finally came to the back of the temple.

Feeling there was still some life in him, his uncle hurriedly sent a man to fetch an old chamber pot. He knew from experience that only the scales inside the pot could save the life of a dying man in such a condition.

Eleventh Boy clenched his teeth so tightly that the liquid could not be poured down his throat.

July Cloud took over and whispered in his ear, "Eleventh Boy, drink it!"

Seeming to hear a faint voice, he opened his eyes. The girl poured it down.

There was no knowing why, but she herself also tasted it.

Then the tinsmiths took off a door, lay Eleventh Boy on it and carried him away.

They reached the east end of the *nur* and were about to move westward, when July Cloud stopped them and said, "Carry him to my home."

The old tinsmith nodded.

July Cloud sold in the market all the fishing nets and reed mats she had woven and bought medicine for Eleventh Boy's injuries.

Women killed their laying hens for him.

The tinsmiths pooled money to buy ginseng.

Porters, tinsmiths, women and girls came to see him in as endless stream, expressing their affection and kindness they seldom showed in their hard, dull lives. They believed that what Eleventh Boy and July Cloud had done was right and they were proud that Big Nur had bred such a fine young pair. They were jubilant as if they were celebrating the New Year!

After the incident, Liu dared not show his face. His gang also barricaded themselves in their quarters with double sentries posted at the gate. Those so-called heroes now turned out to be cowards!

The tinsmiths held a meeting and submitted to the county government a petition demanding that the Chief Trumpeter be handed over to them.

The local government gave no reply.

Then the tinsmiths took to the streets and demonstrated. It was a rare sight, for there were no banners or slogans, just twenty men with their loads, parading slowly through the town. Silent and grave, they were dignified and determined.

The demonstration showed an inspiring solidarity commonly seen among the members of a trade association in the Middle Ages. It lasted three days.

On the third day they sat in front of the screen wall facing the gate of the county government. On the head of each tinsmith was a wooden tray with incense burning in a burner. That was an ancient custom. When people had suffered grievous wrongs, and the officials concerned refused them redress, they had no way out, and could therefore burn down the court with incense and go unpunished.

The county government could very well have ignored this "undesirable custom", as it was nowhere to be found in the Six Law Codes and, what was more, the custom, believed to have been respected in the Qing Dynasty, had long been done away with. But the tinsmiths never wavered. If they took action, the result could be serious. The magistrate invited the local gentry and merchants to talk the matter over and reached a consensus that the case could not be ignored any longer. So the head of the trade association invited an assistant to the magistrate as his representative, the adjutant of the troop, Eleventh Boy's uncle and two of the older tinsmiths, Huang Hailong to represent the porters, and the tinsmiths' two neighbours, the spectacles seller from Baoying and the chopsticks pedlar from Hangzhou, to meet in a big teahouse to settle the whole matter.

Agreement was eventually reached. All medical expenses should be born by the troop (actually the trade association gave the money), and Chief Trumpeter Liu was to leave the area and sign his consent to this arrangement. Feeling avenged, the old tinsmith accepted the terms but insisted that Liu add one more point. If he set foot in this area again, the old tinsmith was free to do whatever he liked with him.

Two days later Liu left quietly, escorted by two of his armed men. He had been transferred to Sanduo to work as a customs officer.

When Eleventh Boy was able to take some food and speak, July Cloud asked him, "They said they'd stop beating you if you would only promise not to come to my home again. Why didn't you agree?"

"Would you have liked me to?"

"No."

"I knew you wouldn't."

"Was it worth it?"

"Yes, it was!"

"Oh, how wonderful you are! I love you! You must get well quickly."

"Kiss me and I'll recover soon."

"Yes, I will!"

There were three mouths to feed now and neither of the men was able to make any money. Like all the families at the east end of the *nur*, they had no savings, and nothing to sell or pawn. Making fishing nets or weaving mats did not bring in money right away. Eleventh Boy's injuries would not heal quickly. And they could not go without food. Without any hesitation July Cloud took the two baskets her father had used, knocked away the dust and went to earn money by carrying loads as her father had done. The local girls and women admired her. At first they were worried, but soon they stopped worrying when they saw her carrying her loads with quick, steady steps. From then on, July Cloud worked as a woman porter, wearing a big red flower on one side of her hair. As she carried purple water chestnuts, green water caltrops and snow-white lotus roots, she walked elegantly like a willow branch in a gentle breeze. Her eyes were as bright as ever, but their expression was more firm and profound. She had become a capable young wife.

Would Eleventh Boy recover?

Certainly!

Translated by Xu Qiaoqi
Illustrated by Zhou Jianfu

WANG RUNZI

(1946 —　)

Wang Runzi was born in 1946 in a village in Wendeng County, Shandong Province. After graduating from the Wendeng Teachers Training School in 1967, he worked first as a teacher and later as a journalist. In 1970, he joined the Writing Section of the Cultural Bureau of Yantai Prefecture. He is now a professional writer in the Drama Writing Department of the Yantai prefectural government. He was admitted to the Union of Chinese Writers in 1982.

Wang Runzi began his writing career in the late 1960s, when, as an amateur, he published a number of poems, reportage and stories. Since 1979, he has written about a dozen short stories including "Early Spring", "Brother Liang and Sister Fang", etc. His "Selling Crabs", published in 1980, was a prizewinner in the nationwide short story competition.

THE WOMAN WHO WEARS
THE TROUSERS

Wang Runzi

I

Sixty-year-old Suocheng had been timid and oversensitive all his life. His wife, Li Qiulan, wore the trousers in the family. As head of the household, her name was entered in the household register instead of his, and her seal was used for the grain and money they received from the production brigade. When Suocheng came home after the day's work in the fields, he ate his supper, wiped his mouth and then turned on the radio. He loved listening to news broadcasts and special programmes for farmers and had no use for songs and operas on the air. The programmes he followed, he said, opened his eyes and widened his vision. That was all he did everyday, and he left to his wife all the household chores, big or small, such as cooking and tending poultry.

Of late, the craze among the farmers far and near had been the sinking of pump-wells, which instantly gave them water for washing so near their homes. Many families in Suocheng's village had sunk such wells. When asked about his opinions, Suocheng merely said, "I'll have to consult my wife."

His wife's answer was: "We'll sink one too. What others can do, we can too. We're just as sound in mind and limb as they are!"

So he told his neighbours with all the confidence in the world, "Of course we will! If you can do it, we can too."

Suocheng sang his wife's praises with deep admiration in his heart, for she was indeed a very capable woman. She had big

263

feet and wore her hair in a bun at the back of her head. Ten years younger than her husband, she had a glib tongue and deft hands. She attended to everything inside and outside the house — getting proper clothes ready before the weather changed with the seasons, thatching roofs, penning piglets. . . . She took care of everything, paying attention to the last detail. Over the years, she had been extremely good at handling their accounts, not wasting a single cent, and yet she could be more generous than any man when necessary.

The evening before the well-sinking, Suocheng pushed away his chopsticks and the rice bowl, sat back with crossed legs, lit his pipe and turned on the radio. At first, he listened attentively enjoying it all, but then he suddenly switched it off.

Qiulan had been enjoying the programme, too, while she was washing dishes in the outer room. She stretched out her hand, still wet, and pulled the string hanging from the wall in the inner room to turn the radio on again. She strained her ears as she continued her washing-up.

Annoyed, Suocheng went on smoking his pipe. After knocking the ash out of the bowl for the third time, he turned off the radio again. Qiulan was exasperated. She rushed in and, wiping her hands on her apron, shouted, "Honestly, that's the limit! You may not want to listen, I do."

"I've a headache," he murmured. "I want to get some sleep." Qiulan's anger instantly melted away and she reached out to feel his forehead. "No temperature. Do you feel sick?"

He muttered, "Um. . . ."

"I'll make some mung bean soup for you. You are always free from care and don't have to worry about anything. Now you're ill!"

After a few moments, she brought him some bean soup, sweetened with two spoonfuls of sugar. Suocheng finished two big bowls. It made him sweat profusely. He lay down, but the whole night he was turning and tossing in bed and could not get to sleep. Now and again, he got out of bed and smoked, knocking the ash out of the bowl onto the window-sill. By dawn, unable to contain himself any more, he woke his wife.

Rubbing her eyes, she asked, "You don't feel any better?"

"I want to talk to you about something."

"Go ahead."

Suocheng cast a glance at her and then lowered his head. He stuck his pipe into his tobacco pouch but couldn't fill it for a while. Impatient, Qiulan sat up and put on her clothes as she asked, "Have you lost your tongue?"

Pulling himself together, Suocheng blurted out, "Let's not sink the well."

"Why not?"

"Didn't you hear what they said on the radio?"

"What did they say?"

"You know as well as I do."

Qiulan pushed aside her quilt and got out of bed. "Then keep it to yourself!"

He clutched her arm. "Don't get so worked up. All right, I'll tell you."

"Out with it! I've no time to waste."

He drew closer and whispered, "The former landlords and rich peasants at Haoshan aren't classified as such anymore, not even Zhao Baiwan, who had been in prison for eight years."

"I know."

"They're in luck now; they're on an equal footing with us former poor peasants and hired hands."

"Yes." Qiulan bit her lips.

Suocheng lit his pipe and started puffing away. "So, we won't sink a well. Perhaps it would all be labour lost."

"Why?"

"You're a woman with a one-track mind. Let me be plain and honest with you. This house of ours was owned by landlord Liu Jingui. He's still alive. I hear that his son is a rich hotel owner in Japan and he has given our county government a car, a television among many other things. Even if Liu Jingui had died, his sons and grandsons would be able to claim back this house of ours. We'll lose it some day. You just wait and see."

"You're imagining things."

"Me, imagining things? No. Don't you know that our government's policies change all the time? You shouldn't be too sure of yourself."

Qiulan lowered her head and could not say anything.

"I've always let you have the final say in our family affairs. But you must listen to me this once. You'll have nothing to lose for that."

Qiulan burst out laughing.

"What's so funny?" Suocheng was puzzled.

Qiulan split her sides as she thumped her husband with her fists. He hastily covered her mouth with his hand, saying, "Don't be silly. The walls have ears. You don't want to wake up our neighbours, do you?"

Qiulan stared at him. "Idiot! I've wasted my bean soup on you. I don't believe that the sun will rise in the west, nor can I believe the Communist Party will plunge us back into misery. Stop dreaming of problems and go back to sleep."

It was already broad daylight when Qiulan got up. She called to the opposite room, "Aren't you going to get up, Xinhuai? The sun is shining on your buttocks!"

Her unmarried youngest son, Xinhuai, entered buttoning his clothes.

"Do you want me, Mum?"

She handed him some money. "Go and buy me some firecrackers."

"What's the occasion? We're not building a house," Suocheng said.

"I just want to hear them crack," barked his wife.

It was customary for peasants to let off firecrackers when they started building a house. No one had ever done so for sinking a well. But Qiulan insisted. She told her son to stand in the middle of the courtyard holding a pole from which hung a long string of firecrackers. Then she asked her husband to light them. Poor Suocheng struck several matches but failed to set them off. Qiulan grabbed the matchbox and lit the firecrackers herself. The noise drew a large crowd into the courtyard, while children ran here and there picking up the unexploded firecrackers. Bits of paper drifted in the smoke, making it a thrilling sight to see!

"Hold the pole higher, Xinhuai," cried Qiulan.

The onlookers whispered among themselves, wondering why a frugal housewife like Qiulan was throwing money away for no purpose whatsoever. Just as the last ones exploded, Qiulan handed Suocheng a spade and said in a loud voice, "Begin digging, Xinhuai's father!"

Somehow, not quite knowing why, Suocheng began digging with vigour.

II

When the well was dug twenty feet deep, they struck rock. As there was still no sign of water, Suocheng wanted to fill up the hole. But Qiulan would not hear anything of it, saying that since the well-site was on the same line as their neighbour's they would sooner or later reach water. It was probably just under that rock. She called a stonemason in to blast it off.

When the explosives were ready, the loudspeaker called for Qiulan to go to the brigade cashier on account of some important matter. As she was busy sticking paper-strips on her glass windows to prevent them from cracking in the dynamiting, she said to her husband, "Go and see what it is all about."

"But it's you they want to see," retorted Suocheng, rubbing his hands in bewilderment.

"Don't be silly. Can't you even take a message?"

Suocheng returned after a while and pulled his wife into the inner room. "Xinhuai's mother, Liu . . . Liu . . . Jingui has . . . come back!" He was so nervous that he could hardly speak.

Stunned, Qiulan leaned against the door.

"He's staying in the county guest-house. He said he'd come to see his old house tomorrow. You can guess what he has in mind. . . ."

Qiulan was tongue-tied.

"What shall we do? Somebody has come from the county. He looked like an important official, and spoke like one too. Right now, he's talking to the Party secretary in the accounting office. He said he'd be coming here in a minute."

"What for?"

"To see our house. They'll entertain Liu Jingui here, he said. There's a truck outside the office. It is piled high with armchairs, carpets and wooden beds — much more impressive furniture than what Liu Jingui had before."

Qiulan thought for a moment. "Are you afraid?"

"Of Liu Jingui? Hm," Suocheng spat. "I wasn't afraid of him when we reasoned with him at the mass meetings in the days of the land reform, so why now? I'm just afraid that we may not be able to get any support this time in our fight against him. The official sounded as if Liu were an emperor and me a mere poor country bumpkin."

"Don't tell me about that pitiful sight! Leave everything to me. Just go and tell the mason to get cracking."

When Suocheng hesitated, Qiulan snapped, "This is our house and our courtyard! We can do whatever we like with it. Why should we be afraid?"

Looking out of the window, Suocheng saw people entering the courtyard! He pulled her sleeves and whispered, "Here they are. The one in front is the official."

Qiulan brushed back a lock of hair hanging low over her brows, walking confidently out of the room and, leaning against the door, strained her eyes to size up the visitors.

The man in front was Sun, Director of the Administrative Office of the county government. As soon as he entered the courtyard, he looked around like a fastidious inspector and said, "What a dirty place! What's the point of sinking a well now? It won't do any good." He walked cautiously to the edge of the well and peered down. Then he turned and asked the old Party secretary, "Can they finish it by tomorrow?"

"No. It will take another four days at least."

Sun thought for a while and said with an air of finality, "Then fill it up. A messy place like this is not fit to be seen by our honoured guest. No people in other countries would sink wells in such a primitive way. It's a disgrace for us Chinese if they see it."

"They have already put in an enormous amount of work."

However, Sun was insistent. "Fill it up. Overall interests should come before partial interests. Now, let's see the house." He was heading for the house when he suddenly found an angry woman blocking his way, with each of her hands holding on to either side of the door frame. She was staring fixedly at him with her narrowed eyes.

Sun was stunned. The Party secretary introduced them to each other. After this little ceremony, Sun broke into a smile. "So you're Comrade Li Qiulan. I've heard a lot about you." He stretched out his hand politely.

However, Qiulan ignored it and refused to move, her face remaining impassive. "Whom do you want to see? Don't you know this house has an owner?"

Sun gaped while Suocheng was pulling her sleeves from behind. Qiulan brushed his hands aside. Looking at Sun squarely in the face, she demanded, "If you know this house has an owner, you should have introduced yourself first. I've never seen such an intruder like you, poking your nose into other people's business in their own house! Who is the owner of this house, I'm asking you."

Sun blushed. His blood boiled, but then he thought as an important official, it would be beneath his dignity to reason with such a ignorant country woman.

"Director Sun is here on business, Qiulan. You should try to understand," said the old secretary.

"I'm a frank person. As far as work is concerned, I've always cooperated with my leaders ever since the land reform movement. While people didn't feel it proper to look the Lius up in those days, they could nevertheless call at my house anytime. I have never kept any watchdogs. Liu Jingui may call on us, now as before, but I'll not receive him as his humble servant! I treat everybody the same, officials or no officials. A couple of days ago when County Party Secretary Zhang came, he swept my courtyard as soon as he entered it. But Director Sun thinks it's too dirty. This is no bachelor's house. How can our courtyard not be messed up by poultry droppings and broken tiles and bricks? Why must we fill up the well? Just because of Liu? If you think my home is a disgrace to you, then take him to the foreign-style houses in the county town. You can entertain him there as an honoured guest. If you bring him here, he should respect me as the mistress of the house. And that's that."

The Party secretary listened in perfect silence, while Suocheng had disappeared in the inner room.

Sun was annoyed, but he controlled himself. "Comrade Qiulan," he said with a forced smile, "I appreciate how you feel. But you mustn't cling to your old peasant mentality. Mr. Liu Jingui is now a patriotic overseas Chinese. To modernize our country. . . ."

Qiulan cut in, "You know state affairs better than I. Just tell me what you want me to do."

There was a lot of hustle and bustle as people unloaded the furniture from the truck and brought it into the courtyard. Pointing to the beds and armchairs, Sun said, "Do your rooms up with these to show Mr. Liu how good life is in our socialist villages."

Qiulan studied the extravagant furniture.

"Well, how do you like it?"

Qiulan asked with a sly smile, "You mean all that furniture will be mine after this? Good! I'll keep it for my Xinhuai when he marries."

"No, no." Sun shook his head vigorously.

Qiulan laughed but then her jaw fell again. "Then why did you bring it here? Just to show off? I've no use for it." With a wave of her hand, she ordered, "Take the furniture away! I don't want it. My courtyard's too dirty. My house isn't a show window."

"Qiulan!" There was a note of severity in the Party secretary's voice.

Sun stamped his foot in anger. "Leave it here. The well must be filled up right away!"

"Right away? Trying to step over me in my house?" Qiulan ran over to the edge of the well and shouted down to the stone-mason. "Light the fuse!"

"O . . . K," the answer trailed off from below.

The onlookers were stupefied.

Suocheng stumbled out and pleaded with his wife, "Don't be so stubborn. Let them have their way."

She pushed him aside. "You're not as alert as you were. Keep off the well now." Then she climbed on to the wall of the pigsty and, cupping her hands over her mouth, cried out at the top of her voice, "We're lighting the fuse, neighbours. Open your windows so the glass won't break."

The fields echoed, "Light the fuse!"

Sun turned pale with rage. "Take the furniture away. Quick!" he shouted to the men who had come with him.

Secretly amused, the old secretary left.

A muffled boom sounded. The ground shook. There was a surge towards the well-site. Qiulan stood under a tree, and tears were rolling down her lined face.

III

It was heavy snow one day many years before all this.

At dusk, a carriage was rolling along a road, with bells jingling on the neck of the horse. The young driver, clad in rags, was shivering in his seat, holding his whip in his arms.

The carriage suddenly halted, and the driver jumped down and poked with the handle of his whip at something covered with snow in the middle of the road. Then he squatted down and pushed the snow away with his hands only to find a little beggar girl, stiff with cold, and there was an empty basket on her arm.

A voice shouted from inside the carriage, "Get a move on."

The driver came back with the little girl in his arms and called respectfully to the carriage, "Sir. . . ."

The window curtain parted briefly to reveal two blinking eyes. "Put her down," ordered Liu Jingui behind the curtain.

"Please save her, Sir. She might live," pleaded the young man.

"If she dies, will you buy her a coffin?"

The young man pleaded again, his eyes all in tears.

Liu swore, "What an unlucky thing to happen before the Spring Festival. Throw her away!"

Gritting his teeth, the young man put the girl back on the road and carefully covered her with his padded jacket. He cracked his whip over the horse and the carriage rumbled over the frozen ground. It was dark when they reached the village. After tethering the horse to a post, the young man hurried back to the same spot where he had left the girl and carried her to his hovel. As there was no fire, he held her close in his arms the whole night to keep her warm. At dawn she opened her eyes. . . .

Excitedly the young man ran to his master. "She's alive! She's alive!" he cried, his eyes glistening with tears of joy. He begged Liu to keep her, offering to work for him in return for the whole year without pay.

Short and thin, the ten-year-old Qiulan — this was the little girl's name — had to work hard all day long, grinding wheat, milling flour, washing clothes, cleaning vegetables. . . . Liu lorded it over her. Even his dog barked threateningly at her. She went about her chores jitteringly. She found warmth only when she returned to the little hovel, where the young driver, Suocheng, had been like a big brother to her. Fate had bound them together.

Seven years later, Qiulan had grown up.

One day she asked Suocheng, "You're almost thirty, Brother Suocheng. Why don't you get married?"

Suocheng replied honestly, "No one will ever marry a poor hired hand like me."

"Do you like me?"

Suocheng was taken aback.

"Marry me if you don't dislike me."

"No, no!" Suocheng protested.

Her eyes brightened as she continued, "Marry me, Brother Suocheng. Let's leave here and set up our own home. I'll devote all my life to you."

He stopped her and his heart was beating fast. "Don't say any more. The master will hear us."

"So what? I've had more than enough here. I would rather go begging."

With a sigh he got out.

One day, Liu asked him, "You want to marry Qiulan, Suocheng?"

"No. . . . No."

Liu laughed.

One evening, when Suocheng came back on an errand, he heard Qiulan crying in the hovel. He went in and saw a bald old man pulling at her and Liu, with one hand holding a water pipe, was pushing her. Qiulan refused to move, her hands clutching at the door frame. At the sight of Suocheng, she freed herself and flew into his arms crying, "Save me, Brother Suocheng!"

Holding her, Suocheng stared at Liu blankly.

Puffing at his pipe, Liu said, "You've come back at the right time. Say good-bye to your sister. She'll soon be married into a good family and will live a happy life. This is Mr. Li."

"He has sold me," Qiulan wept.

It was a bolt from the skies. "Sir, you. . . ." Suocheng could not go on.

Liu continued puffing at his pipe, his head bent.

The bald man looked at Suocheng suspiciously and then asked Qiulan fiercely, "Who is he?"

Liu answered, "Her brother."

Qiulan said nothing but bit her lips.

Mr. Li reached out and held Qiulan's chin up. "Did you sleep with him? Speak up!"

Qiulan elbowed his hand away and replied at the top of her

voice, "Yes. I've slept with him for seven years. I belonged to him long ago."

Liu Jingui was stupefied.

Ashamed, Suocheng stammered, "You . . . You. . . ."

Qiulan buried her head in his arms, weeping bitterly. Suocheng broke down too.

Mr. Li laughed coldly, "Mr. Liu, you want to palm this whore off on me and ask such a high price for her?" He produced the indenture from his pocket, tore it into shreds and turned to leave.

Liu tried to stop him but he strode off without casting a glance behind. Pale with rage, Liu grabbed Qiulan by the hair and hit her on the forehead with his pipe.

* * *

The smoke had dispersed from the courtyard.

Unconsciously Qiulan raised her hand to touch the scar left on her forehead by Liu Jingui's pipe. It still seemed to hurt. Liu might have forgotten the wrongs he had done her, but not Qiulan. . . .

At her gate she looked at the tiled arch over the entrance. She had spent the better part of her life here, in days of the past as a maid, now as the mistress. She had been poor but now, though far from being rich, she was happy. The day she had dashed out of Liu's home with a bleeding forehead, her poor fellow-villagers had helped her to set up a little shed, where she had married Suocheng. The next day, while he had left to do odd jobs, she went out begging again. She was happy to have her own home. When the village was liberated in 1947, the peasants settled their old scores with Liu. The chairman of the Peasants' Association, now the old Party secretary, took Suocheng and Qiulan to Liu's house. "From now on this house belongs to you," he said to Suocheng. "You've earned it with your sweat and blood. It will be yours, your sons' and your grandsons'."

Qiulan threw herself upon the black gate and cried. Since then it had never occurred to her, not even when the situation looked threatening, that the house could ever be taken away from her. In 1948, when the Kuomintang attacked the key liberated areas and the landlords' "home-coming" corps returned, the timid villagers gave back to Liu everything they had received in the days of the land reform. But Qiulan didn't. And Liu Jingui was too cunning to make any rash move. When the Kuomintang troops withdrew from the mainland, he and his son fled first to Taiwan and later went abroad. In 1962, when the Kuomintang sent small armed bands to harass the coastal regions, Suocheng became nervous. But Qiulan hadn't been afraid, believing that the Communist regime could never be shaken. Now all the landlords and rich peasants had been reclassified, not put in the same class as before. This was only reasonable, since they had been downtrodden for years and many of them had turned over a new leaf. But what did Sun have up his sleeve? Had he taken his cue from the Communist Party?

Qiulan felt hot and heavy in the head. Instead of going to the well, she went straight to her room and flung herself on the bed. When Suocheng offered to send for a doctor and cook her some mung bean soup, she said, "Why make such a fuss? Just give me a massage." Suocheng put his thumbs on her forehead and began massaging it.

When the Party secretary came in the evening, Qiulan asked him, "Is it true that the old order is being restored?"

He lit his pipe and sat on the edge of the bed. "I wonder why a strong character like you asked such a question!" he replied with a smile.

Suocheng added, "Qiulan's right. It looks like the political wind is blowing favourably on the rich and powerful again."

"Don't be silly, Suocheng. Remember this is a Communist state."

"I have no respect for a Communist like Director Sun."

"Why, then, didn't you argue with him yesterday?"

Qiulan glared at her husband. "He's too chicken-hearted to speak up."

The Party secretary laughed when he saw Suocheng blush.

Then Qiulan continued, "But Sun came here as a Communist official." The tobacco in the bowl glowed as the secretary puffed at his pipe.

"You've a point there. The prestige of our Party has been undermined by unworthy Communists like him, and people now are not so sure of themselves as they used to be. Sun and his like know only how to sail along, following the political wind. They'll use their power to bully others, all right. None of them is any good. And we mustn't judge the Communist Party by what they do or say. Isn't that right, Suocheng?"

"I agree with you."

Qiulan bit her lips, lost in thought.

The Party secretary knocked the ash from his pipe. "What do you think, Qiulan?" he asked.

"What shall we do tomorrow?" she countered, smiling.

"You're the hostess. We'll let you run the whole show and do whatever you like." He told them that a county clerk had called a moment before to inform him that Zhang, the county Party secretary, had reprimanded Sun, telling him to let the villagers decide how to receive Liu Jingui, who was coming only for a visit. The county government would provide a car for Liu the following day and he would come without the company of any county official.

Qiulan heaved a sigh of relief.

"To be honest, at first I just couldn't see why we should treat our old enemy as an honoured guest," admitted the secretary. "Later, I realized that I was behind the times. We can't always look back and see things in the old light. We've treated people like him as enemies for many years. That's unfair. If they behave themselves and support the Party and socialism, it's not right to discriminate against them for ever. Besides, Liu Jingui is a patriot. He's a Chinese."

Suocheng listened with rapt attention.

Raising her head, Qiulan said, "Please call Secretary Zhang and tell him that I also have the conscience of Chinese and won't let the Communist Party down. And please . . . invite Liu here for me."

The secretary smiled happily.

"What shall we do with the well?" Suocheng asked.

"Go on with your work."

IV

Beside the well was placed an upturned barrow, whose wheel was being used as a pulley for Suocheng and his family to lift baskets of stone from the bottom of the hole. They worked in unison, with Qiulan chanting, "One, two, pull!"

The courtyard was bathed in the morning sunlight. The pigs had eaten their fill and were rubbing themselves against the wall of the sty. A big white rooster was crowing, holding its head up high. As the wind blew, the dew-drops fell from the leaves of the gourd plants that entwined the thatched roof of the hut. The corn hanging under the eaves glittered in the golden rays.

When the empty basket was lowered to the bottom, Qiulan wiped the sweat from her forehead and murmured to herself, "It's more than thirty years. He must look old now."

"He was born in the year of the dog. He must be seventy-one now," Suocheng echoed.

"Perhaps I won't be able to recognize him when I see him."

"Did he get married again in Japan?"

"I don't think he did, from what I heard."

"Why has he given up his comfortable life over there and come back? To get his property back? Secretary Zhang said he had come only for a visit. Do you believe it?"

"It's hard to leave one's homeland. Some of our neighbours saw him weep when he left. Poor man. . . ."

"Why must you pity him while he never showed any pity on us?" Suocheng was indignant.

"It was all past and done with. Why not let bygones be bygones?"

Words of progress of the sinking of the well were being

passed up from below: "We've reached damp earth!" "We can see a trickle of water now."

After three days of hard work the well had been dug thirty feet deep.

At nine o'clock, a car engine was heard. Suocheng whispered nervously, "He's here."

Qiulan thought for a moment, and then said, "Xinhuai's father, you go and change into clean clothes. They're under the cushion of the bed." When he was gone, she told her son, "Get your bike and go and buy me some lean meat in the East Village. I'll make him some dumplings with meat stuffing. That's his favourite." After Xinhuai had left, she picked up a packet of cigarettes from the window-sill and dropped it down the well, shouting to the stonemason below, "I am sorry I've a guest coming. Please call me when you see water." After making all these arrangements, she dusted her clothes and made for the gate.

A shaky, small old man entered, followed by a crowd of children. Was he the arrogant Liu? His head was bald with only a sprinkling of white hair and his eyebrows had almost gone. Visible on his shrivelled face were the age spots. His legs were weak and he had to hold on to his walking-stick, with his back bent. His left hand was still clutching a water pipe, from which a wisp of smoke was curling up.

Qiulan shivered when she saw the pipe.

Liu stopped at the black gate, squinting at the woman standing beside it. He smiled awkwardly and then shook his head, showing no sign of recognition. Suddenly his hands trembled and his pipe dropped to the ground. He closed his lack-lustre eyes in pain, when he saw the scar on her forehead.

Her lips quivering, Qiulan gripped the door frame so hard that her nails almost sank into the wood.

Neither could speak a word.

One of the children was yelling, "Look, the old man has dropped his pipe." The others laughed.

Qiulan was torn by a mixture of feelings. She shooed away the children, who dispersed and watched from a distance.

Then she walked over and picked up the pipe for him. It was still the same one; only his fingers had left more marks on the copper. After so many years, he must have changed too.

Liu held out a trembling hand. "You are Qiulan if I am not mistaken. I'm so glad to see you and my native village again. . . ."

Qiulan's eyes were a little moist with tears as she wiped the dust from the pipe and handed it to him. "Please come in. Suocheng has some good tobacco for you."

"How is Suocheng?" Liu took the pipe with both hands.

"He's fine. It's all thanks to the Party." Qiulan called over her shoulders, "Xinhuai's father, we have a guest."

Buttoning his jacket, Suocheng ran out but halted at the sight of Liu, and for a while remained speechless with amazement.

Liu shook his head with feeling. "You've grown old, too."

After a long time, Suocheng said, "I was born in the year of the rooster. I'm now sixty."

Qiulan laughed.

The tension was gone and they entered the courtyard. When Qiulan told him about the well, Liu nodded in approval. "The water underground is good. I did want to sink a well when I built this house, but I changed my mind for fear that it might bring misfortune to my family." He was laughing at his old superstition now.

"Water, water!" came the voice from the bottom of the well.

Qiulan clapped her hands in excitement and rushed over. Peering down the well, she asked, "Is there much water?"

"Yes. It's gushing out of a tiny hole."

Qiulan turned and called to her husband, "Fetch me a ladle."

Suocheng put a gourd ladle in a basket and lowered it into the well. When he pulled it up again, it was full of water.

"Taste it, Xinhuai's mother. See if it's sweet or salty."

Qiulan took the ladle and offered it to Liu. "Please taste this water from your home village."

Liu was moved but did not dare take it.

"Come on," urged Qiulan. "We'll have plenty of it to drink later."

"Go ahead. You are our guest," Suocheng chimed in.

Liu took the ladle with his trembling hands and began drinking at large gulps, not bothering to wait for the dust in the water to settle. He savoured it, with his eyes half-closed.

"Sweet?" asked Suocheng.

Liu put the ladle to his mouth and took a few more gulps; tears were streaming down his cheeks.

Her eyes filled with tears, Qiulan quickly turned away. . . .

Translated by Liang Liangxing
Illustrated by Cai Rong

DA LI

Da Li is the joint pseudonym of Ma Dajing and his
wife Chen Yuqing.

Ma Dajing was born in
Nanjing in 1947. After
graduating from the Department of Chinese Literature
at Beijing University, he
became editor of the school
paper and librarian at the
Liaoning Teachers' College.
In 1979 he was transferred to the Union of Dalian Writers and
became a professional writer.

Chen Yuqing was born in Shanghai in 1947. After graduating
from the Department of Chinese Literature at Beijing University, she became a high school teacher and also secretary of propaganda in a factory. In 1978 she was appointed editor of the
Seagull magazine. In 1980 she was transferred to the Union
of Dalian Writers and began professional writing.

They began to collaborate in 1978, and published some nov-
elettes, short stories and plays. In 1980, their play *The Light of
Ideals* won first prize in dramatic composition in Liaoning
Province.

BARRIERS ON THE ROAD
Da Li

I

The light yellow mini-bus drove slowly out of the compound of the City Party Committee. Then it picked up speed and raced steadily along the spacious Liberation Street.

Members of the Standing Committee of the City Party Committee in the car were getting prepared for the meeting to discuss the problem of remodelling the minor district Jinjiagou gully. And the first item on the agenda was to pay a visit to the place.

Jinjiagou was situated at the west coastal end of the suburbs; it was within half an hour's ride from the city. After driving across the Mulan River Bridge, the car came on to a strip of slushy dirt road.

It was Qing Ming Festival.* The ice had thawed, and the snow melted. The roads had soaked up all the water. What with the weight of passing cars and the footsteps of pedestrians, they had long since become a stretch of rough gullies. The driver changed gears continually. Finally, he switched to top gear and kept his foot on the accelerator. The motor, under the strain, wheezed. Mud churned up by the rear wheels was spattered onto the back window. Eventually, the car stopped working altogether.

The driver jumped out of the car, and tinkered around madly for a while in the hope of getting it back into motion again. But all to no avail.

---

* Literally Festival of Pure Brightness, a time to visit graves of ancestors and family members.

"Leave it, leave it," said Qin Yue, waving his hand. Vice-Mayor and Secretary of the City Committee, who was in charge of urban construction. "We'd better get out and walk!" So, with Qin Yue in the lead, the members of the Standing Committee went along the slushy path towards Jinjiagou, which was situated between two hills.

In the early days, Jinjiagou was only a small village in the valley. At the turn of the century, after the Japanese had built docks and shipyards near the west coastal end, large batches of workmen continually moved in. They built all sorts of wooden shacks, huts roofed with galvanized iron, and rammed-earth huts, and eventually it became a slum area known far and wide. In the past twenty years, the population had grown while various types of simple structures sprang up here, there, and everywhere, like mushrooms after the rain. Now, Jinjiagou was more crowded and chaotic than ever.

Forty years ago, when Qin Yue was an underground worker here, he knew the locale like the back of his hand. After the fall of the Gang of Four, he came back again. The old-timers, fitters and riveters who used to call him "Big Brother Qin" and "Black Qin" had all turned grey at the temples now. They still lived in the old broken-down huts, which were much more crowded for room as they had by now all acquired grand-children.

An old woman carrying her grand-daughter in her arms invited them to her home, where she entertained them hospitably. A large *kang* (brick bed) took up more than half of the twelve-square-metre room. The old lady said that the entire family, comprising three generations — six people in all — slept on this *kang*. In order to make the best use of space in the room, wooden shelves had been fixed to the walls and on them were safely put their 12-inch TV set and neatly arranged books. Beside the *kang* was a bureau covered with a snow-white eyelet table cloth. The large desk clock and the fish-shaped vase were dusted spotlessly clean.

One could see that the inhabitants of Jinjiagou all nourished dreams of a better future and even under these impossible circumstances they still tried to add colour and beauty to their daily life.

On the way back, none of the committee members said a word. Qin Yue knew that any Communist who had any moral sense in him would not, on seeing such things, remain indifferent. He felt the time had come for a discussion of the plans for the renovation of Jinjiagou.

The next day, the bill on renovation was passed by the committee members without the slightest trouble. Qin Yue immediately contacted the leaders of the Construction Committee, the Urban Construction Bureau, Real Estate Bureau, and the Bureau of Architectural Engineering to work out plans for placement of moving families. Out of the one thousand odd families at Jinjiagou, about one half could live temporarily with their relatives and friends. The remaining six hundred families or more could be housed in temporary quarters in ten or twelve small streets off the less often used roads in the city. Qin Yue suggested that Cuihua Avenue, in the residential district for high-ranking cadres, take the lead in receiving one hundred families.

This immediately threw the conference room into a turmoil. In the end, the majority of the members agreed. A few mentioned the safety control problem; others said that their cerebral nerves were not in too excellent a condition and that they feared too much noise would disturb their sleep, etc.

"Well, you'll just have to put up with it for a while." Qin Yue tried to keep his temper under control as much as he could. "If you can't get to sleep, you can use the time to think of more effective measures for developing Jinjiagou. Of course, if you really can't stand it, you can go to a sanitarium. The Party Committee will get in touch with it. Whoever wishes to go can sign up after the meeting."

II

In less than half a month, the Standing Committee of the City People's Congress had passed the bill on renovation of Jinjiagou and the construction of a new minor ward. Qin Yue was so excited that he immediately phoned the office of Director Gao of the People's Congress. "You old boys are really great! I thought I would have to carry on a protracted war with all of you!"

Then he summoned all those responsible in matters of ship-building, sea port construction, chemical industry, and oil refinery. He bargained with them: "You're all rich guys, and have a strong backing. You've got men, money, and materials. Now let's do our best." He had divided the construction work of Jinjiagou ward and allotted duties to each large enterprise in town. The coordinating plan would be drawn up by the city; houses would be built by the large enterprises and, after they were completed, they would be apportioned to the city and each of the units involved in the work. They quarrelled among themselves for the whole day as to how the buildings were to be apportioned or what percentage each should have, and could not reach any agreement. In the end, Qin Yue flared up: "Listen, you act according to this plan! If you're going to wrangle over trifles any more and reject my proposals, I'll issue a strict order to the effect that none of you will get even one inch of the land! I'll convince the people that they should demand houses from you or move into your offices and homes instead!" had refused at first and now had to suffer the consequences; they were forced to submit after first turning him down. The "rich guys" agreed to the settlement and signed the contract in the end.

There was only one problem left: working out the programme. Although the Bureau of Planning had sent over two sets of plans, neither of them satisfied Qin Yue. The first was too conservative and lacked boldness of vision, while the second was unpractical. He himself could not decide which type it should be. In one of his dreams, he seemed to have seen a new Jinjiagou. He was walking on asphalt roads between big high buildings. Birches were growing on both sides of the roads. Half way between the roads were flower-beds in which cannas and lilies were blooming. It was an ideal place! When he woke up, however, he could not recall everything he had seen in the dream. "Damn it! Are dreams to be trusted?" Yet he did have some faith in his dreams, for didn't Lu Ban, the great master architect in ancient times, get his inspiration for the palace corner tower from dreams, too?

For the past two days, he had been continually thinking of one person: Li Yuanchu, the chief engineer of the Urban Construction Bureau in the fifties. But each time he thought of him, he immediately shook his head with a bitter smile. Wasn't he dreaming again, he wondered.

One day, out of the blue, his old wife, Lin Huixian, Director of the Foreign Affairs Bureau, told him when she came home at dusk, "Lao Qin, Li Yuanchu is applying to go to the States!"

"Who d'you say?" Qin Yue threw down the newspaper in his hand and jumped up from the sofa.

"Li Yuanchu, of course! You know, that chief engineer Li. Why, have you forgotten him?"

"You mean him? Where's he now?"

"He's staying at the City Committee Guest House. Apparently, they gave him redress last month, and now he's just out of jail."

Qin Yue was suddenly assailed by a dizzy sensation. He buried his head in his hands and sank back on the sofa.

"Just out of jail and given redress," he sighed to himself. "That means Li Yuanchu has borne twenty-three years of unrighted wrong!"

Li Yuanchu was a returned graduate from the States. He was about thirty when he came back to China on the eve of Liberation. During that period of reconstruction, this young specialist in city-planning had shown exceptional talent, and therefore he was very soon appointed chief engineer of the Urban Construction Bureau. His programme for the renovation of an old city was awarded a gold medal at the annual conference of international architects held in Warsaw. Then the National Urban Construction Bureau issued orders several times to have him transferred to Beijing, but by means of calculated cajoling and dawdling Qin Yue managed not to follow these orders. At the time, Qin Yue had great confidence in Li Yuanchu, and the two were seen constantly together. After the completion of the First Five-Year Plan, they had acquired sufficient substantial resources. Qin Yue had proposed an ambitious overall plan for a large-scale urban renovation. The first project was to extend Liberation Road, the main thoroughfare at the city's centre, to the sea-port. At the same time, he would like to see high buildings on either side of the road. That was surely the way to demonstrate the superiority of socialism, as manifested in carefully controlled planning. We should have high buildings, he reckoned, instead of the dainty little houses left behind by the foreigners! Besides, the higher authorities had the intention of opening the city to foreigners. Therefore, he argued, we must give it a new look as grand and impressive as possible.

Li Yuanchu firmly opposed Qin Yue's proposals. He held that flanking high building on both sides of the road would destroy its original character. Whatever new buildings designed must not destroy the existing harmony in the area. His opinion was that the most urgent matter of the moment was the reconstruction of Jinjiagou to get rid of the slums.

The two quarrelled fiercely at all the meetings. The irate Qin Yue would foam with rage and bang his fist on the table, whereas the scholarly Li Yuanchu would argue on the basis of reason, not yielding one bit to his opponent.

After the rectification movement had begun, Li Yuanchu made incisive criticisms against Qin Yue's plan during the extended session of the City Committee conference. He said the people needed timely help, not unnecessary adornments. The way Qin Yue was messing things up by giving arbitrary and unreasonable orders essentially showed that he was craving for personal glory. In his pursuit of fame, he had not taken to heart the suffering of the poor; no, not at all!

But then, not long after this, the Anti-Rightist Movement began. As Qin Yue would have it, Li Yuanchu was labelled as an extreme Rightist. Moreover, Qin Yue also officiated at the meeting held by the departments of the architectural committee to criticize Li in the open-air theatre at Zhongshan Park.

Of course, Li Yuanchu did not admit he was wrong. He appealed to every level of court. However, he was convicted as an active counter-revolutionary. He was arrested and appropriately dealt with according to the law. Later on, his sentence was continually lengthened on account of his bad attitude, and so he had been confined in prison for twenty-three years.

Recently, Li Yuanchu's elder brother in the States, upon hearing of his rehabilitation and release from prison, had came to China with the specific intention of taking him back along with him.

"You've agreed to his leaving the country?" Qin Yue asked his wife.

"What reason have we not to?"

"Shut up!" roared Qin Yue. As if making his wife the butt of his anger could rid himself of all his pent-up feelings. Lin Huixian knew what type of temper her husband had; she stood there staring blankly, not daring to utter another word. Qin Yue vehemently hit his broad forehead with his fists and said, "I'll go and see him tomorrow."

III

Qin Yue could hardly believe his eyes. The man in front of him was the former handsome suave young man, the gifted programme expert? Of course. But he was no longer young now. Nearing sixty perhaps? His back was bent, his shoulders drooped and his head was covered with grey hair. A deep scar under his left eye gave his whole face a distorted look. His face was colourless, like that of an excavated mummy's in the historical museum.

His expression was one of apathy. He neither asked Qin Yue to sit down nor gave any water to drink. The cold streaks of light from his eyes seemed to have come from some icy cave.

"I heard only yesterday that you're now back." Qin Yue was very embarrassed, not quite knowing what to say. "Don't hesitate to say anything. You should feel at ease. Things are quite

different now from what they were twenty-three years ago."
Qin Yue looked at him in earnest.

"Let's not talk about the past. Let bygones be bygones." Although Li Yuanchu seemed to be unruffled, still Qin Yue could
see the waves of emotion inside him. A convulsive tremor passed over the corners of his mouth and swiftly went down his
whole body.

"I can't make up for your lost time. But I've come today to
tell you that your dream of twenty-three years ago is going to
come ture."

"What dream?"

"The reconstruction of Jinjiagou and the building up of a
small new ward!"

"Jinjiagou?" His eyes sparkled. Though it lasted only an instant, still Qin Yue was able to detect his excitement. This gave
him a faint ray of hope.

"What about it? Are you interested?" Qin Yue never beat
about the bush. "I know you're going to leave the country, but
it won't be as soon as you think. If you have time, could you
help and work out a plan? It would be sort of — well, leaving
something to remember you by."

"Who's in charge?"

"I am," Qin Yue answered without the slightest hesitation.
Li Yuanchu looked up at Qin Yue and said nothing.

"What about it? Do let me know," pressed Qin Yue. He was
not the type of person to endure such intolerable silence.

"You? No!" Li Yuanchu's voice was low but distinct and
definite.

Qin Yue had never expected he would give such an answer.
But he knew Li Yuanchu was a straightforward person, so he
said, "If I should be arbitrary and give unpractical orders again,
you can scold and curse me as much as you like."

This seemed to pluck one of his heart strings. He perceived
that Qin Yue was not the same man of twenty-three years ago.
Even twenty-three years ago, this man was sincere and genuine.
Could he now blame Qin Yue, and Qin Yue alone, for all his
own misfortune?

"What are you planning this time?" Li Yuanchu inquired earnestly.

At this Qin Yue became quite excited. After all was said and done, Li Yuanchu was Li Yuanchu. Having had dealings with intellectuals for scores of years, Qin Yue was now more familiar with their personalities and ways. They all had an intensive devotion to their own profession which almost amounted to madness. They could bury their true feelings, all right, but they could not suppress their passion for their own profession. Qin Yue came a little closer to Li Yuanchu. He patted him on the shoulder and said, "You're an expert. I've come to ask your advice."

"Making plans is easy. But first of all we should have construction codes." Li Yuanchu seemed to have a well-thought-out plan already.

"Construction codes?" Immediately Qin Yue recalled that this was a focal point of argument on which many of his quarrels with Li Yuanchu in the past had rested. Li had pointed out at the time that in order to launch urban construction on a large scale, there must be construction codes, or else their hands would be tied. But Qin Yue and the Soviet experts criticized him for having adopted capitalist ideas. What construction codes? Surely, by relying on the leadership of the Party, all obstacles could be removed. To stress construction codes would mean doubting the Party's leadership, discarding the Party's leadership. To this day, Qin Yue's stand on this point had hardly changed. He felt, somehow, that setting up codes was a negative measure. As long as one had faith in the Party's leadership and counted on the initiative of the masses, there was no difficulty which could not be overcome. Of course, he no longer thought Li Yuanchu's insistence on construction codes was against the practice of the Party. It was simply that he had studied in the States and had held stubbornly onto their capitalist methods. After all, one should allow them time to change!

"The problem of construction codes can wait. We'll discuss that later. We'd better get down to planning things first." To Qin Yue, the most important thing was to see the blue-print.

This construction codes business was, it seemed to him, a little irrelevant.

"Without those codes, your plans would be useless." Li Yuan-chu did not give in at all. His spirit was as indomitable as it had been twenty-three years before. An inner-combustion engine of 4,000 h.p. would not be able to make him budge.

"Listen, comrade, put your faith in the Party. Do you think I'm a good-for-nothing Party secretary?" Qin Yue did his best to put on a good front to win him over.

"Good-for-nothing?" His lips trembled slightly, revealing an almost imperceptible sardonic smile. "I prefer to be frank. In matters concerning urban construction, you *do* know nothing."

Qin Yue flared up. "I see you've still got the same old temperament!"

"Well, perhaps. And even if you were to place me in confinement for another twenty years, I would still be the same man."

"You'd better not be so muddle-headed!" Qin Yue banged his hand on the table. "True, we did you wrong in the past and we don't deny that! But you'd better get this clear in your head. The Communist Party, not any of your kind, has put things right for you. You'd better try to be a little more reasonable!" Having had his say, Qin Yue slammed the door and got out of the house.

He was still fuming as he got into his car and he could hardly breathe. He lowered the car window hastily, to let in the cool early spring breez for his burning cheeks. He tore at his collar and urged his driver, "Hurry up! Faster! Damn it! He's cockier than ever now!"

IV

The project of renovating Jinjiagou had begun.

Bulldozers, tipcarts, fork-lifts, and cranes were working day and night. The construction site was seething with excitement. The whole place was enveloped in smoke and dust, and the din and clamour filled the air. Fork-lifts threw load after load of bricks and tiles into the tipcarts, and shack after shack was levelled in the twinkling of an eye.

Now, who would expect a newly laid road to Jinjiagou to be blocked in the middle by garages belonging to the Bureau of Commerce? Before the surveying party arrived to mark the lines, they had already dug up the wire entanglement, built a high wall all round, obstructing the route completely.

Qin Yue summoned the director of the Bureau of Commerce and gave him a good dressing-down. "Look here, comrade. Pull down those walls within three days and make way for us." He scratched his black chin, where appeared a short stiff growth of grey beard, and continued, "If you don't get a move on in three days' time, I'll ask the Construction Bureau to send ten bulldozers here at once to pull it down for you!" The director readily promised he would do it and left in haste.

The next day, the secretary in charge of finance and commerce came to ask for a reprieve. They had just built a new garage, and now they had to pull it down immediately. But where was the site for the new garage? So, Qin Yue left it to the architectural committee to look after that. Three sites were subsequently chosen, but none satisfied the Bureau of Commerce. Then, there was also the question of money. The director of the Bureau of Commerce was for ever complaining that he was short of funds and he wanted the city to do something about it. The committee responsible for city-planning approached the Construction Bank, but all it could say was that this was not an item of civil construction, and that it should be cut out altogether. If they wanted to, they could ask for instructions from the main bank. One month elapsed, and nothing happened. What was more, the Bureau of Commerce bribed all quarters concerned with shortage goods. Qin Yue was now at his wits' end, not knowing what to do next.

One trouble followed another. Moving the families out had become a serious problem long before the work of building the road had been completed. Quite a few of them took advantage of the situation and made most unreasonable demands as compensation for their removal. If they had only one room, which was to be torn down, they demanded two in their new abode, and so on. Tearing down a chicken coop meant the payment of two hundred yuan. And compensation for the loss of eight strips of chives was to be five hundred yuan. What was worse, they were all determined not to move out unless their terms were accepted. At first, slight concessions were made. But as soon as news of this spread people made higher demands. Those who had formerly signed their contracts in good faith, now threatened to break them. In the end, statistics indicated that there would not be enough rooms to go around for those who moved, not counting the extra money needed for the tearing down of chicken coops and rabbit hutches! Qin Yue gave orders to take down the names of those who were out to exploit the situation, for he wanted to report them to their work units, and then their own Party Committee would be responsible for moving them out before the dead-line. In spite of all he had done, however, the results were very unsatisfactory; only a few families moved out, certainly not more than the early morning stars. In the meantime, life at Jinjiagou went on as usual — smoke curled upwards from the chimneys at the same old hour; the sound of dogs barking and cocks crowing could be heard at every corner. Families who had vegetable patches went so far as to replough the land and continued growing their vegetables.

Qin Yue became so enraged that his black faces seemed to be turning green. He was losing weight. Gone was his appetite; neither could he get to sleep. Consumed with rage, he summoned the director of the Public Security Bureau.

"Look at that bunch. They're such a disgrace to socialism and the Communist Party! You're director of Public Security. Aren't you going to do something about it?"

Director Lei smiled. "Since the secretary can't do anything, how can you expect me, a mere director, to come up with anything effective?" He took out a copy of the New Constitution from his portfolio and handed it to Qin Yue. "If you can tell me the man who's violated any of the laws stated in here, I'll report him to the procuratorate and have him arrested at once."

Qin Yue took out his presbyopic glasses and spent a long time going over the document, but he could not find one single article under which injunctions could be laid on them. He saw Director Lei to the door in resentment.

"I see! We must draw up a code; otherwise we won't get anywhere!" He suddenly realized now why that stubborn old mule Li Yuanchu had berated him and called him a "good-for-nothing"!

He made up his mind to go and see Li Yuanchu again.

V

Ever since he fell out with Qin Yue in that quarrel, Li Yuanchu had not been able to get to sleep for several nights in a row. The news of the reconstruction of Jinjiagou was like a spark which had rekindled the dead fire in his heart. No, the fire was not dead. It had been smouldering all these years and all it needed was a tiny spark. Then it would burst into a blaze again.

In 1949, Li Yuanchu had just returned from California. He was standing before the window in his apartment on Hengshan Road in Shanghai as he watched soldiers of the People's Liberation Army enter the city in silence. It was drizzling the whole night, but the soldiers remained in the streets, sitting on the ground and holding on to their guns. Although they were soaked to the skin, not one of them got up to knock on people's doors asking for shelter. Li Yuanchu boiled a big pot of beef soup and took it downstairs himself to the soldiers. But they would not accept it. They smiled and thanked him in their simple straightforward manner. It struck him that this was the perfect example of strict discipline, and his eyes were wet with tears. He thought that a party which could train troops like this would certainly be able to lead China into a thriving and prosperous future. He resolutely tore up the plane ticket to Hongkong which his friends had bought for him. He had chosen to remain in China. Not long afterwards, he was transferred to this city by the sea. How he longed to use his talents and skill to the full! Who would ever have dreamed that before he had any chance to realize his aspirations, he would be thrown into prison?

Not too long ago, his brother came from America with the intention of taking him back with him. He had not refused. Yet the agony it had caused was indescribable. If he was to leave now when he was in such a totally helpless state, what would his friends and relatives say! They had once urged him to leave the country. Leaving China now could mean only that he had regretted not following their advice. No! He would not do it! Ever since childhood, he had believed in a kind of philosophy which emphasized strength of character. What he resented most was the pity and sympathy people tried to give him. Furthermore, he never once regretted whatever he himself had done. So to go to the States now would be an open admission that he had made a wrong decision thirty years ago, coming back to China. In the States, he would be expected to say that in his own country he had not been given any opportunity to put his talent to good use. No! He would rather drown himself in the Pacific than do anything of the sort!

In these past twenty-three years, he had continually borne a pain deep in his heart. He hated the ignorance, the irrationality, the tyranny, the decadence and the injustices of the times. Now that these had become things of the past, he wanted to forget as soon as possible the agony they aroused during those years. He was one of those who always stressed efficiency; he could not tolerate wasting time in procrastination. The time life allotted to each man was limited, he believed, and one minute not properly used meant one loss of that very minute itself. Since twenty-three years of his life had been thrown away, he treasured his time more than anyone else. He felt that many people did not understand the interests of an architect like himself. The ordinary man would fancy the bustling metropolis, sky-scrapers, and express-ways, but he as an architect was most interested in open spaces, the wilderness, or even abandoned ruins. Indeed, he had won international praise for his use and remodelling of ruins. After World War II, he accepted an invitation to visit several European cities which had been destroyed by the Fascists' bombing, and on that occasion he worked out a series of outstanding reconstruction programmes. On the eve of Liberation, he chose to come back to this vast land which had been devastated by war. Now that Qin Yue announced that Jinjiagou was to be remodelled, he felt somewhat like a surgeon who had suddenly been given the rare opportunity of operating on a patient — a very difficult case but he knew how to handle it well.

As early as the 1950's, he had already worked out plans for the transformation of Jinjiagou into a minor ward. The trips he had made to the area were no fewer than those made by Qin Yue. Moreover, he had done his survey as an expert planner. He knew how to use the natural environment in designing a proper lay-out of the district, with all the details carefully worked out concerning transport, location of residential areas and amusement centres and so on. In a way, he was like a good tailor who knew how to make the best use of the material available and turn out clothes which were beautiful, economical, practical, and in good taste. He went to Jinjiagou himself in order to have a better picture of the whole situation.

He went three times in succession, congratulating himself each time. Thank Heaven, the place had not changed at all. Apparently, no one in the past twenty-odd years had taken a fancy to this dirty mud hole. If they had built a few factories, or had put up some weird but permanent buildings there, like the ones on Liberation Street, he would have been done for. As it was, the valley was still nothing but slush and waste water, with low barren hills on both sides. The sea behind the hills remained as awe-inspiring and majestic as ever.

"Thank God, Jinjiagou is still a piece of virgin land," Li Yuanchu exclaimed excitedly. "She may be in tatters now, and her face is dirty, her hair dishevelled; but if we get her dressed up again, she will be a dazzling beauty!"

The second time Qin Yue came to see him, he had gone to Jinjiagou again. In the past month or so, he had made a draft for the reconstruction plan and had written out a ten-thousand-word programme. Today, he had taken the draft with him to Jinjiagou to check various details. By the time he got back, it was already evening.

Qin Yue had been waiting in the room for his return. He smoked one cigarette after another, wondering how to apologize to Li Yuanchu. Intellectuals were very sensitive people. They had a strong sense of self-respect and one word inappropriately said would be enough to hurt their feelings. Besides, he had done Li wrong. So what reason did he have to get angry with him now? In truth, he himself had also been criticized many times during the "cultural revolution". He knew what it was like to be wronged and treated unjustly. By comparison, of course, Li Yuanchu's case was much sadder and more pitiful than his own! So he resolved to let Li vent all his grievances and anger; he would listen, even though it might be against his will, and he was determined not to fly into a temper.

At this point, the door opened and in came Li Yuanchu, who was covered all over with slush. On seeing Qin Yue in his room, he was surprised and did not know what to do. Qin Yue, likewise, stared blankly at him, not knowing what was going on. Li Yuanchu had rolled up his trousers, his sneakers were two huge lumps of mud. His shanks were caked with mud, which had begun to crack. There was also mud spattered on his glasses. He was holding a roll of blue-prints tightly to his breast.

"You — you've been to Jinjiagou?" Instantly all became clear to Qin Yue. He went up to greet him in earnest.

Li Yuanchu made no answer, as if still bearing deep enmity towards this uninvited guest. Qin Yue took the roll of papers from Li's hands and opened it. The words flashed a light in his eyes: "Draft for the Jinjiagou Reconstruction Programme". He was dazzled and then felt warm tears welling from his eyes.

He turned round and looked at Li Yuanchu who was still standing in the doorway as if in a daze. Then he seemed to have remembered something; he got Li Yuanchu into the room and came out, shouting to the service desk near the stairs, "Attendant, bring some hot water!"

While Li Yuanchu washed his face, Qin Yue spread the draft out on the table, put on his presbyopic glasses and began to pore over it carefully, inch by inch. It was exactly what he wanted to see and what he had seen in his dreams!

"Fine!" Qin Yue slapped his leg. "Now that we've got the draft you'd better hurry up and draw up a code for me!"

"A hair cut?"* Li Yuanchu could not follow him and was baffled.

"No! I mean 'draw up a code'!" roared Qin Yue in reply. "After we have done that, I can't believe that the mischief-makers won't get what they deserve!"

VI

Li Yuanchu soon drew up a code according to the *Outline of Urban Construction* put out by the National Urban Construction Bureau — it contained detailed rules and regulations worked out for municipal implementation. As soon as Qin Yue got hold of the code, he went to the director of the Standing Committee of the City People's Congress.

"Look here, brother. Let's call a meeting. The sooner you approve this, the better!"

Director Gao skimmed through the document and said, somewhat embarrassed, "This is something new. I'm afraid we old-timers can't understand much of it."

"Well, neither can I. In dealing with such matters we are absolutely useless — rather like trying to blow up a fire with a rolling pin, so to speak. But what do you think of this idea of mine? I'll invite an expert to come and give some lectures. I'll also sit in and listen, try to learn something. 'You build the temple, and I'll invite the gods,' as the saying is. But you'll be responsible for providing the car too, because the few gas cou-

---

* A pun on the two words "li fa". — *Trans.*

pons I've got hardly enough for the trips to Jinjiagou. This time I'll have to be a scrounger!"

For a whole day, Li Yuanchu was giving lectures to members of the Standing Committee of the City People's Congress. Briefly, he summed up the history of urban construction in different countries and the legal measures involved. He also reviewed what had been going on in China for the past thirty years, in matters concerning urban construction: the legal measures adopted, the progress made, the failures encountered and the lesson to be learned from past experiences.

"In the past, I was a negative factor in some of the accounts given by Li Yuanchu. I now admit I was wrong!" Qin Yue suddenly said loudly. For a moment, people were dumbfounded. Then a long-lasting applause broke out.

After that, Li Yuanchu explained the importance and function of codes. Qin Yue promptly recounted, by way of support, a series of recent incidents and appealed to the Standing Committee of the City People's Congress for the examination and approval, as soon as possible, of the code that Li Yuanchu had drawn up.

Qin Yue had obtained executive power at last. He instructed the City Committee Printing Press to print several thousand copies of the bill and distribute them to each unit concerned. At the same time, through the Jinjiagou neighbourhood committee they were distributed to each household, and all the residents were urged to discuss the contents. Reports were to be made after their discussions. When all arrangements had been made, Qin Yue issued an official order via the Urban Construction Bureau to announce definite dates for moving and demolition.

Meanwhile, the Bureau of Commerce was still determined not to cooperate. Qin Yue got the leaders of both the Commercial and the Construction bureaus to come with him to the garage built by the Bureau of Commerce. "Just when are you going to pull it down?" he asked the director of the Bureau of Commerce.

"As soon as we can choose a new site and put up a new garage."

"Will three days be enough?"

"Three days?"

"Yes. Even that is too long, it seems to me." Qin Yue raised his voice. "If the road is obstructed, neither people nor materials can get through. Now, what are you going to do about that?"

"We'll try our very best to pull it down as soon as possible."

"Oh, leave it. You don't have to do that!" Qin Yue waved his hand impatiently. He turned to the head of the Construction Bureau and said, "Give them the bill for land tax."

Upon looking at the bill, the director of the Bureau of Commerce had a fright.

Qin Yue sneered and said, "Understand now? Beginning from this very moment, you'll have to pay 30,000 yuan monthly for this land. If you don't, according to the laws of urban control, it'll be sealed for safe-keeping, and the use of the land will be suspended."

"Goodness!" exclaimed the director. "Is there gold or silver in this land which calls for such a high tax?"

"No, there's neither gold nor silver here. Quite simply, this land belongs to the People's Republic of China! Whoever wants to exercise feudal separatist rule will have to pay for it!"

The next day, the director of the Bureau of Commerce reported to Qin Yue that the Bureau Party Committee had decided unanimously to pull down the walls of the garage and recede thirty metres to ensure a passage-way. "Oh, what a worthy comrade you are!" said Qin Yue, pointing his finger at the director's forehead. "You won't be convinced until you're faced with grim reality. You won't retract until you collide into a wall! Thirty metres is too much; we'd be satisfied with twenty." He raised his head and laughed heartily. In the two months of carrying out the Jinjiagou project, this was the first time he laughed so happily or was so care-free.

The daily quota of the number of households to be moved was one hundred. Qin Yue got hold of the director of the Construction Bureau, asked him to organize an efficient construction contingent and put up temporary shelters along the small street already chosen for this purpose. One hundred families per day; you could get more removed, but not less, and no delay would be tolerated. Each household should have two rooms, a ground stove in the outer room, and a heatable brick bed in the inner room. They must guarantee the flue would never be blocked, and that there would be a public toilet and water tap to every ten households. Also, there must be preventive measures against water pipes freezing.

The whole process of moving progressed quite successfully. Scores of trucks sent here from all over the town shuttled back and forth. The director of the Public Security Bureau specially picked a group of experienced policemen to deal with the safety and traffic problems.

The Urban Construction Code was working like a huge steam-roller! It crushed all the obstacles on the road. The majority of the inhabitants signed their contracts with the units of urban construction, agreeing to move out; they looked forward to their future life in new houses, and therefore, they left happily. As for the very few who continued to make trouble deliberately, various departments of urban construction resorted to legal measures and eventually they had to go. They did not receive any compensation since they had to pay for the dismantling, according to the code, with the torn-down material. A good example that the pursuit of self-seeking would lead to deprivation!

VII

On the last day of moving, Qin Yue came to check up on things at Jinjiagou. Old Yang, who was in charge of the moving process at the headquarters, reported to the secretary of the City Committee that everything would be finished today. However, three families had caused some problems. "What problems?" asked Qin Yue. Old Yang took out his memorandum pad and went through his notes. He was on the point of elaborating on these problems when Qin Yue interrupted him. "Come, take me along and let me talk to them."

Arriving at the first family, Qin Yue saw at a glance that it was the house of his former landlord when he joined the workers' movement. People said he was now an old retired dock-worker living with his wife.

Qin Yue was about to step inside when Old Yang called him back saying, "It isn't the old couple who are reluctant to move out; only we'd thought —"

"Thought what?"

"Well, this is where you established our first Party branch. It is a place worth preserving. If we pulled it down, then, in future —"

"What about the future?" Not waiting for him to finish, Qin Yue went on, "Still yearning to build memorial halls and museum? The past will never be able to explain the present or the future. To live on patched-up dreams all the time is what the spineless good-for-nothings hanker after!" Qin Yue looked at him sharply. "Whose stinking idea was it? Was it yours? Huh?"

"No, I — we were afraid that in future —" Old Yang mumbled, not knowing what to say.

"No use in licking my boots! I won't raise your salary, or promote you! Listen, you. Tear it down; tear it down as fast as you can!"

They then came to the second family. There was only an old lady and her eight-year-old granddaughter. The old lady's son was working out of town. People said these two did not have the heart to leave a pomegranate tree behind. So they were reluctant to move.

Upon hearing this, Qin Yue laughed so hard that he almost fell. He pushed open the fence door and saw that the blossoms on the tree were beginning to fade. A few green pomegranates half showed themselves behind the leaves. He

stooped down and patted the rosy cheeks of the little girl and asked. "What's your name, little girl?"

"Pomegranate," The little girl raised her head reluctantly. Crystal-like tears filled her eyes.

"No wonder you hate to move, because you're pomegranate, too!" Qin Yue laughed even more heartily. This job of his was really very interesting: you came across all kinds of people in such a short time!

Before Qin Yue said anything further, however, the old lady suddenly covered her face and began weeping. At this, Pomegranate also burst into tears. She cried so pathetically that Qin Yue also felt a wave of indescribable sadness sweeping over him.

"What in the world is the matter? Speak up, won't you?" Qin Yue could make neither head nor tail of things. He sensed that perhaps things were not as simple as he had expected.

After careful questioning, they found out that the little girl's mother was a surgeon at the city's No. 4 Hospital. After the great earthquake had struck Tangshan, she joined the medical relief corps, and was unfortunately killed there. A little tree had been planted in the same year her daughter was born, and Pomegranate was the name she had given to her little daughter.

Qin Yue was silent after listening to this account of their past. A long pause, and he sighed heavily. He patted Pomegranate on her head and said, "Don't you worry. We'll make sure the tree will go with you."

Turning round to Old Yang, he said, "Go immediately to the Gardening Department and buy a large-sized wooden tub. Transplant the pomegranate in it." He had already gone out of the door, when he turned round and said to the old woman, "I'll come again tomorrow to look at your tree. I'll tell them not to hurt one single leaf!"

"I'll guarantee we'll do the job well." Old Yang very seriously accepted this special order of the city secretary.

In the afternoon, Qin Yue received an urgent phone call

from the director of the Bureau of Architectural Engineering. He had supervised the building of temporary shelters in the high-ranking cadres' residential district, Cuihua Avenue. Everything had progressed very smoothly. But at four o'clock, when workers of the construction unit were about to go home after the day's work, City Secretary Liu's wife came home from her office. As soon as she saw a row of simple structures put up in front of her home, she flew into a rage, summoned the director of the Bureau of Architectural Engineering before her and ordered him to tear them down instantly.

"Did you tear them down?" Qin Yue queried.

"We really couldn't go against her —"

"No? I see. But building temporary houses on Cuihua Avenue is a resolution passed by the Standing Committee. Secretary Liu was at the meeting, too!"

"Yes, but Secretary Liu's gone to Beijing now and it's so difficult to explain things to her. She said her daughter-in-law's just had a baby, and that she didn't want excessive noise, and that —"

Qin Yue realized at once that Secretary Liu's wife was throwing her weight about. Their daughter-in-law was Qin Yue's only child. Considering this special relationship with the Lius, surely, Qin Yue would not be so adamant in his stand. The thought of this brought on a flood of irritation such as he had never experienced before. Ever since he was reinstated, Qin Yue had the feeling that a large unseen net was closing in upon him. All kinds of personal relationship, all sorts of gains and losses were tightly woven together in this fine net, in which he would be caught sooner or later. Secretary Liu was an honest and sincere man, all right, but his wife had a reputation far and wide as the Liu family's "political commissar". She was involved in practically everything, public or private. True, she was infinitely resourceful. But once she got hold of you, you would hardly know whether to laugh or cry.

Qin Yue did not wish to commit an error of this nature; he must not make what his in-laws intended to do an exception to the rules. He cut the message short irritably. "You're the head of the Architectural Engineering Bureau, not the president of the maternity hospital. You needn't bother about post-natal matters! Of course, her daughter-in-law needs a bit of peace and quiet now, but the families that have moved out of Jinjiagou have no place to live! Don't you know that? How many houses have you pulled down already?"

"Five."

"Is there any more space on Cuihua Avenue?"

"None."

"What about the space outside my house?"

"It's all occupied."

"All right. Build back the houses you have torn down, then."

"What?"

"Just say it's my order. You must arrange a place for those five families before it's dark. Whoever doesn't agree can come directly to me and talk to me about it!" With that remark, Qin Yue threw the receiver back onto the desk with a bang.

According to Old Yang, the last family they went to was occupied by Hou Ruiping, nephew of a certain vice-minister in Beijing. He had come here only a month ago. When people tried to persuade him to move, he asked for two apartments in exchange; or else he would not budge.

"Hou Ruiping?" Qin Yue remembered the young man had tried to use the name of his uncle to get a flat for himself. On that occasion Qin Yue rebuked him knowing that he already had an apartment in a new building in Railroad Station Square. Obviously, the young man intended to exchange the two flats for a Western-style house! But what in the world had brought him here?

They found out in their investigations that after failing to get the rooms, Hou Ruiping had taken the advice of a "house monger", and had exchanged rooms with a family in Jinjiagou a month ago, in order to demand exorbitant compensation when he was asked to move out.

"The house property of Jinjiagou was frozen two months ago. How could he manage the exchange?" asked Qin Yue.

"They say he did it via back-door connections with a chief of the Bureau of Housing Administration."

"Cheaters! Come on, let's go and sort them out!"

Hou Ruiping's house was locked. Qin Yue looked round outside. It turned out to be nothing but a dilapidated old grey wooden house. The eaves were rotten and about to fall down any minute. It was beyond him that Hou Ruiping should exchange a new two-room apartment in Railroad Station Square for such a broken-down hovel as this. He must have had something else in mind.

"Get a few workers to wait here," Qin Yue said loudly. "When Hou Ruiping gets back, tell him the terms clearly. We'll give him one room for each one that's hauled. If he doesn't like it, we'll tear the whole thing down and that's that."

VIII

It was like a noisy evening bazaar in front of Qin Yue's house. Those families who had not finished with their moving were busy putting things together. The space before his doorway was cluttered up with furniture boards, branches for kindling, big pickling vats, broken bricks for the chicken coop, etc. His chauffeur had to stop the Toyota "Crown" way out at the entrance of the alley and watch him from afar as he picked his way through heaps of firewood and water vats before squeezing into his own door.

As Qin Yue came into the kitchen, his wife was just taking off the lid of the steaming pot, and snatching out some steamed buns. The kitchen was filled with hot steam. "Here, hurry. Lend me a hand." His wife thrust a huge bamboo basket at him. "Put the buns in here!"

"Why do you make so many?"

"There're several families who've just moved in outside our door. They haven't had anything to eat yet." Lin Huixian took off her apron, picked up a large aluminium pan of fried mince meat and vermicelli, and then walked out of the kitchen. She turned her head and called out, "Why don't you hurry up? It's just the right moment to 'warm the pots' for them!"

"Warm their pots?" Qin Yue stood dumbfounded. In an instant he recalled the old local custom: whenever people move house, friends and relatives would go to the new house to congratulate them on moving. It was known as "warming the host's pot". Vermicelli and steamed buns were indispensable for relatives and friends to take along with them on such occasions. It was said that vermicelli signified long-lasting prosperity, while buns meant accumulation of wealth.

Qin Yue recalled a snowy day more than ten years ago. His family of three was sent off to the countryside in a big truck. When they arrived at their destination, they noticed that the frost had not been swept off the walls of the house in which they were to live; nor had the broken windows been papered over. But as soon as they arrived, the landlady came in and gave their buns that were frozen stiff and vermicelli made of yam paste to "warm their pot" for them.   She also wished them luck and hoped that they would feel warm and happy.

Using this "pot warming" as an opportunity, Qin Yue went round the families, inquiring as to whether the brick bed drew fire or not, or whether the smoke seeped back down the flue, or if the door latch had been put on, and whether the window bolt fitted or not. . . .

Amidst all the talk, Qin Yue suddenly spied Old Yang with a green water pail in his hand. He was watering the pomegranate tree in a wooden tub. Standing by his side was Little Pomegranate with a pair of little brush-like braids.

"Haven't gone home yet?" Qin Yue went over to him and asked.

Old Yang put down the sprinkling can and, pointing to the pomegranate tree, said, "I'm waiting for you to come and check the job. If you say it's OK, my job's done."

"You'll have to ask her," answered Qin Yue, as he touched Pomegranate's head. "If she's satisfied, then it's OK."

Little Pomegranate lifted her smiling face. It looked like a pomegranate blossom in full bloom.

"Little Pomegranate, we're neighbours now. Welcome to my home!" So saying, Qin Yue pulled on Old Yang. "Come, let's have supper at my place first. I don't think I've had lunch to-day!"

To do honours to Old Yang, Qin Yue personally stir-fried meat shreds and hot pickled mustard green and shelled a few lime-preserved eggs, in addition to preparing the minced meat and vermicelli. Lin Huixian also strained a dish of Sichuan cabbage from the pickling vat.

Qin Yue had just seated himself at the table when he sud-denly thought of something. He asked his wife for twenty yuan and thrust it at Old Yang. "Take it," he said, "or else I'll forget what it's for."

"What's it for?" Old Yang could make neither head nor tail of it.

"It's for the flower pot and tub from the Gardening Depart-ment."

"Can we have it reimbursed?"

"Never mind. There may not be a regulation which looks after that!"

Old Yang knew very well Qin's temper, so he did not re-fuse, but took up his bowl and began to eat. They were in the middle of the meal when the phone rang madly.

The phone call was from Director Lei of the Public Security Bureau. Hou Ruiping swore he would not move. He threatened to make a long-distance call to his uncle and lodge a complaint against the house-moving headquarters for infringing on human rights. If they did not agree with his term, then he would stay put and they could do whatever they liked! The headquarter's bulldozers were still waiting there, not daring to move an inch. So the director of the Public Security Bureau asked for help. "Shame on him! Pure blackmail! Bullying us and relying on the strength of other's position and power! Bah! . . ." Qin Yue began to curse into the receiver and banged his fist so loud on the table that both Old Yang and Lin Huixian came running up to him to see what had happened.

"We act according to the construction codes. Even if he were related to God Almighty, he wouldn't be allowed to have his own way." Protected by the construction codes, Qin Yue felt safe. He gave Director Lei firm orders: "Get on with the orders! I'm still in control!"

IX

Qin Yue went to Jinjiagou immediately. On the way there he lowered all the windows of the car; but his blood was boiling and nothing could cool him down. He tried hard to control his temper. Hou Ruiping's uncle was one of his former superiors, and if things got out of hand, he would have to take the consequences. He hoped that everything could be solved peacefully without resort to extreme measures.

By now Jinjiagou had been levelled. It looked all the more quiet and deserted at night. Rows of construction engines stood by the roadside; they looked like steel monsters lying in ambush in the dark.

As soon as the jeep reached the valley, Qin Yue spotted Hou Ruiping's solitary dilapidated wood house. It looked like a lone grave in the wilds or a pillbox on open terrain. Qin Yue had been a leader of an armed working team during the War of Resistance Against Japan, and had blown up countless Japanese pillboxes. Before him now was this obstinate barrier which looked so very much like the pillboxes of the past. Suddenly all kinds of emotions came over him.

He knocked on the door himself. It was tightly bolted. After a while, came a low, hoarse voice asking, "What are you here again for? I told you my terms long ago!"

"I'm Qin Yue. Tell Hou Ruiping to come out!"

The window opened. Through the window, Qin Yue could see a barn lantern shining. The walls were bare and the room was filled with smoke. Seven or eight young men were sitting at a round table on which cups and dishes were stacked up higgledy-piggledy, with all remnants of the meal in them.

Hou Ruiping stuck his head out of the window and asked, "Uncle Qin, what is it?"

"You ought to know!"

"They've shown no respect for democracy, infringed our rights and violated the Constitution. We have a right to defend ourselves!"

"It was you who violated the urban construction administrative laws in the first place!"

"All right, then. If you agree to my terms, I'll move out right away."

"This isn't the free market! There's no need for any bargaining." Qin Yue felt a flame of fury burning inside him. He was about to explode. He was grinding his teeth in order to keep down his fury.

"OK. Give me two apartments and I'll move."

"That apartment you already have is good enough for you. Compared with other inhabitants of Jinjiagou, you ought to be satisfied. As a cadre's son, you ought to consider the bad influence —"

"So you're going to give me all that official jargon? Well, too bad! Sorry, I can't oblige you!" So saying, he closed the window with a bang.

"Another tyrant! Hmm!" Qin Yue cursed viciously, grinding his teeth. Waving his hand at the workmen behind him, he yelled, "Break the door open!"

A group of workmen rushed forward. They were battering at the door and the lime and dust were falling down on them.

All of a sudden, a window opened, and an empty wine bottle was thrown out, landing in the midst of the workers.

"Watch it!" shouted Qin Yue. "Damn it! They're a lawless lot!" He raised his hand and anxiously looked at his watch.

Just at this moment, the noise of roaring motors filled the air. The headlights of the engines lit up Jinjiagou. A contingent of fully armed policemen came whizzing past. Director Lei jumped out of the commanding car with a walkie-talkie in his hand. He hurried over to the City Party Secretary and said: "Secretary Qin, what's your order?"

"Demolish this fortified house!" The valley echoed as his order boomed out.

Director Lei transmitted the order via the walkie-talkie. A dozen or so armed policemen surrounded the wood house immediately. They first issued a warning through a semi-transistor amplifier. Having received no response after several attempts, they broke in upon the occupants as sudden as lightning and drove Hou Ruiping and his gang out of the house.

Immediately, three caterpillar-type bulldozers, under surveillance of the armed police in motorcycles, charged at the house.

A booming crash rocked Jinjiagou. The ramshackle house let out a few piercing sad moans and crumbled as the bulldozers moved on. A screen of smoky dust rose up in the air; it writhed and danced in the blinding light of the cars. The bulldozers growled angrily as they threw piles of rubbish by the roadside.

The wind from the sea coming from between the hills soon drove away the smoky dust, and once again Jinjiagou regained its peace in the silvery moonlight.

Qin Yue loosened his collar and took a deep breath of the moist sea air. He felt refreshed and relieved instantly. The last "nail", so to speak, had been taken out. Jinjiagou was now laying itself bare, with all its original glory. To Qin Yue it suddenly seemed rather unfamiliar. Yet it was also lovable and it looked like an innocent and obedient child waiting for her mother to dress her up.

He let out a long breath. The big job was completed at last! — people had moved, and the road had been built. To clear away all the barriers, how people had had to suffer, and what painstaking labour they had had to undertake!

He wished very much to relax a bit, or even go to a sanitarium during the summer time to cure his rheumatism. But no, he could not. Pulling down the old Jinjiagou had been difficult enough. Could the setting up of a new Jinjiagou be accomplished without any pain at all? No! He had already begun to visualize the difficulties and obstacles he would meet.

Would there be a steady supply of construction materials? Problems of cement, reinforcing bars, and bricks might not be too difficult to solve. But wood was very scarce. He had already suggested to certain units concerned to experiment with steel window frames; but he did not know the result yet. Besides, would the municipal administration be able to supply them with appliances in time? Things like gas, electricity, and running water would often land you in headache departments! He decidedly did not wish to have the new apartments of Jinjiagou share the same fate as that of Qiansanmen in Beijing which were "ghost buildings" — they were still pitch-dark in the evenings one year after completion. In addition, there was the setting up of service trades and commercial network centres, as originally designed, etc. Indeed, there were numerous things he would have to worry about. Fortunately, Li Yuanchu had previously made provisions for them in his construction plans. But in order to implement things, he, as secretary of the City Committee, would have to work for all he was worth. He might meet with rebuffs again, or encounter obstacles. Yet, the comforting thought was that the road was completed. Barriers of any sort would certainly be cleared away sooner or later. On this point Qin Yue was quite sure. He firmly believed he was a man of principle, totally uncompromising. He was ready to risk everything in his fight for ideals, destroying barriers. He was destined to lead the contingent and together they would get the job done!

Translated by Li Meiyu
Illustrated by Zhao Ruichun

HANG YING

(1944 —   )

Hang Ying was born in Tianjin in 1944. After graduating from junior middle school in 1959, she worked as a stage designer at the Tianjin People's Art Theatre, where in 1970 she became a script writer. She was admitted into the Union of Chinese Dramatists in 1980. A council member of the Union of Tianjin Writers, she now engages in full-time writing.

Hang Ying's 1978 play *Wedding* won second prize in the script competition, sponsored by the Ministry of Culture in celebration of the 30th anniversary of the People's Republic. Since 1980, she has published a number of short stories, including "Off to a Flying Start" and "A Clever Blind Girl".

A SALESWOMAN

Hang Ying

I

The result of the week-long opinion poll, so unexpected, put me in a very awkward position. She came in first with 1,899 votes, far ahead of the next two on the list. I was flabbergasted.

To ask the customers to vote for the best shop assistant had been the idea of our new manager and Party secretary, Guo. "The customers know who's best," he said. "Their participation in running our store will help us improve our work." He had us put at the store entrance a big ballot box to which he assigned a special man to collect the votes every day. So that customers could identify the shop assistants for the contest he had each of them wear a badge with a number on it.

I was put in a spot by this novel idea of Guo's because as the secretary of the Youth League I had always been sure of the outcome of any vote before people raised their hands. Taking my cues from the Party secretary I did a lot of spadework by finding a likely candidate and recommending him or her at Party or League meetings. People then would take my lead and know who to choose. But now it was different. Guo had dropped me no hints. All he said was, "Let the customers decide." And now they had singled out a girl who was neither a Communist nor a Youth Leaguer, not even a prospective one!

I thought for sure people would vote for Wang Xianshu, No. 59, who had been played up by the store management during the previous six months. On the suggestion of Gao, the former Party secretary, she was being groomed to be a second Wang

314

Shuxian, which was me. Our names were almost the same. I was in my thirties. I had no boyfriend, but I had lots of titles: secretary of the store Youth League committee, member of the store Party committee, veteran advanced worker, member of the city Youth League committee, member of the district women's association, woman pacesetter, model of late marriage. . . . I wanted Wang Xianshu to shine like me. She stood at my old counter and succeeded me as group leader. Arriving before dawn, staying on late, mopping the floor, cleaning the toilets, filing regular ideological reports to the League branch, she followed my example in every way. . . . Like me, she wore her hair back without bangs, her short pigtails tied with dark rubber bands. She also wore a plain blouse under a work jacket the colour of which had faded with washing. Indeed, she was the very image of a model worker. But she got only half the votes.

The winner was Jin Lu, or Golden Deer, the girl at the candy counter. Her number was 163, but the young men who often breezed in from the steel rolling mill nearby called her "No. 1". I didn't know what they meant until I found out that they were grading our girls on the looks. This alone made her unqualified to be honoured with the title of model worker. But now this pretty face was challenging me!

II

The awards were to be presented the following week at a meeting attended by our leaders, press and radio journalists, colleagues from other stores and customers' representatives. I sought Guo out and suggested that we postpone announcing the results until we had discussed the problem first so that things would not turn out badly for us. Guo agreed and called an enlarged Party committee meeting for that evening.

At the meeting, staff members of the Political Work Section and I raised three points against Jin. First, she was frivolous and too preoccupied with clothes. She had been chosen as the beauty queen of our store by some customers. Her votes might have been fixed by people with other motives. Second, she didn't like her job, but was more enthusiastic about appearing before the footlights at the Cultural Centre. Third, she was a flirt. Several times she had invited boys to her room to eat sweets.

The trade union official and men of the Propaganda Section disagreed. They said her votes showed that she sold the most and that she was popular, quick and capable, and devoted to her work. Socialist competition means to compete well in work, they said. Since the customers had chosen her, they argued, we should announce the result of the poll honestly.

Guo, all smiles, wound up by saying, "We should see that the poll is conducted in a democratic way and with Party guidance. Before we call the meeting to give out the awards, we'll ask Wang Shuxian to find out more about Jin Lu, and the trade union and Propaganda Section the views of our customers."

That evening, I tossed and turned in bed. I was at once happy and worried — happy because I would be able to prove my point, worried because, though new to our store, Guo knew quite a lot about it and may have drawn his own conclusions. Jin may have wormed her way into his favour. I would need unrefutable arguments to convince him.

At the first glimmer of dawn I cycled to the store to check the account books of the candy counter, hoping to hit Jin where I thought she was weakest.

As I got off my bike, I saw a bright red one already in the parking shed. Only she dared ride such a flashy bike, with various gadgets attached — a reflectors, a transistor horn, a down tube wrapped in red velvet, a "Deer" brand electroplated lock, an unusual taillight, topped off with a galloping metal deer at the head of the front fender. The bike was just like her. What annoyed me more was that she had come so early. Why? To tamper with her account books?. . . I hurried to the candy counter. I saw no one, and the account books were under lock and key. I stopped by to look into the changing room, the table tennis room and the library. No sign of her. The store was not open yet. The corridors were empty. Where could she have gone?

Then I heard a faint sound of singing floating down from the fifth floor. I ran up to the auditorium. No one was there. The singing was coming from higher up. Out of curiosity, I went up two flights of iron stairs to the roof, where I saw her singing.

As she sang, she twisted her body as if dancing. I'd never been to a dance, and I'd seen few foreign films. She was probably doing the strange disco dance that people were so crazy about these days. I hid myself behind the chimney. She was absorbed in her performance, unaware of being watched.

The sky was now rosy with the rising sun, throwing into relief the sexy curves of her body. Blushing to the tips of my ears, I closed my eyes.

Yes, she was beautiful, young and vivacious, but being prejudiced, I found her disgusting. Her rosy cheeks and lips looked as if she wore make-up. Her eyes were large and bright and her long eyelashes were seductive. Even more repugnant was the wild expression in her eyes, eyes that always looked people square in the face. And her fashionable clothes and that flashy bike of hers! She really had no sense of what was proper. So she had come here early in the morning when no one was around to indulge in such an indecent act. How could a person like her be a model worker?

I was fuming when she suddenly stopped singing and staggered towards the railing as if intending to throw herself over. My heart jumped to my throat. I was wondering whether I should rush over to stop her, when she suddenly turned round. Leaning against the railing she sighed, brushed back her long hair, and said, "I feel empty and oppressed. Time hangs heavy on my hands. Very soon, my face will be covered with wrinkles and my hair will turn grey. . . ." She broke down and began sobbing. Without realizing what I was doing, I passed my fingers over my face and felt a nostalgia for my lost youth.

I tried hard to control my feelings — I couldn't miss this

fine opportunity to probe into her innermost thoughts. Suddenly she stopped crying and stretched her arms towards the sky, sighing, "Let me pass my time in music and dancing. . . ." Again she twisted her body crazily, waltzing round and round, her dishevelled hair covering her face. I became worried. What had happened to her? Why was she so distressed? Perhaps . . . she had gone mad? But then I contradicted myself: No, this was her true rotten self.

My investigation was more successful than I had expected. I stole down the stairs with a contented simle.

III

The head of the candy counter and I looked through the account books the whole morning but found nothing wrong with them. When I asked him if Jin had ever been found stealing sweets, his answer was negative. So I let him return to his counter.

My head swam after tackling figures for hours and finding nothing suspicious. The matter didn't seem so simple as I had thought. I decided to go back to the candy counter to see why she was so popular.

The store was crowded, the candy counter even more so. People visiting the city on business or pleasure, those about to get married or calling on friends and relatives, parents shopping with their children — all wanted to buy sweets. Being short I could not see clearly who was at the counter behind the throng of customers. Then I caught a glimpse of a head of rich curly hair fastened by a golden clip characteristic of the Dai girls of Xishuangbanna in Yunnan, complete with a little chain which swung as her head moved. This deliberate showiness got my back up.

As I stood there trying to find fault with her, I had to admit that she worked efficiently. Smiling, she asked the first customer in line what he wanted. As she measured it for him, she asked the second what he needed and told the third to

make up his mind. At the same time she figured out how much the first customer should pay, checked it skilfully on the abacus, and gave each customer an account of what his change was. Her skill earned her much praise.

With my professional eye I noticed that she did not keep her head bent over the scale but looked up now and again to smile at customers when she talked to them. All shop assistants were required to be friendly. It had taken me a long time to learn this before I was commended as a model worker. She must have taken great pains, too.

But my favourable impression was soon gone when I recalled her indecent performance on the roof. She was an entirely different person then. If I had not seen it with my own eyes, I would never have believed it. One should be judged not only by her work but, more important, by her ideology. However well she acted, there was still something which threw a revealing light on her true character — the dazzling hairpin. And that golden chain behind her ear that drew men's attention to her snowwhite neck! What a shameless coquette!

Perhaps out of admiration or curiosity, onlookers who had not intended to buy anything queued up too. This increased business, of course, but wasn't her way of attracting customers disgusting?

I snapped out of my musings when, impatient for his sweets, a child in his mother's arms at the end of the line began crying. When her efforts to soothe him failed, the mother slapped him, which made him howl like mad. Jin asked the other customers, "Comrades, how about letting this lady be the first in line? It's not good for this little boy to cry so much."

When they agreed, She thanked them and asked the grateful mother to come to the front. But the boy still wailed. Jin gave him two sweets to stop him.

My heart sank. It was necessary to maintain order in the store, but she should not give away sweets like that. I wondered — did she do it often?

The woman protested. Meanwhile, as Jin finished measuring the sweets, she took two back and asked the woman, "Isn't that only fair?" After wrapping a few pieces of candy in a small piece of paper, she put the rest into a bag which she neatly tied before helping the woman put it into her satchel. She slipped the smaller bag into the mother's pocket, saying, "This is for your little boy to eat on the way home, so you won't have to open the big bag."

"That's very thoughtful of you," the woman said, thanking her.

I had to yield my plan to her.

A soldier carrying a suitcase entered the store. He took his place at the end of the queue, looking at his watch again and again. After serving two more customers, Jin noticed he was about to leave. "Are you in a hurry?" she called out to him.

"Yes. I've got to rush to catch a train back to camp. I want to take some sweets to my friends."

With the consent of the other customers, she let the soldier jump to the front of the line. He saluted her and left smiling with his sweets.

To think that such a decadent person was so efficient and enthusiastic about her work! Who was the real Jin, the one on the roof or the one behind the counter? Could there be beautiful jade inside a crude stone? The doubts born out of my prejudice were being dispelled as the satisfied customers streamed past her.

IV

Just after the soldier left, a gang of youths from the steel rolling mill crowded forward demanding, "We're in a hurry too! We want to be taken care of first." The enraged customers shouted, "Come on — get to the back of the queue!"

A tall, dark young man in steel worker's overalls dragged their brown-haired leader out and said in an authoritative voice, "Shape up and stand in line."

Brown Hair and his gang quieted down but continued to hang around.

Jin seemed to know the young man. "On your day off, Mr. Dai?" she asked to ease the tension.

Brown Hair laughed at this. "He isn't Mr. Dai. He's called Daiyu,"* he said, pointing at the young man.

The customers laughed. The young man's dark face turned red with anger. He stared at Jin, then darted towards Brown Hair who retreated crying, "Daiyu in classical Chinese means 'black shining jade'."

Jin giggled while the young man cast her another angry glance and ran after Brown Hair.

Brown Hair dodged behind a pillar. "Since you've come to the rescue of No. 1, if you propose now, she'll accept you for sure," he said, taunting the young man.

"Shut up or I'll lift your hide off!"

Brown Hair whispered something to him. "Dare you do it?" he asked the young man.

The two young men went back to stand at the end of the queue, each holding a ten-yuan note in his hand and a crafty grin on his mouth.

Somehow, I felt worried for Jin. I had been a salesgirl myself. I would have got cold feet in such circumstances.

But she threw them a casual glance as if she had not sensed anything unusual. "Can I help you?" she asked politely when the young man's turn came.

He blushed. Brown Hair poked him in the back. "Which are the best sweets? Please tell me the speciality of each variety so that I can make a choice," he asked.

She nodded. Speaking to him as well as to all her customers she began, "It all depends on your taste. Generally speaking, sweets from the north are sweeter than those from the south. The ones from the northeast are the sweetest. If you have a sweet tooth, buy those from Beijing or the north-

---

* Daiyu is the heroine of the classical Chinese novel *A Dream of Red Mansions,* a girl who is noted for her beauty and delicate health.

east. In the south where sugarcane grows, people care more about better ingredients and flavour than sweetness. Beijing is famous for its crisps, butter balls, and fruit drops. Tianjin is known for its coffee-flavoured sweets and wine-flavoured chocolates from the Qishiling Confectionery. Shanghai is famous for its toffees. Chongqing has good sweets too, while fruit drops from Guangdong are the best in the country. . . . We have more than twenty varieties of toffees alone. So which do you want?"

It was as if she was reciting a poem with her perfect Beijing pronunciation in her musical voice. The customers were impressed by her detailed presentation. The young man stood transfixed until his companion gave him challenging looks.

"One ounce of each please," he said.

"All in one bag?"

"No. In separate bags."

A murmur ran through the crowd.

"Is that the way you buy things? You're just out to make trouble," one old man said.

"Don't serve him," others shouted.

The young man looked embarrassed, but Brown Hair put his hand on the scale and replied, "It's none of your business. Why can't we buy things that way?"

A man went up to reason with him, and the gang crowded forward. It looked like a fight. I elbowed my way to the counter to intervene. At the sight of me, Jin smiled and calmly addressed her customers, "Don't worry. This will only take a minute." When the commotion subsided, she asked the rest of the gang, "What about you?"

"The same. We want to taste every kind," they said.

"One ounce each?"

"Two ounces each. Four ounces in a bag," Brown Hair cried.

"Three ounces each. Nine ounces in a bag."

"Four ounces each. One pound two ounces in a bag."

Goodness! That would mean her measuring the sweets many times and tying many bags. And how could she work out the prices and give out the change quickly? Quietly she asked the fifth member of the gang, "And you? Half a pound each? There are more than twenty varieties. Please have thirty yuan ready."

The man felt in his pocket and made a face. "I don't have a sweet tooth. Please give me 1.3 ounces each."

What impudence! These scoundrels jostled the young man in admiration, while making faces and urging Jin, "Please hurry!"

"OK," she answered, adjusting the scale. The customers watched her movements, some curious, some anxious, some fuming. In a jiffy, miracle seemed to happen. She put a bunch of small bags on the counter with her left hand, while with her right hand she took a handful of sweets and put it on the scale. It was always just right. Then with her left hand she picked up a bag, filled it with sweets and tied it up neatly in a second.

The customers held their breath, while I wondered when she had learned this skill. Her movements were so deft and elegant she was more like a dancer than a salesgirl.

But something even more amazing was yet to come. She called out the unit price of each variety of candy and its weight as she tied the bags up, announcing the total cost while checking the figure on her abacus with her fingers flying over the rattling beads. Her calculations were always accurate. Taking the money, she told each how much change he would get. She was still cool as a cucumber as she finished serving all those rascals.

The customers, gaping all the while, broke into applause as if they had just seen a superb performance in a theatre.

She fixed her eyes on the dark young man till he blushed. His companions were stunned.

"Do you need something else?" she asked with a smile, seeing the gang rooted to the spot. "We have chocolate bars. boxed sweets, assorted toffees, jelly drops, sesame sweets, mint drops. . . ." Then she solemnly produced five lollipops for children. The customers split their sides while Brown Hair and his gang ran away.

In a polite way, she had called them silly boys, smart girl! I was sure they would never dare bother her again.

Before I knew what I was doing, I was giving her a friendly smile.

V

Back in my office, I sent for Jin's roommate, Ren Xiaomei, and asked her whether Jin had often invited boys to eat sweets in her room. I didn't know why I was so keen on clearing up the question, but the answer pleased me. Ren said that Jin had invited young friends to sing and play music. She had treated them to more than two hundred kinds of sweets she had bought, asking them to sample them and write down their comments in a notebook. Ren also told me that many nights she had practised wrapping up stones and weighing them. . . .

The scales fell from my eyes. I was ready to blame the head of the candy counter for not having told me about her exemplary behaviour. But then I remembered he had recommended her for a demonstration of her skill. I had struck out her name because. . . . I was conscience-striken.

At a store cadres meeting that evening, I came out with a report on the results of my investigation to the approval of Party secretary Guo. It was decided that the outcome of the poll would be announced the following morning, and the meeting to give out awards held as planned. I volunteered to help Jin draft her speech so that I could have a chance to talk to her frankly.

The following morning, photographs of those chosen by the customers were put up on the "board of honour" at the store entrance. Jin, as the winner, attracted much attention, but she worked as usual, unaffected by her fame. She also was dressed as smartly as ever. Didn't she realize that a model worker should play down her dress? I felt I must talk to her as soon as possible and incidentally tell her to get her speech ready. The moment the store closed I went straight to her room.

She had put on an even more beautiful dress and was polishing her shoes.

"You're going out?" I asked.

She laughed and made me sit down on her bed. She was nonchalant when I offered my congratulations.

I told her that she was to speak at the meeting and asked her what she was going to say.

"No, no! I am a poor speaker," she said, blushing and shaking her head.

"You spoke very well at the counter the other day," I said. "You came out first in the poll. You must speak. It's our leaders' decision."

She looked at me helplessly. "I must speak?"

I nodded.

"All right then."

When I offered to help her with her speech, she asked, "You mean I have to prepare something ahead of time?"

"Write it out or at least make an outline, so that you won't go astray," I said.

"I'll just say what's on my mind."

"That won't do."

I decided to write it for her, but I had to know her thoughts. I couldn't tell her I'd seen her dance on the roof, so I asked her tentatively, "Has anything been weighing on your mind lately?"

"Why, no," she said, puzzled.

"Yesterday morning. . . ." I hedged.

"Yes?" Her eyes opened wide.

I was pondering how to put it mildly when someone knocked at the door.

"Come in," she said.

The door remained closed. She got up and called, "Who is it? Why don't you come in?" When she opened the door, she was amazed.

There stood the dark young man, his face crimson. He bowed his big body and muttered, "Sorry, No. 163, Comrade Jin Lu. I learned your name from the board of honour."

Her shocked expression turned into a sardonic one as she asked him in politely.

His face a deep red, he backed away protesting. "No, no! I don't want to disturb you. I've only come to express. . . ."

My spinster's heart pounded. What did he want to express? Jin smiled and looked at him steadily.

Embarrassed, he showed his white teeth in a grin and shoved a package into her hand. Only then did I notice he had shaved and had his hair cut, looking very handsome in a woollen jacket. She didn't open the package but held it in her hand, as if measuring its weight.

"Is it a bomb?" she asked with a gleam in her eyes.

"Yes. Dare you open it," he asked.

She opened it right away. It was the sweets he had bought. "A small gift. My name's on it," he pointed at the wrapping paper and went away.

"Hey, come back . . ." she ran after him, but he was already down the stairs.

Jin spread out her hands in a helpless gesture. I opened the wrapper: it was a certificate given by the steel rolling mill to outstanding workers. His name was Shi Yongli.

"It never occurred to me he did his work so well," she said as she smoothed it out.

I agreed, then added, "But he shouldn't hold the paper so cheap."

My solemn expression made her laugh.

"Yes. The great Youth League secretary can't bear to see that," she said, "but I like people who make light of fame and honour."

My mouth dropped when she used the word "like" so casually. As if reading my thoughts, she added with a smile, "I meant it in the broadest sense of the word."

I was about to offer more advice when she said, "Well, humans are complicated. Some very outstanding people have glaring faults." She stopped abruptly, blushing, and ran out the door.

I was still in the dark about what she was going to say at the meeting.

VI

Although the meeting was going to be held the following day, Jin still hadn't written out her speech. According to the usual practice. I decided to get the speakers together to go over their speeches with them that evening. I had to see that their speeches were politically sound.

Jin sought me out and told me apologetically that she had an appointment and could not come.

"What? Are you asking leave of absence from such an important meeting?" I asked.

"I'm taking part in a dress rehearsal for a play at the Cultural Centre, so I can't come to your dress rehearsal," she said.

Dress rehearsal? How could she put it like that? "No. You must come," I said firmly.

She became impatient. "I can tell you right now what I'm going to say, but since I'm in the leading role in the play, I must go," she said.

"What kind of a role?" I persisted.

"A girl who has lost sight of her aim in life and kills her time sprucing herself up and dancing. . . ."

The situation dawned on me as recalled her bizarre dancing on the roof. "Very soon, my face will be covered with wrinkles and my hair will turn grey . . . ," I recited.

She grabbed my hand, her eyes bright. "You've seen us rehearsing?"

"I . . . heard about it," I said, hesitating. So she was only reciting her lines that morning! I stroked her hand and told her, "OK. Go to your rehearsal."

She hugged me and wheeled me round in a quick waltz, making my head reel. I stopped her.

"Stay away from these activities in future," I said.

She gave a start, "Why?"

I couldn't understand her disturbance. "You are a model worker now and must be strict with yourself in everything. You must not only work well, but also behave well." I gave a meaningful look at her dress.

She paid no attention and replied, "Can't a model worker have a hobby?"

"Certainly you can. But your prestige is more important. You must work hard to keep it, otherwise you will be a flash in the pan."

"I hate people who put up a front to seek prestige," she said. "It never occurred to me that I would become a model worker. And I don't think it should be a lifelong title. . . . Of course I'll work hard to keep it, but if I have to choose between being a model worker or an actress, I'll choose the latter."

"What?" I couldn't believe my ears. Yet I couldn't lose my temper, so I tried to appease her. "That's not what I mean."

She brightened up. Sitting down beside me, she asked in a respectful tone, "What else do our leaders expect of me?"

Her submissiveness pleased me. Removing her golden hair clip, I told her like a big sister, "Many leaders and guests will come to our meeting, better not wear this. . . ."

"Why?. . ."

"Why must you wear it?" I countered with a smile.

"Because it makes me pretty. It also reminds me not to lower my head when I serve my customers. I tend to forget when I am busy. When I lower my head, the chain touches my ear to remind me."

So that's how it was! She had many good ideas to tell her audience. "All right, just tell your listeners how this golden chain reminds you to look at your customers when you serve them. But don't mention that it's pretty."

"But that's my main reason for wearing it," she insisted.

I gave her a tap on the forehead. "Silly girl! Keep it secret from others. How can you say it in a meeting?"

"Why not?" she said, chuckling. "I want to tell everybody.

I like to be pretty. Only those who love life care about their looks."

Perhaps all amateur actresses are like that, I thought. "Tell me what you're going to talk about." Seeing her pondering over the question, I added, "Just say how you came to love your work."

"Well, it is a long story." After a sigh she went on, "I wanted to be an actress, but I lost the chance. Now I'm too old to be one."

"But you have worked well," I said.

"I realized not everyone can do what he wants even in developed countries, not to mention in a country like ours."

"So how did you come to love your work?"

Her answer again surprised me. "You grow to like anything you're familiar with. No matter what kind of work you do, when you get the hang of it, you come to love it."

"Not all young people are like that," I said, shaking my head. "You must say why you are so kind to the customers."

She thought for a moment. "Well, I'd better tell you first how they helped me," she said.

"The customers helped you?"

"Take my regular customers," she said, "one middle-aged woman teacher, her face always pale as a sheet, came to buy a few sweets on pay day every month. But once she failed to turn up. Instead, her little daughter came together with her mother-in-law. The old lady told me through her tears, "She is always busy, preparing her lessons late every night in her eight-square-metre room. Her pay is low. She buys sweets only for me and the children. Because she is now hospitalized for hypoglycemia, I've come to buy her some candy. She needs them for her ailment. . . . One old worker often comes with her grandson who only wants chocolates. His grandfather told him, 'You are born under a lucky star. I never tasted sweets until my twenties, not to mention chocolates! There were several young men who came to buy sweets to celebrate their being admitted to universities. Those who failed said, 'It'll be our treat next year.' Two more were admitted this year, still the last one said, 'Come and eat my sweets next year.' "

Her eyes were moist. "They taught me many things about life. I am only too happy to serve ordinary people like them," she said.

She spoke as if to herself. She turned her gaze outside the window, the tears in her eyes glistening in the glow of the setting sun. I knew what she would talk about at the meeting — her love for people, life and beauty. I had misunderstood her. I blushed when I realized my rigid thinking. . . .

"You have spoken very well. Thank you." I felt a lump in my throat.

Embarrassed, she scribbled on a piece of paper on the desk. I urged her to go to her dress rehearsal.

She flashed me a grateful smile. "Can I come to see your play?" I asked.

Surprised and overjoyed she gave me two tickets. "The première is tomorrow. I hope you'll tell me what you think of it."

"Thank you." I saw her to the door. There seemed to be something more I wanted to say to her, but instead I asked, "Why are you always so happy?"

She was silent for a moment, then laughed. "I don't know. I just find life sweet," she said.

She left. I heard her laughed again when she met someone in the corridor. I picked up the piece of paper and saw a deer, its horns crowned with a rose. I repeated to myself, "Life is sweet."

Golden Deer, her heart brimming with roses, will plunge into the world with firm steps. . . .

Translated by Liang Liangxing
Illustrated by Zheng Shufang

JIANG ZILONG

(1941 —   )

Jiang Zilong was born in 1941 in a village of Cangxian County, Hebei Province. In 1958 he became a worker for Tianjin Heavy Machinery Factory. He enlisted in the army in 1960. In the summer of 1965, he returned to the factory and served successively as production section chief, factory director's clerk, workshop general branch vice-secretary, workshop vice-director, etc.

Jiang Zilong began to publish his works in 1962. His story "A Day in the Life of the Machinery and Electricity Bureau Chief", which came out in 1976, aroused an intense social reaction. In 1973, "Manager Qiao Assumes Office" won a first class prize in the national outstanding short story competition. That same year he joined the Union of Chinese Writers. In 1980, "Pioneers" won a second class prize in the national outstanding novelette competition (1977-80).

THE DIARY OF A FACTORY CLERK

Jiang Zilong

March 4, 1979

Today, I got to the factory an hour early because Director Wang was to be transferred. People like him, I surmised, would not wait till everybody had come in before making the exit. Almost certainly, he would prefer to leave the factory before the work hours began.

Director Wang himself sent in the application to the company requesting the transfer. I understood very well indeed that he must have felt that if he stayed on he would be idling away his time in the factory. Of course, he had been squeezed out by Vice-Director Luo. Everybody in the factory was probably well aware of that, but nobody dared pierce the paper covering the glassless window, as it were, particularly in the presence of Director Wang, to let in a breath of truth. That was the tacit understanding all right, which had nevertheless made things even more unbearable for everybody around.

In the four years that I've been clerk I've seen two directors leave. Director Wang is the third. Honourably, he assumed office, full of vigour and enthusiasm, but now, disheartened, he left, making way for his successor. Those who seek authority play games with power but power retaliates with games of her own played on the seekers themselves. What with transfers and re-elections, the replacement of leaders seems to be the simplest way of solving problems. Perhaps this has always been the practice past and present, at home and abroad. Yet each time a director leaves, transferred somewhere, a soul is laid bare. It will take me a while to calm down. I am determined to use my power for the first time, as a clerk, to have the factory's only jeep arranged to pick up Director Wang and take him to his new unit.

However, the man in the reception booth told me as I came in, "Director Wang left an hour ago."

"Alone?"

"Secretary Liu was carrying his stuff for him."

"And the factory jeep?"

"It was sent off by Vice-Director Luo last night."

A pang of guilt stung my conscience. I had thought of coming in an hour early only to give Director Wang a hand, while the man who was bent on humiliating him had already carried through his plans the day before. Somehow, I also felt a sudden surge of resentment towards Party Secretary Liu: you honest and ineffectual official! Your province of Shandong has produced heroic men since ancient times, but why haven't you got one whit of their mettle. Not only did our senior official send off the director personally, he even carried his luggage and got him onto a crowded public bus!

Lost in thought I stood beside the factory gate when a light wind ushered in the jeep. Vice-Director Luo jumped down from the vehicle beaming with self-content and a smile spread across his pale pock-marked face. He laughed on seeing me and said, "Lao Wei, you're here awfully early today. Have you come to see Director Wang off? Has he left already?"

"He's left." I didn't want to say much especially when I was in my lousy mood. Neither do I want to get into unnecessary trouble by saying anything a clerk shouldn't.

Vice-Director Luo got a couple of "double-bang" firecrackers out of his pocket. Handing me a couple he said, "Here're two for you."

I didn't take them saying, "I don't dare let them off."

"Oh," he tittered, "don't tell me you're too grown up for that!"

"Do you always carry such playthings around with you?" I asked.

"They're left over from the Spring Festival," he said. "I'm blowing them off today to drive away bad fortune!"

Ke. . . . BAM!

"Hee! Hee! Hee!"

Like a cold gust of wind, that sound bore through my ears and chilled me to the marrow. It was a good thing Director Wang had left early; I hate to think how he would've felt if he had heard those "double-bang" crackers exploding.

Factory director! Who could have thought the position would have inspire such perverse behaviour! In order to obtain that title and cast off the prefix "vice", Luo has already forced three men to leave. But the company had twice appointed a new director to come before. Will it bring in yet another replacement for Director Wang or will it, as Vice-Director Luo hopes, drop that loathed prefix "vice" from his title? If that is going to happen I'll have to begin thinking of my escape from this office and my return to my old job as statistician in the production section.

March 11, 1979

"Lao Wei, is it true that Vice-Director Luo has been promoted director?" Even more workers have been asking me this question.

I invariably answered, "I don't know." Which was usually followed by, "Come on. Don't tell me you don't know by now!"

My dear pitiful fellow-countrymen. Honestly. . . . You're not in charge of anything but you're so inquisitive. You want to pick up any gossip about anything. You'll have to work whoever becomes the director. What has the appointment got to do with you? These last few days, the halls have been echoing with yells of "Director Luo, telephone!" In some of the workshop reports the address has been changed from "vice-director" to "Director Luo". Even more pitiful than the workers are these scheming cadres whose loyalties shift with the wind.

"Lao Wei, have you noticed Director Luo has really taken charge lately? From morning to night he is all over the factory overseeing everything."

"I haven't noticed." Isn't everyone making too much of all

this? You ought to know you come to the factory to work, not to look at other people's faces! Maybe it's because I'm a clerk that I am so oblivious or at least indifferent. I hear all that is said, see everyone's expression yet I'm able to hear without listening, see without noticing, at all times maintain my detachment.

What pain! Some day if I can prove myself worthy and become a factory director myself, I will make sure nobody will suffer that! I'll buy a robot to work for me as my clerk, with no heart or breath, no mouth or ears, and an expression eternally that of a steel sheet. In short, one who will change only according to the natural, but not political climate.

Meanwhile I know somebody is paying very close attention to my tone of voice and my expressions. When I refer to Luo Ming I still use his full title, "Vice-Director Luo". All the documents which ought to be looked over by the director, I passed on to the Party Secretary Liu, perfectly in accordance with regulations. Then I pass them on to whomever he says should handle them. I do not take them straight to Luo Ming or offer my suggestions, because I know my place. Luo has probably noticed this but there is nothing he can do. I haven't received notification of his appointment from our superiors yet.

I do not object to Luo Ming becoming director because I don't have that authority, but if my opinion were solicited by my superiors, I would say, "True, Luo Ming has been with the factory a long time. He is also well acquainted with everything here and he has a lot of people backing him up, but he is not good enough to be this factory's director. He is concerned only with a director's power, not with his responsibilities. He does not have the right calibre or the ability of good director."

March 12, 1979

Strange indeed! Today Vice-Director Luo's daughter, Luo Jingyu, came into my office and kept me occupied for half a day.

Two years ago she managed to be sent back to the city from the countryside. Since then she has not been assigned any job, apparently because her standards are too high. She will not join any collectively-owned units. She refuses work that is either not to her liking or too far away from home. Since she rarely came to the factory, I had no idea why she was sitting before me talking at random for such a long time.

She sat chatting about this and that until she "happened" to hit upon the subject of work, and then she came straight to the point, "I'd like to join your factory," she said.

"I hope you're not joking," I said in disbelief, "ours is a very small factory. Sure, it's state-operated but we've got only 200 workers. You'll find it very limited, I'm afraid. Besides, we're a chemical factory, and surely this is hardly the kind of job you're looking for."

She replied quite frankly, "I've waited already two years to get into a good unit. I'm 26 this year, you know. I can't go on waiting like this forever. At any rate, this factory does have its advantages: expenses are low, the pay is good, and the workers are given a lot of bonuses."

"Well, if that's what you want, why don't you talk it over with your father?"

"You know that wouldn't look good. Lao Wei, you do it for me."

Here was an opportunity to ingratiate myself with a superior in order to gain personal advancement. For when a factory director wants to get something done but finds it improper to do it himself, then his clerk should be the person entrusted with the job. He should, according to the needs, do whatever he can to help the director. But four years ago, unable to go against the Party's order, I had to accept the transfer and reluctantly became clerk here. At the time I made one promise to myself: no matter whom I worked for I would maintain a purely official relationship, and I would not be drawn into any private dealings. I would take care of the factory business according to official principles no matter whom I was dealing with and I would never let personal considerations interfere with the execution of my public duty. So I answered her, "I'll have to ask for instructions from the Party branch first. Then we can talk more about it."

Luo Jingyu was taken aback. Obviously, she had chosen this moment, with her new status as the daughter of a man about to become director, to come to the factory. After all, according to the concept of order in today's society, the factory director's daughter is above the director's clerk, who should therefore serve her as well. The only hitch is I don't want this extra, new title of the director's daughter's clerk. Luo Jingyu was not at all pleased and, with the same cold laugh as her father's, she flung the door open and left.

March 15, 1979

Secretary Liu told me delightfully today in a whisper, "The new director will be here soon!" This simple man at times is rather like a child. Already he has as happily welcomed three others and three times he has seen them off with a heavy heart, no doubt, carrying their luggage. Now when he hears a new director is coming he is elated all over again.

Perhaps I am indifferent to both joy and disappointment.

March 18, 1979

"Dinglingling. . . . Dinglingling. . . ."

Far away from the office, I could hear the telephone in my office ringing. We always sneer at people who turn up at work not one minute earlier. We jokingly call it "stepping on the bell". The truth is, however, the phone is ringing eight days out of ten before I walk into the office. Most of the calls at this hour are for the directors, because the easiest time to catch them is just at the shift begins. Finding them only half an hour after work has begun can be a problem. I don't know what it is they have to disappear to do, much less whether they are busy taking care of official or private business.

"Dinglingling. . . . Dinglingling. . . ."

Clerks can become stone deaf when they choose to. No matter how persistently it rings, I always open the door as unhurriedly as usual, hang up my bag, take out a piece of bread or a stick of fried dough and have a bite before answering the telephone.

"Hello, hello, is this Lao Wei? Can I ask you to do me a favour. My father passed away yesterday and I want to have him cremated today. Could you speak to the director and ask him if I could use the factory's car?"

"Who is this?" I asked, a little surprised.

"I'm Big Pang, Pang Wancheng. Sorry to bother you."

"Why didn't you make this request earlier?" I replied, grudgingly.

"I didn't know he was going to die so soon!"

I realized that was a difficult problem and said, "You know as well as I do that the factory has got only one jeep and one car. They were both sent out to the provinces to pick up some raw materials yesterday. They won't be back for a day or two. There is nothing I can do, I'm afraid."

Big Pang is an honest and hardworking crane operator. He would not have asked for help unless there was no other way. He is also stubborn. I explained the whole situation to him but he would not give up and continued to implore piteously, "Lao Wei, I can't talk to Director Luo. Whatever else people may say, you've been the director's clerk for all these years and you've got more pull than I do. You're my only hope. It's not easy to arrange a time for the cremation. My relatives are coming, and if we can't find a car there's no way to get to the crematorium. What can I do? Lao Wei, I'm relying on you. Please try to help."

It was up to me now to make sure that his old man would be cremated, but I had no idea how I could find a car. In the eyes of the workers, the power of a clerk is impressive. They don't understand that I am nothing more than the director's servant, come to think of it. But at a time like this, truth was not an argument which could convince Big Pang. Apparently, I was the only "big-wig" he knew. He had no other strings to pull.

I held the receiver feeling somewhat vexed when a squat plump man came around from behind me. (I don't know when he entered the office). Laughing happily he said, "Here, let me say a few words to him." I was a little annoyed and plainly said, "What can I do for you?"

This fat little man had a pair of large, bright goldfish eyes that bulged out from a face so round it resembled a leavened wheat pancake. He seemed extremely genial and smiled as though he had just run into an old friend. I figured he must be the worker in charge of supplies and marketing and that he had come to the factory to take care of some business. I pointed out to the left with my hand and said, "The production section is the third door on the left."

The little man shook his head. "My name is Jin Fengchi, I've been assigned to work at the Eastern Chemical Factory by the Chemical Bureau."

So this was the new director! I was floored. I silently cursed myself for picking today to judge people on their appearance. More than anyone else, a clerk must avoid snobbishness.

I handed the receiver to Jin Fenchi. He picked it up and said in a voice which was serious though comforting, "Don't worry, Comrade Pang, tell me when you need the car." He took a ball point pen from his pocket and I handed him a sheet of paper. As he wrote, he repeated what Big Pang said.

"You need the car at 10:00, O.K. Where is your house? Jinzhou Road, Section 5, Number 8, all right. Now what's your full name? Pang Wancheng, good. Oh, Wancheng, wait outside by the front door to your house at 10:00. The car will definitely be there on time. You're welcome. No, no, don't mention it. Now is there anything else I can do for you? It doesn't matter who I am just as long as I can lend you a hand. One more thing. There is no need for sorrow when old people pass away. Don't get too upset. Take care of yourself and rest for a few days. . . ."

Jin Fengchi switched the receiver to his left hand and dialled another number. "Chemical Machinery Repair Shop? Who's this? Lao Du? Do you know who I am? Ha! Ha! Yes, I've just taken on the new post. I had to go; there was no other way. I hated like hell to leave you guys and our factory. Hey, something's come up and I need to borrow our van. Is that all right? It is? Great! Have Little Sun take it down to Jinzhou Road, Sec. 5, No. 8 at 10:00. He's looking for a fellow named Pang Wancheng. Thanks a lot, just give me a call if I can ever help you out."

He hung up, turned round and asked, "How many telephone lines do we have here?"

"This is a small factory," I said. "There're only three: this one, the one in the Production Department and the one in the reception booth."

He pulled up a stool and sat down, slipped a pack of cigarettes out of his pocket and insisted I take one. Then he lit one up himself. He looked at me a bit, his bulging eyes twinkling with laughter. Finally he said, "I don't have to ask, do I? You must be Comrade Wei, the clerk in charge of everything around here."

"My name is Wei Jixiang," I said politely. "But I'm afraid I've been assigned to a job that I'm not much good at. You'll have to make do with what you've got." It was clear from my tone of voice that I am not excited about my position as clerk.

Director Jin said politely, "I've just got here and I'm not familiar with this place at all. I'll be constantly asking you for your help."

I promptly waved my hand and said I was not looking forward to it.

Director Jin looked displeased. All the more earnestly he said, "Let me speak honestly. The masses are cadres' teachers, clerks are the instructors of directors. Whenever a meeting is called or a report given, a director relies on his clerk to write up a draft of what he is to say. If the clerk is talented then the director will appear competent, but if the clerk is no good then there's not much hope for the director. All official documents go through your hands first, and it's up to you to distribute them to whichever manager is in charge. Really, you are the supervisor of the director. While a director manages the workers, the clerk manages the director."

I could not sit still as he was talking. I had felt assured at first but that quickly turned to uneasiness and my face began to burn. I wasn't sure if he was flattering me or being sarcastic. In the factory I am nothing more than an intellectual performing a job I was never trained for. I was bewildered by this talk of the newly-arrived director. Even now I can't say with certainty what sort of impressions I have of this man. It seems he is at least a man who can get things done.

At noon, after the cremation of his father, Pang Wancheng came straight back to the factory without even having changed his mourning clothes. Director Jin had gone off with Secretary Liu to familiarize himself with the situation in the workshops. When the workers saw me leading Big Pang still dressed in his suit of mourning in search of the director, they were curious as to what was going on and all crowded around us.

When Big Pang saw the director, he ran straight over to him and threw himself down on the floor, in the old Tianjin style obeisance, knocking his head on the floor with loud thumps. It was astonishing that this old custom of filial kowtowing following a death in the family had made its way to our factory. That was the last thing I ever expected of Big Pang. Director Jin was also caught off guard. Flustered, he helped him to his feet. "Comrade Pang! What are you doing?"

At first, Big Pang was overcome with gratitude. On seeing that the director was himself somewhat moved, he could only stammer, "Director Jin, thank you, sir! If you hadn't sent that van to my house, my father would still be lying there for who knows how many days. He would've begun to stink because we couldn't have done anything with the body. My buried father, I'm sure, would thank you, sir! Thank you. . . ."

Jin tried to comfort Big Pang by patting him on the shoulder but the stumpy director couldn't quite reach up that high on the towering worker; so he grabbed his arm vigorously and said sincerely, "Big Pang, that's enough of this sort of talk. Nowadays, those who have connections, take advantage of them and those with power, use it. But what about the workers themselves who don't have any connections or influence? The way I see it is: one, it's no wonder there is some antagonism between the workers and their leaders; and two, naturally the workers aren't working as hard as they were before 1958. We complain that they are only concerned about their own affairs and are too self-centred, but it seems to me that no one cares about them when they have problems. If they don't look after themselves, who will?"

I was astonished at the boldness of Director Jin's speech. He had only just arrived and here he was in front of everybody talking frankly with the workers as if he were chatting with old pals, and in a tone that sounded indignant on their behalf.

Sure enough, all of this went straight to the hearts of the workers. I could tell from the look in their eyes and the sound of their whispering that Director Jin had made a better impact than if he had delivered an official speech on assuming office.

Secretary Liu was pleased to see the workers greet the newly-arrived director so warmly. "Old Jin," he said, "You see the workers in this factory aren't such bad fellows. Everyone is welcoming you."

Director Jin turned to Big Pang and repeated in front of the crowd what he had told him earlier on the telephone, "Wancheng, when people pass away, there is no coming back for them. Don't let it get to you. Take a few days off to rest at home and finish up all the funeral arrangements. Just make sure you take care of yourself."

Pang Wancheng, blushing brightly, was moved almost beyond words. "No," he said. "I don't want to rest. I came here to work." Having said that, he took off his mourning clothes and changed into his work clothes. Even though Director Jin told him to rest a few more days, he did not take time off more than was necessary. Of the allotted three-day leave for mourning he stayed out only a day and a half.

Old Liu escorted Director Jin off to another workshop. I turned around to head back to the office, when I suddenly noticed Vice-Director Luo standing behind the crowd. He was watching the receding figures of Liu and Jin, furiously inhaling a cigarette. Each of the pocks on his face stood out distinctly. These pock-marks are a barometer of his moods. When he is pleased, the light coloured pocks almost seem to disappear, but when annoyed or angry his face reddens and so each mark glaringly stands out.

He walked over to Big Pang and said as he laughed, "Pang Wancheng, I would never have thought a strong man like you had such weak legs. Someone lets you borrow a car and down you go on your knees."

Pang Wancheng was terrified. "Vice-Director Luo," he stuttered. "What do you...?"

Luo has the temperament of a dog. Without any warning he'll bark at you viciously and without any reason he's liable to bite. I pretended not to see them, turned my head and returned to the office. However, he ran up from behind and fell in step beside me.

"Lao Wei, our new boss sure knows how to win over popular support."

I didn't answer. When directors lock horns, I take no part in the tangle. I never lean towards one side or the other. I can see, though, that our small chemical factory is about to enter turbulent times.

March 23, 1979

"Director Jin's first act on assuming office was to have a car sent over from another work unit so that one of our docile workers could borrow it!" This story has spread throughout the factory, embellished somewhat at each re-telling. The people here are easily satisfied and more easily aroused.

April 2, 1979

I went with Director Jin to the company to give a work report today. Neither one of us said anything for quite a while as we rode in the jeep. Suddenly he turned to me and asked a question I had never expected.

"That line 'Even the mighty dragon cannot crush a snake in its own nest', what opera is it from?"

"*Shajiabang*," I turned to him and said.

Again we lapsed back into silence, but I understood completely what he had meant.

Once there we jumped down from the jeep and stepped into the office building. Director Jin said, "We must give our report first. Everyone is always more polite in the beginning. All the big shots won't want to start things off because they'll want to hear what the others have to say first. A little factory like ours can squeeze right in. Besides, when the meeting has just begun all the officials are paying attention and listening closely. Later on the old men are all tired, smoking cigarettes, drinking tea, or going to the toilet, so no one pays attention to the reports."

I respected his analysis but was still a little worried for him. He had not been at the factory a month yet. What could he have to report?

The company had called all the directors to come to this meeting. Secretary Liu was afraid that Director Jin had not spent enough time at the factory and so was not yet familiar with the situation. He suggested in his straightforward way that Vice-Director Luo should be called on to go on his behalf. I know Luo was very anxious to attend the meeting. But Director Jin simply laughed. "I'll go just the same," he said. I don't know if he wanted to deprive Luo Ming of the opportunity to appear before the company acting as director, or whether he did not want to lose this chance to present himself in his new position. I was an extraordinarily subtle move.

He was, after all, the first one to speak when the meeting began. He gave a lively report. He spoke of how Pang Wancheng had taken only one and a half days off when he was entitled to three days of mourning. He praised the workers while he said nothing about himself, but he left the leaders with the impression that he was quite capable. Afterwards the company officials commended our factory, and that was very uncommon for a small insignificant unit like ours.

I realized more and more that Director Jin is not all that simple. Just as the second report began he whispered to me, "Old

Wei, I'm going out for a while. Take good notes and pay especial attention to the reports on the experiences of the other factories and the suggestions of officials." Then he left for several hours, coming back only as the meeting was about to come to an end.

April 25, 1979

One strange thing follows another; these last few days Vice-Director Luo's pock-marks seem less have not been so noticeable. How could the storm of rivalry for authority have passed so quickly? Luo Ming is not the type that admits defeat easily. Has he conceded to Director Jin? It doesn't seem possible.

When I came back to the office from the cafeteria at noon today, Director Jin was on the phone in my office. Vice-Director Luo stood almost fawningly by his side. ". . . her name is Luo Jingyu. Yes, that's right, Luo-Jing-Yu. She is a relative of mine. Well, whether you can do it or not, I'm afraid it must be done. I want to hear from you by the end of the week. Good, O.K., it's settled."

That explained a lot of things. I don't approve of Director Jin always winning people over in this way but I respect his ability to calculate. Luo Ming is not an easy assistant to work with but he knows this factory inside out and he has his own clique ready to back him up. If Director Jin can buy off Lou Ming, then he'll have a solid foothold here. It hadn't occurred to me that he would do things this way. No wonder some of the workers have been saying behind his back that he is "slippery"!

May 10, 1979

Director Jin and I went to the bureau for a meeting. After sitting there for a bit he whispered in my ear, "Lao Wei, take good notes. I'm going out for a second." He plays the same trick whether it's a meeting at the company or the bureau. What was he doing out there?

After waiting a moment, I left the meeting room too. I thought I'd see what he was up to. Many of the offices in the chemical bureau building had their doors wide open as the weather was already getting rather hot. Director Jin was going from floor to floor paying everyone a visit. From the first floor to the fourth he went from room to room, everywhere acting as if he were walking into the home of old friends. He warmly greeted every section chief and every cadre, laughing and talking with them. Wherever he went he took expensive cigarettes from his pocket, liberally pressing them on people who smoked. From time to time he'd pick up someone else's cup of hot tea and drink from it freely, as one does with old friends. Of course, he wasn't the only one passing out cigarettes; others were giving theirs to him too. But he was obviously well acquainted with the people of every section. Sometimes he'd discuss a serious matter earnestly; sometimes it was pure idle chatter full of joking and laughing. In no time a few hours had passed.

Our little unit is probably insignificantly small in the eyes of the chemical bureau. That this unimportant factory director can wander through the bureau freely laughing and chatting with friends in every section, some of whom are cadres with status much higher than his own, is remarkable. I've got to admit in this respect he's quite extraordinary.

After the meeting, I asked Director Jin on the ride back to the office, "I've heard you've a lot of friends in the bureau and the company. Is that true?"

He looked at me and laughed, "Didn't you see them all today?"

I couldn't hide my embarrassment.

He said openly, "Lao Wei, in the little time I've known you, I have seen that you are a good worker. When you write, you write quickly and with style. All day long you're hard at work, busier than any director. But you are a bit of a bookworm and rather unimaginative in your approach to things. Let me tell you something that I've learned. In capitalist societies the key which opens all doors is money. In this country the key to all doors is connections. This situation is not going to change in the next four or five years. We are a little factory with unimportant cadres. We don't have status and we don't have power. If we don't take advantage of the connections we do have, if we don't pull the strings, we'll never make any headway."

A frightening outlook! I'm not sure if I am disgusted with him or admire him.

May 12, 1979

Vice-Director Luo's pock-marks had almost disappeared on his smiling face. He said to me gleefully, "Lao Wei, I've got something for you to do. Would you take Director Jin over to my house for dinner tonight? I'm afraid he won't come, so I want you to drag him over."

"You are a petty man," I thought to myself. "You are paying him back for arranging your daughter's employment." Then considering that Luo Ming is just an old unskilled pump worker who, through sheer luck, was admitted to the Party and subsequently promoted vice-director, what more should I expect? Still I didn't want to go to his house for dinner.

In the past when faced with this kind of unwanted invitation, I always used the wife and kid as an excuse to turn it down. If I didn't say my wife was sick then I'd say the kid had a fever. One way or another they have to be dragged into it on my account. I had to come up with a good one today to get out of this, so I said firmly, "Oh, dear! My little one's picked up a case of pneumonia. I've got to go home right after work and take him to the hospital."

Luo instantly looked severe. "I know it's awfully impertinent of me, a mere vice-director, to ask an important clerk like you to come to my house, so let's do this: bring Old Jin to my place first and then do whatever you have to do."

There was no way out! All I could do as I watched Luo Ming leave was curse myself, "If my son decides to become a clerk in the future I'll cut his fingers off!"

Before the end of the day, I went to invite Director Jin on behalf of Vice-Director Luo. He accepted it with pleasure and asked me to go with him. I repeated my excuse. Director Jin's eyes narrowed until they were only slits and he laughed, "You really aren't much of a liar, Lao Wei. From now on you'd better stick to the truth. Your face gives you away: red then white, white then red."

"Director Jin, it's the truth," I lied.

He laughed even more heartily, "Your excuses are always the same, you don't even change their pattern. You should keep your ear to the ground. Everyone in the whole factory knows that Lao Wei has only one all-weather excuse. No matter what comes up, if you don't want to take part, you'll say your wife or kid is sick. Someone as intelligent as you ought to be able to come up with a better excuse than that. Why always bring such calamities to your family?"

All I could do was given an awkward laugh and shake my head.

He patted me on the shoulder. "Don't be such a bookworm. When the vice-director gives a meal you don't accomplish anything by not going. We'll refuse to touch a drop of liquor that isn't worth a couple of yuan. Come on, we'll go together. You won't have to say a thing once we're in the door. Just keep your head down and eat your food. You can't turn down a free lunch you know!"

In the end I did not go, but I know the motivation behind Luo Ming's invitation. His daughter reported for work today at the state-operated No. 10 radio factory. Director Jin certainly can get things done; he has single-handedly tamed a fellow like Luo Ming.

When Party spirit, discipline and laws don't work, he resorts to personal loyalty and favours. I'm not sure why, but Director Jin has not earned my respect. My impression of his sincerity and geniality when he first arrived has been worn away by the events since then.

(The entries for June through September '79 have been deleted)

October 9, 1979

The superiors set the example for everyone below them. As

relations among leaders and cadres become more complex, society will accordingly produce the corresponding complexity. In turn, that will also be reflected in the people's political and philosophical thinking.

Luo Ming and Director Jin behave like close friends now, but Secretary Liu and Director Jin's relationship has become increasingly strained. At the cadres' meeting today the conflict between the secretary and the director came out into the open while they were discussing bonuses.

The higher authorities handed down a document in September which allows factories to give out workers' bonuses from the profit made. Our factory operates by using whatever materials are available, and most of our raw materials are picked up from what other factories throw away as waste. Our outlay is low, but we pull in a very good profit. The smaller a factory, the fewer the workers, and the easier it is to give out bonuses. When the September accounts were settled, it was discovered that every worker could get a bonus of 50 yuan. Even the office personnel could collect up to 40 yuan. For the majority of the workers, this was equal to doubling their month's salary.

Secretary Liu, the simple and honest man of Shandong, was astonished when he heard the figures. Although his own living condition is the lowest of factory-level cadres, he shook his head in objection. "This is not acceptable. It's too much money to give as a bonus!"

I could see from the expressions on not a few faces that most of the people disagreed with Liu. "Why is it too much? Money is not evil. It is no sin to give more. Who wouldn't be happier with an extra 40 yuan a month?" But none of the committee members opened their mouths to express either agreement or disagreement. They all watched the director and the secretary, waiting for them to settle the whole issue. They would have liked to receive more money of course, but no one was willing to say that.

Director Jin said to Luo Ming, "Lao Luo, what do you think?"

Vice-Director Luo replied frankly, "We should award the bonuses in accordance with instructions."

Secretary Liu said, "The documents were directed at enterprises in general, and our factory has its own special conditions. We shouldn't exploit this ambiguity. If the authorities knew we wanted to issue so much money there would be trouble."

"If we don't give the money out in bonuses what are we going to do with it? Just hand it over to the authorities?" Luo Ming retorted.

Secretary Liu answered, "We'll put it in the bank. We can use it in future for the benefit of everyone."

Director Jin sat without saying a word, smoking his cigarette. No one could guess where he stood. He was a man who dealt in connections, and he was adept at weighing the pros and cons. He wouldn't take risks to issue the workers a few dozen yuan in bonuses every month. What would he do if this adversely affected his relationship with the leaders of the bureau and the company? Was it not against the state interest? Might it not hurt the relationship between the workers and the state? Which way would he go? It seemed obvious. He could not sacrifice the war for this battle. Especially now that the Party secretary had made his stand clear, it was hard to believe he would oppose it openly. Everyone including me felt Director Jin would not approve the bonuses.

When Director Jin stated his position his first words were just what I had expected. He said, "Lao Liu is right. The bonuses are a bit large. . . ."

Vice-Director Luo turned red, "What . . . You. . . ."

Director Jin turned to him and waved his hand. Apparently they had discussed this matter privately beforehand. Having already convinced Luo Ming previously, could he turn round and recklessly exploit the present situation? Perhaps he had only used poor Luo Ming as a decoy to test how far the secretary was prepared to go.

Director Jin went on, "We are the leaders of the Eastern Chemical Factory. We ought to let the state worry about its own affairs. What we should concern ourselves with are the workers of the Eastern Chemical Factory. If we upset them, that would be very unfortunate. The instructions have already been announced to the workers. If we don't award bonuses according to those instructions then we will be breaking a promise. Not only would we be cursed but when the workers' dissatisfaction spread, production would be seriously affected. Therefore, I recommend that the entire bonus, all 50 yuan, be issued. If the company raises any objections we will say we have acted according to instructions from our superiors. If other factories report us then we will respond justifiably, 'We have worked harder; now we're enjoying the benefits. We've made a lot of money for the state and naturally our bonuses are larger!' What do you say to that?''

The majority of the committee men agreed to Director Jin's proposal and it was passed. Secretary Liu still felt that such large bonuses were not appropriate but he could not come up with any reason for objection. Although Director Jin's proposal was passed with a majority vote, after the meeting Liu asked him to stay behind.

After work I had to jot down some data for the company, so I still did not leave. I opened the door to Liu's office a little and listened to the conversation in the next room while I attended to the files. I was worried about Secretary Liu's temperament; he was too conscientious, honest to a fault. Director Wang, who had been transferred to another unit, was most suited to his temperament. He was straightforward, honest and frank to both his superiors and those below him. He never resorted to deception, but he had been too narrow-minded, and even at times somewhat sulky. Before the year was up he had been forced out by Luo Ming.

Now comes Director Jin who is quick and very capable. He's made very valuable connections with people both above and below. Even Luo Ming has been won over. The director and the vice-director in fact work together very well. Lao Liu could have done without his worries. He is making too much of it all, really. In the past he and Director Wang together proved to be no match against Luo Ming. So how can he single handedly oppose both Director Jin and Luo Ming now? An honest man can't win against a dirty fighter. I'm worried for him, and for our factory.

In the room next door, Lao Liu's voice was rising higher and higher, "the most important thing for a leader is to have the correct attitude. You cannot pander to the whims of one group. You've got to consider all sides. It is even more important not to take what belongs to the state and use it to cultivate people! Lao Jin, some people have come to me with reports of this problem. You must be more conscientious!"

This was a serious accusation for a senior official, all right. I quickly grabbed the now finished data and rushed them over to the next room, to relieve the tense atmosphere.

However, Director Jin was very cool. After listening to all that talk, he did not seem to be in the least concerned. He looked at me and said as he laughed, "Lao Wei, you've come just at the right moment. Let's have a little talk. Our Secretary Liu here is simply impossible. It's not surprising that our former colleagues here at the factory couldn't work with him. Our supervisor is more interested in having everyone below him kiss his ass than in really leading them a hand. Let me ask you, is there any evidence which suggests that I'm not doing my job properly? Would you say I've been taking what belongs to the state to curry favour with the workers? Am I not carrying out the instructions handed down to us correctly?"

"Ai!" Lao Liu waved his hand. "When it comes to money, the more you hand out the less everyone complains. Reduce it by just a fraction and the workers all start grumbling. But as leaders, we've got to think of their long-term welfare. We've got to teach and guide the workers. Doesn't the document say also that we should take some of the money for the collective benefit?"

"If you don't hand out the whole 50 yuan, the workers will curse us. Besides, if you do deduct some money, what do you use the rest of it for?"

"Save it for a rainy day. Of course, if something comes up in the next month or there is a task left unfinished, we could still award the bonuses. Once we've collected enough money in the bank we could build some dormitories for the workers."

"Forget it, Secretary Liu, you can't see you're creating trouble for yourself." Jin turned to me and said, "You're a clerk and this should be clear to you. Power's not worth a damn if you wait too long to use it. If you're told to award bonuses now, then you award them. If you don't award them the winds will shift and the order will be reversed. You still want to build a dormitory? For a little factory like ours it would be hard to build more than twenty or thirty apartments. The local construction bureau is going to want a few, the electricians and plumbers will each want a couple, and then the coal store and the grocery will want some. How many apartments will be left for us? We'll spend our money right now! We won't waste our time! Is it worth the cursing? Our workers aren't going to get anything out of it. If we take that money and put it in their hands, it will be secure and more beneficial!"

Secretary Liu expressed neither agreement nor disagreement. Director Jin pulled out a pack of cigarettes and offered one to each of us. Lao Liu declined, brought out one of his own, and smoked it. Director Jin took no notice, however, and stuck the cigarette he had offered to Liu into his own mouth. He lit it up, inhaled deeply, and then said, "What you're suggesting would have worked before 1958 but it won't work now. We have a challenging problem here; we cannot ignore the instructions of our superiors, nor can we carry them out completely. Lao Liu, how such trouble have you created for yourself in this type of situation? When some people were allowed to return to the city after the "cultural revolution", you didn't arrange jobs for them quickly enough, did you? There's something else, I tell you. About the wages which had been frozen. Those who pressed their claims fast got their money; those who acted slowly never got any. This sort of thing happens all the time. Whoever is not on his toes, suffers."

Director Jin spoke sincerely. He truly wanted to persuade Secretary Liu to be more flexible. Yet I felt Lao Liu was not impressed and his opposition only intensified.

Oct. 10, 1979

The whole factory is engaged in discussions after the announcement that the bonus would be given. What is exasperating is everyone knows about the argument concerning the bonus at the Party meeting yesterday, more than I do or can record. Secretary Liu has been generally cursed, and Director Jin has become the man of the hour!

I am outraged over the injustice done to Secretary Liu.

Making the most of the situation, Director Jin held a meeting for workers and staff in order to rally enough support behind him. Without asking me to write up the draft he delivered a short but deeply persuasive speech, truly displaying his adeptness.

He said, "the bonus given out this month is not one penny withheld. We have awarded all of it. Some people will be surprised when they receive this much money. All we ask is that everyone work hard. If we raise our factory's profits still higher, next month the bonus will be even larger. Rest assured, as long as I'm in charge of the money not one penny will be deducted, not one minute will be delayed in giving it all to you! . . ."

Nov. 2, 1979

It was a most disheartening Sunday. From 4:00 in th morning to 3:00 in the afternoon, I caught only three or four small carp. As I was on my way home I bumped into Director Jin. His day's catch filled a basket. I asked him where he had caught them. He laughed but didn't answer. I suppose he must be on good terms with whoever guards the fishpond and caught them there. Despite my refusal, he divided his catch and forced half of it on me. As we walked by his house he invited me in to sit for a while. I could not turn him down easily and in any case I wanted to see what his house was like. I figured a man as infinitely resourceful as he would definitely have a splendid home.

On stepping through the doorway, I discovered his house was extraordinarily plain. It was so austere I didn't dare believe it was the director's house.

His daughter was at home doing her homework. He told her to cook us some food and give us a little liquor. She gave him a quick glare, grabbed her book bag and went off to her grandmother's room.

Director Jin asked his mother to fix us something to eat and drink. The old lady agreed but never stopped grumbling. It wasn't long before his mother explained what the trouble was.

Of the 70 plus yuan that Director Jin makes each month, he hands over only a tiny fraction to his family. What's left over is for expensive cigarettes and good liquor. Every night when he is through with drinking at a local restaurant, he comes home and had a bite and that's all. The grandmother and his two children mainly rely on his wife's income to get by. His status at home is far below the status he enjoys at the factory.

It never occurred to me that he was that type of person. Ironically, it also gave me a somewhat favourable impression of him. While I sympathize with his family I admire the fact that he reserves his resourcefulness in monetary terms for the factory, rather than using it to his family's advantage.

Dec. 31, 1979

The bell rang announcing the end of the shift, but none of the cadres left his work because of Director Jin's earlier telephone call from the bank. He had gone there with the administrator of the finance section shortly after coming into office in the morning. The factory had decided to issue a hundred yuan for the year's bonus but the bank was not going to approve it. The director had taken all the documents himself for the negotiation. He stayed at the bank all morning and could not come back for lunch at noon. I didn't know why he had asked the cadres to wait.

After a little while, the director returned. His face was beaming with pleasure and he said, "Everybody get to work. No matter what, we're going to get this money divided up and handed out today."

The cadres were all delighted and, under the direction of the finance administrator, started counting out the money, sticking each stack of 100 yuan into a red envelope.

Secretary Liu brought the director into my office and said excitedly, "Lao Jin, we can't do this! It's wrong to give bonuses at random! The documents do not say that you can hand out so much money at the end of the year!"

Director Jin, who was in a rush, said curtly, "The documents do not say that I cannot hand it out, either."

"Lao Jin, this is a mistake! Is the factory going to close down after the New Year?"

"Damn it! You are just impossible!" Director Jin was struggling to suppress his anger. "How many times have I told you, we've got to issue what we have. Moreover, we've got to do it today. Otherwise, why do you think I wasted my time at the bank? There is no telling which way our superiors will turn next. It shifts constantly. See? Who knows what next year's regulations will be? If a new document arrives saying we should freeze the bonuses, then we won't be able to issue them even if we want to. Then we'd have to face all the workers' curses."

"If you're afraid of their curses, then let them curse me."

"The decision was made at the Party branch meeting, and you cannot reverse this by yourself. It's going to be issued!" Director Jin stormed out of the door. It was the first time I'd seen him lose his temper.

Jan. 3, 1980

As soon as I got in to work today I was given several documents. Among them was one announcing a freeze on the 1979 bonuses.

I brought the document to Director Jin. "I predicted that would happen!" he said, laughing.

After this was announced publicly, the acclaim for Director Jin grew throughout the factory. The cadres all discussed the matter too. Everybody was saying, "That 100 yuan was issued just in time. One day later, and we would have missed our chance. Director Jin has both foresight and the courage to act."

Then the election for the people's representatives was held in the afternoon. In accordance with the number of staff and workers in our factory the district gave us only one representative. This year's election was truly democratic; the superiors had not even picked the candidates; everything was left completely to the people.

The factory was divided up into four voting blocks. The workshops made up three while the cadres from all sections constituted the remaining one. Director Jin took the vote in each of the three workers' blocks with an overwhelming majority. In the cadres' block he won all but three vote. This was the result everyone had expected. One thing came as a surprise, though on one of the ballots, a worker had written, "Jin Fengchi is an old fox." Since the few workers who were responsible for counting the ballots could not keep this to themselves, this attack on Director Jin was quickly spread around.

After work, Director Jin came into my office with a couple of bottles of expensive liquor. "Don't leave yet, Lao Wei. Have a drink with your poor homeless director." He pulled out a couple of bags of peanuts from his pocket.

"Why can't you go home?" I asked.

"I had an argument with my wife yesterday, I'd better not go back yet. Otherwise, we'd start arguing again." He filled a teacup with the liquor and he threw back his head and poured it down his throat.

"Director Jin," I said, "it just isn't right the way you neglect your family. Starting next month I'll take a good portion out of your salary to give it to your family."

He laughed, "Come, come, drink up. Even an upright official

finds it hard to settle a family quarrel. My wife and I have been fighting for twenty years; that hasn't made me mend my ways. What makes you think you can help? Come on, drink up!''

Even without eating much of anything, he was able to put away his liquor. He'd drink two shots and then eat a peanut. The more he drank, the more he wanted to drink. In no time his bulging goldfish eyes turned red. Suddenly, he looked me straight in the eye and said, "Lao Wei, people nowadays are awfully hard to please. There are all kinds out there. No matter how you do things, you can't please everyone.''

I knew what he was referring to, but I didn't know what to say in reply.

He had another shot of liquor and said, "In order to please the workers, I've offended all the officials; on the other hand, if I wanted to please the officials I'd be upsetting the workers. Do you know which three cadres didn't vote for me today?''

I was astonished. How could he know who did not vote for him? Certainly he suspected Secretary Liu. It was obvious that the staid and proper secretary would not have cast his vote for him. All I could say was, "I don't know.''

Director Jin grinned. "One of the ballots was Luo Ming's; there is no doubt about that.''

I certainly had not thought of that, nor did I altogether believe it. "I thought he admired you quite a bit.''

"That's because I've done a few things for him; he doesn't have as many tricks as I do. But he is a somewhat malicious man. He's much too envious. Today he was right not to vote for me, though.''

"Who cast the third vote?'' I asked.

Touching the tip of his nose with his finger he said, "Me!''

He was either drunk or making fun of me, I thought.

"I'm telling you the truth.'' He gulped down another shot and continued a bit drunkenly. "I know that even you look down on me. You think I'm slippery, wheeler-dealer, don't you? I wasn't always this slippery, you know. The more I deal with people in this society, the thicker the grease is spread over my body. A loach is slippery so it can bury itself farther into the mud and escape the hands of men. When a man has been knocked around enough, he learns to be more slippery too. As society becomes more complex, men becomes more slippery. Simple as that. Secretary Liu is a good man, I know, but he didn't get as many votes as I did. What does this tell us about being a good man? If I ran the factory his way, did everything by the rules, it would result in bad management. The workers wouldn't be satisfied and the officials would be displeased. Don't think I'm happy because I've got the most votes. On the contrary, deep down I'm utterly despondent. I know Secretary Liu didn't cast his vote for me, but I cast my vote for him!"

"Director Jin, you've had too much to drink." I helped him to the bed where the night duty person sleeps. "You lie here for a while. I'll go home and get you something to eat."

I regretted voting for him this afternoon. Although he had won by a landslide, he would never be an appropriate "people's representative".

I truly believe that he will lose the elections next time!

Translated by Richard Belsky
Illustrated by Cai Rong

LI BINKUI
(1945 —   )

Li Binkui was born in 1945, in Heyang County, Shaanxi Province. After he graduated from a senior middle school in 1964, he returned to his native place and was engaged in farming. Four years later he joined the army. In 1974 he was transferred to the Drama Troupe of the Urumqi Military Area and since then he has been working as a staff writer.

His writing career began in 1964. In addition to the operetta *Red Lantern in a Snow-capped Mountain* and the play *The Green Land of Hazhina,* which is a joint work, he has published a dozen pieces of literary works, including a few short stories and two pieces of prose writing, namely "On Leave" and "A Fountain of Fire".

A SOLDIER IN THE TIANSHAN MOUNTAINS

Li Binkui

I

Plucking up courage, I hitch-hiked all by myself and arrived at Dry Gully. I headed straight for the troops' quarters, but to my great disappointment I found the barracks deserted, for the soldiers had all gone to the worksite in the depth of the Tianshan Mountains.

In the whole hostel, which was merely a few rows of prefabs, there was only one other guest. She was a rather attractive woman of about thirty, with an oval face and fine features. She had a little white flower pinned on her black woollen jacket. What puzzled me, however, was that her eyes were swollen with tears. She was mumbling to herself, "Haizhou, I shouldn't have left you. I've let you down."

The fierce wind was roaring over the vast Gobi Desert in the sandstorm and dust was swirling everywhere. I pushed the table and the spare bed board against the window and the door to give them proper support. Then I put on a gauze mask, and lay on the bed fully clothed. I stared blankly at the ceiling.

I had asked my factory management for permission to come and attend the conference on the improvement of shears in Xinjiang, because Zhitong had written to me several times, saying, "Please come, Qian. It's a good chance to see for yourself how we soldiers live and work in the Tianshan Mountains. I'm sure you'll be able to understand me better after this...."

The evening I set off, his mother came to see me with a large bag of toffees and asked me to give it to him personally.

It was bad enough, this sandstorm raging outside the troops' headquarters. What the devil would it be like up in the mountains? It so happened that Han, the Fifth Company Commander had just come down to the hostel to see the young woman. So I began wondering whether I should ask him to give the sweets to Zhitong. Then I decided that I shouldn't as he had phoned Zhitong shortly after my arrival, shouting merrily into the receiver: "Deputy Battalion Commander, your girl-friend is here to see you. All the way from Beijing! She has brought with her a bag of wedding sweets!" Oh, my gracious! For three months, I had not written him even a short note.

I came here simply because I wanted to put an end to our whole affair. There was a good deal of truth in what my friend Xiao Tian had said. He pointed out that it would be another year before Zhitong, now thirty-one, came to see his relatives in Beijing and that if I were to wait till then to let him know how I felt, it would mean another year's debt of emotion, so to speak. But what could I possibly say when I saw him again, here? Better write him a letter instead. That was a good idea! I threw off my quilt and got out of bed.

"Comrade Zheng Zhitong . . ." I began. But what an awkward address! And my words sounded cold and heartless. No, I should have written "Dear Zhitong". Every time I began my letter with his name, he would appear in my mind: a stalwart young man with a pair of penetrating eyes. His exploding merry laughter would also ring in my ears. At this moment I seemed to see him standing beside me, fondling my black hair and saying to me, "Qian, it is awfully heartless of you! I've made up my mind to go back to Beijing with you. I'll never leave you again."

"Impossible," I said to myself. Then I changed my mind as I pursued my thoughts. "Why be so pessimistic when you are coming to meet him in the mountains?" I argued within myself. Many a time had I argued thus and now I went over the arguments all over again. Suddenly, I hurled down my pen, crumbled the paper and flung myself onto the bed. I began weeping.

Inside, the lamp cast its dim, pale light on the young woman who looked like a bronze statue lying down; outside, the wind howled all night long vehemently shaking the low hut.

Early the next morning, a leading comrade from the worksite arrived in a jeep and went away with the woman guest I was feeling so miserable and began pacing the room, when Company Commander Han rushed in, his weather-beaten face lit up with a mysterious smile. He handed me a flattened matchbox, on which were these words:

Qian, sorry to have kept you waiting. Something has cropped up and needed immediate attention. See you tomorrow.
Zhitong

The scratchy handwriting obviously was a sign of the great hurry he must have been in. I felt uneasy. "What could have happened?" I wondered. "Apparently, there hasn't been any transport service for the past couple of days...." said Han. His hasty explanation and the white flower on the young woman's jacket increased my anxiety. I could not wait a minute longer. I wished I could see him right away. "Let's go at once!" I said and hurried out.

Without the slightest hesitation, I climbed into the cabin of a lorry, which was loaded with food supplies.

II

The lorry was racing into the mountains.

The asphalt road, wider than I had expected, took a serpentine course along the mountainside. All around were dense woods of firs which blotted out the sun; at the bottom of the valley flowed a river carrying with it chunks of ice. Because the road was not yet open to traffic, there were only a few trucks passing by. The gloomy ravine was quiet and chilly.

So this was the road built by Zhitong! This was the road which many a time his letters had made me visualize in my excited imagination! A new feeling came over me, as if I had entered the world of poetry or some dream-land. Indeed, our romance was like a dream. . . .

In 1971, there was a great stir in our school. At the meeting convened with a view to urging the school-graduates to go to the countryside, someone suddenly expressed his doubts. "We school-graduates should certainly receive re-education from the poor and lower-middle peasants," he remarked. "But what about the problem of unemployment in China?" The whole school was stunned and Zhitong's name spread around the campus. A meeting was then called to criticize him. Everyone was curious to see what that bold, unorthodox, reactionary element would do. By a stroke of luck, I was the first to denounce him. But my solemn speech, reinforced by gesticulating, was interrupted by giggles from the audience. I glowered at them in my indignation and found Zheng Zhitong sitting in the middle of the first row. He was shaking his close-shaved head superciliously, his face turned upward, as if he had nothing to do with the meeting. So, after this, the meeting was not taken too seriously. I took him to the Red Guards' headquarters. "Trying to be different and provocative, eh?" I demanded, banging the table. "What about you? A girl with a boy's haircut, aren't you trying to be different and provocative?" he sneered and looked at me with his piercing eyes. I blushed, my lips blue with rage, but I couldn't find any words for a retort. A few days later, Zheng Zhitong put up a big character poster announcing that he would live and work in the countryside of Shaanxi, the sacred place of the Chinese revolution.

He and I happened to have been assigned to the same village. I felt triumphant. He had, after all, repented and volunteered to re-educate himself! "Zheng Zhitong, you should have stayed behind for your employment prospects," I said to him, tongue in cheek, on the way to the countryside of Shaanxi. "What on earth has made you choose the Loess Plateau?" "Do you know how the Americans developed their Western areas?"

he laughed and went on. "Look at our forefathers who went to the border areas and kept watch on the frontier!" I ignored his remarks and chuckled to myself. Then he burst into laughter. I had never heard a laugh so strange and so loud ever since I was born. I was annoyed; but some of the schoolmates cheered him, others whistled and even stamped the floor. "Don't be conceited!" I cursed under my breath, "I may be a junior middle school graduate, but I look down upon those college students or even their professors. You have got nothing to be proud of. You are dull-minded, like a sturdy bull."

Two years went by. All the political movements had not turned anything for the better. School graduates, bottles in hand, tried to cultivate influential people in order to get themselves transferred back to Beijing. Those with their precious connections jeered at me and left; those without vented their spleen on me for the simple reason that I had taken the lead in upholding principles. My enthusiasm was gradually waning, and finally I became disillusioned too. Since I had refused to wheedle my way back to Beijing, I had no other alternative but to stick it out. I wished I were dead! In retrospect, I could not help feeling sorry for what I had done to Zheng Zhitong. So I began observing how he reacted to things around. He was no longer what he used to be: no inspiring speeches, no high-sounding comments. He became taciturn; day in and day out he farmed in the fields and didn't say a word even at meals. All his spare time was devoted to the perusal of philosophical books or magazines, which he kept under his pillow and worn-out mattress. There was a deep frown on his brow all day long, and he was lost in thought as if he had to solve all the world's problems.

One summer afternoon, there was a sudden rainstorm and presently water was cascading from the eaves. A thunderbolt struck an elm tree in the courtyard. Zheng Zhitong, barefooted, in his vest and shorts, was making his way down the village. Sheer danger and stupidity! I cried and rushed out into the rain, chasing him. I spotted him standing on a precipice, gesticulating, looking at the sky. When I had come close, I heard him reciting a poem of the Song period: "The great river flows eastward, washing away traces of the great men, generations past. . . ." "Are you crazy?" I ran up and caught his arm, wondering how I had plucked up my courage. Perplexed, he looked at me and said, "You yourself are crazy, too." "You must have gone mad rushing into the rainstorm like this. Aren't you trying to kill yourself?" "Killing myself? I'm just having a rain bath in the storm!" He looked calm but serious as he uttered every word clearly. I tried to size him up again. When he realized what I had been worrying about, he burst into his usual ear-piercing laughter. "You are making a fool of yourself, Cultivator," he said. (Cultivator was the name I chose for myself when I began work in the village.) "The open country, now glorying in this lightning, rainstorm and howling wind, is a poem in itself! It has bred heroes for so many generations. Why should we be scared and stay away from these testing forces of nature, here in this very sacred place of the revolution which has given us a new China? Come along, let's have a walk!" His romantic and warm words drove away my cold and for the first time I had a glimpse of his strength of mind and purity of heart.

We walked chattering idly, for two hours or so. Later, I got a high fever, which lasted a few days. To make things even worse, he came up sneezing and said to me, "I find that I have been sloppy and undisciplined. I should live a soldier's life. I'll join the army." I didn't want him to leave me; I didn't know why. So I said to him sarcastically that he was only trying to zigzag back to Beijing. "Nonsense! Some people may do it for personal gain, but I join the army in order to know more of our society. . . ." In my desperation I reminded him, "You were criticized and disciplined at school, weren't you?" Immediately, he bit his middle finger and wrote on a piece of paper: "Man should go out to face the world." He decided to present it to the army officers who were recruiting in the area. "All right," I said with tears in my eyes. "You can all leave me. I'll kill myself." He replied sternly, giving me a good dressing down, "Suicide! It's very nice of you to say that! Look at those country folk. They supported the revolutionary wars whole-heartedly. And now they're still hungry. They can barely find enough black soya beans or millet to fill up their stomaches. What can they do? Commit suicide? Crawl to the cities or towns and try to live and work there? My dear Cultivator, over the past few years I have seen clearly for myself the plight of those who have a low station in life. Probably I feel more miserable than you do. The 'cultural revolution' may ruin us, but it is likely that some real fine men will come out of it. We should think hard and look into things and work for the benefit of our country and the people." I knew him well: a man who would pursue an unswerving course once he felt he had made the right decision. So with tears in my eyes, I walked with him for three kilometres and saw him off. He left. His unit was stationed at Qaidam in Qinghai. It was extremely cold there and people had to wear cotton-padded coats all the year round. He wrote me a few letters, but they were all impersonal. My heart turned cold. And yet who could ever forget the very first person to whom one had lost one's heart?

III

The lorry raced on, leaving the fir woods far behind. After we had gone up a frozen river, there came into view a huge glistening slope and a snow-covered mountain ridge. Suddenly, the sky looked wider, with a deeper blue set off against the white sheen of snow.

In 1977 I was transferred to Beijing. One winter evening I attended a party at Xiao Tian's home and danced till midnight. When I got home, I pushed open the door, which was unlocked. I found my mother moaning in bed, surrounded by my father, younger brother and sister and a soldier. Upon seeing me, the soldier called, "Cultivator Li . . ." His resonant voice gave me a start. Zheng Zhitong, it was Zhitong! He still remembered the name I gave myself when we were working in the village. "Your mother fell down when she was trying to get on a crowded bus and hurt her side," my father explained. "It was Zheng who carried her home on his back. My mother forced herself to sit up and said, "He wanted to leave until he heard you were my daughter."

I wondered if I was in a dream-land. He looked tall and sturdy in his uniform. His square face suggested masculine strength. There seemed to be a hunter's toughness about him. He was looking me up and down. Then our eyes met.

It was an embarrassing moment, all right, but my mother had to go on, "Qian's still single. She snubs anyone who would mention the word marriage. How about you? Have you got a family?" As he rubbed his hands in great embarrassment, my heart was throbbing. After a long while he stammered, "It is a rule in the army that unmarried soldiers have a leave every two years. Our commander insisted that I not return until I have found myself a wife." I could hardly suppress a giggle; I was relieved. My younger sister sniggered so hard that Zhitong blushed.

The night deepened, and there was not a soul in the street when I walked him out of the alley.

"Come again on Sunday."

"Sorry, I'm afraid I can't. My leave is over."

"You mean you have found a wife?" No sooner had I said this than I regretted having made such a flippant remark. Smiling bitterly, he said, "It is hard to win the heart of a girl here in Beijing. Who wants to marry a foot-slogger like me from Xinjiang?"

"Oh, come off it, officer," I said jovially, pretending to be casual. "I'm afraid you are too choosy."

"Nonsense!" he hastened to explain. "I don't want girls to be introduced to me. I prefer a girl who once worked with me and therefore understands me. . . ." His eager eyes looked into my face. Disconcerted, I looked away, pretending to tidy my hair.

Both of us stood speechless, each waiting for the other to speak, our hearts beating faster. But Zhitong was a man of remarkable self-control and, having looked at his watch, he shook my hand and left.

The day Zhitong returned to the army, I went to the railway station to see him off. On the way back his mother kept grumbling, "Now he is deputy battalion commander, and a model officer of the engineer corps, but what is the use of that? He is twenty-nine and still single. Nowadays soldiers are nothing but trash in the eyes of the girls. Even country girls won't have them; they were looking for city boys! Who'll follow him to Xinjiang? Alas. . . ."

Often, in the still of the night, the twinkling stars reminded me of the old days Zhitong and I shared in the countryside. At last I could not bear waiting any longer. I wrote him a letter trying to find out how he felt. One month passed, and then another, without any reply from Xinjiang. I got so cross that I wouldn't allow anyone to mention his name.

Barely two months later, came the spring of 1978. One day after work my younger sister came home and, making face at me, said, "Great news! I just ran into Zheng Zhitong in the subway. He is studying at a military academy. He asked after you." "Did he? I'm not interested." Feeling snubbed, she turned away. That evening Zhitong turned up suddenly and he was all smiles. Indifferently, I showed him to my room, deliberately avoiding his eyes.

"I know you feel annoyed," he said, trying to make amends. I began to yield. But when I asked him why he didn't answer my letter, his smile vanished and on his face appeared the familiar frown. After a while, he said decidedly, "We soldiers are straightforward. I hope you don't mind what I'm going to say even if in doing so I'm making a blunder. Before the 'cultural revolution', soldiers from the border areas or the northwestern plateaus were held in high esteem. They would introduce themselves readily, sticking out their chests, when they took lodgings or looked for girl-friends. 'I'm from the border areas.' For that statement alone would make people admire them. But now we have to say humbly, 'I'm from the border areas; you may not like that.' " He breathed heavily, his face reddened with rage. "To tell you the truth, I don't need any sympathy; nor do I need charity," he continued. "When I was in Beijing last time, I was fed up with the cool detachment some people displayed for soldiers. I simply can't stand such insults!" He banged at the table, his body trembling all over. "Well, you can't stand it, so you suppose I can?" I retorted. "Cultivator, I know it's not easy for you to be transferred to Beijing. Why should I be in the way of your future happiness? So. . . ." "So what? Why bother to explain, since you think you know all?" That was all I could say.

My sarcastic words silenced him. Several times, he rose to go, but dawdled and sat down again, lowering his head in great embarrassment. After I calmed down, I regretted having hurt him so much. Obviously, he had all along loved me, but he didn't like to put me in a dilemma. Probably he had suffered a great deal after reading my letter and it was long before he regained his self-control. But in the end he could come up only with a lame explanation which was more like a confession. A man of his sense of self-respect must have passed through terrible ordeals putting up with a girl's sarcasm! I began to feel uneasy.

Spring, after all, was a season for love. So let me shut my eyes and be carried away by the current of emotion. Let me be driven to where he was. I prayed that it wouldn't lead to misfortune.

IV

The lorry was racing on and on. . . .

The red sun peeped out from the clouds. Its golden rays fell on the white snow, which sent back dazzling, bright lights. New-comers naturally compared the beauty of the snow scene to that of a charming girl. Little could they imagine that at the shout of "avalanche!" its ugly face would show itself glorying in its destructive power.

As Zhitong had foreseen, my mother, though delighted to see us in love, was worried that Xinjiang was too far away. My younger sister, however, had other ideas. She believed that Zhitong would surely be posted to work in the academy and, even if that did not work out, he could still leave the army and return to Beijing. Mimi, my best girl friend, urged me to give him up. She advised me, "Why, things have changed. It's no longer fashionable to court a foot-slogger. If I were as pretty as you, I would certainly choose a high official, an overseas Chinese, or at least a college graduate. Give him up!" Xiao Tian even went so far as to make fun of me by saying, "Hey, why don't you let us meet your hero lover?" Since Zhitong didn't mind my friendship with Xiao Tian, I decided to introduce him to my circle of friends. When we arrived, Mimi and some others were dancing. She said saucily, "How marvellous to have a guest from Xinjiang, a land of song and dance! Come on, give us a performance!" The others were laughing heartily. I felt humiliated. Who would have thought that Zhitong would accept the request! Casually, he began waltzing with me. He danced with grace, following the rhythm of the sweet music, and moved lightly and nimbly almost like a dragonfly skimming the surface of the water. I was fascinated by his elegance. Gently, he gave me a sweet smile and whispered, "Shall we go to a concert next time?" Indeed, my cup of happiness was full.

Xiao Tian felt jealous. Snapping his fingers, he cried, "That's no good. Let's have some real music." "Let's have 'Good Wine and Coffee'," one of them echoed. The tape recorder started playing and all at once a trembling voice, more like crying, wailed: "Who loves me? Who will love me? . . ." Mimi was now swaying her sensual hips, her gilt necklace rippling, and, making eyes at Zhitong, invited him to dance with her.

Zhitong knitted his brows, looking very displeased. "Sorry, I must be off now." Then he swept out of the room, slamming the carved door.

I ran after him and soon caught up with him; but before I could say anything, he bawled, "No need to explain! I won't listen anyway! That's no recreation. They are a rotten lot, bored and frustrated. What would our soldiers in Tianshan think if they saw such rot?" Tianshan again! I was sick to death of it. "Do you love me or your Tianshan? Your buddies may think whatever they like. It's none of my business!" I mounted my bicycle and pedaled away. He was standing there, still fuming. It served him right!

After this, for two whole weeks we didn't see each other. Often I skipped supper. I picked up an English textbook and tried to read but my mind was elsewhere. It was dreary weather. There was no wind, and the heat was stifling. Then he suddenly turned up with two pink tickets in his hand.

"There is a concert tonight. Let's go." He seemed to be in high spirits, as if nothing had ever happened between us. "Go away! I'm trying to get some sleep." I was lying in bed and pulled the quilt over my head. He kept silent for a long while. It was heart-rending to hear his chair creaking. "All right," he said at last. "I'm sorry I was rude, but I do think that you have changed a great deal over the past few years. You have lost your spiritual mainstay," he said gently and every word of his touched the chord of my heart.

I had to admit that he was right. There was no need for him to remind me of the days I spent in the countryside. I had been feeling low since I returned to Beijing. Work, meals and wages had somehow become the routine of my life. I felt empty after the parties at Xiao Tian's home. As a way out, I sometimes shut myself up in my room, practising calligraphy or reading English. Late at night, lying in bed, I felt as if I were in a boat which had lost its direction, drifting away in the ocean. Sometimes I did want to exert myself and find some real purpose in life. But what could one do? True, the Gang of Four had been overthrown, but what did that mean to me? I had had a terrible time working like a slave in the countryside for six years, but some people still thought that had been a completely unnecessary sacrifice. Now look at

Xiao Tian! He escaped being sent to the countryside by enlisting in the army through his influential connections. He remained in the city and even managed to join the Party. Then, once again through mysterious channels, he had found an easy job in the Tourist Bureau! My transfer to Beijing couldn't have been made possible without my appeal to him — I had to put on a forced smile when I went to see him. The fact that I had taken the lead in going to the countryside was still a laughing-stock. So much for all that talk about noble ideals and revolution! What a joke!

"Well, reality is never as rosy as we would like to imagine." Zhitong sighed. Then he began to give an account of what he himself had gone through over the past few years.

"I simply thought the army a paradise when I first joined up in 1973. Shortly after I was enrolled in a company, I was transferred to the regiment's spare-time propaganda team. Everyday, when the soldiers were eating their meals the chickens raised by the regiment commander would come into the mess looking for food. Very soon, their droppings were everywhere. I was hot-tempered, as you know. So I flared up and on the spot killed one of them with a big broom. Then I put up a big-character poster at the entrance criticizing the commander. As a result, I was made to write a self-criticism and sent back to the company 'to be disciplined'. This drove me mad. To hell with the commander! A civilian official like him would have been labelled as a capitalist-roader, pure and simple; as my thought ran wild, I came to believe that our country was a hopeless case since a regiment commander could be so rotten. Later, our regiment was transferred to Xinjiang. The troops had hardly entered the mountains when they were caught in an awful snowstorm. Our trucks moved along at a snail's pace. For a day and a night we covered only five kilometres. Before long, we ran out of food. The orderly went under a truck and cooked some soya beans with a blowlamp for the commander. But he gave all the beans to the drivers. He also joined us in digging away the snow and pushing the trucks. I was so moved at the time that I could have shouted:

'Long live the commander!' For me there was no doubt that his was the very image of a veteran revolutionary. Afterwards I often wondered what sort of man he really was; but the more I thought, the more perplexed I got. As time passed, I gradually found the answer: the worse after-effect of the 'cultural revolution' was that our ways of thinking had become mechanical. We tended to go to extremes. When you were praised, you were nothing but good; when criticized, you were anything but good. Girls wearing a boy's hair-cut and dancing the 'Loyal Dance' were supposed to be the most radical; at present, however, wearing long hair and dancing rock-and-roll is thought to be a sign of the complete emancipation of mind. Things keep changing and you will soon learn the safest way is to follow the trend of the day. But I still don't see what is wrong with going down to the countryside and what is wrong with carrying out the revolutionary drive to build up the rural areas. Are we left now with nothing but broken dreams and a bitter past? If that were the conclusion reached by the young people of our generation, what could the country expect of them? How can the country build a new spiritual life on such an ideological ruin?"

One after another, his solemn words found their way into my heart and together with the patter of the rain outside they brought me back to the days when I was a radical student, when Zhitong and I lived and worked on the northwestern plateaus. Oh, that unforgettable night when he had a rain bath in the storm!! And here in this room were the two of us again, of the same generation but now how different from each other! Why was I so bitter and frustrated, grumbling at the social injustice I had suffered, while all along he had been unswerving in his pursuit of the truth in life and found it! Failing to control myself, I began to cry.

Zhitong lifted the quilt gently and brushed my forehead and cheeks with his handkerchief. As if coaxing a child, he said soothingly, "Ah I see you've embroidered the English words 'Good night' on your quilt cover. It's careless of me not to have noticed that you have been learning English and studying hard." "Boo, you are the greatest!" I retorted. He gently held my hand in his own saying, "I'm not good enough for you, Qian. You're still the best!" I must have appeared like a spoilt child and after a while putting my hands around his neck, tried to sit up.

Since then I had been madly in love with him. One day we were rowing on the Kunming Lake at the Summer Palace, I was so overcome by emotion that I dropped a hint about marriage. He told me in all seriousness that he had to rejoin his men in a few days. "Will you like to live with me in the mountains all your life?" he asked. I had never thought of this before and my mind began to reel again. . . .

"Hold on tight!" The driver's warning pulled me back to present from my reverie. I found the lorry moving along a not properly surfaced road. Glancing at my watch, I inquired anxiously, "Are we getting near the worksite?"

"This is the Dotted-line District before us," the driver answered, his eyes fixed on the road ahead. His short moustache twitched faintly.

"Is your battalion stationed in the Dotted-line District?"

"Yes."

"Are you very busy?"

"Not really. Two shifts a day, twelve hours a shift, not including emergency work." His sarcasm got on my nerves. A new recruit trying to impress people. That's all, I thought.

V

The lorry pulled up before piles of frozen rock and sandstones. We had arrived at last! But I began to feel uneasy and a little confused.

Han jumped down from the lorry, his lips betraying the effects of the cold. He told me that it was already 3,000 metres above sea-level and that the Dotted-line District was so named because it was impossible to make an on-the-spot survey of the precipices and the steep cliffs and therefore they had to map it out in dotted lines. "Wait for me here. I'm going to find the deputy battalion commander." He started off running and moving nimbly among the rocks and finally joined the soldiers on the other side. I couldn't hear what they were talking about because of the howling wind. However, I could see one of them pointing somewhere in the mid-air. I looked up.

Good gracious! What did I see but a precipitous cliff such as I had never seen before? It tilted backward menacingly like an injured wild beast and it was puffing out clouds of smoke and vapour. Barely visible in the misty clouds was a snow-covered man clinging to the cliff unsteadily against the cold wind blowing in gusts. He was trying to hit an overhanging piece of a rock with a steel pole. Any minute he could be swept away like a fallen leaf. "Well, could it be Zhitong?" All of a sudden, I was overcome with fear. Hastily, I ran forward to get a closer look despite my benumbed legs.

"Stop, it's dangerous!" Han yelled, running towards me. Before I realized what was going on, the whole valley was shaken by a thunderous crash. Instantly, thick clouds of dust and snow went up and Zhitong vanished from my sight. I screamed and, covering my eyes with my hands, fainted.

I didn't know how long it was before I came to and heard a familiar voice shouting, "What's happened? Is anyone hurt?" Then the voice was filled with surprise and delight, "Oh, how come you're here?" Han and others were chuckling. I blushed and had a quick look at him. His appearance astonished me. He was wearing a worn-out osier hat, with a broad, thick safety-belt fastened around his waist over a threadbare cotton-padded coat. His galoshes were covered with slush, his face and body with scraps of ice and rock. But for his black shining eyes, I wouldn't have been able to recognize him. I was deeply grieved.

Oddly enough, on seeing me, he did not appear as excited as I had expected. I could still remember the night shortly before he finished his study at the academy. It was eleven at night when somebody was knocking on my door. Something dreadful must have happened, I thought. But it was only

Zhitong, who said casually, "Nothing the matter, only I desperately want to see you.... Don't ask me why, but I've got the premonition that we'll never see each other again." I walked with him for the rest of the night. It was not until then that I realized that he had been madly in love with me, too....

And now, it might be a woman's instinct, but I was certain that he was preoccupied by some troubles; otherwise he wouldn't have been so indifferent. "Let Han take you to the battalion headquarters," he said coldly. "I've to look after the work here first." "Just as you please!" was my colder answer. He hesitated for a while, and I could see he wanted to talk to me. But then he changed his mind. Stepping up to Han, he said, "The out-hanging rock has been removed. Tell the soldiers to set their minds at ease. You must get the road-bed cleared before four this afternoon. You'll be in charge now. I'm going to call up the political instructor."

The ice and snow scraps swirling in the wind were beating full in my face. Before long, my legs were benumbed with cold, but my heart felt colder. When he finished talking with Han, I picked up my bag, getting ready to go with him. He seemed to take no notice of me, as he headed for a dug-out to make his phone call. The sympathy I felt for him was now turned into resentment. He must have heard something about what I had been doing and guessed why I had come. So he was giving me the cold shoulder on purpose!

Shortly after we parted from each other last time, his regiment commander came to Beijing to attend a conference. He paid me a personal visit and urged me to get married and live in the barracks. It so happened that Mimi had been pestering me with the request to accept a date with one of Xiao Tian's classmates, who was due to study abroad and whose father was a high-ranking official. In a dilemma, I turned down both. Soon after this Zhitong wrote to me, insisting that I should break with Xiao Tian and Mimi. Alas, what a predicament I was thrown in! My younger sister, who thought highly of Zhitong, commented that he was a fine man but would make a lousy husband....

Now, so much the better, I thought. Since he had deliberately left me out in the cold, I would tell him clearly what was on my mind and then leave him in the afternoon. This damned place was not fit for living. . . . No, I began to change my mind. No, I'd better think it over again before rushing to a final decision. Such a break would mean a severe blow to a person's most tender feelings. What would become of him then?

Bang! Another blast somewhere. I looked at the cliff whose overhanging rock had just been removed. Zhitong came running up and, passing me his sweaty helmet, lifted my bag and turned away. Not until we were safely out of the Dotted-line District did he explain to me, "I know you were anxious to meet me down in the hostel. I was in the worksite when Han phoned me. So I scribbled a note for the driver to take down to you. . . . The Dotted-line District is perilously covered with scraps of frozen rock and there have been a few accidents. As there hasn't been any transport service for the past few days fuel and equipment cannot be brought here. Besides, we are running out of food supplies. Though he tried to force a smile, his tone betrayed his great worry. I should have said something to lighten the awkward atmosphere, but suddenly I felt suffocated and was going to throw up. He looked at me and said most casually, "You'll be all right. It's high altitude. New-comers always feel it. As a rule, women suffer less than men." I squatted at the roadside, fuming. I retched but didn't throw up anything, for I had not had a meal since the previous evening. He bent to pat, or rather beat, me on the back. Glowering at him, I protested, "Not so hard!"

It was a summer's day after all. As we descended, I noticed the snow was melting. There were patches of green here and there on the slopes. Little flowers were peeping out between the icicles by the roadside; even the sun seemed warmer. Zhitong's sense of humour came back. He skipped and leapt and slid on the ice, asking me questions all the time. He was most interested in what was going on in Beijing, and was filled with envy upon hearing about the recent performance of a foreign symphony orchestra. "How very nice if one could get some live television coverage and watch the performance here in the mountains!" Was he making roundabout references to the purpose of my coming here or dropping a hint about coming back to Beijing?

As the snow melted, water kept trickling down the rugged slopes. The dripping sound could be heard everywhere. I could hardly find a dry place to put my feet on. "You'll sprain your ankles, walking in your high-heels. Let me carry you across!" I could not tell whether he was joking or mocking at me. Pretending not to have heard him, I lifted my foot, trying to step on a stone. "That won't do!" he chuckled, winking at me. "You'd better put on my galoshes. I'll walk barefoot." In a huff, I leapt forward valiantly, when a truck passed by at top speed, splashing the slush. Startled, I fell off the stone, spattered all over, my feet landing in a puddle. Zheng Zhitong laughed until tears came into his eyes. "Serves you right! Now you know our Tianshan Mountains, eh?" What a cruel and boisterous laugh! That was too much for me. So sneering, I retorted, "Yes, I know you only too well, don't I?" Shocked, he ran up, all in a fluster. "I was only teasing you. Why did you say that?" I didn't reply, trudging mechanically along the muddy road, my mind having become a blank. He glanced at me from time to time without saying anything. He sighed audibly. . . .

VI

Their battalion headquarters consisted of only a few bleached tents pitched on a terrace levelled on a slope. At the entrance was a frame, over three metres high, made of three pieces of wood. In the middle of the horizontal piece, to my surprise, hung a big white paper flower; on each of the two vertical ones was posted a long, worn-out, sad-looking elegiac line, written in black characters on white paper. These lines read:

He shed his blood on Tianshan; for what did he lay down his life? For the name of his country and the army.

He lived ten years away from his wife; where did he find happiness? In the union of countless couples outside.

I recognized Zhitong's firm, strong handwriting immediately. He paused before it for a short while, looking melancholy again. "Someone has died?" I was just wondering, when the political instructor came out to meet us.

Promptly heads appeared at the door curtains and window flaps. It seemed as if everyone were looking at me. The messenger was staring at my sunglasses. I felt completely out of place among those smelly, boisterous soldiers. I sat at the table, without saying a word.

"Why, a girl from Beijing shouldn't be so shy, should she?"

"Stop talking nonsense! She is feeling car sick. Have some sweets, please . . ." Zhitong managed a smile and tried to get me out of the embarrassment. But when they saw the sweets, they became even more cheerful. "Good, you're throwing a party before the wedding ceremony, eh? So much the better! we'll visit your bridal chamber for fun, all the same! Following tradition, you know. You'd better warn your fiancee beforehand. We are a rough bunch and she shouldn't lose her temper, when we celebrate your wedding." Zheng Zhitong kept nodding his head all the time. Finally, the political instructor came to our rescue. Beaming with joy, they went back to work. Then came the last straw when I overheard Zhitong and the political instructor arranging my lodgings.

"How ridiculous! The whole lot of you!" I stopped them, as he was about to enter the tent. "They teased you because they were pleased to meet you," he explained. "You see, Han has spread the news that you are coming here to marry me!" he said, laughing to himself. "Gosh!" I interrupted. "Who told him that I'd come to marry you?" His face froze at my impertinent remarks; he wanted to say something but did not. He snorted, shook his head, and went out.

As the sun's rays came into the padded tent through a small

window, it was getting so hot that I took off my woolen sweater and still perspired profusely.   When Zhitong came back again, he lifted the bucket of melted ice off the stove and smothered the fire by putting a layer of damp coal on it.   "That's the weather here in the mountains.   You go through the four seasons in a single day and have to change your clothes accordingly."   After washing his face, he took out a pair of slippers from under the bed, saying, "Put them on.   I'll take your leather shoes out in the sun." So he had softened up.   "I don't like to change my shoes," I sneered. "Take them off.   They are soaked through. You'll catch cold." Then he coaxed, "You are the same stubborn girl, aren't you? All right, I was wrong, OK?" He stooped to unfasten my shoe laces.   My legs jerked and nearly hit him on his forehead.   I was nervous, but he was still squatting in front of me, his intelligent and gentle eyes staring into my face.   He seemed to me like a kind elder brother cajoling his mischievous little sister.   I was moved.

Indeed, he looked lean and haggard! Long exposure to the sun and the storms on the plateau had tanned his skin.   With sallow cheeks and a stubbly beard, he looked like a man of forty.   His bright eyes were blood-shot from excessive fatigue and anxiety and his voice had become husky.   Since we got to the battalion headquarters, he had been so busy looking after me that he had not thought of changing his own clothes. Now the melting ice began dripping down from his padded coat. I could not let him suffer any longer. "Well, I'll change my shoes, then," I said in a reconciled tone.   "You'd better change your clothes, too.   How terrible you look in them!" He grinned. "No hurry! I'll have to see about supper first." "Aren't you crazy? Take off your padded coat!" I demanded and tried to strip it off, but he quickly moved away. I felt annoyed.   After a long while, he complied most reluctantly, grinning sheepishly, with his hands behind his back.

I pretended to ignore him at first and then, quite abruptly, dived behind his back and pulled apart his hands.   I was stunned! Good gracious! His side had been seriously injured, his shirt was stuck to the unhealed wound, and around the blackened scabs were traces of blood and sweat. So that was why he had always been wearing a broad leather belt! He took it calmly, however. "Nothing serious!" he said, trying to make me feel at ease. "Only a scratch, that's all." It was obvious that he had been working without letting anybody know about it. I dipped a towel into the hot water and loosened the smelly shirt from the skin by pressing the towel hard against it. When I applied balm to his wound, my tears kept dropping on his bare back. I didn't quite see why he should risk his life in so wretched a place. Zhitong was leaning on the table, listening to my complaints quietly. It was long before he spoke again. "There was a terrible avalanche in the Dotted-line District last Sunday," he said slowly, "Yu Haizhou, political instructor of the Fifth Company, was killed; the rock was all red with his blood. The accident happened when his wife had just come to visit him. She is staying in the tent down there."

"So that's the woman I met in the hostel!" My teeth chattered. Zhitong heaved violently as he nodded and then, straightening up, said, "They married young. Their son is already two years old, but they had lived apart from each other for ten years. Yu had always been in poor health. This time all his wife wanted to bring him was a bag of Chinese medicinal herbs. Who would have thought. . . ." He broke down. "I got injured when I was digging out the corpse. It's nothing serious. As a matter of fact, Qian, the very thought of Yu's death helps me to stick it out. You didn't write me a single word for months. This drove me mad." Excited, he turned round and grasped my hands and, biting his lips, made great efforts to curb his emotion, but his eyes were still swollen with tears. "Qian, you must stay here longer this time. I've got so much to talk to you. . . ."

I felt sort of choked. What should I say to him in face of his outburst of emotion? I was feeling guilty and ashamed as well as embarrassed. Unable to endure such mental torture any longer, I flung myself into his arms and cried. I wept and kept knocking my head against his broad chest as I urged him,

"Let's go back! I'll do anything so long as you leave the army. I can't bear to see you suffer so much."

He smiled. Holding my face in his rough hands, he wiped the tears off my face with his fingers and said, "That's real baby talk. Do you think I'll leave?" "Why not?" I asked, without giving him a chance to explain, and went on. "Who knows, indeed who cares, that you soldiers are risking your lives? By hook or by crook, lots of ex-service cadres are trying to get back and work in Beijing. There are people who don't want to live in their own country, too. Xiao Tian and some others are now applying for passports. Don't be a fool, Zhitong. You'd better get out of Tianshan and take a look at the outside world." My voice had become a shout.

"Different people have different ways of looking at the world. For me, I believe some people have to build roads so that others could travel more easily. As for Xiao Tian and his like, better forget about them." Zhitong gave a grim smile and, turning to me, said warmly, "Qian, let's talk about ourselves."

Just then the driver who had given me a lift up the mountains called for Zhitong. He went out of the tent. What a nuisance!

I leaned against the desk, my mind in a muddle. There was a faint fragrance oozing out of the snowdrops on his clean desk. My eyes fell on a photo of a smiling girl whose black eyes revealed a mixture of annoyance and conceit. It was me; Zhitong took the picture when we were rowing on the Kunming Lake at the Summer Palace. That day for the first time he hugged me tight in his strong arms. I couldn't believe at the time that a soldier like him would be capable of such passionate love. He kissed my hair, smiling, ". . . Why call us foot-sloggers? Are we all brawn and no brain? Actually, we understand love the most. . . ." "Talking big, eh?" I teased him, making a face. "It's true. One will never join the army unless one can love others." He had a heart of gold and he loved me truly and intensely. But was I that selfish and that mean? Why couldn't we play our part if we lived in the city? Didn't I deserve some happiness that I could call my own?

Zhitong came back, looking worried. He kept pacing the room, his heavy steps foreboding a storm. Gingerly, I asked him what had happened. Scowling, he bawled, "That's really too much! A recruit who has been in the army for only one year has applied for demob and he has been making so much fuss about it. Nowadays, men recruited from the countryside want to quit, complaining about the shortage of labour-hands in their families, now that the 'system of responsibility' is widely practised; those from cities or towns simply don't like to work in the army. Some even deserted this year. Officers don't feel at ease serving in the border areas. Such people don't give a fig about the country's problems. They care only for themselves. Let him go and good riddance!" After venting his spleen, he tapped at his own forehead regretfully and sat down in a chair, looking distracted.

By now the messenger had prepared a rich dinner, but neither of us felt like eating anything. The messenger was a little bewildered. To cheer me up, he brought me a marmot, which he had caught. Zhitong shook his head, smiling wrily and then beckoned me to go out with him for a walk.

VII

Down the mountain, turning a bend, one could see a vast stretch of grassland. I could hardly believe my eyes. Grass rippled in the breeze and scarlet wild peonies showed off here and there against the wavy green. There in the distance many white tents were pitched on either bank of the Alstan River; from the bridge worksite came the hum of traffic and a medley of human voices. . . .

Zhitong was in high spirits again. He inhaled deeply the fresh air and pulling me by the hand ran after a marmot. Soon I was out of breath and, clutching my chest, waved to stop him. Not until then did he stop running and throw himself on to the grass as if he were going to embrace the whole pasture. "Qian, look at the lovely grass. After the road is built, the herdsmen won't have to worry about entering the mountains. The whole grassland will soon be turned into a mechanical stock-raising area. . . ." He was glorying in his visions. "What is so good about living in the city? Pollution, noise, three generations of a family living in a small room; more people than flowers in parks, where two pairs of lovers have to share one bench! Now here in the mountains, just look at this green land and all your worries, boredom and what not will be gone in an instant. Of course, some would call me a nut. But I don't care." He flung his arms up and sat up. He hugged his legs, pondering. After a long while, he said as if to himself, "You know, China produced a great traveller called Xuan Zang in the Tang Dynasty and again a famous navigator named Zheng He, in the Ming Dynasty. For the past century, however, our country has been bullied and disgraced. It is true that history is made by the people, but history, in its turn, can influence a nation's spirit. Are we in a rut now? Have we completely freed ourselves from the inferiority complex and obsequiousness that plague the people of the semi-colonial countries? People are usually content with things as they are and don't like to see any changes. Where is the spirit of the pioneer who works with great perseverance, the adventurer who keeps exploring new worlds, or the hero who wants to prove that his country is second to none in the world. Perhaps I'm going too far, but I do think it imperative to imbue the young people with such a spirit if we genuinely want to make our country strong each making his contribution in his own way. Don't you think so?"

I said nothing. I appreciated his words but quietly I was thinking of finding my way out. On the one hand, I realized I loved Zhitong more than I had ever before; several times I was on the point of saying I would marry him. On the other hand, I knew it was impossible to change his mind. Love was more than embraces and kisses. Separation, bringing up children, always on the move with the army. . . . I simply did not have the spirit of an explorer. I couldn't afford to be a heroine again. Life was ruthless; I was not in a position to sum up the history of mankind and make my impact. Discussions of a nation's spirit meant to me no more than an increase of a few yuan in our bonus system. I fully accepted the simple truth that I was not born for greatness. And that it would be better for me to return to my snug nest for an easy life. What was wrong with that? But my misery drove me to despair. I really should leave him. But then I couldn't make up my mind.

The sun gradually sank behind the icy peaks. Zhitong walked on in silence. It was worse than calling me names. He stopped at Yu Haizhou's grave, overwhelmed with utter grief. I dared not glance at him. Just then Doctor Zhao, the regiment commander's wife, turned up. She caught hold of my hand and said, "Hey, I was looking for you up on the mountain. Come and stay with us tonight. Our clinic is not far, just beside the worksite. We've tidied up a tent for you. My old man says he wants to meet you."

"I've got only a day's leave and I've to get back today. Thank you all the same." I said to her politely, for I realized that I shouldn't stay and make Zhitong suffer any longer.

Disappointed, Doctor Zhao went away. "Let's go! Hurry up!" Zhitong said firmly, suddenly making up his mind. "I'll have to go to the worksite at four." Just then, the young messenger ran up, panting, "Deputy battalion commander, the regiment commander asked me to tell you that you should stay at home and accompany. . . ." He glanced at me and chuckled. Zhitong stopped him and said, "Hurry back and report to the commander that I'll be at the worksite soon." "That won't do! You haven't had a meal, not even a wink of sleep; besides. . . ." "Nonsense! You hurry along!" Zhitong flared up suddenly, but the messenger murmured and didn't move. Zhitong was about to give him a dressing-down, but he changed his mind and, forcing a smile, said cordially, "Hurry up, will you? Don't you know there will be a meeting at the worksite?" Disappointed, the messenger turned and made his way towards the worksite.

A bugle sounded. From the loudspeakers came the military music. Lines of soldiers, with tools on their shoulders and white flowers pinned on their chests, were heading for the Dotted-line District. As soon as I entered the barracks, I felt the solemn and stirring atmosphere. When Zhitong put on his safety-belt and took a small white flower from the drawer, something ominous shadowed my mind. "What meeting are you going to hold? Why do you insist on going?" After hesitating for a short while, he said, "The whole regiment is holding an oath-taking rally on the spot where the political instructor died. We'll swear to conquer the Dotted-line District. From today on I'll be acting as the political instructor of the Fifth Company. After the rally I'll take the soldiers to work. I must go, mustn't I?"

"Zhitong, you . . . you mustn't!" I snatched the white flower from his hand. "Give it back to me, Qian." He caught my hand angrily. "No, I won't. . . ." Despite his fierce looks I burst out into tears and cried, "Zhitong, let's leave this place, I beg of you. We'll have a good talk and sort things out. I can't live without you . . . I can't. . . ." I hugged his broad shoulders, looking at him imploringly. His chest heaved as emotion surged up within him. Through the window he gazed at the mountains in the distance. Finally, he said, weighing every word, his voice low and quivering, "To tell you the truth, over the past six months I've been torn by indecision myself. I've suffered more than you have. There had been moments when I almost decided to quit. My mother, like you, has wept many, many times. Nevertheless, I've made up my mind and I must say to you that you shouldn't mention my quitting again. . . . Not long ago, a few officers and technicians went to inspect the roads and the patrol routes at the border. It was raining and by accident our jeep got bogged down in the mire near the watch tower across the border. When we tried to push the jeep out of the mud, they laughed, whistled and even took photos. They made their soldiers watch us pushing the jeep forward in the rain. They laughed at us for having these bad roads and poor equipment. This was an insult, not for me as an individual, but for the army and country as a whole. Isn't it true? Now the big power to the North holds us in derision while the pint-sized country to the South tries to brow-beat us. Some of our fellow-countrymen still fail to see that we are living under threats. Without a strong army, without the soldiers toiling and risking their lives to build and guard the border areas, there will be no national security, let alone the 'four modernizations', no personal happiness and sweet love. I know views on these things vary from man to man, I won't impose mine on you. As a soldier of new China, I'd rather give up my life for our country's modernized defence than be crushed down by the invaders' tanks or armoured cars. . . ."

"Oh, please, Zhitong," I begged. "Don't press me any more. Let me calm down and think it over again. . . ." I threw myself into his arms, all my grievances erupting like a volcano. . . .

Outside, a jeep horn hooted. Snow-flakes started dancing frantically again and soon the road was covered and the sky blotted out. I collapsed in the cabin of a lorry, which took me far, far away.

Bang! There came another sound of a blast. The army flag was fluttering in the cold wind and rumbling machines of all kinds made a thrilling melody. I couldn't help sticking my head out of the cabin window. My eyes swept over the thousands of soldiers, as I tried to find Zhitong. Oh, over there in the Dotted-line District, high above on an outhanging piece of a rock was my dearest Zhitong waving to me, all white with snow except for the red star cap insignia shining liking a burning flame. . . .

Translated by Gu Tingfu
Illustrated by Zheng Xin

LI GUOWEN

(1930 — 　)

Born in Shanghai in 1930, Li Guowen studied in Nanjing National Drama School in 1947 and, two years later, worked in the Research Department of the Central Drama Institute. In 1952, he joined the Chinese People's Volunteers and served as a writer in the army art troupe. In 1954, he was appointed literary editor in the propaganda section of the Federation of Railway Workers' Trade Unions. Three years later, in 1957, he was sent away to do manual labour for a long period. In 1979 he was a writer of the Chinese Railway Art Troupe.

His short story, "Re-election", published in 1957, won him much recognition. Then, he stopped writing altogether until 1979. Since he resumed writing, he has published "The Bus Reached Fenshuiling", "Hollow Valley and Fair Orchid" and other short stories. His long novel *Spring in Winter* came out in 1981.

THE MOON ECLIPSE

Li Guowen

I

The early frost of Mount Taihang sprinkled on the ranges, the forests, and the terraced fields which had just been cleared after the harvest. Yi Ru looked out of the bus window. The desolate autumn scene, bare and white, reminding one of the alkaline bank of a salt-pond, was enough to damp anybody's spirits. There was no sign of life except that the persimmons could find by the road-side, blankly fixed their eyes on the bus as it went past.

Yi Ru somewhat regretted that he was making this trip in such haste. He should have written a letter or sent a telegram beforehand! But to whom? Perhaps Aunt Guo had already passed away!

As the bus was approaching his destination, he felt more and more depressed. He should not have come to the old Revolutionary Base to explore something of his spiritual world! It was foolish of him to have acted on impulse, since it was impossible to recover anything of his past, now long lost. The bus arrived at S County, but still he could not figure out what that something was that he had come back to look for. True, he could not forget his lost love, but the other things which he tried to recall rather confused him. He could not sort out his feelings.

He stood by the square in front of the gate of the bus station and shivered in the bitter mountain wind. As it was much colder in the mountain area, the drivers had already put on their goat fur-lined coats turned inside out. He walked towards them, and inquired whether they could take him to Lotus Pond, if they were going that way, but his request unexpectedly provoked a loud roar of laughter. The mountain dwellers — that was how he used to address the beloved and respected country folks in the old Revolutionary Base — had a peculiar sense of humour and resilience. They said to him, "Old Brother! We don't want your money! Go and get an eight-*jiao* ticket, ride on that four-wheeled iron animal, and you will get there by lunch time."

Yi Ru laughed. The last time he left S County, there was no bus station. Now, the highway led directly to Lotus Pond or probably to Yangjiaonao, the small mountain village, and that was there he wanted to go.

After he had paid eight *jiao* at the window of the ticket office, he hesitated. Then he was given the ticket, and he finally decided that he should go. Of course, he still could not say exactly why he was returning to Yangjiaonao. What kind of situation would he have to face upon arrival? Could he find that something which seemed to be eluding him?

It had been his long-cherished dream to come back to this place; otherwise he would feel as if he had lost something. So, after he put the ticket into his pocket, seeing that he still had plenty of time, he walked along Xiguan, a narrow street, now called Sixin Road, which led him into the town. This very uneven flagstone road had been used by many generals or ministers in the past either riding on horses or walking on foot. The S County's steamed millet, though not quite easy to swallow, was delicious and they enjoyed it immensely in those days. Yi Ru wanted to have something to eat, though he was not quite hungry, for he knew that he would be on the bus for several hours and that he might miss lunch after his arrival at Lotus Pond. After all, he would need the energy to climb over the main peak to get to Yangjiaonao.

Suddenly, an idea came into his mind. In the vicinity of Xiguan, he recalled, there was a Moslem restaurant, famous for its mutton soup. In 1947, when he and Bi Jing, director of the regional propaganda department — he remembered him with a smile — came to S County for the first time, the director patted him on the shoulder and said, "Yi Ru! You'll be my guest. I want to invite you to have some mutton soup of Xiguan with me." The director, he remembered, threw on the table a large pile of Border Area Banknotes printed on sheep wool paper. The vinegar and sauce jars were shaking. "Come and bring us two large bowls of soup with plenty of spices in it." This was indeed the most delicious meal he had ever had! The mutton soup tasted so good that he swallowed all the sheep's entrails in it before he had time to appreciate their sweet flavour.

As Bi had stomach trouble, he dared not eat too much, but Yi Ru, having finished his fill, licked his lips with relish. "Little rascal! I'll order another bowl for you!" He laughed and his eyes narrowed into a slit. Yi Ru was embarrassed! The waiter hurried in with another bowl of soup saying: "Little Eighth Route comrade, please help yourself." He lowered his head and within minutes the soup was gone. Large beads of sweat appeared on his forehead.

So now, Yi Ru decided to taste this soup once more though he himself was troubled with stomach-ache, a kind of occupational disease of the drivers and repair-workers.

S County was a small county town in the Mount Taihang regions, so small that it was only a tiny dot on the map, as if it was too shy to make its appearance. The mountain dwellers themselves did not think much of their tiny town. Yi Ru went back and forth from Xiguan to Dongguan but still he could not find the Moslem restaurant. He asked a seller of baked sweet potatoes. The man had a wrinkled face stained with coal dust, like those of the mountain dwellers. He thought Yi Ru was ridiculing him on purpose and replied, "A Moslem restaurant? Mine is state-owned enterprise, serving workers, peasants and businessmen. It's one of the experiments of the Brigade. I can't tell you the special term they use. But it's not private business. If you want to buy something here, go ahead; if not, please yourself. Only don't look down on me!"

He thought Yi Ru meant to ridicule him and deliberately took him for some one who was running the restaurant individually. But when Yi Ru took out two *jiao* and bought two pieces of baked sweet potatoes, he realized he had been mistaken and that this man from another part of the country honestly meant what he said. He sighed, "The Moslem restaurant has incorporated with the cooperative enterprises. Just like mine, it was closed down ten years ago. I have re-opened for business now. We are doing well with these worker-peasant-businessman co-operatives and make money for the Brigade." Like this old mountain dweller, Yi Ru has recently resumed his old profession as a journalist. He was very pleased to hear the new term "peasant-worker-businessman cooperatives", which had been transported from the Adriatic coast. New things would bring in new hopes, like the mild morning sunlight of early autumn shining on this small town, however isolated and backward, giving it warmth and the promise of a new day. This baking cooker might very well turn out to be the precursor of a modern oven in a modern kitchen as a result of joint enterprises in the few years to come. Yi Ru left him, holding the red hot sweet potatoes in his hands. The man was crying in a hoarse voice: "Hot! Sugar pulp like honey!" Probably because he had been out of business for a long time and therefore out of practice, his voice was hollow and dry. Yi Ru began to wonder whether he too would be affected by the lack of practice for so many years. When he took up his pen again and resumed his old profession as a journalist, could he regain his former brilliance in writing in the 1950's?

He got on the bus. As it moved on, the bus engine boomed with a loud noise.

Yi Ru noticed, at first sight, that this bus had been re-moulded from an old Dodge. This age-old bus was going up a very steep slope and the woman driver was trying to do her best to keep it moving. He knew that soon there would be some trouble with the cylinder and the vaporizer might be soiled. But this 20-year-old woman driver was vigorous and energetic. Her short hair, her scarf round her neck, and her flower blouse discoloured with the heat of the sun and the drenching of sweat: all these made him recall somebody he had known before. He opened his eyes wider, gazing intently at her from the back. She was more like a country girl, unlike those professional women-drivers who wore sunglasses and who tried to look superior. Perhaps she had just obtained her driver's licence? Judging from the way she drove the bus, Yi Ru thought that surely she would be able to drive such tractors as "Dongfanghong" or "Tieniu 55". Her bushy black hair, too thick to be cut with scissors, her powerful build and her round shoulders reminded him of a woman's figure which had been deeply engraved upon his heart. She had given him the most beautiful chapter in the book of his memory, which had made him feel all these years that life was still worth living. That woman was his Niuniu at Yangjiaonao!

Was he coming back for her sake? Perhaps so or perhaps not entirely so? He felt a heavy burden in his heart. Then, somehow, he finally realized the main purpose of this tiresome trip was to find his Niuniu of Yangjiaonao. Outside the bus window, the main peak of Lotus Pond, like a quiet, sensitive young peasant girl in the mountain village, appeared above the shadowy clouds. Seeing the peak, he felt he was coming home again — much the same as he had felt upon receiving the Party organization's official notice that he was allowed to re-join the Party, which had been his home. But what was Niuniu doing now after such a long absence of twenty-two years? Yi Ru was a man of deep emotion — this was his fatal weakness! He would not be Yi Ru, however, if he had not felt that he should come back to express his gratitude to Niuniu, who had saved his life and loved him truly. Perhaps, his return might disturb her peace of mind, for surely she must be a mother of many children now! That was why throughout the journey he regretted his recklessness and blamed himself for having decided to come back. Now, the main peak was beckoning him. He thought he had made the right decision, after all! For soon he would be again with the people he loved. Niuniu, Aunt Guo, who had looked after him as if he were her son, and those villagers who had seen this little Eighth Route boy-soldier grow up. Yes, there were many kinds of love: Niuniu's love, Aunt Guo's love and people's love for the Eighth Route Army and the Communist Party. He was coming back to find his lost love! Here in Yangjiaonao, too, he had followed Bi Jing, engaged first in guerilla fighting, and then in land reform and the building up of political power.

"Niuniu! Do you still remember the little boy-soldier with a carbine?" he kept wondering.

While he was thus buried in thought, the long-distance bus was climbing up towards the Lotus Pond Commune, with a buzzing noise which lulled other people to sleep.

II

Yi Ru had never imagined that one day he could come back to this town from Qaidam.

He stood in front of the grey building, which he had left a long time before. After casting a quick look at the building, which had turned more grey with the passage of time, he mounted the steps quickly. He pushed open that glass door for the first time after twenty-two years of absence and felt that he was his old self again with untrimmed long hair and untidy clothes. The door glass mirrored a pair of kind and innocent eyes, shining with pleasant lustre. He smiled as he looked for the old, familiar faces but found none. He pushed open several other doors, and was greeted with the same icy-cold voice, "Whom do you want to see?" or, worse still, merely a cold stare.

He went upstairs to his former editor's office, where he finally found several familiar faces. However, none of them noticed that he had come in. The office table where he used to work was occupied by a woman who looked at him with surprise. He could not make out who she was. She wore a pair of golden-framed spectacles, imported from a foreign country, which covered up one-third of her face. As she stared at him, he felt rather uneasy. He wanted to repeat in a loud voice what had so often been proclaimed in real earnest by Director Bi in the 1950's: "If you turned the newspaper office into some sort of yamen, you would not hear the voice of the people. You must mix with the people, as we used to do in the old Liberated Areas, sleeping on the same *kang* (brick bed), and getting along wonderfully well. . . ." Yi Ru gazed at the woman wondering, "Why do you stare at me like that, comrade! I'm not going to swallow you up, nor will I steal your purse!"

"Yi Ru, is that you?" cried someone excitedly

"Yes, it's me, 'Three-Feet Ice'!"

Many of them laughed. In those days, his nickname "Three-Feet Ice" was used not only by his old colleagues but also by those who had never seen him. It was said that when Yi Ru was about 16 or 17, no taller than a carbine, he edited war news for the *Shanxi-Qahar-Hebei Daily*. In the 1950's, he rose to distinction as an important newsman in the newspaper office. In those years he travelled widely on reporting tours, and he wrote enthusiastically about the various projects undertaken by the Government. He was also sent to Korea to cover the peace negotiations at Panmunjom. Young journalists all looked up to him as a true professional.

Yi Ru had been a "professional correspondent", and he could make friends with strangers very easily. In this old room, he shook hands with his new friends one by one. When he walked to the table by the side of the window, the beautiful slender woman stood up, and turned towards him. The moment she took off her golden-brimmed glasses, he recognized the familiar charming face.

"Ling Song! . . ."

She remained silent and smiled sweetly. Her warm smile showed that they had known each other very well in the past and now no language was needed to express the joy of their meeting. He remembered, twenty years ago, as the poets put it, in the time of blooming youth, after he had polished her manuscripts, or rather, after he had rewritten her paragraphs before sending her articles to the printers, she would smile sweetly as she did now. Then, so many years ago, after the work was over, she would quietly tell him about what was going on in the newspaper office. He was charmed by her beautiful hair, fascinated by her laughs, ringing like silver bells, and stirred by the smell of her fragrant perfume. He did not like the feelings she had aroused in him because, after all, she was the wife of his best friend. Like all the women who were pursuing fame, she wanted to become a well-known journalist.

Ling Song was the most splendidly and richly dressed among the women in the editor's office, it seemed. But when she took off her glasses, Yi Ru noticed that time had left its marks on her face; wrinkles were visible, though faintly. However she knew how to present herself in the best light. Her becoming dress made her look vigorous and younger than her age, especially when she smiled softly.

In the whole office was there anyone who did not know the love affair between them after the death of Ling Song's husband in 1957? Such kind of news would soon spread. Yi Ru would not mind at the time.

"How are you?" he shook her hand, greeting her politely.

She smiled pleasantly. She revealed in her expression that silence could convey more sentiment than words. Yi Ru turned round and asked the other people, "Where's comrade Bi Jing's office?"

People had different opinions about his whereabouts. For days they had not seen their leader. Recently, there had been a rise in the prestige of the newspaper among the people. The increase in sale and in individual subscription proved that the great improvement in publication had produced good results. But where was comrade Bi Jing? Had he gone somewhere to contact people asking them to write articles? Surely, Ling Song ought to know.

"I heard Sister He Ru say Bi has gone somewhere!" Then, she raised her arms, touching her fashionable hair curls with her hands. She asked, "Do you know where they're living now? They've moved to a new place, and that is not easy to find. Look, I've just finished this article. . . ." She handed to the group leader her article, on the scientific explanation of moon eclipse.

Yi Ru thought they might have had moon eclipse recently. After so many years, Ling Song was still writing such routine articles. It seemed that she had made little intellectual progress and that she had been wasting her time on her curling hair. Then, she threw a quick glance at Yi Ru. Her eyes were sparkling, her nostrils quivered, and her lips slightly parted as she smiled, revealing her white teeth. Apparently she meant to say, "You will have to ask me to accompany you!" Sometimes, a clever beautiful woman could express herself that way!

"Please tell me their address! Though I come from Qaidam, I can find the place all right." After he left the newspaper agency, he thought he was right in taking his stand, for, after all, there was something which must be thoroughly forgotten.

The town looked the same but the streets were crowded. Yi Ru had lived in the vast deserted Qaidam Basin for more than 20 years, where he seldom saw a man after he had walked for miles. To him, even the barking of a dog in a distance was something to look forward to. Now, when he was walking among the dense crowd, he felt so suffocating as if he had tumbled into a salt pond, where he could neither sink nor float.

He felt relieved, though, when Sister He opened the door for him. The hair of this hot-tempered aggressive old sister had turned grey.

"Did you receive Old Bi's telegram? He thought you would be coming back by air!"

"I bought the air ticket but I sent it back. Granddad Wangdui, a Tibetan old man, once said to me, 'A yak may not move faster than a horse but it can reach Lhasa step by step! Young man, just count how many horse-riders have rolled down from their horse backs?' I think there's a lot of truth in what he said. . . ."

"Nonsense! I think you're afraid of travelling by air. But you were never afraid of anything in the past."

"Never mind, where's Bi?"

"He waited for you for several days. As you didn't appear, he went away."

"But where is he now?" He found that Bi Jing still had that restless spirit.

"Who knows? He's getting old but he's still got plenty of energy!"

Yi Ru understood this old leader. "He's got something urgent to attend to?"

"Don't know. But he's been working as hard as ever. Look! He's in such a hurry that he forgot his pills for his stomach ache." Then she added, "Have you been to the newspaper agency?"

Yi Ru nodded. He looked around and saw there was nothing in the room except books, paintings and drawings, just as it was many years before. This was Bi's old style of work.

"Didn't you see her?" He Ru looked with great concern at Yi Ru, who had always been regarded as a member of their family. Their friendship was built long ago during the past when fightings were carried on intensely.

She was one of those wives who were fond of exercising certain power on their husbands. Well, there were times when the moon was hidden by the clouds and there was even moon eclipse. Then, he recalled Aunt Guo's story about the Dog of Heaven eating up the moon; hence the eclipse. Perhaps it was his recollection of Aunt Guo's explanation that led to his thought of coming back to Yangjiaonao.

Ling Song was walking gently towards him, smiling as she came closer. She was wearing a tight white woolen shirt, which showed off her charming, graceful figure well. Above her high dress-collar, he could see her slender neck. She still had a beautiful face, which looked like a flower wet with morning dew. The face drew nearer and nearer. He could not move away. Her icy cold face was pressing close to him. He quickly shook his head and instantly woke up. He did not realize that he had fallen asleep and his face was now pressed against the window of the bus.

It was a funny dream! But, to some extent, it nevertheless

reflected the world of reality. He questioned himself, "Perhaps that's the truth about dreams?"

The old car suddenly stopped. Some passengers got out and sat on the terraced field, smoking their long-stemmed pipes and looking at the distant sky, murmuring: "Young driver, take your time! We're in no hurry. Even a donkey sometimes refuses to work. The bus needs a rest." Just for fun, the other passengers crowded around the woman driver to see how she fixed the engine. She squatted herself down on the ground in front of the bus, opened the bonnet of the engine and tried to find out what had gone wrong. Her pretty face was covered with grease and sweat. She looked up, shouting, "Mamma! Step on it once more."

The driver's mother, Yi Ru noticed, was the only other person on the bus. Short-haired, broad-shouldered like her daughter, she was sitting on the driver's seat. She stepped on the brake by mistake, whereupon the driver leapt up like a leopard and snarled at her mother, "The accelerator not the brake! . . ." As Yi Ru was anxious to get away from there as soon as possible, he decided to give the girl some help, and came out of the bus. He was experienced in fixing broken-down cars, having worked in Qaidam for 20 years.

"Xinxin! Haven't you finished the work?" The driver's mother was getting impatient.

The girl looked up and said, "Mamma, please, the passengers aren't complaining."

The woman climbed down from the side-door by the driver's seat. "They can wait, but I can't. I'd better be off now and climb over the hill." It seemed that she was not patient enough to wait till the car was repaired. Suddenly Yi Ru was startled! Why did her voice sound so familiar?

"Mamma! . . ." her daughter grumbled.

"Xinxin! Take it easy! I'm going now." She hurried away. How Yi Ru wished she would turn round so that he could see her face! But it seemed that she had deliberately chosen not to do so. When he walked to the front of the bus, the woman

was a long way off. He watched her back and felt it looked familiar.

The old Dodge finally started working again. Xinxin stood up straight triumphantly, proudly waving her hand to her mother who had gone far away. Then she called the passengers back to the bus and apologized to them for the time she had taken. The patience and tolerance of those mountain-dwellers surprised Yi Ru. Instead of complaining, they consoled her, "Unlike your mother, we can still wait. Is it all right now?" But Yi Ru knew better. He warned them like a professional, "It won't go very far, I'm afraid."

Xinxin stared at him angrily and said, "How do you know? Get on the bus, otherwise, we'll go without you!" She snarled at him as she jumped on her seat.

He laughed, waving his hand. "Please yourself."

Soon, the old Dodge stopped again. Xinxin got off the bus and came to him smilingly. "Are you sent by the bus company to see how the peasant-worker-businessman cooperatives work?"

Again, this new term from the Adriatic coast! Yi Ru laughed. Then, he was informed that this short-distance transportation, provided by the Tractors' Station, was intended to save the country-folks the trouble of carrying things on their shoulders or backs. During the Anti-Japanese War, Yi Ru had carried grain and food up the hill. He knew how he felt as he went up the mountain path step by step. The young girl's frankness and her smile had fascinated him. So, at her request, he came to the bus engine. As a car repairer for 20 years, he knew what to do. He was in no hurry, though, as he took out two baked sweet potatoes, giving one to Xinxin, "Xinxin, help yourself! You may be hungry."

Without showing the least modesty, she took it and ate a large mouthful. Then before she swallowed it she exclaimed: "Sugar pulp like honey! This is from our Yangjiaonao!"

Yi Ru looked at her in astonishment. "Are you a native of that small mountain village?"

As her mouth was full, she could not speak. So she nodded. "Your mother is also from Yangjiaonao?"

She burst into laughter, for she thought it was a funny question. "This 'sugar pulp like honey' is a new product, cultivated by my mother. Do you know what they call this kind of sweet potatoes? They call it 'Niuniu', my mother's name!"

Upon hearing that name Yi Ru was tongue-tied. He stared into the distance, trying to find his Niuniu, who had walked half way up the hill, and saw a small shadow of a figure, walking up step by step with much difficulty. Yi Ru suddenly turned round and gazed at Xinxin steadily. He thought, "She has a daughter now! No wonder she turned her back on me and left in such a hurry. . . ."

He ate a mouthful of sweet potato. It tasted sweet but all its sweetness could not remove the bitter regret in his heart! He should not have come! Why should he disturb her peace of mind?

III

Outside the window, the trees were dancing gracefully in the beautiful moonlight. Yi Ru was unable to get to sleep in the commune's guest room. Was it because the sight of Niuniu and her beloved daughter had filled his heart with sadness? Was it because he was upset by the sad news that Aunt Guo had passed away? Or was it simply the guest's snore in the next room which reminded him of Bi Jing?

In the old days in such a beautiful moonlight night, he would get up, hastily put on his clothes and picked his way with Bi over the main peak to get back to Yangjiaonao. He would stop by the pond, which looked like lotus petals, and drink a few mouthfuls of the sweet clear cool water. Then they would run directly to Yangjiaonao. On his way, he would open his coat a little and enjoy the cool breeze, blowing softly on him. Bi Jing was chatting about the love affairs between Pavel and Tonya in N. Ostrovsky's novel *How the Steel Was Tempered* and about Ah Q embodying the soul of the Chinese peasants. . . . Then, after a while they would be home. There, both Aunt Guo and Niuniu were waiting for them. They would enjoy the sweet fragrant wine, which, soon make them drowsy. Before long, Bi would be lying on the *kang*, snoring heavily.

The man in the next room was snoring, but it was not as loud as Bi's. When Yi Ru first came to Yangjiaonao, he was not much older than the leader of the Boys' League. His Niuniu, who was then a small girl with pigtails, smiled. "Director Bi," she used to say. "Your snoring is excellent!"

Bi Jing laughed, "Aunt Guo! Sorry about my snoring. Please be patient. When I was in Yan'an, I went to see several foreign doctors, but they could do nothing about it. Just wait till the Japanese are defeated!"

"Why?" asked Niuniu. "Then you would not snore any more?"

He pinched her nose. "No. Then I'll leave Yangjiaonao. And I can't enjoy the lovely date wine any more."

"And I'll miss your snoring. . . ." Yi Ru did not understand what Aunt Guo was trying to say. But much later, he understood her hidden meaning.

"Indeed, that's the past. . . ." Yi Ru remembered at one of the Party's branch meeting in 1957, he started talking about snoring. "Now, Director Bi's thunder-like snoring cannot be heard by Aunt Guo any more. Even I, having served as his secretary for so many years, can seldom hear it. He is far too busy these days, fully holding meetings or organizing political studies. For the rest of his time, he has to run various errands for Comrade He Ru. Last time Aunt Guo came to see him, he couldn't spare even five minutes to sit down and talk with her. He told me to take care of Aunt Guo who had brought him four bottles of date wine as well as dried persimmons and walnuts.

As he had worked under Bi Jing for many years, Yi Ru had learned from him not to say too much. He would not mention to anybody, for example, how Bi took out a pile of five-yuan banknotes and put them in his hand, with embarrassment.

"Please give these to her and ask her to stay with you. Do take eight or ten days off and keep her company. I'll get permission from the editing office. Try to get her whatever she wants. It's unfortunate He Ru wouldn't let her stay with us. Take the wine, too, for my wife won't have any except the prize-winners at the Panama Exhibition."

Yi Ru could imagine how much pressure He Ru must have put on Bi. He refused to take the banknotes and said, "You think I have no money?"

Bi Jing sighed, "These banknotes can by no means assuage my regret!" He went on angrily, "We can fight the Japs, defeat the enemies but we can do nothing about the vulgarity of the petty bourgeoisie."

Yi Ru looked at Bi Jing sympathetically. He himself was going through an emotional crisis. Ling Song, whose husband had just passed away, clung to him closely, and she was trying to force him to make a choice between her and Niuniu.

Aunt Guo could understand and forgive Bi because this was the third time she had come to town to visit him after Liberation. She followed Yi Ru to the single men's dormitory building at the back of the newspaper agency. While climbing up the five-storied stairs, she murmured, "I know, Old Bi is a very important cadre now. An old woman like me from the deserted mountain valley is not respectable enough to stay in that magnificent house of theirs." Yi Ru understood quite well what she meant. If his pretty young wife were not living there, Aunt Guo might stay with Bi Jing for her whole life. Yi Ru remembered how Aunt Guo offended He Ru on her first visit after Liberation. She thought their servant was He Ru's mother and said to her that she had a very beautiful daughter. Then, she pointed at He Ru, saying that it was such good luck that she had chosen Bi as her husband, who was an excellent man. Well, he snored, but snoring wouldn't hurt badly once she got used to it. This was, of course, a terrible mistake, but He Ru did not mind. She merely laughed and it was then forgotten. But she was hurt by Aunt Guo's other remarks. When Aunt Guo learned that the elderly woman was their servant, she shook her head and said to He Ru, "You are young and strong. You shouldn't have hired her to wait on you." Then she turned to Bi and said reproachfully, "This isn't like our Eighth Route Army man, eh?"

In 1954, she went to see Bi for the second time. As it was a time of national prosperity, Aunt Guo brought a full load of things: millet, dates, potatoes, date wine, fried pancake, boiled eggs and all sorts of treasures that could be found at Yangjiaonao. She was exceedingly happy, even happier than He Ru who had just given birth to a fat little baby-boy. Probably because Aunt Guo's husband and sons had died during the revolutionary war, she was particularly fond of babies. She held the baby close to her heart, kissing him and caressing him in a way as she had done to Yi Ru, the small boy-soldier, in the past. Yi Ru noticed He Ru's face suddenly turned grey in terror. She was afraid that Aunt Guo might be carrying some kind of disease.

On this second visit, Niuniu came with Aunt Guo. It was she who carried the full load of presents. Short-haired, broadshouldered, she was blushing as she came in.

This time Aunt Guo stayed only a short time because Niuniu was always worried about the seeds she had planted. After Aunt Guo and Niuniu returned to Yangjiaonao, He Ru finally picked a quarrel with her husband. It so happened that Yi Ru had come over to inquire about a manuscript, and he saw her fierce temper. A guerilla leader most feared by the enemies, an extremely persuasive speaker and a well-known chief editor of a famous newspaper, Bi Jing could do nothing about his wife's scolding except sighing deeply. Yi Ru, too, was included in her severe chiding. "I hear you intend to marry that block-headed girl."

"Sister He! You say she is block-headed?"

"You're a correspondent of rising fame. Can this match do you any good?"

Bi Jing tried to stop her but she insisted, "You keep out of this. I want to speak my mind."

"Sister He!" Yi Ru asked her smilingly, "Why do you think

it's not a good match? By the way, can you tell me the name of the blue flowers in your terrace?"

She could not, nor could Bi.

Yi Ru said proudly, "But she can!"

He Ru retorted angrily, "If you want to marry her, that's your business. . . ."

The day before this scene, Yi Ru had accompanied Niuniu to visit the town. They went to the newly-built botanical garden. Casually, she said, "It's the first time in my life that I saw such beautiful blue flowers!"

"Where are they?" Yi Ru looked around.

She smiled sweetly. "Not here. But in Director Bi's courtyard. Do you know the name of those flowers? Oh! Even a famous reporter like you can't tell! I looked up the dictionary and found it. It's a very pleasant name!"

Yi Ru waited.

"Forget-me-not!" She said gently.

"Ah! Niuniu! You're afraid that I might forget you!"

Under a tree with red beans, she smiled with deep emotion just as she had done years ago when they were standing by the clear fountain on the main peak of the Lotus Pond. "You're a famous man now. I often see your name in the newspaper!"

"Niuniu, your name means so much to me."

In 1957 Aunt Guo came alone, after she had recovered from a serious illness, narrowly escaping from death. Perhaps she felt that she would not live much longer. She bought a coffin for herself with all her savings. What was left to be done, she thought, was to make sure these two orphans would get married. Yi Ru's parents were in the Red Army and they were killed in the revolutionary war. Niuniu's parents were poor coal miners, who lost their lives while at work, suffocated by poisonous gas. On that tragic day, Aunt Guo, found little Niuniu lying by the cave-door dying. She carried her home and brought her up as her adopted daughter.

On her third visit, Aunt Guo was very happy to be with Yi Ru again. She went from room to room in the men's dormitory, collecting the dirty bed-covers, towels, shirts and trousers of the editors, artists, photographers, proof-readers, and the others. She washed them clean, just as she had done for the servicemen at Yangjiaonao in the past.

Serving these young people, Aunt Guo felt it was like old times, she would like to hear them sing, though. In the past the armymen sang wherever they went and people's hearts would be burning with revolutionary fire. She asked Yi Ru, "Do sing the song, 'The Wind Is Roaring'! I haven't heard it for so many years!" So they started singing in high spirits. They saw the old revolutionary mother was smiling and hot tears were rolling down her cheeks. Nobody ever noticed that Bi Jing was standing at the doorway, wiping away the hot tears from his cheeks.

Well, they saw the chief editor now and they began to leave Yi Ru's room. When the three of them were finally left alone, he said to Yi Ru, sighing deeply: "What you told me last time is perfectly right. We must try to find the reason from within not from without. Haven't we lost what means most to us?"

"What do you mean, Director Bi?"

"Haven't you got some wine?"

"I have no such prize-winner from the Panama Exhibition!"

Just as in the past when they ate steamed millet at her home at Yangjiaonao, Aunt Guo watched them as they drank the date wine and ate the chicken legs. They talked about things which she sometimes couldn't understand.

"Aunty! Are you mad with me?" asked Bi. "I've become an important man. But I know I've lost touch with the common people and I don't like it."

Aunt Guo partly understood what he meant. "Never mind. A family may quarrel sometimes! We'll be all the better for it afterwards."

At the Party's branch meeting, Yi Ru made a speech: ". . . To be honest, since we came to town, how much have we considered the interests of our fellow country-folks? We have lost touch with the common people who, during the revolution, had fed us with steamed millet, carried us on their wheel-barrows or with the stretchers. By relying on them, our Party defeated the enemies and won victories. That is why we are repeatedly told by our Party that we must work closely with the masses. If we lose this excellent tradition, we'll be utterly lost." He looked at Ling Song who was sitting opposite him. As she had been recently admitted to the Party, she was dressed quite simply. After the meeting, she gave him a note: "If you don't mind, I'll come and see Aunty."

When she pushed open the glass door and walked down the steps, she turned around to wink at him. She seemed to be asking him: "Am I welcome?" Yi Ru spread out his hands to show he didn't care.

While her husband was lying sick in the hospital, she had become so attached to him that it made him feel uneasy. After the death of her husband, she had been chasing him with her eyes. No matter how he tried to avoid her, he always felt her eyes fixed on him.

When she finally came to Yi Ru's room, she treated Aunt Guo with such sincerity and warmth that the old woman was greatly moved. Yi Ru was wondering what she was up to, when she suddenly produced a ticket and exclaimed, "Goodness! I almost forgot to give you this ticket I got for you. It's for an opera. Do you want to go?"

She hailed a pedicab and sent Aunt Guo away.

When she returned, she took off her jacket. Yi Ru saw a beautiful young woman standing before him, her white woolen shirt showing off her round shoulders, her fascinating breasts, and her slender waist. Her large sparkling eyes were fixed on him. "Yi Ru, you talked about 'forget-me-not' this afternoon. Do I look like that flower?"

He shook his head.

"Then, your 'forget-me-not' must be Niuniu, as Aunt Guo told me a while ago? But do compare! Who is more beautiful? She or I? Who's better?"

Yi Ru was not accustomed to this kind of confrontation. "Ling Song! Maybe you're a 1,000 times or even 10,000 times more beautiful than Niuniu. But love is a different matter. Well, I respect you! I'm grateful to you! Let's be good friends."

"I love you, Yi Ru. If my husband had been alive, I would have divorced him, and married you. I love you. Love is cruel! I know I may not be as good as your Niuniu, but I feel you are mine! I've come to your room now to show everybody that I'm yours. Let's get married tomorrow. A woman has the right to win her love, her happiness and her man!" Then, she came over, embraced Yi Ru closely, pressing her tearful face against his.

IV

Xinxin was pleased with the work that Yi Ru had done. After he had fixed the engine of the bus she jumped up with joy. As the bus reached the Lotus Pond, she asked him ardently to cross over the hill to her home at Yangjiaonao. He would love to, of course, but he decided to stay overnight at the Lotus Pond. A man approaching 50 understood the word "cautious".

He left the guest room and continued his journey. As he climbed up the main peak, he enjoyed the cool invigorating morning breeze. This was the first time he walked on the mountain path after twenty-two years!

The last time Yi Ru left Yangjiaonao, he and Niuniu believed that they would be together again in ten days or a fortnight. After he had walked away two steps, he turned round and saw Niuniu still standing there smilingly. He shouted, "Niuniu! I'll be back after I finish my work in the two weeks at the most."

But he did not come back till now, twenty-two years later! He recalled the evening when he freed himself from Ling Song's love snare. When Aunt Guo finally came back from the theatre she saw Yi Ru was getting ready to leave.

"What are you doing?"

"Going back to Yangjiaonao!"

"What for?"

"I want to marry Niuniu!"

Aunt Guo was overjoyed as she exclaimed, "I have said it

before. Heaven forbid that Yi Ru should ever forget his Niuniu! Yi Ru has been saved by Niuniu twice!"

Yes, he had been saved by her twice: once from the local landlords' Homecoming Corps, as she fought with them desperately like a leopard and the second time she found him half dead among the corpses during the Longtankou Campaign.

Then, Yi Ru told Aunt Guo what had happened ten minutes before she came in. As Ling Song was leaving his room, she said to him scornfully, "You saint! Tomorrow everybody would know that I had spent the night with you!" So, Aunt Guo and Yi Ru wanted to leave at once. They carried their things on their backs and came to Director Bi's house to say good-bye to him. He Ru was lying on the sofa. She was quite delighted to see Yi Ru, but as soon as she saw Aunt Guo her smile disappeared. She stood up and offered her the seat. When Yi Ru told her about their intention, she said, "Is it necessary to wait for Old Bi? He has to attend endless meetings." "Let's wait!" Aunt Guo replied, for she wanted to see him again.

He Ru took out two five-yuan banknotes from her drawer and gave them to Aunt Guo, "I'll not see you off. Please take them! You may need them on your way. Or, buy youself some cloth and make yourself a jacket!"

Yi Ru was infuriated. He noticed that Aunt Guo's hands were trembling. What an insult to the people coming from the mountain valley! In the past she had risked her life, not divulging where Bi was when questioned by his enemies. Consequently, she was beaten up severely. And these banknotes were to be her reward for having saved his life?

On their way home, Aunt Guo did not smile. When they arrived at Yangjiaonao, entered the room and saw Niuniu, her face brightened up.

"Niuniu! See, what I've caught for you?"

However, Niuniu was not the least surprised. Hadn't he forgotten that light bluish forget-me-not?

"Ah? Where's my captive?" Aunt Guo turned round.

At the thought that he was going to marry his beloved Niuniu, Yi Ru felt embarrassed, so he put down his wallet, picked up the buckets and went to the well to fetch water as the soldiers used to do in the past when they entered the village. In the evening the three of them sat closely in a circle at the head of the *kang*, eating steamed millet. Niuniu filled up his bowl after he had finished it, blushing as she gave him more food. According to the custom of the mountain village, a husband must be served by his wife. At first, Yi Ru rushed forward to serve himself, but Aunt Guo stopped him. "Let Niuniu do it. The two of you should have been husband and wife long ago!"

Some beautiful moments in one's long life could never be forgotten. The happiness of a day or two would be kept safe for ever in one's memory. . . .

On the evening of the third day when Yi Ru and Niuniu were together, a telegram came from the newspaper agency. Yi Ru realized he had to leave her. They were standing by the pond for a few more moments. Yi Ru could only say, "It's fate, Niuniu!"

"It doesn't matter! You'll be back soon," she tried to comfort him.

"Yes, I will, Niuniu."

"I've given you my body and soul. I'm yours forever," said she, her eyes shining with confidence, fully revealing her wifely virtues of honesty and gentleness.

This was true love, the only love in Yi Ru's life.

Yi Ru hurried to the newspaper agency. His efficiency was well known to everyone. Not long after, he was branded as a rightist.

But that was some time ago. Now, coming back, he learned from He Ru that Ling Song married an old man in 1958, twenty years older than she. He had plenty of money but whether she had found love and happiness, nobody knew. At the beginning of the "cultural revolution", the old man was severely criticized. Then he had a heart attack and collapsed in the place where he was confined. He was all right now and the Government had given him 10,000 yuan. . . . He Ru had more to say, but Yi

Ru interrupted her and said, "I don't want to repair the temples for the monks!"

When Yi Ru reached the peak, he saw a man striding down-hill towards Yangjiaonao. He reminded Yi Ru of someone he had known very well.

V

Yi Ru felt the man looked like Bi Jing. Impossible! He looked carefully again, using his hands as a shade, but, in a moment, the shadow of the man passed over the tomb-stones of a graveyard and disappeared into the village.

Yi Ru was quite certain that the man was Bi. He recalled that Bi Jing was branded as a "rightist" during the "cultural revolution" and was sent to be reformed through labour at the Preparedness Against War Grain Storage in a meadow south of the Qilian Mountains. Whenever the bandits were coming, the labour leader would telephone to call in soldiers for help. However, Bi Jing had a better solution. He waved his arms and gave orders, "Those who are true communists come forward! The grain belongs to the people, to the state, and we're not going to let the rebel bandits have it. Let us communists show our true colours! Those who have guns and grenade go in front; those who have no weapons use wooden staffs. Comrades, follow me!"

Director Bi was in action again in spite of his poor condition. With a staff in his hand, he led the group and marched out, ready to fight the bandits. Yi Ru was with him, too, as he had come over to see his old leader.

"Let's fight!" roared Bi Jing.

Upon seeing this regiment, the bandits rode away. When they returned to the grain storage, the leader was still on the phone: "Send some armed units here quickly. . . ."

So, that was Bi Jing, a man with an iron will.

Since Yi Ru left the newspaper agency for the reform-through-labour camp at Qaidam Basin in 1958, he had lost con-

tact with the outside world.   He wrote Niuniu only once and
in the letter he said he was very grateful to her.   However,
for her own good, she'd better regard him as dead and that
she should not wait for him.   It was somewhat like a farewell
speech.

It was at the end of 1959 that Bi Jing was sent away in exile.
He knew Yi Ru was staying at Qaidam, but he didn't have his
address.   So he wrote about 100 slips, posting each on the back
of the cars carrying grain to Qaidam.   On the slips he gave
his address and his message, "Yi Ru! Come and see me as soon
as you can.   I'm now staying in the Preparedness Against War
Grain Storage in a meadow south of the Qilian Mountains."

Six months later, as Yi Ru was repairing the engine of one
of the cars, he found one of these slips written by his old leader.
He went to see Bi.   When they met again, Bi Jing said, "Come,
Yi Ru! Let's embrace each other three times!" He took out from
his inner pocket a small packet wrapped with cloth.   "Six
months ago, Aunt Guo came to see me from Yangjiaonao and
stayed with me for several days.   We had a good talk.   Before
she left, she said, 'I may not live long enough to see the day
when you're reinstated.   But I'll pray for you.' Then she took
out two packets. She had sold her coffin for 180 yuan and
divided the money for the two of us. . . ." Bi Jing could not hold
back his tears.

"Our Party will never forget us! The people will never forget
us! Yi Ru! Always remember that the people are our beloved
parents."

He opened the packet and Yi Ru noticed that the ninety-
yuan banknotes were neatly put together. Bi was thinking deeply.

When Yi Ru was about to leave, he saw that Bi Jing had
something to say but finally he held back.   He only made a
hint that he would dearly love to return to Yangjiaonao. Yi Ru's
eyes fell on Bi's two swollen legs and said, "Old director! Do
take good care of yourself."

"I'll be all right," Bi thanked him.

When they said good-bye, Yi Ru stuffed into his old leader's hands 12-catty grain coupons, which was all he had, and jumped into the car. Bi Jing was moved and yelled, "Yi Ru, but how can you manage without these?"

"Don't worry! Do take care of yourself!" As the car started moving, he waved his hand to him.

Bi Jing shouted after him: "Remember, the people would never forget what we have done!"

That was some time ago. . . . Now in the middle of July, as was the custom, people would pay respect to their dead relatives in the graveyard. Probably that was why Director Bi had come to visit Aunt Guo's grave?

Yi Ru was now approaching the little mountain village of Yangjiaonao. He had been away for more than 20 years. He was not sure whether he should go and see Niuniu again. He sat on a rock, gazing at the familiar mountain village. For 20 years he had been doing duties for the Transportation Brigade visiting many places, and now he had finally come back.

He entered a small courtyard in the centre of the village. The yard was quiet. There was a lock hanging on the door. Then he found the key hidden in a hole on the trunk of the date tree. Everything looked the same. When he was about to open the door, suddenly he felt it might not be proper for it was no longer his home. After a while, he decided to go in.

The room looked exactly the same as he had left it so many years before. Then he saw a note on the table, written by Niuniu in her neat handwriting. "I'm going out with Xinxin to buy something for Aunt Guo's grave. Your meal is in the pan. Heat it up and help yourself. If you can't wait, you can meet us at her grave."

Apparently Niuniu had left this note for her husband. Yi Ru smiled painfully. Through the door curtain he peeped into the inner room where formerly Aunt Guo and Niuniu had lived. The door curtain was half open, and he saw many pairs of new shoes, which looked somewhat like those made by the Women Salvation Corps for the soldiers during the War of Resistance Against Japan.

He walked into the room, stood by the side of the *kang* and examined the shoes. They were of the same size and shape. What surprised him most, however, was that on each pair was marked the year of production: 1957, 1958, 1959. . . . He counted them. There were twenty-two pairs altogether. Now Yi Ru understood everything. Overwhelmed with emotion, he almost collapsed. He fell, overturning the lid of the pan on the cooking stove. The cooked sweet potatoes were still warm then he saw a note above the stove:

Daddy:
This is the "sugar pulp like honey" which you like so much. Do you know its name? It's called Niuniu.

Your daughter Xinxin

He walked into the outer room and found hanging on the wall his own picture, taken in Korea in front of the Conference Hall of Panmunjam. He was then wearing his army coat without a hat, and his hair was sticking up like a cock's tail. By the side of his picture was a certificate awarded for distinguished service as an excellent tractor driver. He saw on it the name Yi Xinxin!

For a long time, Yi Ru didn't know what to do. Then he rushed out. The sun was setting in the west. He hastened to Longtankou where he thought Aunt Guo must be buried. Her husband and her sons, killed in battle at Longtankou, were buried on top of the hill in the vicinity of the battlefield. He was going to see his wife, the woman who had sewn twenty-two pairs of shoes while waiting in despair for his return. He was going to see his daughter, the tractor driver, and to see the grave of Aunt Guo — yes, Aunt Guo, who had been like a mother to him. Now he understood that because she did not want to disturb his work, she must have forbidden Bi Jing to remind him that he had a wife waiting for him and a daughter he had never seen. Like a real mother, she knew too well these two orphans, Niuniu and himself! What a pity she was now dead and couldn't see the two of them together again.

The evening sun was shedding its dim light on the hills. Yi Ru finally arrived at Longtankou.

It was the 15th day of the lunar month, which promised a full moon. The sun was down and the moon began to rise from the east. As the evening deepened, the sky shone in the beautiful twilight. Yi Ru was looking for Aunt Guo's grave, when he heard someone call "Daddy!" Then he saw Xinxin running towards him. Niuniu was standing by a grave, looking calm. She was repeating to herself what she had said twenty-two years before when they parted: "You will come back, I know you will!"

Xinxin whispered, "Daddy! Yesterday, mother dared not talk to you. She told me afterwards that you hadn't changed a bit!"

"Of course. How could I? That's why we gave you your name Xinxin, meaning two hearts in one!"

From not too far away, suddenly came a voice: "No! They will never change, for better days will come. . . ."

"Director Bi! . . ." exclaimed Yi Ru and Niuniu almost at the same time.

Hastily, Bi Jing walked over, almost running towards them. He held Niuniu in one hand and Yi Ru in the other, overjoyed.

Suddenly Xinxin said: "Mammy! Daddy! The moon! Look at the moon! . . ." Then, they heard the striking of gongs and crackling of fireworks. People were shouting: "Look! The moon is going to be swallowed up by the Dog of Heaven! . . ."

It was the eclipse of the moon. The mountain ranges soon looked gloomy. From six to seven, the whole family, sitting on Aunt Guo's grave, were shrouded in complete darkness.

Finally, about a quarter past seven the moon reappeared, shedding a tiny ray of light on Xinxin's eyes.

At half past eight, a brighter moon was shining brighter than ever in the sky. Xinxin jumped up, speaking loudly, as if she wanted it to be heard by her grandmother lying underground, "It's all over! The moon is shining on us again!"

Yes, it was a beautiful night. And it promised a sunny day!

— Abridged and translated by Zhang Liang
Illustrated by Cai Rong

ZHANG LIN

(1939 —   )

Zhang Lin was born in 1939 in Faku County, Liaoning Province. After graduation from a senior middle school in 1959, he worked on the railway, first as a train attendant and then as chief of a dining car. Zhang is now chief of train attendants of passenger trains of the Qiqihar Railway.

He began writing in 1977, and has published a novelette *Flame Flower* in 1978, "Snow", "A Lone Swan" and other short stories in 1980.

ARE YOU A COMMUNIST
PARTY MEMBER?

Zhang Lin

I

Liu Dashan, Director of the Northern Railway Bureau, will be sixty in two years, and will then be joining the rank of the old. To him, his past life has been marked by numerous twists and turns; all very complicated indeed, and yet he also feels that essentially it has been a simple life.

In his early years, when he was not even as tall as the small carbine he firmly held in his hands, he took part in the guerilla war against the Japanese, together with a group of sturdy and strong young men. That war over, almost immediately he found himself fighting against the Kuomintang. On a rainy night, when the Liaoxi-Shenyang battle was about to begin and the army was getting ready to leave for the South, the regiment commander summoned Liu to the headquarters and told him that he was to remain with the divisional commander and that his job from now on was to look after the railways. Upon hearing this, tears came to his eyes as he was holding his rifle in his hands. The whole night he wept, and his tears came faster than the rain outside. He obstinately demanded that he should be marching south with the regiment. His tears moved his comrades-in-arms, who went to appeal to the regiment commander on his behalf. But they were reprimanded and came back in silence.

Early the next morning, the divisional commander came to their barracks. He shouted as soon as he entered the room, "Who is Liu Dashan?"

Liu stood up sulkily. The divisional commander shrugged his shoulders under his overcoat and walked towards him. He shook his broad and black eyebrows and bawled, "Weeping like a young wife! Are you a Communist Party member?" Then he left.

Liu Dashan was dumbfounded, his ears filled with the echoes of the roar of the divisional commander. Finally, he stealthily kissed his rifle, handed it over to another soldier, and stayed behind with the divisional commander to look after the railway tracks. Gradually he developed a fondness for iron rails, as if he could feel the warmth of the icy cold tracks, as if he could hear a heart throbbing therein. The former divisional commander, caretaker director of the railways, passed away many years ago. Liu, however, still frequently thought about him, that very hot-tempered old man.

Liu Dashan was born in the Jiaodong district of Shandong Province. His father was a farmer; so, too, his grandfather and his ancestors. In appearance, he was a typical tall and sturdy man from Shandong, with a large nose, a wide mouth and a head of thick, bristly black hair. At one time, he wanted to have a more stylish hair-cut, but his hair was too wiry and it could not be pressed down. So he had to be content with a crew-cut, and let his hair stand erect like the bristles of a shoe brush. Appropriately, however, the stiff hair signified his strong character. Totally uncompromising, he would never desert his principles. During the ten years of the "cultural revolution", he refused to bend to the political opportunists' will and, naturally, had to suffer on account of his "stubbornness". That nightmare over, after the implementation of the Party's policy, he was given a very high post which did not involve much work. He did not like it and said that it was worse than the job of digging graves. It was only very recently that he had been reappointed Director of the Railway Bureau.

Though young, the secretaries of the Railway Bureau were all smart and knew very well the ways of the world. But they did not know much about Liu Dashan. From what they heard, he liked to swear. He would swear when he was angry, and swear when he was in a good mood — there was a difference in tone of course. Before his arrival, the secretaries had rearranged everything in the office for him. There was a desk bigger than a double bed with legs shaped like those of a tiger. On the desk were three telephones. The walls had been painted cream yellow, which, scientifically speaking, was a warm colour, and it was supposed to help create a genial atmosphere for the irritable director. However, the director stayed in this "warm nest" only one day. The next morning he summoned Secretary Zhou Feng to his office and said, "Let's move out! We'll use that room near the railway station."

The secretaries were busy again for a whole morning. The work of changing the office room was finally done and they were all exhausted. The new office was a smaller room overlooking the station. The walls were not painted. Through the wide window, which looked rather like a big TV screen, one could see clearly everything that was going on in the station. The voices of the dispatchers, the cries of the loaders, the shouts of the inspectors and, above all, the loud whistles of the locomotives — all these combined to pierce the air. Now Director Liu felt comfortable and relaxed as if he had drunk some good wine or was listening to some soothing music. Sitting in his chair facing the window, and grinning from ear to ear, he exclaimed, "Good! That's how it should be!"

It was not difficult for the secretaries to find out more about their new director. Before long, they succeeded in digging out some particulars about his past, among which two incidents were of particular importance.

Incident No. 1: In the extremely cold winter days of 1965, the railway lines in the area were all covered with snow and the switches were not working properly. The trains, when ascending the slopes, soon got stuck. In that terrible weather, there was once a serious accident, but at the time the director of the Longhe branch bureau was not in his office. He was fast asleep at home. When Liu heard about this, he was livid with rage, and at six o'clock that evening when the shifts changed, he rang up the director. As soon as he answered, Liu cleared his throat, frowned and started swearing at him, "Damn you! Our men are out there day and night in the wind and snow, but you, as soon as the shift was over, hurried off and back home after drinking two ounces of your damned smelly wine, snuggled down in bed under your wife's quilt. . . . Are you a Party member? From now on, all branch bureau directors will be on night duty. I'll call the roll by telephone at twelve o'clock every night. If you're tired, you can sleep with the tracks! No one is allowed to go home!"

So the directors of the branch bureaus were at their posts, there were no more accidents and things ran smoothly.

Incident No. 2: In 1964, many workers grumbled that the hospital of the Railway Bureau was in a state of disorder. The medical services were very poor and the staff didn't care very much about their patients. Two patients had died because of a wrong diagnosis. One of the doctors even examined his patient without even using the stethoscope. When Liu heard about these reports, he did not swear; instead, he bit his lip. One night, several days later, he suddenly complained of a stomach-ache. He did not take a car or allow anyone to accompany him to the hospital. He walked slowly to the emergency ward. The doctor on duty was of course sleeping soundly, his mouth foaming. Liu called him several times. The doctor opened his heavy eyes, closed them again, and began to inquire what his trouble was. Then, showing signs of impatience, he told Liu to lie down on the bed, casually examined his abdomen, yawned, and concluded that the patient had appendicitis and should have an emergency operation. Liu jumped up on the bed, glaring at him, and shouted, "Damn you! You and your appendicitis! What kind of doctor are you? You are a disgrace to your white overcoat!"

The doctor instantly woke up and, rather confused, stared at the unusual patient. "You? . . ."

"Yes, I'm Liu Dashan. I have come especially to call on you today, my dear doctor!"

The doctor's face turned pale, and his shoulders slumped.

Liu jumped down from the bed, buttoning up his clothes, "Go and ring the administrator and ask him to come here!"

After a while, the administrator arrived in a car. He did not know what had happened because the nervous doctor had not told him anything. When he pushed open the door, he found the Director of the Railway Bureau standing before him in a rage.

"Are you a Communist Party member?" Liu asked him in a mild tone.

The administrator nodded his head, not knowing why Liu was asking such a question. Liu frowned and said coldly, "You say you are a Communist Party member, but I think you look more like a member of the Kuomintang!"

There could have been some minor inaccurate details as reported in the above accounts. Exaggerations were inevitable as the stories circulated among the railway workers. It was also known that Liu had been told off by the authorities that his rudeness and his partiality for swearing were the habits of guerilla fighters. Liu accepted this criticism and expressed his determination to get rid of these undesirable habits. But not more than a week later, he was cursing and swearing again. He felt that he could express himself more forcibly by using such language, just as some writers were fond of using exclamation marks! When the "cultural revolution" began, he was one of the first persons to have a large board hung round his neck, as a sign of public disgrace. His "crimes", as listed, were numerous; even that slight remark of his about a Communist Party member behaving more like a member of the Kuomintang was enough to make him suffer hell on earth. When he was publicly criticized for this very crime, the hospital administrator jumped up on the platform and testified on his behalf that he did not mean that as an insult to the Party and that his criticism of the hospital was very fair indeed. But then, as a result of his defence, the administrator was condemned as a "royalist" and he, too, had a board hung on him. Liu Dashan was very appreciative of his integrity and bawled at the so-called revolutionists, "Damn you lot! This is utter nonsense!" Of course, what happened after that could be easily imagined.

All these were things of the past. Liu Dashan had become a legendary hero and his numerous anecdotes were well known in the Railway Bureau.

II

Liu also had the habit of dropping in each day on the various departments and offices of the Bureau to see how the workers were getting on. As he saw it, the railways were the main arteries of a country, and they'd better be functioning well. So, too, the bureau that looked after them. The bureau should not slack off in attending to all its duties.

One afternoon at four o'clock, after inspecting the transportation and finance departments, Liu came to the typing room. He did not come here often. When he entered the room, he saw a typist, more than forty years old, trying on a light blue embroidered woollen coat. She took a long time in trying it on, her eyes gleaming with excitement. Another girl, about twenty years old, clapped her hands lightly in admiration. Liu felt very awkward, but he did not shout or swear, for he knew that if he did, they would be very upset. He usually tried to control himself in front of women. He was thinking of saying, "If you must try that on, please do it at home. The office is not a place for this sort of thing." He also intended to speak gently. But before he could open his mouth to say anything, the two typists had already noticed his presence. The younger one stuck out her tongue, and they both sat down hurriedly at their typewriters and began to work as if nothing had happened. Liu left the room without saying anything. He thought to himself: a woman of her age still wearing light blue coloured clothes embroidered with cream yellow flowers? Was that really appropriate? People said she was an old maid and, in her younger days, had tried to find herself a handsome young man. Surely, such a man existed only in her dreams, for God had not yet created him! Now that she was already over forty, of course she realized she couldn't be so choosy in her search for a partner. She only wished to have a cadre, even an elderly one, for husband. Liu was a little preoccupied with these thoughts, as he went to the secretariat. There was no one there, however. He was told that the transportation department had managed to get some fresh fish and that the whole staff had gone there to have a share each. Liu felt his anger mounting. He thought: How irresponsible! Leaving their work at the smell of some fish! I'll sit here and see when they will return! He sat on a chair, and looked at a picture under the thick glass on the desk. It was the picture of a pretty girl, looking like a ballet dancer. It was probably cut out from a pictorial magazine. Then he saw a letter on the desk, addressed to "Director Liu Dashan". He opened it and read it at once. And he was mad with anger.

"Damn it!" he swore as he read the letter. It was a letter giving him all the details of a train collision that had happened at the Baita Railway Station the previous month. It exposed how the Baita Railway Station and the Beicang Branch Bureau had together tried to deceive the authorities by describing a major accident as a minor one, in their report. Liu had already dealt with this accident, as he had been led to believe that it was something ordinary. But, according to the letter, it was a major accident indeed! He banged his fist on the desk, and the ink bottles were jumping. "Damn it!" he yelled. "You've played a dirty trick on me! I have been totally deceived! If what this letter says is true, just you watch out!" Then he wondered if the letter was giving a false accusation. After all, since the "cultural revolution", false accusations had been quite common. He read the letter again to see whether or not it was signed. If there was a signature and address, it was at least eighty or ninety per cent true.

Yes, the letter was signed: "Lü Jiucai, a pointsman at the Baita Railway Station." Liu licked his lips and exclaimed, "Good! He has the guts to put down his name and address. He's a man!"

There was the clatter of heels in the corridor, rather like that of girls. Secretary Zhou Feng came in joyfully holding in his hand several fat fish on several strings; the tail of one of them was still wriggling. Zhou Feng produced the best of the lot and said, "Director Liu, these are yours."

Liu Dashan kept a straight face and asked, "Where on earth did you get these?"

Zhou Feng did not reply, but smiled awkwardly. Liu's face twitched, the corners of his mouth also quivering, "I've caught quite a big fish too, and, in addition, some small ones. . . ." He waved the letter in his hand. Zhou Feng was somewhat taken by surprise and he nearly dropped the fish.

"When did this letter arrive?" asked Liu.

". . . . ."

"Tell me the truth!"

Zhou Feng looked at Liu and felt that it would not do him any good to tell a lie. So, he answered, "Three days."

"Why didn't you pass it on to me immediately?"

"Bai Fan, the Chief of the Beicang Branch Bureau, telephoned me to say that a worker there was making a fuss about the whole matter. I thought that since you were in detention for two years together with Bai during the "cultural revolution", you'd be embarrassed if I gave you this letter. . . ."

Liu blinked his eyes, "Did Bai Fan know about this letter?"

Zhou Feng looked timidly at Liu and nodded. "Yes. He telephoned to say that the branch bureau would soon be given a red banner for winning the competition. But if this leaked out. . . ."

Liu Dashan's facial expression changed again. He was biting his lip, breathing heavily through his nose. "Humph! You couldn't care less about principles when people flatter you and give you presents. I see, you have been an excellent secretary! How long have you been in this dirty business?"

He was walking about, absolutely furious. The trains were whistling outside. A train-load of wood had just left the station. Suddenly, he walked towards the secretary and asked him, "Have you seen the film *Lenin in 1918*? Rememeber that captain of the guard at the Kremlin? He was truly a fine fellow, a man of iron! The capitalists offered him pots of money. Did he waver? Wouldn't you waver if so much money were given to you?" He yelled so loudly that he did not notice the door had been stealthily pushed open and then closed again by someone. The secretary stood there petrified unable to utter a word. He had seen the picture, but he had never thought about what he would do if he were the captain of the guard. Liu paced the room. Then he suddenly picked up the telephone receiver and said, "Hello. Is that the Party school? This is Liu Dashan. I want to recommend a student to you."

A somewhat husky voice replied, "Our classes began a week ago."

"That doesn't matter. His name is Zhou Feng."

Liu put down the receiver, blinked and said, "Listen, my handsome young fellow, you can go to the Party school tomorrow to register. Knock some sense into that head of yours, will you? Go and see *Lenin in 1918* a few more times."

Zhou Feng nodded and picked up the fish again. He was about to say something, when Liu shook his head, "Send them back to where they came from! I've already caught my big white fish."*

Zhou Feng's white face was sweating. He thought, "Oh shit! When there are so many people in the world, why did I have to come up against him?"

III

That afternoon, Liu called a meeting and organized a special investigation group which included the chief of the transportation section, the chief of the technical section and, of course, the chief of the discipline inspection section. They were to proceed to the Baita Railway Station. Before they started, Liu

---

* "Big white fish", refers to the Branch Bureau chief, Bai Fan, the character "bai" means "white". — *Trans.*

called them to his office and warned them, "You are all Communist Party members. . . . Good! When you are at the Baita Railway Station, don't drink. Whoever invites you to a meal, refuse. Keep your mouths shut. If you accept somebody's hospitality, you will find it difficult to say anything against him later. Make sure you won't be bribed. If you really want a drink, I'll treat you when you come back."

They set off that afternoon on a freight train, because there was no passenger train available. Two days later, they returned and went straight to Liu's office. He was at a meeting. After a while, he came back, his face flushed. The meeting was not yet over, in fact, and there were probably some very heated discussions going on. He left because he heard that the investigation group was back. They reported to him in detail all that they had learned. The statements made by the pointsman were true. The group had questioned the workers and examined the scene of the accident and the damaged trains. The accident was truly a major one. While there, somebody did try to invite them to dine at his home. That man was none other than the station-master, a smart fellow and a lively and persuasive talker. His words were like the grapes of Turpan, much sweeter than any produced elsewhere. Of course, the members of the group did not accept the invitation. The report on the accident was written by this very man, who had also made a verbal report by telephone to Bai, giving his reasons for what he had written. He then received the following praise from Bai: "You've got a good head on your shoulders!"

"Damn them! These people always mess up everything!" Liu exploded after listening to the report. Suddenly he stood up, stroked his bristly hair and said, "Get me through to the Baita Station and ask Lü Jiucai to come here at once. Dismiss that smart-ass, the station-master, and appoint an honest man for his job!"

Everyone left except Liu. He closed his eyes, listening to the whistle of the trains. He thought: How shall I deal with this big white fish? Yes, I was demobilized and transferred to work on the railways with him, and we were in detention, through no faults of our own, for two years together. There we talked endlessly and it appeared as if we had talked about all the problems in the world. We said that the earth was round. I said that it was a place filled with all sorts of problems. Wasn't that so? Some questions we could answer, but most of them we could not. When we were unable to answer a question, we felt miserable. Gradually we started to drink. We used to ask that sissy young man, who was supposed to be keeping an eye on us, to get us some wine without being noticed. The wine cost us one yuan a catty and so we called it "the yuan spirit". We often drank from the bottle when we could not get to sleep at night. After having some wine to warm our stomachs, we would talk passionately about this and that. Sometimes, Bai drank so much that his face became as red as a lobster. He would half close his eyes and sigh repeatedly, "*Ai, ai*! Old Liu, when we do get out of here, will you still work on the railways? I've had enough of it. I've worked on the railways for twenty years, and all I've got to show for it is this!"

Liu would then gulp down another mouthful, smacking his lips, and move nearer to Bai, confiding, "I can't leave these tracks any more than I can leave my wife. . . . Tell me, Old Bai, do you ever think of your wife?"

Bai's eyes would redden, and he would ask in reply, "Do you?"

"And how I do! How can a man not think of his wife!" Then, they stopped talking; the wine was all drunk and they fell silent, in deep thought. After a while, several rats appeared and ran along the foot of the wall. Then their squeakings were heard. Liu thought, "Those squeaks probably come from baby rats, looking for their mother. That's their world. But isn't that the same in our world? There are men and there are rats. There are good men and also bad men. There may be more good men than bad men. But wouldn't it be better to have still more good men?"

After their release from confinement, they also frequently met and drank together. They used to drink straight from the bottle. They were not accustomed to the use of fine wine glasses. Although it was proper to drink from these glasses, it was not mouth-filling. Later, Liu's wife admonished him that drinking from the bottle was the way of the American soldiers. So they used white porcelain jars on their drinking sessions. Sometimes, when Bai had drunk a good deal, he would unbutton his clothes and show the scars on his body, the marks of the beatings he had received from the so-called revolutionists. But Liu refrained from showing his, saying with a flushed face, "Why bother? They only reveal the dreadful past!"

An ear-piercing whistle brought him back to the present. Liu stood up, and walked towards the window. The railway station lay before him; it was a key railway transportation station. Several hundred trains arrived and departed daily, but all its installations were old, looking somewhat like present-day people dressed in the clothes of the Qing Dynasty. The dense smoke from the stream locomotives rose, blackening half of the sky. Some of the engines were from the days of the anti-Japanese war.

He muttered to himself, "Oh, so backward! China's backwardness is the shame of us Communist Party members. There are men who tell lies openly, and there are also those who listen happily to those lies and believe in them. What is evidently false is taken seriously as if it were true. Damn them! A branch bureau chief has cheated his subordinates and fooled his superiors. What will the men think of us? The Party's prestige is already low and it will suffer even more if things continue like this. People will lose all their faith in us. This is the greatest shame for Communist Party members! Bai, I've caught you today and I won't let you get away with it. I'll have to deal with you, and announce it in the bureau bulletin."

He picked up the telephone receiver and rang up Bai, "Hello, I want to speak to Bai Fan. Old Bai? You can change your job! . . . What new job are you after? . . . Go and be an actor! . . . You're laughing? What a good actor you are! You can turn lies into truth! Damn you! I was nearly taken in by you! Where did you learn such tricks? You've lied to the bureau over the Baita Station accident. One Communist

Party member cheating another! . . . I've investigated the whole matter thoroughly. I heard you wanted to give Lü Jiucai trouble. Damn you! You just try it! But I'm on his side. Your little glib-tongued station-master must be dismissed, and you also will have to face punishment!" Bai's arguing and pleading could be heard over the telephone. Liu threw the receiver down on the table, walked round the room, and picked it up again, "Listen Old Bai, are you still a Communist Party member? Wait till you see the consequences!" Then, he banged down the receiver.

A meeting of the bureau Party committee was held that evening, and a decision was reached regarding the penalty to be imposed on the Beicang Branch Bureau for not giving the real facts of the accident. Someone felt that the penalty was too severe and that it might affect the present emphasis of our unity and stability, but Liu looked grim and held on to his opinion. He said, penalty and unity and stability were two different matters; they should be considered separately. In order to maintain discipline, a serious warning was to be given to Bai Fan and recorded in his file. The chief of the safety supervisory office of the Beicang Branch Bureau was to be dismissed, as was the station-master of the Baita Railway Station. Furthermore, a reward of fifty yuan was to be given to Lü Jiucai. The above measures were to be published in the bureau bulletin the following day.

After the meeting Liu felt tired. His back ached. He returned to his office, pummelling his back. He had only just sat down when a stranger wearing a railway worker's uniform came in. He took off his cap, showing his white hair and he had a wrinkled face. Holding the cap in his hand, he walked towards Liu and said, "I want to see Director Liu."

"Here I am. Please take a seat." Liu pointed to the chair opposite him. The old man, however, did not sit down.

"My name is Lü Jiucai, I am the pointsman of the Baita Railway Station," the old worker said slowly and softly.

Liu slowly stood up, looked tenderly at the old worker and asked in a low voice, "Are you a Communist Party member?"

"Yes, I joined the Party in 1950."

"Me too. I joined the Party in 1942."

The two men remained silent. They felt that words were unnecessary; it was just right to be silent. The power of language was limited, but the power of sentiment was boundless. The two men looked at each other, each finding in the opposite's face the honest eyes of a Communist Party member. Suddenly Liu embraced the old worker, and, with tears in his eyes, said, "Old comrade, you are really good." Then, controlling himself, he asked, "How old are you now?"

"Fifty-nine years and four months."

"You are older than me by one year. You're my elder brother, my elder brother!" Liu exclaimed joyfully.

He gazed at the old worker, at his grey hair and the many wrinkles on his face, and said sadly, "What a pity! If only you were ten, even five years younger! How do we need honest men like you in so many places!"

The old worker shook his head. His lips trembled slightly, "Don't wish me any younger, that's impossible; but try to help the younger men to mature faster than they can. It's up to you!"

Liu nodded his head in approval.

The old worker continued, "I'll retire next year. I've been working on the railway switches for thirty-two years. I know how many pebbles there are in the switch-room. I really hate to leave. . . ."

Liu's mind was in a turmoil. He wanted to pay respect to this old Party member. Embracing him again, Liu said, "You rest here in our hostel tonight and go back tomorrow."

After saying this, he took up the telephone. "Hello, is that the hostel? This is Liu Dashan speaking. We have a guest who will be staying here tonight. Prepare dinner for him. . . . What? What rank of cadre is he? Wait a minute. . . ."

Liu smiled, covered the mouthpiece with his hand and winked at Lü Jiucai. "They're asking what rank you are."

"I am only a worker," said Lü.

Liu again spoke into the telephone, "What rank? He's my superior!"

IV

At ten o'clock that night, Liu Dashan walked back home with an empty stomach. His wife had already warmed the wine for him. Although Liu was tired out, he looked relaxed and he grinned at his old wife.

Liu fell in love with a peasant girl many years ago when his army unit was stationed in a village. But his unit commander, on learning this, cautioned him that they were fighting a war and that it was not the right time to consider having a wife. That must wait until the war was over. Though Liu had to leave, he left his heart behind. After he was demobilized and transferred to work on the railways, he went again, in 1950, to that village to look for the girl. The villagers told him that she was already married and about to give birth to a child. On hearing this news, he left the village like a wounded animal. Finally, he pulled himself together and took a train to his native village in Jiaodong, where he married a girl who was now his old mate. Although she was not as pretty as the girl of his first love, she was simple, honest and very considerate. His love for her grew and he knew that he could never leave her.

Liu drank his wine; his wife was beside him. She had something to say to him today, but she would wait until he had drunk so much that his face was red and his eyes beamed with smile. About half an hour later, she looked at his face and began, "You've done it again. The same old mistake."

"What mistake?" Liu asked, holding his wine jug before his mouth.

"What mistake? Your bad temper. Why did you penalize Old Bai?"

Liu stared at his wife, banged his wine jug on the table and declared, "Women should keep themselves out of politics!

When women interfere in politics, they're bound to mess up everything!"

His wife knew that he was in a comparatively better mood after drinking, so she continued, "Don't forget the lessons of the 'cultural revolution'. . . ."

Liu raised his voice and said slowly as if singing, "We cannot allow bad people to do as they like even if there is another 'cultural revolution'. I'll give up only when I die."

"No! You must help Old Bai and do something about his penalty."

Liu raised his eyebrows and said grimly, "I'll do nothing! It was I who proposed his penalty to the Party committee!"

"Then. . . ." His wife was not going to give up.

Liu pushed the wine jug away from him. He would not drink any more. "If you say one more word, damn it, I'll divorce you!"

Unable to bear it any longer, his wife retired to the inner room to weep. Liu sat still for a while, thinking: "Shit! The guerilla habit has got me again!" Then, he went inside and lovingly embraced his wife. "I'm sorry I lost my temper. I wouldn't part with you for all the young girls in the world! You are my dearest treasure!"

His wife looked hurriedly at the door, and said reproachfully, "Let go. What if our granddaughter should see us!"

Several timid knocks were heard, so Liu went outside with his wife and opened the gate. A young man entered, his head down. He was about thirty years old. Quite lean, he had a small white face and was carrying a large bag.

"Whom are you looking for?" Liu asked.

The young man did not answer. Suddenly he covered up his face and began to cry bitterly. This made Liu feel very uncomfortable. He gave the young man a chair and asked, "What's the matter? Come on, tell me."

"I was the station-master of the Baita Railway Station. . . . But now I am no longer. . . . I've made a mistake. . . ." He sobbed still more, as if his parents had just passed away.

Although Liu was a man of experience, he was rather taken

aback by this peculiar scene. He walked round the young man, studying him from different angles. Suddenly he stopped before him, "You bastard! Are you crying because you've lost your job? Or are you sorry for your mistakes? Don't put on an act! Will crying help you get your job back? Don't think I'm a merciful-faced Buddha!"

The young man's shoulders heaved for a while and then he stopped crying. Liu couldn't help laughing. He thought to himself: What an actor! How many good actors had been trained these past ten years!

The young man moved his hands away from his face. There were no tears on it, though it was quite flushed. He darted a brief glance at Liu and then pursed his lips in disapproval. "Director Liu," he cautioned, "if you go on like this. . . ."

"What will happen? Tell me."

The young man shook his head and sighed as if he pitied Liu.

Liu began to laugh. He stroked his hair. "So you think the sky's going to come crashing down just because I've kicked you out! You're not very old, but you're a tricky customer. You began by flattering me; when that failed, you resorted to tears, then threats. Damn you! Are you a Party member?"

The young man looked up and met the furious gaze of Liu. Then he timidly bent his head again.

"Go on, try to be an honest man! Don't give me this nonsense any more. I'm sick of it!"

The young man had prepared some other "moves", but as soon as he put them forward, they were dismissed by this big Shandong man. He left, finally, and when he was far away from the house, he took out two bottles of wine and several cakes from his bag and hurled them away, swearing, "Let the blasted dogs eat them!"

Soon, the aroma of strong sweet wine filled the night air.

V

When the penalty was published in the bureau bulletin, it seemed that a minor earthquake had occurred all along the tracks. Some people were awakened from their deep slumber, and one man seemed to have been struck by lightning. Bai Fan collapsed with a coronary heart disease that very day. When Liu heard of this news, he thought: Was he faking illness because he was ashamed, or because he felt he had been wronged? How many incidents of this kind had occurred in our society these last few years? People had the tendency of falling ill, in order to prove they had been overworked!

Liu decided to visit Bai that night to see for himself how he was getting on. Most people would avoid such a confrontation, but not Liu.

At night, the stars and the moon were in the sky. There were not many people on the road. A few pairs of young men and women were heading for the woods not too far away.

Liu reached a newly-completed apartment block. He went to the first floor and walked straight into a room without knocking at the door. There he found Bai lying in bed, with several pillows placed under his head. On the bedside table were many bottles of medicine, including some imported Japanese and German ones. The seriousness of his illness was quite evident. When Bai Fan saw Liu he tried to lift his body towards the wall and he closed his eyes. Then, the door leading to the inner room opened. Lingling, a pretty, young girl stuck her head out. On seeing Liu, she shut the door again with a bang. Liu stood there, thinking, "Such haughty airs!" Then he took a chair and sat down. On the table he saw a photo of a pretty woman. She was Bai's wife, who died two years ago. When she was still a girl, she was a well-known beauty. Bai Fan was originally named Bai Erzhu. In wooing this girl Bai changed his original name to Bai Fan, in order to give it a somewhat romantic air. Liu Dashan objected to the change at that time. Bai Fan asked for the help of a university student to draft his letter to the girl. The letter began with the words "My dear . . ." so that the girl thought that Bai had been to Europe for study. She disliked the words "My dear" very much. Because of these unlucky words, she prolonged her period of examination of Bai Fan by three months. Now this beauty had vanished from this world, and could only look at her home with sorrowful eyes as if saying to Bai Fan and her daughter Lingling, "Without me, how can you go on living?"

Liu sat for quite a long while. Bai did not move. Liu looked at the door, coughed and called, "Lingling, we have a guest here. Can you bring in some tea?"

There was still no response from the inner room. Liu raised his voice and called again, "Lingling, have you also got coronary heart disease?"

Nothing stirred in the inner room. Suddenly, Bai turned round and called loudly, "Lingling, this is something between grown-ups. Keep out of it and bring in some tea!" His voice was very stern. Then he turned his back again and closed his eyes.

Lingling appeared, pouting. She poured out a cup of water and placed it before Liu. He noticed she had tears in her eyes.

"Uncle Liu," she said, wiping the tears from her face. "You treat my father like this. . . . If he dies, what shall I do?"

Liu stroked her head and said very much moved, "No, he won't die." Then he added, "If he dies, I'll be a father to you."

Lingling smiled. Liu moved his chair nearer the bed and said to Bai, "Damn it! You should at least speak to me."

Bai moved a little, but he did not turn his face. Liu continued, "You're suffering, I know. But do you think I'm so happy? When Lingling wept, I also felt very bad! But what can we do? Give up our ideals and principles? Quit the Party? You know more than I do. Come. . . . Let's have a drink."

"Drink?" Bai turned to face Liu and asked, "For friendship? For our two years in detention? For your penalizing me?"

Liu did not answer. After a while, he said, "Damn it! Why are you so stubborn?" He opened the cupboard, took out a porcelain jar and a bottle of *erguotou*.* He removed the cork and poured out half a jar of wine. Then he picked it up and toasted, "To our friendship!"

---

* A strong spirit usually made from sorghum. — *Trans.*

Liu drank a large mouthful and pushed the jar towards Bai, who did not move. Liu again toasted, "To the end of the steam locomotives and to automatic switching!" He gulped another big swig and again offered Bai the jar. Bai still refused to pay any attention. Liu then took up the jar for the third time and declared, "To both of us, members of the Communist Party and to my recommendation, quite rightly I hope, of you for membership of the Party! He drank and held out the jar to Bai. This time, Bai rose his face all red, his hands trembling, as he took the jar and slowly drank the wine.

Liu stood up, took his leave and went out. He did not hear anyone follow him. He left and, after going some distance, turned round and saw Bai, supported by Lingling, standing outside the door looking in his direction. Liu again felt touched, "Ah! so he's not a log of rotten wood."

The night deepened. Liu felt that there was something on his mind as he was walking home. A pair of lovers went past him, the girl with her head on the young man's shoulder; neither of them was saying a word. Liu did not give them another look. He was reminiscing about his past life. He saw in his mind's eye the land of Jiaodong, red dates and the faces of his dying fellow fighters. He saw the face of the old divisional commander and heard his roar, "Are you a Communist Party member?"

He felt that he must answer this question properly, as should Bai and every one who had joined the Communist Party.

Translated by Hu Zhemou
Illustrated by Zheng Xian

中国获奖短篇小说选
（1980—1981）
柯云路　张贤亮等著
蔡　荣　赵瑞椿　周建夫
郑叔方　郑　沂　插图

＊

外文出版社出版
（中国北京百万庄路24号）
外文印刷厂印刷
中国国际图书贸易总公司
（中国国际书店）发行
北京399信箱
1985年（28开）第一版
编号：（英）10050—1150